## THE FINAL MASTERPIECE BY SPECULATIVE VISIONARY OCTAVIA E. BUTLER

# *fledgling*

"Book of the year . . . a harrowing meditation on dominance, sex, addiction, miscegenation, and race."
—Junot Díaz, *The Observer*

"A finely crafted character study, a parable about race and an exciting family saga. Exquisitely moving fiction."
—*Kirkus Reviews* (starred review)

"Cleverly constructed and carefully extrapolated . . . full of action and suspense . . . a compelling, tough-minded meditation on 'otherness.' "
—*San Francisco Chronicle*

"A unique vision of the modern vampire, and a kick-ass heroine to boot."
—*Seattle Weekly*

"FLEDGLING woos the reader with one of fiction's greatest entice-ments: the pleasure of a totally page-turning plot."
—*San Francisco Bay Guardian*

"A literary gem that is accessible to all readers."
—*Black Issues Book Review*

"Vivid and tense . . . laced with emotionally and erotically charged encounters . . . It's a fascinating read, uncomfortable, horrifying, and ugly at times, but always compelling."
—*Detroit News*

BOOKS BY OCTAVIA E. BUTLER

*Fledgling**

*Parable of the Talents**

*Parable of the Sower**

*Lilith's Brood**
Dawn
Adulthood Rites
Imago

*Seed to Harvest**
Wild Seed
Mind of My Mind
Clay's Ark
Patternmaster

*Kindred*

*Survivor*

*Bloodchild and Other Stories*

*available from Hachette Book Group

# OCTAVIA E. BUTLER

## *fledgling*

**GRAND CENTRAL**
PUBLISHING

NEW YORK   BOSTON

Grand Central Publishing Edition

This Grand Central Publishing edition is published by arrangement with Seven Stories Press, 140 Watts Street, New York, NY 10013

Grand Central Publishing
Hachette Book Group
1290 Avenue of the Americas
New York, NY 10104
www.HachetteBookGroup.com

Printed in the United States of America

First Hachette Book Group Edition: January 2007
14

Grand Central Publishing is a division of Hachette Book Group, Inc.
The Grand Central Publishing name and logo is a trademark of Hachette Book Group, Inc.

The Hachette Speakers Bureau provides a wide range of authors for speaking events. To find out more, go to www.hachettespeakersbureau.com or call (866) 376-6591.

The publisher is not responsible for websites (or their content) that are not owned by the publisher.

ISBN 978-0-446-69616-6
LCCN: 2006928308

Cover design by Don Puckey/Julie Metz
Cover photo by Marc Yankus

*To Frances Louis
for listening*

# *one*

**I** awoke to darkness.

I was hungry—starving!—and I was in pain. There was nothing in my world but hunger and pain, no other people, no other time, no other feelings.

I was lying on something hard and uneven, and it hurt me. One side of me was hot, burning. I tried to drag myself away from the heat source, whatever it was, moving slowly, feeling my way until I found coolness, smoothness, less pain.

It hurt to move. It hurt even to breathe. My head pounded and throbbed, and I held it between my hands, whimpering. The sound of my voice, even the touch of my hands seemed to make the pain worse. In two places my head felt crusty and lumpy and . . . almost soft.

And I was so *hungry*.

The hunger was a violent twisting inside me. I curled my empty, wounded body tightly, knees against chest, and whimpered in pain. I clutched at whatever I was lying on. After a time, I came to understand, to remember, that what I was lying on should have been a *bed*. I remembered little by little what a bed was. My hands were grasping not at a mattress, not at pillows, sheets, or blankets, but at things that I didn't recognize, at first. Hardness, powder, something light and brittle. Gradually, I understood that I must be lying on the ground—on stone, earth, and perhaps dry leaves.

The worst was, no matter where I looked, there was no hint of light. I couldn't see my own hands as I held them up in front of me. Was it so dark, then? Or was there something wrong with my eyes? Was I blind?

I lay in the dark, trembling. What if I were blind?

Then I heard something coming toward me, something large and noisy, some animal. I couldn't see it, but after a moment, I could smell it. It smelled . . . not exactly good, but at least edible. Starved as I was, I was in no condition to hunt. I lay trembling and whimpering as the pain of my hunger grew and eclipsed everything.

It seemed that I should be able to locate the creature by the noise it was making. Then, if it wasn't frightened off by the noise I was making, maybe I could catch it and kill it and eat it.

Or maybe not. I tried to get up, fell back, groaning, discovering all over again how badly every part of my body hurt. I lay still, trying to keep quiet, trying to relax my body and not tremble. And the creature wandered closer.

I waited. I knew I couldn't chase it, but if it came close enough, I might really be able to get my hands on it.

After what seemed a long time, it found me. It came to me like a tame thing, and I lay almost out of control, trembling and gasping, and thinking only, *food!* So much food. It touched my face, my wrist, my throat, causing me pain somehow each time it touched me and making noises of its own.

The pain of my hunger won over all my other pain. I discovered that I was strong in spite of all the things that were wrong with me. I seized the animal. It fought me, tore at me, struggled to escape, but I had it. I clung to it, rode it, found its throat, tasted its blood, smelled its terror. I tore at its throat with my teeth until it collapsed. Then, at last, I fed, gorged myself on the fresh meat that I needed.

I ate as much meat as I could. Then, my hunger sated and my pain dulled, I slept alongside what remained of my prey.

When I awoke, my darkness had begun to give way. I could see light again, and I could see blurred shadowy shapes that blocked the light. I didn't know what the shapes were, but I could see them. I began to believe then that my eyes had been injured somehow, but that they were healing. After a while there was too much light. It burned not only my eyes, but my skin.

I turned away from the light, dragged myself and my prey farther into the cool dimness that seemed to be so close to me, but took so much effort to reach. When I had gone far enough to escape the light, I fed again, slept again, awoke, and fed. I lost count of the number of times I did this. But after a while, something went wrong with the meat. It began to smell so bad that, even though I was still hungry, I couldn't make myself touch it again. In fact, the smell of it was making me sick. I needed to get away from it. I remembered enough to understand that it was rotting. Meat rotted after a while, it stank and the insects got into it.

I needed fresh meat.

My injuries seemed to be healing, and it was easier for me to move around. I could see much better, especially when there wasn't so much light. I had come to remember sometime during one of my meals that the time of less light was called night and that I preferred it to the day. I wasn't only healing, I was remembering things. And now, at least during the night, I could hunt.

My head still hurt, throbbed dully most of the time, but the pain was bearable. It was not the agony it had been.

I got wet as soon as I crawled out of my shelter where the remains of my prey lay rotting. I sat still for a while, feeling the wetness—water falling on my head, my back, and into my lap. After a while, I understood that it was raining—raining very hard. I could not recall feeling rain on my skin before—water falling from the sky, gently pounding my skin.

I decided I liked it. I climbed to my feet slowly, my knees protesting the movement with individual outbursts of pain. Once I was up, I stood still for a while, trying to get used to balancing on my legs. I held on to the rocks that happened to be next to me and stood looking around, trying to understand where I was. I was standing on the side of a hill, from which rose a solid, vertical mass of rock. I had to look at these things, let the sight of them remind me what they were called—the hillside, the rock face, the trees—pine?—that grew on the hill as far as the sheer wall of rock. I saw all this, but still, I had no idea where I was or where I should be or how I had come to be there or even why I was there—there was so much that I didn't know.

The rain came down harder. It still seemed good to me. I let it wash away my prey's blood and my own, let it clean off the crust of dirt that I had picked up from where I had lain. When I was a little cleaner, I cupped my hands together, caught water in them, and drank it. That was so good that I spent a long time just catching rain and drinking it.

After a while, the rain lessened, and I decided that it was time for me to go. I began to walk down the hill. It wasn't an easy walk at first. My knees still hurt, and it was hard for me to keep my balance. I stopped once and looked back. I could see then that I had come from a shallow hillside cave. It was almost invisible to me now, concealed behind a screen of trees. It had been a good place to hide and heal. It had kept me safe, that small hidden place. But how had I come to be in it? Where had I come from? How had I been hurt and left alone, starving? And now that I was better, where should I go?

I wandered, not aware of going anywhere in particular, except down the hill. I knew no other people, could remember no other people. I frowned, picking my way among the trees, bushes, and rocks over the wet ground. I was recognizing things now, at least by category—bushes, rocks, mud . . . I tried to remember something more about myself—anything that had happened to me before I awoke in the cave. Nothing at all occurred to me.

As I walked, it suddenly occurred to me that my feet were bare. I was walking carefully, not stepping on anything that would hurt me, but I could see and understand now that my feet and legs were bare. I knew I should have shoes on. In fact, I knew I should be dressed. But I was bare all over. I was naked.

I stopped and looked at myself. My skin was scarred, badly scarred over every part of my body that I could see. The scars were broad, creased, shiny patches of mottled red-brown skin. Had I always been scarred? Was my face scarred? I touched one of the broad scars across my abdomen, then touched my face. It felt the same. My face might be scarred. I wondered how I looked. I felt my head and discovered that I had almost no hair. I had touched my head, expecting hair. There should have been hair. But I was bald except for a small patch of hair on the back of my head. And higher up on my head there was a misshapen place, an indentation that hurt when I touched it and seemed even more wrong than my hairlessness or my scars. I remembered discovering, as I lay in the cave, that my head felt lumpy and soft in two places, as though the flesh had been damaged and the skull broken. There was no softness now. My head, like the rest of me, was healing.

Somehow, I had been hurt very badly, and yet I couldn't remember how. I needed to remember and I needed to cover myself. Being naked had seemed completely normal until I became aware of it. Then it seemed intolerable. But most important, I needed to eat again.

I resumed my downhill walk. Eventually I came to flatter, open land—farmland with something growing in some of the fields and other fields, already harvested or empty for some other reason. Again, I was remembering things—fragments—understanding a little of what I saw, perhaps just because I saw it.

Off to one side there was a collection of what I gradually recognized as the burned remains of several houses and outbuildings. All of these had been burned so thoroughly that as far as I could see, they offered no real shelter. This had been a little village surrounded by farmland and woods. There were animal pens and the good smells of animals that could be eaten, but the pens were empty. I thought the place must once have provided comfortable homes for several people. That felt right. It felt like something I would want—living together with other people instead of wandering alone. The idea was a little frightening, though. I didn't know any other people. I knew they existed, but thinking about them, wondering about them scared me almost as much as it interested me.

People had lived in these houses sometime not long ago. Now plants had begun to grow and to cover the burned spaces. Where were the people who had lived here? Had I lived here?

It occurred to me that I had come to this place hoping to kill an animal and eat it. Somehow, I had expected to find food here. And yet I remembered nothing about this place. I recognized nothing except in the most general way—animal pens, fields, burned remnants of buildings. So why would I expect to find food here? How had I known to come here? Either I had visited here before or this place had been my home. If it was my home, why didn't I recognize it as home? Had my injuries come from the fire that destroyed this place? I had an endless stream of questions and no answers.

I turned away, meaning to go back into the trees and hunt an animal—a deer, I thought suddenly. The word came into my thoughts, and at once, I knew what a deer was. It was a large animal. It would provide meat for several meals.

Then I stopped. As hungry as I was, I wanted to go down and take a closer look at the burned houses. They must have something to do with me or they would not hold my interest the way they did.

I walked down toward the burned buildings. I might at least be able to find something to wear. I was not cold. Even walking in the rain had not made me cold, but I wanted clothing badly. I felt very vulnerable without it. I did not want to be naked when I found other people, and I thought I must, sooner or later, find other people.

Eight of the buildings had been large houses. Their fireplaces, sinks, and bathtubs told me that much. I walked through each of them, hoping to see something familiar, something that triggered a memory, a memory about people. In one, at the bottom of a pile of charred rubble, I found a pair of jeans that were only burned a little at the bottoms of the legs, and I found three slightly burned shirts that were wearable. All of it was too large in every way—too broad, too long...Another person my size would have fit easily into the shirts with me. And there were no wearable underwear, no wearable shoes. And, of course, there was nothing to eat.

Feeding my hunger suddenly became more important than anything. I put on the pants and two of the shirts. I used the third shirt to keep the pants up, tying it around my waist and turning the top of the pants down over it. I rolled up the legs of the pants, then I went back into the trees. After a time I scented a doe. I stalked her, killed her, ate as much of her flesh as I could. I took part of the carcass up a tree with me to keep it safe from scavenging animals. I slept in the tree for a while.

Then the sun rose, and it burned my skin and my eyes. I climbed down and used a tree branch and my hands to dig a shallow trench. When I finished it, I lay down in it and covered myself with leaf litter and earth. That and my clothing—I folded one of my shirts over my face—proved to be enough of a shield to protect me from sunlight.

I lived that way for the next three days and nights, eating, hunting, examining the ruin during the night, and hiding myself in the earth during the day. Sometimes I slept. Sometimes I lay awake, listening to the sounds around me. I couldn't identify most of them, but I listened.

On the fourth night curiosity and restlessness got the better of me. I had begun to feel dissatisfied, hungry for something other than deer flesh. I didn't know what I wanted, but I went exploring. That was how, for the first time in my memory, I met another person.

## two

It was raining again—a steady, gentle rain that had been coming down for some time.

I had discovered a paved road that led away from the burned houses. I had walked on it for some time before I remembered the word "road," and that led to my remembering cars and trucks, although I hadn't yet seen either. The road I was on led to a metal gate, which I climbed over, then to another, slightly wider road, and I had to choose a direction. I chose the downslope direction and walked along for a while in contentment until I came to a third still wider road. Again, I chose to go downhill. It was easier to walk along the road than to pick my way through the rocks, trees, underbrush, and creeks, although the pavement was hard against my bare feet.

A blue car came along the road behind me, and I walked well to one side so that I could look at it, and it would pass me without hitting me. It couldn't have been the first car I had ever seen. I knew that because I recognized it as a car and found nothing surprising about it. But it was the first car I could remember seeing.

I was surprised when the car stopped alongside me.

The person inside was, at first, just a face, shoulders, a pair of hands. Then I understood that I was seeing a young man, pale-skinned, brown-haired, broad, and tall. His hair brushed against the top of the inside of his car. His shoulders were so broad that even alone in the car, he looked crowded. His car seemed to fit him almost as badly as my clothing fitted me. He lowered his window, looked out at me, and asked, "Are you all right?"

I heard the words, but at first, they meant nothing at all. They were noise. After a moment, though, they seemed to click into place as language.

I understood them. It took me a moment longer before I realized that I should answer. I couldn't remember ever speaking to another person, and at first, I wasn't sure I could do it.

I opened my mouth, cleared my throat, coughed, then finally managed to say, "I . . . am. Yes, I am all right." My voice sounded strange and hoarse to my own ears. It wasn't only that I couldn't recall speaking to anyone else. I couldn't remember ever speaking at all. Yet it seemed that I knew how.

"No, you're not," the man said. "You're soaking wet and filthy, and . . . God, how old are you?"

I opened my mouth, then closed it again. I didn't have any idea how old I was or why my age should matter.

"Is that blood on your shirt?" he asked.

I looked down. "I killed a deer," I said. In all, I had killed two deer. And I did have their blood on my clothing. The rain hadn't washed it away.

He stared at me for several seconds. "Look, is there someplace I can take you? Do you have family or friends somewhere around here?"

I shook my head. "I don't know. I don't think so."

"You shouldn't be out here in the middle of the night in the rain!" he said. "You can't be any more than ten or eleven. Where are you going?"

"Just walking," I said because I didn't know what else to say. Where was I going? Where would he think I should be going? Home, perhaps. "Home," I lied. "I'm going home." Then I wondered why I had lied. Was it important for this stranger to think that I had a home and was going there? Or was it only that I didn't want him to realize how little I knew about myself, about anything?

"I'll take you home," he said. "Get in."

I surprised myself completely by instantly wanting to go with him. I went around to the passenger side of his car and opened the door. Then I stopped, confused. "I don't really have a home," I said. I closed the door and stepped back.

He leaned over and opened the door. "Look," he said, "I can't leave you out here. You're a kid, for Godsake. Come on, I'll at least take you some-place dry." He reached into the backseat and picked up a big piece of thick cloth. "Here's a blanket. Get in and wrap up."

I wasn't uncomfortable. Being wet didn't bother me, and I wasn't cold.

Yet I wanted to get into the car with him. I didn't want him to drive away without me. Now that I'd had a few more moments to absorb his scent I realized he smelled . . . really interesting. Also, I didn't want to stop talking to him. I felt almost as hungry for conversation as I was for food. A taste of it had only whetted my appetite.

I wrapped the blanket around me and got into the car.

"Did someone hurt you?" he asked when he had gotten the car moving again. "Were you in someone's car?"

"I was hurt," I said. "I'm all right now."

He glanced at me. "Are you sure? I can take you to a hospital."

"I don't need a hospital," I said quickly, even though, at first, I wasn't sure what a hospital was. Then I knew that it was a place where the sick and injured were taken for care. There would be a lot of people all around me at a hospital. That was enough to make it frightening. "No hospital."

Another glance. "Okay," he said. "What's your name?"

I opened my mouth to answer, then closed it. After a while, I admitted, "I don't know what my name is. I don't remember."

He glanced at me several times before saying anything about that. After a while he said, "Okay, you don't want to tell me, then. Did you run away? Get tired of home and strike out on your own?"

"I don't think so," I frowned. "I don't think I would do that. I don't remember, really, but that doesn't feel like something I would do."

There was another long silence. "You really don't remember? You're not kidding?"

"I'm not. My . . . my injuries are healed now, but I still don't remember things."

He didn't say anything for a while. Then, "You really don't know what your own name is?"

"That's right."

"Then you do need a hospital."

"No, I don't. No!"

"Why? The doctors there might be able to help you."

Might they? Then why did the idea of going among them scare me so? I knew absolutely that I didn't want to put myself into the hands of strangers. I didn't want to be even near large numbers of strangers. "No hospital," I repeated.

Again, he didn't say anything, but this time, there was something different about his silence. I looked at him and suddenly believed that he meant to deliver me to a hospital anyway, and I panicked. I unfastened the seat belt that he had insisted I buckle and pushed aside the blanket. I turned to open the car door. He grabbed my arm before I could figure out how to get it open. He had huge hands that wrapped completely around my arm. He pulled me back, pulled me hard against the little low wall that divided his legs from mine.

He scared me. I was less than half his size, and he meant to force me to go where I didn't want to go. I pulled away from him, dodged his hand as he grasped at me, tried again to open the door, only to be caught again.

I caught his wrist, squeezed it, and yanked it away from my arm. He yelped, said "Shit!" and managed to rub his wrist with the hand still holding the steering wheel. "What the hell's wrong with you?" he demanded.

I put my back against the door that I had been trying to open. "Are you going to take me to the hospital even though I don't want to go?" I asked.

He nodded, still rubbing his wrist. "The hospital or the police station. Your choice."

"Neither!" Being turned over to the police scared me even more than the idea of going to the hospital did. I turned to try again to get the door open.

And again, he grasped my left upper arm, pulling me back from the door. His fingers wrapped all the way around my upper arm and held me tightly, pulling me away from the door. I understood him a little better now that I'd had my hands on him. I thought I could break his wrist if I wanted to. He was big but not that strong. Or, at least, I was stronger. But I didn't want to break his bones. He seemed to want to help me, although he didn't know how. And he did smell good. I didn't have the words to say how good he smelled. Breaking his bones would be wrong.

I bit him—just a quick bite and release on the meaty part of his hand where his thumb was.

"Goddamnit!" he shouted, jerking his hand away. Then he made another grab for me before I could get the door open. There were several buttons on the door, and I didn't know which of them would make it open. None of them seemed to work. That gave him a chance to get his hand on me a third time.

"Be still!" he ordered and gave me a hard shake. "You'll kill yourself! If you're crazy enough to try to jump out of a moving car, you should be in mental hospital."

I stared down at the bleeding marks I'd made on his hand, and suddenly I was unable to think about anything else. I ducked my head and licked away the blood, licked the wound I had made. He tensed, almost pulling his hand away. Then he stopped, seemed to relax. He let me take his hand between my own. I looked at him, saw him glancing at me, felt the car zigzag a little on the road.

He frowned and pulled away from me, all the while looking uncertain, unhappy. I caught his hand again between mine and held it. I felt him try to pull away. He shook me, actually lifting me into the air a little, trying to get away from me, but I didn't let go. I licked at the blood welling up where my teeth had cut him.

He made a noise, a kind of gasp. Abruptly, he drove completely across the road to a spot where there was room to stop the car without blocking other cars—the few other cars that came along. He made a huge fist of the hand that was no longer needed to steer the car. I watched him draw it back to hit me. I thought I should be afraid, should try to stop him, but I was calm. Somehow, I couldn't believe he would hit me.

He frowned, shook his head. After a while he dropped his hand to his lap and glared at me. "What are you doing?" he demanded, watching me, not pulling away at all now, but looking as though he wanted to—or as though he thought he should want to.

I didn't answer. I wasn't getting enough blood from his hand. I wanted to bite him again, but I didn't want him afraid or angry. I didn't know why I cared about that, but it seemed important. Also, I knew hands weren't as good for getting blood as wrists and throats were. I looked at him and saw that he was looking intently at me.

"It doesn't hurt anymore," he said. "It feels good. Which is weird. How do you do that?"

"I don't know," I told him. "You taste good."

"Do I?" He lifted me, squeezed past the division between the seats to my side of the car, and put me on his lap.

"Let me bite you again," I whispered.

He smiled. "If I do, what will you let me do?"

I heard consent in his voice, and I hauled myself up and kissed the side of his neck, searching with my tongue and my nose for the largest blood source there. A moment later, I bit hard into the side of his neck. He convulsed and I held on to him. He writhed under me, not struggling, but holding me as I took more of his blood. I took enough blood to satisfy a hunger I hadn't realized I had until a few moments before. I could have taken more, but I didn't want to hurt him. He tasted wonderful, and he had fed me without trying to escape or to hurt me. I licked the bite until it stopped bleeding. I wished I could make it heal, wished I could repay him by healing him.

He sighed and held me, leaning back in his seat and letting me lean against him. "So what was that?" he asked after a while. "How did you do that? And why the hell did it feel so fantastic?"

He had enjoyed it—maybe as much as I had. I felt pleased, felt myself smile. That was right somehow. I'd done it right. That meant I'd done it before, even though I couldn't remember.

"Keep me with you," I said, and I knew I meant it the moment I said it. He would have a place to live. If I could go there with him, maybe the things I saw there would help me begin to get my memory back—and I would have a home.

"Do you really not have anywhere to go or anyone looking for you?" he asked.

"I don't think I have anyone," I said. "I don't remember. I need to find out who I am and what happened to me and . . . and everything."

"Do you always bite?"

I leaned back against him. "I don't know."

"You're a vampire, you know."

I thought about that. The word stirred no memories. "What's a vampire?"

He laughed. "You. You bite. You drink blood. He grimaced and shook his head. "My God, you drink blood."

"I guess I do." I licked at his neck.

"And you're way too young," he said. "Jailbait. Super jailbait."

Since I didn't know what "jailbait" was and I had no idea how old I was, I didn't say anything.

"Do you remember how you got that blood on your clothes? Who else have you been chewing on?"

"I killed a deer. In fact, I killed two deer."

"Sure you did."

"Keep me with you."

I was watching his face as I said it. He looked confused again, worried, but he held me against his body and nodded. "Yeah," he said. "I'm not sure how I'm going to do that, but yeah. I want you with me. I don't think I should keep you. Hell, I know I shouldn't. But I'll do it anyway."

"I don't think I'm supposed to be alone," I said. "I don't know who I should be with, though, because I can't remember ever having been with anyone."

"So you'll be with me." He smiled and his confusion seemed to be gone. "I'll need to call you something. What do you want to be called?"

"I don't know."

"Do you want me to give you a name?"

I smiled, liking him, feeling completely at ease with him. "Give me a name," I said. I licked at his neck a little more.

"Renee," he said. "A friend of mine told me it meant 'reborn.' That's sort of what's happened to you. You've been reborn into a new life. You'll probably remember your old life pretty soon, but for now, you're Renee." He shivered against me as I licked his neck. "Damn that feels good," he said. Then, "I rent a cabin from my uncle. If I take you there, you'll have to stay inside during the day. If he and my aunt see you, they'll probably throw us both out."

"I can sleep during the day. I won't go out until dark."

"Just right for a vampire," he said. "How did you kill those deer?"

I shrugged. "Ran them down and broke their necks."

"Uh-huh. Then what?"

"Ate some of their meat. Hid the rest in a tree until I was hungry again. Ate it until the parts I wanted were gone."

"How did you cook it? It's been raining like hell for the past few days. How did you find dry wood for your fire?"

"No fire. I didn't need a fire."

"You ate the deer raw?"

"Yes."

"Oh God, no you didn't." Something seemed to occur to him suddenly. "Show me your knife."

I hesitated. "Knife?"

"To clean and skin the deer."

"A thing? A tool?"

"A tool for cutting, yes."

"I don't have a knife."

He held me away from him and stared at me. "Show me your teeth," he said.

I bared my teeth for him.

"Good God," he said. "Are those what you bit me with?" He put his hand to his neck. "You *are* a damned vampire."

"Didn't hurt you," I said. He looked afraid. He started to push me away, then got that confused look again and pulled me back to him. "Do vampires eat deer?" I asked. I licked at his neck again.

He raised a hand to stop me, then dropped the hand to his side. "What are you, then?" he whispered.

And I said the only thing I could: "I don't know." I drew back, held his face between my hands, liking him, glad that I had found him. "Help me find out."

# three

On the drive to his cabin, the man told me that his name was Wright Hamlin and that he was a construction worker. He had been a student in a nearby place called Seattle at something called the University of Washington for two years. Then he had dropped out because he didn't know where he was heading or even where he wanted to be heading. His father had been disgusted with him and had sent him to work for his uncle who owned a construction company. He'd worked for his uncle for three years now, and his current job was helping to build houses in a new community to the south of where he'd picked me up.

"I like the work," he told me as he drove. "I still don't know where I'm headed, but the work I'm doing is worth something. People will live in those houses someday."

I understood only that he liked the work he was doing. As he told me a little about it, though, I realized I would have to be careful about taking blood from him. I understood—or perhaps remembered—that people could be weakened by blood loss. If I made Wright weak, he might get hurt. When I thought about it, I knew I would want more blood—want it as badly as I had previously wanted meat. And as I thought about meat, I realized that I didn't want it anymore. The idea of eating it disgusted me. Taking Wright's blood had been the most satisfying thing I could remember doing. I didn't know what that meant—whether it made me what Wright thought of as a vampire or not. I realized that to avoid hurting Wright, to avoid hurting anyone, I would have to find several people to take blood from. I wasn't sure how to do that, but it had to be done.

Wright told me what he remembered about vampires—that they're immortal unless someone stabs them in the heart with a wooden stake, and yet even without being stabbed they're dead, or undead. Whatever that means. They drink blood, they have no reflection in mirrors, they can become bats or wolves, they turn other people into vampires either by drinking their blood or by making the convert drink the vampire's blood. This last detail seemed to depend on which story you were reading or which movie you were watching. That was the other thing about vampires. They were fictional beings. Folklore. There were no vampires.

So what was I?

It bothered Wright that all he wanted to do now was keep me with him, that he was taking me to his home and not to the police or to a hospital. "I'm going to get into trouble," he said. "It's just a matter of when."

"What will happen to you?" I asked.

He shrugged. "I don't know. Jail, maybe. You're so young. I should care about that. It should be scaring the hell out of me. It is scaring me, but not enough to make me dump you."

I thought about that for a while. He had let me bite him. I knew from the way he touched me and looked at me that he would let me bite him again when I wanted to. And he would do what he could to help me find out who I was and what had happened to me.

"How can I keep you from getting into trouble?" I asked.

He shook his head. "In the long run, you probably can't. For now, though, get down on the floor."

I looked at him.

"Get down, now. I can't let my uncle and aunt or the neighbors see you."

I slid from the seat and curled myself up on the floor of his car. If I had been a little bigger, it wouldn't have been possible. As it was, it wasn't comfortable. But it didn't matter. He threw the blanket over me. After that, I could feel the car making several turns, slowing, turning once more, then stopping.

"Okay," he said. "We're at the carport behind my cabin. No one can see us."

I unfolded myself, got back up onto the seat, and looked around. There was a scattering of trees, lights from distant houses, and next to us, a small house. Wright got out of the car, and I looked quickly to see which button or lever he used to open the door. It was one I had tried when he was threatening to take me to a hospital or the police. It hadn't worked then, but it worked now. The door opened.

I got out and asked, "Why wouldn't it open before?"

"I locked it," he said. "I didn't want you smearing yourself all over the pavement."

". . . what?"

"I locked the door to keep you safe. You were trying to jump from a moving car, for Godsake. You would have been badly hurt or killed if you had succeeded."

"Oh."

He took me by the arm and led me into his house.

Once I was inside, I looked around and immediately recognized that I was in a kitchen. Even though I could not recall ever having been in an intact kitchen before, I recognized it and the things in it—the refrigerator, the stove, the sink, a counter where a few dishes sat on a dish towel, a dish cabinet above the counter, and beside it, a second cabinet where my nose told me food was sometimes stored. I remembered the blackened refrigerators and sinks at the burned ruin. But this was what a kitchen should look like when everything worked.

The kitchen was small—just a corner of the cabin, really. Beyond it was a wooden table with four chairs. Alongside the kitchen on the opposite side of the cabin was a small room—a bathroom, I saw when I looked in. Beyond the bathroom was the rest of the cabin—a combination living room-bedroom containing a bed, a chest of drawers, a soft chair facing a stone fireplace, and a small television on top of a black bookcase filled with books. I recognized all these things as soon as I saw them.

I went through the cabin, touching things, wondering about the few that I did not recognize. Wright would tell me and show me. He was exactly what I needed right now. I turned to face him again. "Tell me what else to do to keep you out of trouble."

"Just don't let anyone see you," he said. "Don't go out until after dark and don't . . ." He looked at me silently for a while. "Don't hurt anyone."

That surprised me. I had no intention of hurting anyone. "All right," I said.

He smiled. "You look so innocent and so young. But you're dangerous, aren't you? I felt how strong you are. And look what you've done to me."

"What have I done?"

"You bit me. Now you're all I can think about. You're going to do it again, aren't you?"

"I am."

He drew an uneven breath. "Yeah. I thought so. I probably shouldn't let you."

I looked up at him.

He took another breath. "Shit, you can do it right now if you want to."

I rested my head against his arm and sighed. "It might hurt you to lose more blood so soon. I don't want to hurt you."

"Don't you? Why not? You don't even know me."

"You're helping me, and you don't know me. You let me into your car and now into your house."

"Yeah. I wonder how much that's going to cost me." He put his hand on my shoulder and walked me over to the table. There he sat down and drew me close so that he could open one of my filthy shirts, then the other. Having reached skin, he stroked my chest. "No breasts," he said. "Pity. I guess you really are a kid. Or maybe . . . Are you sure you're female?"

"I'm female," I said. "Of course I am."

He peeled off my two shirts and threw them into the trash can. "I'll give you a T-shirt to sleep in," he said. "One of my T-shirts should be about the size of a nightgown for you. Tomorrow I'll buy you a few things."

He seemed to think of something suddenly. He took my arm and led me into the bathroom. There, over the sink, was a large mirror. He stood me in front of it and seemed relieved to see that the mirror reflected two people instead of only one.

I touched my face and the short fuzz of black hair on my head, and I tried to see someone I recognized. I was a lean, sharp-faced, large-eyed, brown-skinned person—a complete stranger. Did I look like a child of about ten or eleven? Was I? How could I know? I examined my teeth and saw nothing startling about them until I asked Wright to show me his.

Mine looked sharper, but smaller. My canine teeth—Wright told me they were called that—were longer and sharper than his. Would people notice the difference? It wasn't a big difference. Would it frighten people? I hoped not. And how was it that I could recognize a refrigerator, a sink, even a mirror, but fail to recognize my own face in the mirror?

"I don't know this person," I said. "It's as though I've never seen her before." Then I had another thought. "My scars are gone."

"What?" he asked. "What scars?"

"I was all scarred. A few nights ago . . . three nights before this one, I was scarred. I remember thinking that I must have been burned—all over. And I couldn't see for a while when I first woke up, so maybe my eyes were scarred, too." I sighed. "That's why I hurt so much and why I was so hungry and so tired. All I've done is eat and sleep. My body had so much healing to do."

"Scars don't vanish just because wounds heal," he said. "Especially not burn scars." He pushed up the sleeve of his right arm to display a shiny, creased patch of skin bigger than my hand. "I got this when I was ten, fooling around our barbecue pit. Caught my sleeve on fire."

I took his arm and looked at the scar, touched it. I didn't like it. It felt the way my own skin had when I examined my scars. I had the feeling I should be able to make his scars go away too, but I didn't know how. I turned his hand to look at the bite mark I'd made, and he gasped. The wound seemed to me to be healing as it should, but he snatched his arm from me and examined the hand.

"It's already healing!" he said.

"It should be healing," I said. "Are you hungry?"

"Now that you mention it, I am. I had a big meal at a café not far from the job site, but I'm hungry again."

"You should eat."

"Yeah, but I'm not into raw meat."

"Eat what's right for you. Eat what your body wants."

"But you ate raw meat to heal?" he asked.

His words triggered something in me—a memory. It felt real, true. I spoke it aloud: "All I need is fresh human blood when I'm healthy and everything's normal. I need fresh meat for healing injuries and illnesses, for sustaining growth spurts, and for carrying a child."

He put his hands on my shoulders. "You know that? You remember it?"

"I think so. It sounds right. It feels right."

"So, then," he said, "what are you?"

I looked up at him, saw that I had scared him, and took one of his huge hands between mine. "I don't know what I am. I don't know why I remembered just now about flesh and blood. But you helped me do it. You asked me questions and you made me look into the mirror. Maybe now, with you to help me, I'll remember more and more."

"If you're right about what you've remembered so far, you're not human," he said.

"What if I'm not?" I asked. "What would that mean?"

"I don't know." He reached down and tugged at my jeans. "Take these off," he said.

I undid the shirt that I had twisted and tied around me to keep the jeans up, then I took them off.

He first seemed frozen with surprise that I had done as he said. Then, slowly, he walked around me, looking. "Well, you're a girl, all right," he whispered. At last, he took me by the hand and led me back to the main room of the cabin.

He led me to the chest of drawers next to the bed. There, in the top drawer, he found a white T-shirt. "Put this on," he said, handing it to me.

I put it on. It fell past my knees, and I looked up at him.

"You tired?" he asked. "You want to go to sleep?"

"Not sleepy," I said. "Can I wash?" I hadn't minded being dirty until the clean shirt made me think about just how dirty I was.

"Sure," he said. "Go take a shower. Then come keep me company while I eat."

I went into the bathroom, recognized the shower head over the bathtub, and figured out how to turn the shower on. Then I took off the T-shirt and stepped in. It was a hot, controlled rain, wonderful for getting clean and feeling better. I stayed under the shower longer than necessary just because it felt so good. Then, finally, I dried myself on the big blue towel that was there and that smelled of Wright.

I put the T-shirt back on and went out to Wright who was sitting at his table, eating things that I recognized first by scent then by sight. He was eating scrambled eggs and chunks of ham together between thick slices of bread.

"Can you eat any of this?" Wright asked as he enjoyed the food and drank from a brown bottle of beer.

I smiled. "No, but I think I must have known people who ate things like that because I recognize them. Right now, I'll get some water. That's all I want."

"Until you want to chew on me again, eh?"

I got up to get the water and touched his shoulder as I passed him. It was good to see him eat, to know that he was well. It made me feel relieved. I hadn't hurt him. That was more important to me than I'd realized.

I sat down with a glass of water and sipped it.

"Why'd you do that?" he asked after a long silence. "Why'd you let me undress you like that?"

"You wanted to," I said.

"You would let anyone who wanted to, do that?"

I frowned, then shook my head. "I bit you—twice."

"So?"

"Taking my clothes off with you is all right."

"Is it?"

I frowned, remembering how badly I had wanted to cover myself when I was naked in the woods. I must have been used to wearing clothes in my life before the cave. I had wanted to be dressed as soon as I knew I was naked. Yet when Wright had taken my shirts, I hadn't minded. And I hadn't minded taking off the jeans when he asked me to. It had felt like what I should do.

"I don't think I'm as young as you believe," I said. "I mean, I may be, but I don't think so."

"You don't have any body hair at all," he told me.

"Should I?" I asked.

"Most people over eleven or twelve do."

I thought about that. "I don't know," I said finally. "I don't know enough about myself to say what my age might be or even whether I'm human. But I'm old enough to have sex with you if you want to."

He choked on his sandwich and spent time coughing and taking swallows of beer.

"I think you're supposed to," I continued, then frowned. "No, that's not right. I mean, I think you're supposed to be free to, if you want to."

"Because I let you bite me?"

"I don't know. Maybe."

"A reward for my suffering."

I leaned back, looking at him. "Does it hurt?"

"You know damn well it doesn't."

He drank a couple of swallows more, then stood up, took my hand, and led me to his bed. I sat on the bed, and he started to pull the T-shirt over my head.

"No," I said, and he stopped and stood looking at me, waiting. "Let me see you." I pulled at his shirt and unbuttoned one of the buttons. "You've seen me."

He nodded, finished unbuttoning his shirt, and pulled his undershirt over his head.

His broad chest was covered with a mat of brown hair so thick that it was almost like fur, and I stroked it and felt him shiver.

He kicked off his shoes and stripped off his pants and underwear. There was a great deal more fur on him everywhere, and he was already erect and eager.

I had seen a man this way before. I could not remember who he had been, could not recall a specific face or body. But all this was familiar and good to me, and I felt my own eagerness and growing excitement. I pulled the T-shirt over my head and let him push me back onto the bed, let him touch me while I petted and played with his fur and explored his body until, gasping, he caught my hands and held them. He covered me with his huge, furry blanket of a body. He was so tall that he took care to hold himself up on his elbows so that my face was not crushed into his chest.

He was very careful at first, afraid of hurting me, still afraid that I might be too young for this, too small. Then, when it was clear that I was not being hurt at all, when I had wrapped my arms and legs around him, he forgot his fears, forgot everything.

I forgot myself, too. I bit him again just beneath his left nipple and took a little more blood. He shouted and squeezed the breath from me. Then he collapsed on me, empty, spent.

It bothered me later, as he lay sleeping beside me, that I had taken more blood. If I didn't find another source of blood soon, I would weaken him too much.

I got up quietly, washed, and put on his T-shirt. I would not let myself be seen, but I had to go out and look around. I had to see who and what else might be nearby.

# four

**W**right lived in an area where houses were widely scattered along a road. They sat well back from the road, and sometimes they were surrounded by trees. It was as though the people in each of these houses were pretending they lived alone in the woods. Most of the other houses were much larger than Wright's cabin. His closest neighbor was one of these larger houses—a two-story house made of wood, painted white, and now full of light. This must be where Wright's aunt and uncle lived. I could hear people talking downstairs and music coming from upstairs. Best to let these people alone, at least until they slept.

Three houses away there were no lights, and the people were already asleep. I could hear the soft, even breathing of two of them upstairs in a front bedroom.

I went around the house looking for a quiet way in. The house had plenty of windows, but the ones on the lower floor were closed and locked. On one side, though, where the trees screened the house from the road and the neighbors, I found a little platform next to a second-floor window, and the window was partly open. I stared up at the platform, recognizing it, remembering that it was called a "balcony," but knowing nothing about it beyond that. Things kept coming to me in this frustrating, almost useless way.

I shook my head in annoyance and decided that I could leap the distance from the ground to the balcony. I'd made longer leaps on my two deer hunts, and the balcony, at least, wasn't moving. But I was concerned that I might make too much noise.

Well, if I awoke more than one person, I would run. If I were quick enough, maybe no one would catch me.

That's when I remembered that more might happen to me than just capture. I might be shot. I recalled being shot once before—perhaps more than once. This, like the balcony, proved to be another of my limited, nearly useless slivers of memory. I remembered the hammering impact of the bullet. I remembered that it hurt me more than anything had ever hurt me. But who had shot me? Why? Where had I been when it happened? Did it have something to do with my winding up in the cave?

Nothing.

No answers.

Just slivers of memory, tormenting me.

I stood slightly back from the balcony, seeing and understanding how far up it was, how I must grasp the somehow familiar wrought iron, hold it, and haul myself up. It was like watching a deer and figuring out where to leap so that I could seize it, or at least run it down with the least effort.

I stooped, looked up at the place on the balcony where I intended to land, jumped, landed there, caught the wrought-iron railing, pulled myself up and over it. Then I froze. Had anyone heard me?

I didn't move for several seconds—not until I was sure no one was moving nearby. The breathing I could hear was the even, undisturbed breathing of sleeping people. The room I slipped into was occupied by one person—a woman, sleeping alone. I crept closer to her bed and took a deep breath.

This woman didn't smell as enticing as Wright had. She was older, no longer able to have children, but not yet truly old. For her age, though, she was healthy and strong, and from what I could see of her body stretched out on the bed, she was almost as tall as Wright, but slender. I didn't like her age, and I thought she was too thin, but her height and her good health beckoned to me. And her aloneness was good, somehow. There were other people in the house, but none of them had been in her room for a long time. She didn't smell of other people. Perhaps it was only because she had bathed, but I got the impression that no one had touched her in a long while.

Most important, though, she could feed me without harm to herself. Wright was larger and could give more blood, but this woman had possibilities. I needed to know several more people like her.

I moved closer to the bed and the sleeping woman—and knew suddenly that there was a gun in the room. I smelled it. It was a terrifyingly familiar smell.

I almost turned and ran out. Being shot had apparently done me more harm than I realized. It had left me an irrational fear to deal with. The pain had been very bad, but I was not in danger of being shot now. No one was holding this gun. It was out of sight somewhere, perhaps in one of the drawers of the little table that sat next to the head of the woman's bed.

I stood still until my fear quieted. I would not be shot tonight.

When I was calm, I lay down beside the woman and covered her mouth with my hand as she woke. I held on to her with my other arm and both my legs as she began to struggle. Once I was sure of my hold on her, I bit into her neck. She struggled wildly at first, tried to bite me, tried to scream. But after I had fed for a few seconds, she stopped struggling. I held her a little longer, to be sure she was subdued; then, when she gave no more trouble, I let her go. She lay still, eyes closed.

I fed slowly, licking rather than sucking. I wasn't hungry. Perhaps tomorrow I would come back and take a full meal from her. Now I was only making certain of her, seeing to it that she would be here, available to me when I needed her. After a while, I whispered to her, "Is it good?"

She moaned—a satisfied little sound.

"Leave your balcony door unlocked from now on, and don't tell anyone about me."

"You'll come back?"

"Shall I?"

"Come back tomorrow."

"Maybe. Soon."

She started to turn to face me.

"No," I said. "No, stay as you are."

She obeyed.

I licked at her neck for a while, then asked, "What's your name?"

"Theodora Harden."

"I'll see you again, Theodora."

"Don't go. Not yet."

I left her, content that she would welcome me when I came back. I wandered up and down both sides of the road until I had found four more—two men and two women—who were young enough, healthy, and big enough. One by one, I collected them. I would stay with Wright but go to these others when I needed them. Were they enough? I didn't know.

I went back to Wright's cabin, still wide awake, and sat at his table. I wanted to think about what I had done. It bothered me somehow that it had all been so easy, that I had had no trouble taking blood from six people including Wright. Once I had tasted them, they enjoyed the way I made them feel. Instead of being afraid or angry, they were first confused, then trusting and welcoming, eager for more of the pleasure that I could give them. It happened that way each time. I didn't understand it, but I had done it in a comfortable, knowing way. I had done it as though it was what I was supposed to do.

Was there something in my saliva that pacified people and pleasured them? What else could it be? It must also help them heal. Wright had been surprised with how quickly his hand was healing. That meant healing must normally take longer for him. And that meant I could at least help the people who helped me. That felt important.

On the other hand, it felt wrong to me that I was blundering around, knowing almost nothing, yet involving other people in my life. And yet it seemed I had to involve them. I hadn't hurt anyone so far, but I could have. And I probably would unless I could remember something useful.

I thought back as far as I could remember, closed my eyes and thought myself back to the blindness and pain of the little cave. I had emerged from it almost like a child being born. Should I go back there? Could I even find the place now? Yes, I thought I could find it. But why go back? Could there be anything there that would help me remember how I'd gotten there?

I had gone from the cave down to the site of the burned houses. I had found nothing that looked familiar at the houses, but maybe it would help me to know when the houses burned and why and who had done it. Also, it might help to know who had lived at the houses. I had found no burned bodies, although there had been places that smelled of burned flesh. So maybe the people who lived there had been hurt but had gotten away, or maybe they had been killed and were taken away. If I had lived there, I had certainly gotten away. Maybe in the confusion of the fire, we'd gotten separated. But why hadn't the others—whoever they were—looked for me, searched the forest and the hillside? Why had I been left to fend for myself after being so badly injured? Maybe they were all dead.

I went back again, to my memory of the cave. I had awakened in terrible pain—blind, lost, naked. And then some animal had come to me, had come right up to me, making me a gift of its flesh. And I had killed it and eaten it.

I thought about the animal and its odd behavior. Then, in memory, I saw the remains of the animal, scattered around the cave. I had seen it briefly, just before I left the cave. I had been able to see then, but I had not been aware enough to understand what I was seeing. What I had killed . . . and eaten . . . in the cave had not been an animal. It had been a man.

I had not seen his face, but I had seen his short, straight black hair. I had seen his feet, his genitals, one of his hands . . .

A man.

He had come up through the trees and spotted me in the shallow cave. He came to me. He touched my face, sought a pulse in my wrist, then my throat. It hurt when he touched me because my burns were still raw. He had whispered something. I hadn't understood the words at the time, hadn't even understood that they were words. He bent over me. I could feel him there, warm—a large, edible-smelling patch of warmth—so tempting to my starving, damaged body and to my damaged mind. Close enough to touch. And I grabbed him and I tore out his throat and I ate him.

I was capable of that. I had done that.

I sat for a long time, stunned, not knowing what to think. The words that the man had whispered when he found me were, "Oh my God, it's her. Please let her be alive." That was what he said just before I killed him.

I put my head down on the table. The man had known me. He had cared about me. Perhaps I had had a relationship with him like the one I was developing with Wright. I must have had such relationships with someone—several someones.

How could I have killed such a person?

I couldn't kill Wright. Could I? I'd been with him for only one night, and yet there was a bond between us. But I had not recognized the other man. I couldn't see his face—had no memory of ever seeing his face—

but his scent should have told me what he was. How was it that he had smelled only like food to me and not like a person at all?

I heard Wright wake up. Heard his breathing change. After a moment, he got up and came over to me. The room was dim but not dark. There was a window in the kitchen area where the moonlight shone in.

"What's going on?" he asked. He put his hands on my shoulders and rubbed me pleasantly.

I sat up. "I've been trying to remember things," I said.

"Any luck?"

"Pain, hunger, bad things. Nothing from before I woke up hurt and blind in the cave." I couldn't tell him about the man I'd killed. How could I ever tell him about a thing like that?

"Give it time," he said. "You'll get it back. If you'd see a doctor—"

"No! No hospital. No doctor."

"Why?"

"Why?" I stood up, turning to face him. He stepped back, startled, and I realized I had moved too quickly—faster than he expected me to move. No matter. It helped me make my point. "Wright, I don't know what I am, but I'm not like you. I think maybe . . . maybe I look a lot more human than I am. I don't want to draw attention to myself, maybe have people try to lock me up because they're afraid of me."

"For Godsake, girl, no one's going to lock you up."

"No? I look like a child. I might be locked up for my own safety even if they weren't afraid of my differences. You thought I was a child."

He grinned. "I don't any more." Then he hugged himself, hands rubbing his furry forearms a little.

I realized that he had gotten cold standing naked in the unheated room while he talked with me. "Come back to bed and get warm," I said.

He got back into bed, pulling me against him as I slid in beside him.

"Can you get information for me?" I asked.

"Information?"

"About memory and not being able to remember things."

"Amnesia," he said, and just like that, the word was familiar to me.

"Amnesia, yes. And about vampires," I said. "Most of what you told me . . . I don't think it has anything to do with me. But I do need blood. Maybe there are bits of truth mixed into the movies and folktales."

"I'd like to know how old you are," he said.

"When I know, I'll tell you. But, Wright, don't tell anyone about me. Don't tell your friends or your family or anyone."

"You know I wouldn't. I'm more likely to get into trouble than you are if anyone found out about you."

"I think your trouble would be shorter-lived than mine," I said.

"I won't say a word."

After a while, I thought of something else. "There was a fire, Wright. Some houses surrounded by farmland and woods. Eight houses not far from where you picked me up. Do you remember hearing about it?"

He shook his head. "Sounds big, but no, I don't remember hearing anything about it. Do you know when the fire happened?"

"No. I found the ruin when I was able to get up and walk around. There weren't any bodies or bones or anything. It was just a burned-out ruin."

"How close is it to where I picked you up?"

"I don't know. I had been wandering away from it since just after sundown when I met you. I wasn't going anywhere in particular. I was feeling frustrated. I'd been hunting, eating, sleeping, and going over the ruin for three days, not even knowing what I was looking for." I shook my head against the pillow. "I believe I could find the place because I've been there. It seems that I have a very good memory for the little I've done and sensed in the past few days."

"Maybe this weekend you could show me the ruin."

"All right."

"Meanwhile, it's almost time for me to get up and get ready for work."

"It's not dawn yet."

"Yeah, how about that? But before I go, I'm going to show you how to use my computer. Do you remember computers?"

I frowned, then nodded. "I remember what they are. Like refrigerators. But I don't think I know how to use one."

"Like refrigerators?"

"I mean, sometimes when you say something or I see something— like when I saw your refrigerator—I know what it is, what it's for, but I don't remember how I know or if I've ever had one."

"Okay. Let's get you online, and you can gather some information yourself." We got up again, and he put on a white terry-cloth robe and put one of his vast plaid shirts on me. I wasn't cold, but I didn't mind. His computer was a slender laptop that he took from the back of the black bookcase where I had not noticed it. He opened it on his kitchen counter where there was an electrical outlet and a phone jack. He turned it on, making sure I saw everything he did and what he typed in to get online. Then he shut everything down and made me do it. It all felt vaguely familiar to me. I was comfortable with it. When I'd gone through the process, he was happy.

"I don't use the thing much anymore," he said. "I thought for a moment I'd forgotten my password."

It occurred to me just then that his memory would improve. I managed not to say it, but, yes, his memory should improve because I was with him, because now and then, I would bite him, injecting whatever I injected into people when I bit them. I didn't say anything about it because I didn't want him to ask me questions I couldn't answer—like what other changes might be in store for him.

"I'm going to stop by the library on my way home," he said. "I'll see what I can find for you about vampires and amnesia. Maybe I can even scare up something on your fire."

"Thank you."

He grinned. "We aim to please." He went off to take a shower and get dressed.

By the time he came out, clean and shaved, dressed in blue jeans and a red plaid shirt like the one I had on, I had already looked through a huge amount of nonsense about vampires. Apparently they were in fashion with some people. There were television shows, movies, plays, and novels about them. There were groups devoted to talking about them endlessly in online chat groups. There were even people who tried to look the way they thought a vampire should look—a cloaked figure with long, sharp teeth, and long, dark hair . . .

"Anything useful?" Wright asked me.

"Nothing," I said. "Worthless stuff."

He nodded. "Stay away from the TV stuff and movies. Go with folklore and mythology, maybe anthropology. And there are some medical conditions I've heard of. There's one that makes people so allergic to sunlight that they only go out at night, and maybe superstitious people of the past thought they were vampires. There's also a disease or a psychological condition that makes people think they're vampires."

"You mean they're insane?"

"I don't know. If a psychiatrist found out what you eat and drink, he might think you're insane."

"Even if I bit him?"

He looked away. "I don't know. I think that might convince him whether he liked it or not. Renee, are you going to go unconscious during the day?"

"I'll probably sleep for a while."

"But will it be normal sleep? I mean, would you be able to wake up if the house were on fire or if someone broke in—not that either of those things is likely?"

"I just sleep," I said. "Normal sleep. The sun hurts my eyes and my skin, and I seem to prefer to sleep during the day—the way you prefer to sleep at night. I don't catch fire or turn to ash or dust or anything like what I've read about so far on your computer. Anything that would wake you up would wake me up."

"Okay, good. Lock the door when I leave. Nobody should be coming in here when I'm not home. If someone knocks, ignore them. If the phone rings, don't answer it." He started to leave, then turned back, frowning. "Ordinary sun exposure burns your skin even though you're black?"

"I'm . . ." I stopped. I had been about to protest that I was brown, not black, but before I could speak, I understood what he meant. Then his question triggered another memory. I looked at him. "I think I'm an experiment. I think I can withstand the sun better than . . . others of my kind. I burn, but I don't burn as fast as they do. It's like an allergy we all have to the sun. I don't know who the experimenters are, though, the ones who made me black."

He became intensely interested. "Do you know if the experimenters were like you—sort of vampires—or were they like me?"

"Don't know." I looked at him. "But keep asking me things. Whenever you think of a question, ask me. Sometimes it helps."

He nodded, then kissed me. "I've got to go."

"Breakfast?" I said.

"I ate it last night. I'll pick something up on the way to work. I've got to go grocery shopping this evening. It's a good thing you don't eat."

And he went out the door and was gone.

# five

I spent most of the day at the computer making no real progress. There were diseases that people might once have mistaken for vampirism. One of them was called porphyria. It was probably what Wright thought of as a sun-allergy disease. In fact, it was a group of diseases caused by pigments that settled in peoples' teeth, bones, and skin. The worst of the porphyriac diseases made people so vulnerable to light that they developed huge sores as parts of their flesh eroded away. They might lose their noses or their lips or patches of their cheeks. They would look grotesque.

That was interesting, but it awakened no memories in me. After all, I had already proved that if I were badly burned or wounded, I would heal.

There were river-borne microorganisms that caused people to develop problems with their memories just as there were microorganisms that could cause people to look hideous and, in the past perhaps, be mistaken for vampires. But that had nothing to do with me either. Whoever and whatever I was, no one seemed to be writing about my kind. Perhaps my kind did not want to be written about.

I wandered from site to site, picking up more bits of interesting, but useless, information. Finally, I switched to hunting through information about recent fires. I found a couple of articles that probably referred to what I was coming to think of as "my fire."

They said the houses had been abandoned. The fire had happened three weeks ago and had definitely been arson. Gasoline had been splashed about liberally, then set alight. Fortunately, the fire had not spread to the surrounding forest—as it probably would have if the houses had truly been abandoned. There would have been plenty of bushes, vines, grasses, and young trees to carry the fire straight into the woods.

Instead, there had been a broad clearing around the houses, and there had been farm fields, stubbly and bare.

The houses had not been abandoned. I was not wrong about the scents of burned flesh that I had found here and there in them. Those houses were close to the cave where I had awakened. I had gone straight to them from the cave as though my body knew where it was going even though my memory was gone. I must have either been living in one of those houses or visiting one. And there had definitely been other people around at the time of the fire. Why would the articles deny this?

Wright had said we could go back to the ruin on the weekend. According to the computer, today was Thursday. The weekend was only a day away.

I wanted to go back now, on foot, and comb through the ruin again. I was more alert and aware now. My body had finished healing. Maybe I could find something.

But it was daytime, almost noon. I felt tired from all my running around the night before and stiff from sitting for hours at the computer. I turned it off, got up, and decided to soak for a while in the tub before I went to bed. That may have been a mistake. Someone knocked on the door while I was filling the tub. I turned the water off, afraid they'd already heard it, afraid they would know someone was in the cabin when it was supposed to be empty.

The knock came again, and a woman's voice called out, "Wright? Are you home?"

I kept quiet. After a while, I heard her go away. I soaked nervously in the water I had already drawn and went to bed.

◎     ◎     ◎

When Wright got home—long after sunset—he brought groceries, an "everything" pizza, a library book about vampires written by an anthropologist, and some clothing for me. There were two pairs of jeans, four T-shirts, socks, underwear, a pair of Reebok athletic shoes, and a jacket with a hood. Everything except the shoes were a little big. Somehow he'd gotten shoes that were just the right size. He'd held each of my feet in his hands, and that must have helped. And he'd bought a belt. That would keep the jeans up. The rest of it worked fine even though it was a little large.

"You're even smaller than I thought," he said. "I'm usually pretty good at estimating the size of things I've seen and handled."

"I'm lean," I said. "I feed on blood most of the time. I don't think I could get fat."

"Probably not." He stowed the groceries in his refrigerator, then turned and looked at me. "My neck is completely healed."

"I thought it would be."

"I mean, no scar. Nothing. No scar on my hand, either."

I went to him and looked for myself. "Good," I said when I had seen. "I don't want to leave you all scarred. How do you feel?"

"Fine. I thought I might feel a little weak, like I did when I donated blood, but I'm fine. I don't think you took very much."

"I think I probably took more than I should have from you yesterday. Who did you donate blood to?"

"Friend of mine was in a car wreck. They saved him, but he lost a lot of blood."

"He took blood from you?"

"No, nothing like that. He . . . do you know what a transfusion is?"

I thought about it and then realized that I did know. "In the hospital, blood was sent from a container directly into your friend's veins."

"That's right, but it wasn't my blood. He and I aren't even the same blood type. I just gave to offset a little of what he had used." He bent, picked me up, and kissed me. "It isn't nearly as much fun as what you do."

I had already found that I enjoyed any skin-to-skin contact with him. For a few moments, I gave myself up to that enjoyment. Then, reluctantly, I drew back. "Someone was here today," I said. "A woman came to the door while I was filling the tub for a bath. I think she heard the water running. She knocked and called your name."

"Older woman?" he asked.

"I couldn't see her."

"My aunt, maybe. My aunt and uncle live it the big house out front." He gestured toward the front of the cabin with the arm that wasn't holding me. Then he put me down. "You probably saw it last night. They had company so it was all lit up."

"Can she get in here? Does she have a key?"

"Yeah. My uncle does anyway. But they don't snoop. I think you'll be okay in here."

I wasn't so sure, but I let it go. If the woman ever came into the cabin while Wright was at work, I would bite her. Then she would accept my being here, keep it secret, feed me, and then maybe help me find some of the answers I was looking for.

"I'm glad we're going back to the site of the fire this weekend," I said. "I found articles that said the place was abandoned and that vandals set it afire."

"Good work," he said. "I thought you'd find something online."

"But why would it say that?" I demanded. "I'm sure it wasn't abandoned. In fact, I'm pretty sure I was there. It was close to the cave where I woke up and not really close to anything else."

He thought about that, then shook his head. "I found articles at the library that said the same thing," he said. "They were from two small newspapers in the area. The reporters wouldn't have any reason to lie."

I shook my head. "If I can find them, I can get them to tell me why they lied. But first I want to go to the ruin. I'm connected with that place somehow. I'm sure I am. And Wright, the clothing I was wearing when you found me, I got it at one of the burned houses. It had been folded and put away . . . maybe in a drawer or on a shelf. When I found it, it was at the bottom of a big pile of half-charred clothing, and it had only been burned a little. Why should an abandoned house have piles of clean, folded clothing in it?"

Wright nodded. "I'll take you back there then," he said. "Saturday?"

"Friday night." I stood on tiptoe and still could not reach him. I was annoyed for once that he was so tall, but he picked me up again and held me against him. I bit him a little at the base of his throat, drew a few drops of blood. It wasn't necessary, but we both enjoyed it. He stood still, holding me, letting me lick at the wound.

After a while, he sighed. "Okay, Friday. Are you going to let me eat my pizza while it's hot?"

I licked once more, then pulled away from him reluctantly and slid down his body. "Eat," I said, and picked up the vampire book. "I'll read and wait for you."

The book was interesting but not that helpful. Many cultures seemed to have folklore about vampires of one kind or another. Some could hypnotize people by staring at them. Some read and controlled people's thoughts. It would be handy to be able to do things like that. Easier than biting them and waiting for the chemicals in my saliva to do their work.

Not all vampires drank blood according to the book. Some ate flesh either from the living or from the dead. Some took in a kind of spiritual essence or energy—whatever that meant. All took something from their subjects, usually not caring how they injured the subject. Many killed their subjects. Many were dead themselves, but magically reanimated by the blood, flesh, or energy they took. One feeding usually meant the taking of one life. And that made no sense, at least for those who took blood. Who could need that much blood? Why kill a person who would willingly feed you again and again if you handled them carefully? No wonder vampires in folklore were feared, hated, and hunted.

Then my thoughts drifted back to the man I had killed at the cave. I killed and fed as viciously as any fictional vampire. I ate a man without ever recognizing him as a man. I'd not yet read of a vampire doing that, but I had done it.

Did others of my kind do such things? Had I done such a thing before? Had someone found out about us and tried to kill us back at the ruin? That would seem almost . . . just. But what about the other people who had been at the ruin? Had they been like Wright or like me? Had the ruin been a nest of vampires? I could still remember the scents I had found here and there around the ruin where flesh had been burned. Now I tried to sort through them, understand who was who.

After a while, I understood that some of them had been like me and some like Wright—vampires and other people living and dying together. What did that mean?

Wright got up, came to stand beside me, and took the book out of my hands. He laid it open, its pages facedown on the table. "I think I'm strong enough to take you on now," he said.

Perhaps he was, but I took only a few drops more of his blood while I enjoyed sex with him. It seemed necessary to take small amounts of his blood often. I felt a need for it that was something beyond hunger. It was a need for his blood specifically. No one else's. I took it slowly and gave him as much pleasure as I could. In fact, I took delight in leaving him pleasurably exhausted.

I went out later when Wright was asleep and took a full meal from Theodora. She was smaller and older than Wright, and she would probably feel a little weak tomorrow, tired perhaps.

"What work do you do?" I asked her when she looked ready to drift off to sleep.

"I work for the county library," she said. Then she laughed. "It doesn't pay very well, but I enjoy it." And then, as though my question had opened the door for her to talk to me, she said, "I didn't think you were real. I thought I'd dreamed you."

"I could be just a dream," I said. I stroked her shoulder and licked the bite. I wondered what work was done in libraries, then knew. I had been in libraries. I had memories of rooms filled with books. Theodora worked with books and with people who used books.

"You're a vampire," she said, breaking into my thoughts.

"Am I?" I went on licking her bite.

"Are you going to kill me?" she asked as though she didn't care what the answer might be. And there was no tension in her.

"Of course not. But you shouldn't go to work tomorrow. You might be a little weak."

"I'll be all right. I don't like to take time off."

"Yes, you will be all right. Stay home tomorrow."

She said nothing for a moment. She moved restlessly against me, moved away, then came back, accepting again, at ease. "All right. Will you come back to me again? Please come back."

"In a week, maybe."

"That long?"

"I want you healthy."

She kissed me. After a moment of surprise, I kissed her back. I held her, and she seemed very comfortable in my arms.

"Be real," she said. "Please be real."

"I'm real," I told her. "Sleep now. I'm real, and I'll come to you again. Sleep."

She went to sleep, happily fitted against me, one arm over and around

me. I lay with her a few moments, then slipped free and went home to
Wright's cabin.

⊚        ⊚        ⊚

On Friday evening after dark, Wright drove me back along the road
where he had found me. The road was almost as empty on Friday as it
had been when I walked it, barefoot and soaking wet. One or two cars
every now and then. At least it wasn't raining tonight.

"I picked you up near here," Wright said.

I looked around and couldn't make out much beyond his headlights.
"Pull off the road when you can and turn your lights off," I said.

"You can see in the dark like a cat, can't you?" he asked.

"I can see in the dark," I said. "I don't know anything about cats so I
can't compare myself to them."

He found a spot where there was room to pull completely off the
road and park. There, he stopped and turned off his headlights. Across the
road from us there was a hillside and, on our side of the road, a steep
slope downward toward a little creek. This was a heavily wooded area,
although there was a clear-cut area not far behind us.

"We're not far from the national forest," he said. "We're running par-
allel to it. Does anything look familiar?"

"Nothing yet," I said. I got out of the car and looked down into the
trees, letting my eyes adjust to the darkness.

I had walked this road. I began to walk it now, backtracking. After a
while, Wright began to follow me in the car. He didn't turn his lights on
but seemed to have no trouble seeing me. I began to jog, always looking
around, knowing that at some point it would be time for me to turn off
onto a side road and go down into the woods.

I jogged for several minutes, then, on impulse, began to run. Wright
followed until finally I spotted the side road that led to the ruin. I turned
but he didn't.

When he didn't follow, I stopped and waited for him to realize he'd
lost me. It seemed to take a surprisingly long time. Finally, the car came
back, lights on now, driving slowly. Then he spotted me, and I beckoned
to him to turn. Once he had turned, I went to the car and got in.

"I didn't even see this road," he said. "I had no idea where you'd gone. Do you know you were running about fifteen miles an hour?"

"I don't know what that means," I said.

"I suspect it means you should try out for the Olympic Games. Are you tired?"

"I'm not. It was a good run, though. What are the Olympic Games?"

"Never mind. Probably too public for you. For someone your size, though, that was a fantastic run."

"It was easier than running down a deer."

"Where are we going? Don't let me pass the place."

"I won't." I not only watched, I opened my window and smelled the air. "Here," I said. "This little road coming up."

"Private road," Wright said. "Open the gate for me, would you?"

I did, but the gate made me think for a moment. I had not opened a gate going out. I had climbed over it. It wasn't a real barrier. Anyone could climb it or walk around it or open it and drive through.

Wright drove through, and I closed the gate and got back into the car. Just a few moments later, we were as close to the ruin as it was safe to drive. There were places where rubble from the houses lay in the road, and Wright said he wanted to be careful with his tires.

"This was a whole community," he said. "Plus a lot of land."

I led him around, showing him the place, choosing the easiest paths I could find, but I discovered that he couldn't see very well. The moon wasn't up yet, and it was too dark for him. He kept stumbling over the rubble, over stones, over the unevenness of the ground. He would have fallen several times had I not steadied him. He wasn't happy with my doing that.

"You're a hell of a lot stronger than you have any right to be," he said.

"I couldn't carry you," I said. "You're too big. So I need to keep you from getting hurt."

He looked down at me and smiled. "Somehow, I suspect you would find a way to carry me if you had to."

I laughed in spite of myself.

"You're pretty sure this was your home, then?"

I looked around. "I'm not sure, but I think it was. I don't remember. It's just a feeling." Then I stopped. I'd caught a scent that I hadn't noticed before, one that I didn't understand.

"Someone's been here," I said. "Someone . . ." I took a deep breath, then several small, sampling breaths. Then I looked up at Wright. "I don't know for sure, but I think it may have been someone like me."

"How can you tell?"

"I smell him. It's a different scent—more like me than like you even though he's male."

"You know he's male? You can tell that from a smell?"

"Yes. Males smell male. It isn't something I could miss. You smell male."

He looked uncomfortable. "Is that good or bad?"

I smiled. "I enjoy your scent. It reminds me of all sorts of good feelings."

He gave me a long, hungry look. "Go have the rest of your look-around on your own. You'll finish faster without me. Suddenly I want to get out of here. I'm eager to get back home."

"All right," I said. "We can go as soon as I find out about our visitor."

"This other guy, yeah." Suddenly, he sounded less happy.

"He may be able to tell me about myself, Wright. He may be my relative."

He nodded slowly. "Okay. When was he here?"

"Not that long ago. Last night I think. I need to know where he came from and where he went. Stay here. I won't go far, but I need to follow the scent."

"I think I'll come with you after all."

I put my hand on his arm. "You said you'd wait. Stay here, Wright."

He stared at me, clearly unhappy, but after a moment he nodded. "Watch yourself," he said.

I turned away from him and began to zigzag through the rubble until I felt I had the direction of the scent—the direction from which the man had come and in which he had gone. It was like a thread that drew me.

I followed it as quickly as I could to the opposite end of the ruin and beyond, through a stand of trees and on to a broad, open meadow. It ended there. I walked through the trees and into the meadow, confused, no longer understanding what I was looking for. I found marks on the ground, marks that were wrong for a car or a truck. There were two of them—long, narrow indentations too narrow and far apart to be tire marks. The word helicopter occurred to me suddenly, and I found that I knew what a helicopter was. I had a picture of one in my mind—clear bubble, rotor blades on top, metal structure sweeping back to the tail rotor, and two long runners instead of wheels. When had I ever seen such a thing?

Had a helicopter landed here, then? Had a man of my people gotten out and looked around the ruin, then gotten back into the copter and flown away?

That had probably happened. I couldn't think of any reason why it would be impossible.

Would he come back, then? Was he my relative? Had he been looking for me? Or had he had something to do with setting the fire?

If I had stayed in the area instead of wandering out to the highway and getting into Wright's car, I might have already been in contact with people who knew who I was, knew much more about me than I did. Or I might have been hurt again or killed.

I walked around where the copter had landed, looking to see whether anything had been dropped or thrown away. But there was nothing except that faint ghostly scent.

Then I caught another scent, fresh this time. Two scents. Another person—a male like Wright, but not Wright. And there was a gun of some kind. Where had the man come from? The wind—what there was of it—came to me from beyond where the helicopter had landed. That was how I had come to notice the scent of the first stranger. This new man must have passed me on his way to the ruin. If he had passed far enough away, I wouldn't have noticed, focused as I was on the helicopter and its occupant. But now I thought he must be somewhere near Wright. He and his gun must be somewhere near Wright.

I turned, ran back through the trees toward Wright. I spotted the man with the gun before I got near him. He was moving closer to Wright, not making himself known, watching Wright from hiding.

I meant to confront the man with the gun and perhaps take his gun away. I was intensely uncomfortable with his having it and being able to see Wright while Wright could not see him. I saw him as I emerged from the trees. I saw him raise the gun—a rifle, long and deadly looking. He pointed it at Wright, and I was too far away to stop him. I ran flat out, as fast as I could.

I headed toward Wright and tried to put myself between him and the gun. I expected to be shot at any moment, but I had time to hit Wright in his midsection and knock him down, knock the air out of him just as the rifle went off. Then, with Wright safely on the ground, I went after the shooter.

He fired once more before I reached him, and this time, in spite of my speed, he hit me. An instant later, I hit him with my whole body. And while I could still think, while I was aware enough to be careful, I sank my teeth into his throat and took his blood—only his blood.

# six

I didn't care whether I hurt or killed the gunman. I had knocked him unconscious when I hit him. Now I took his blood because he'd spilled mine, and because suddenly, I was in pain. Suddenly, I needed to heal. He was lucky I was aware enough not to take his flesh.

Moments later, I heard Wright's uneven steps coming toward me, and I was afraid. I went on taking the gunman's blood because it seemed to be the least harmful thing I could do at the moment.

I let the man go when Wright stood over us. I looked up at him then and, to my relief, did not in the slightest want to eat him. He stared at me, eyes wide.

"Are you shot?" he asked.

"My right leg," I said.

He was on his knees, lifting me, pulling my jeans down to examine my bloody leg. It hurt almost too much. I screamed, but I didn't harm him.

"I'm sorry," he said. "I'm so sorry. I thought you might be bleeding—losing too much blood." He hesitated. "Why aren't you bleeding more?"

"I don't ever bleed much."

"Oh." He stared at the wound. "That makes sense, I guess. Your body would know how to conserve blood if anyone's did. The bullet went all the way through. You have to go to a doctor now."

I shook my head. "I'll heal. I just need meat. Fresh meat."

He looked at the gunman. "It's a shame you can't eat him."

I stared down at him. "I can," I said. The gunman didn't wash himself often enough, but he was young and strong. His bite wound was already beginning to close. He wasn't going to die, even though I'd taken quite a bit more blood from him than I would from Wright or Theodora. If he had managed to shoot Wright, I would have made sure he died. "I can," I repeated. "But I really don't want to."

Wright smiled a little as though he thought I was joking. Then, still looking at the wound, he said, "Renee, you'll get an infection. There are probably all kinds of germs already crawling around in that wound and maybe pieces of your jeans, too. Look, I'll get you fresh meat if you'll just see a doctor."

"No doctor. I've been shot before. Some of the wounds I woke up with in the cave were bullet wounds. I need fresh meat and sleep, that's all. My body will heal itself."

There was a long silence. I lay where I was, feeling leaden, wanting to sleep. I had taken perhaps twice as much blood from the gunman as I would have dared to take from Wright or Theodora, and I still wasn't satisfied. I needed to sleep for a while, though, and let my body heal a little before I ate flesh.

The gunman would awaken thirsty and weak, maybe feeling sick.

And how did I know that?

It was one more sliver of memory, incomplete, but at least, this time, not useless.

"Shall I take you home?" Wright asked finally. "I can stop at the store for a couple of steaks."

I shook my head. "I don't want to be with you when I wake up. I'll be too hungry. I might hurt you."

"I don't think there's much chance of that," he said with just a hint of a smile.

He didn't understand. "I'm serious, Wright, I could hurt you. I . . . I might not be thinking clearly when I wake up."

"What do you want me to do?"

"Look around for a sheltered place here in the ruins. I'll need to be out of the sun when it comes up. You might have to heap some of the rubble up around me to make enough shade."

"You want me to leave you here? You want to spend . . . what, tonight and tomorrow out here?"

"I will spend tonight and tomorrow out here. Come back for me Sunday morning before sunrise."

"But there's no need—"

"Don't buy steaks unless you want them for yourself. I'll hunt. There are plenty of deer in the woods."

"Renee—!"

"Build a shelter," I said. "Put me in it. Then go home. Come back Sunday morning before sunrise."

There were several seconds of silence. Finally, he said, "What about this guy?" He nudged the gunman with his foot. "What do we do with him? Why did he want to shoot you anyway? Was it just because you scared him?"

"Me?" I said surprised. "He was aiming at you when I hit you. I couldn't reach him in time to stop him from shooting you. That's why I knocked you down—so he'd miss. Then I went after him."

He took a moment to absorb this. "God, I didn't know what the hell happened. What if he'd killed you?"

"He could have, I guess, but I didn't think he'd be fast enough. And he wasn't."

"He shot you!"

"Annoying," I said. "It really hurts. You'd better take his gun and keep it."

"Good idea." He picked it up.

"Find me a place that will be out of the sun. Otherwise, I'll have to heal a burn as well as a bullet wound."

He nodded. "Okay, but you haven't answered. What about him?" He nodded toward the gunman.

"I'll talk to him. I want to know why he tried to shoot you."

"You aren't afraid to have him here?"

"I don't want him here, but he's here. I'll try not to hurt him, but if I do, I do."

"When you're asleep, he might decide to finish what he started."

"He won't. As long as you've got his rifle, he can't."

"You bit him. That's why you aren't afraid of him, isn't it?"

"I'm afraid *for* him. I'm afraid I might not be able to stop myself from killing him."

"You know what I mean."

I did know what he meant. He was beginning to understand his relationship with me—as I had already begun to understand it.

"Because I bit him, he'll obey me," I said. "He won't hurt me if I tell him not to."

He fingered the place where I'd last bitten him and stared down at me.

I took a deep breath. "I think you can still walk away from me, Wright, if you want to," I said. I wet my lips. "If you do it now, you can still go."

"Be free of you?" he asked.

"If you want to be free of me, yes. I'll even help you."

"Why? You want to get rid of me?"

"You know I don't."

"But you want to help me leave you?" He made it a flat statement, not a question.

"If that's what you want."

"Why?"

I took a deep breath, trying to stay alert. "Because I think . . . I think it would be wrong for me to keep you with me against your will."

"You think that, do you?" Again, it wasn't a real question.

So I didn't bother to answer it.

"How?" he asked.

"What?"

"How can you help me leave you?"

"I can tell you to go. I think I can make it . . . maybe not comfortable, but at least possible for you to go and have your life back and just . . . forget about me."

"I didn't know what it would be like with you. I didn't know I would feel . . . almost as though I can't make it without you."

"I know." I closed my eyes in pain. "I didn't know what I was starting when I bit you the first couple of times. I didn't remember. I still don't remember much, but I know the bites tie you to me. That comforted me—that you were with me. But now, maybe you don't want to be with me. If that's what you've decided, tell me. Tell me now, and I'll try to help you go."

There was nothing from him for a long time. I felt as though I were drifting. My body wanted to go to sleep, demanded sleep, and somehow, I did doze a little. When he put his palm against my face, I jerked awake.

"I'm going to take you to one of the chimneys," he said. "I'll make a shelter for you there."

"If you want to go," I said, "you should tell me now." I paused. "I won't be able to stay awake long. And . . . Wright, if you don't take this chance, I don't think you'll be able to leave me. Ever. I won't be able to let you, and you couldn't stand separation from me. I know that much. Even now, it's probably hard for you to make the decision, but you should go if you want to go. It's all right."

"It's not all right," he said.

"Wright, it is. You should——"

"No!" He shook his head. "Don't tell me that. Do not tell me that!" He grasped my face between his hands, made me look at him.

"What shall I do?" I asked.

"I don't know. I don't want to lose you."

"Freedom, Wright. Now or never."

"I don't want to lose you. I truly don't. I've only known you for a few days, but I know I want you with me."

I kissed his hand, glad of his decision. It would have been hard to let him go—perhaps the hardest thing I could recall doing. I would have done it, but it would have been terrible. All I could do now was make things as safe as possible for both of us.

"Okay, then. Choose a good spot and build a shelter around me—something that won't let the sun in."

He walked around the ruin, stumbling and cursing now and then, but not falling. Eventually he found a reasonably intact little corner with two wall fragments still standing. That was better than a chimney because it was less of a potential trap. There was no part of it that I couldn't break through if I had to. It might once have been part of a closet. I drifted off to sleep while he was cleaning the debris out of it. I awoke again when he lifted me and put me in the corner.

Once I had found a comfortable position, he walled me in with stones, pieces of charred wood, tree branches, and pipe. After a while the little shelter he was building was perfect for keeping the sun out. When he finished, he reached in through the small opening he'd left and woke me up again.

"Go home," I told him, and before he could protest, I added, "Come back Sunday morning. I'll have found something to eat by then. Deer, rabbits, something."

"Just in case, I'll bring you a steak or two."

"All right." I wouldn't be wanting the steaks, but it had finally occurred to me that getting them and bringing them would make him feel better.

"What can we do to make you safer from this idiot?" he asked about the still-unconscious shooter.

"Take the gun. That will be enough."

"He could knock this shelter down at high noon while you're asleep."

"If he does that, I'll kill him. I'll have no choice. I'll get a nasty sunburn, and it will take me a little longer to heal, but that's the worst. Let me sleep, Wright."

I listened and heard him leave. He didn't want to, but he left.

Two or three hours later, the man who'd shot me finally woke up. He coughed several times and cursed. That's what woke me—the noise he made. Because I didn't dare confront him yet, I kept quiet. He got up, stumbled fell, then staggered away, his uneven steps fading as he moved away from me. He didn't seem to notice that his rifle was gone. And he didn't come near my little enclosure at all.

I slept through the rest of the night and the day. By the time the sun went down, I was starving—literally. My body had been hard at work repairing itself, and now it had to have food. I pushed away the wall of rubble that Wright had built and stood up. I was trembling with hunger as I fastened the jeans that Wright had pulled up after he examined my leg but had left loose for comfort. I took a few deep breaths, then first limped, then walked, then jogged off in the one direction I didn't smell human beings.

Hunting steadied me, focused me. And hunting was good because it meant I would eat soon.

I wound up eating most of someone's little nanny goat. I didn't mean to take a domestic animal, but it was all I found after hours of searching. It must have escaped from some farm. Better the goat than its owner.

Relieved and sated, I began hiking back toward the ruin to wait for Wright. Then I caught the scent of other people nearby. Farms. I had avoided them while I was hunting, but now I let myself take in the scents and sort them out, see whether I recognized any of them.

And I found the gunman.

It wasn't midnight yet—too early for Wright to have arrived. I had time to talk to the man who had caused me so much pain and nearly cost Wright his life. I turned toward the farm and began to jog.

I came out of the woods and ran through the farm fields toward the scent. It came from a one-story, gray farmhouse with a red roof. That meant I might be able to go straight into the room where the gunman was snoring. There were three other people in the house, so I would have to be careful. At least everyone was asleep.

I found a window to the gunman's bedroom, but it was closed and locked. I could think of no way to open it quietly. The doors were also locked. I went around the house and found no open door or window. I could get into the house easily, but not quietly.

I went back to the gunman's bedroom window—a big window. I pulled my jacket sleeve down over my hand and closed my hand around the sleeve opening so that my fist was completely covered. This was made easier by the fact that the jacket, like the rest of my clothing, was a little too big. With one quick blow, I broke the window near where I saw the latch. Then I ducked below the windowsill and froze, listening. If people were alerted by the noise, I wanted to know at once.

There was no change in anyone's breathing except the gunman's. His snoring stopped, then began again. I waited, not wanting there to be too many alien sounds too close together. Then I reached in, turned the window latch, and raised the window. The window opened easily, silently. I stepped in and closed it after me.

At that point, the man in the bed stopped snoring again. The colder air from outside had probably roused him.

As quickly as I could, I crossed the room to the bed, turned his face to the pillow, grabbed his hands, dropped my weight onto him, and bit him.

He bucked and struggled, and I worried that if he kept it up, he would either buck me off or force me to break his bones. But I had already bitten him once. He should be ready to listen to me.

"Be still," I whispered, "and be quiet."

And he obeyed. He lay still and silent while I took a little more of his blood. Then I sat up and looked around. His door was closed, but there were people in the room next to his. I had heard their breathing when

I was outside—two people. On the other hand, because his closet and theirs separated the two rooms, I could barely hear them now. Maybe they wouldn't hear us.

"Sit up and keep your voice low," I said to the gunman. "What's your name?"

He put his hand to his neck. "What did you do?" he whispered.

What's your name?" I repeated.

"Raleigh Curtis."

"Who else is in this house?"

"My brother. My sister-in-law. Their kid."

"So is this their house?"

"Yeah. I got laid off my job, so they let me stay here."

"All right. Why did you shoot me, Raleigh?"

He squinted, trying to see me in the dark, then reached for his bed-side lamp.

"No," I said. "No light. Just talk to me."

"I didn't know what you were," he said. "You just shot out of nowhere. I thought you were some kind of wild cat." He paused. "Hey, do that thing again on my neck."

I shrugged. Why not? He would definitely be sick the next day, but I didn't care. I took a little more of his blood while he lay back trembling and writhing and whispering over and over, "Oh my God, oh my God, oh my God."

When I stopped, he begged, "Do it some more. Jesus, that's the best feeling I've ever had in my life."

"No more now," I said. "Talk to me. You said you shot me because I scared you."

"Yeah. Where'd you come from like that?"

"Why were you aiming your rifle at the man? He didn't scare you."

"Had to."

"Why?"

He frowned and rubbed his head. "Had to."

"Tell me why."

He hesitated, still frowning. "He was there. He shouldn't have been there. It wasn't his property."

"It wasn't yours either." This was only a guess, but it seemed reasonable.

"He shouldn't have been there."

"Why was it your job to drive him off or kill him?"

Silence.

"Tell me why." After three bites, he should have been eager to tell me. Instead, he almost seemed to be in pain.

He held his head between his hands and whimpered. "I can't tell you," he said. "I want to, but I can't. My head hurts."

Something occurred to me suddenly. "Did you see the man in the helicopter?"

He put his face into the pillow, whimpering. "I saw him," he said, his voice muffled, barely understandable.

"When did he come? Thursday night?"

He looked up at me, gray-faced, and rubbed his neck, not where I had bitten him, but on the opposite side. "Yeah. Thursday."

"Did he see you, talk to you?"

He moaned, face twisted in pain. He seemed to be about to cry. "Please don't ask me. I can't say. I can't say."

The man, the male of my kind, had found him, bitten him, and ordered him to guard the ruin and not tell anyone why he was doing it. But what was there to guard? What was there to shoot a person over?

In spite of myself, I began to feel sorry for Raleigh. His head probably did hurt. He was torn between obeying me and obeying the man from the helicopter. That kind of thing wasn't supposed to happen. Just thinking about it made me intensely uncomfortable, and, of course, I didn't know why. I waited, hoping to remember more. But there was no more, except that I began to feel ashamed of myself, began to feel as though I owed Raleigh an apology.

"Raleigh."

"Yeah?"

"It's all right. I won't ask you about the man in the helicopter any more. It's all right."

"Okay." He looked as though he hadn't taken a breath for too long, and now, suddenly, he could breathe again. He also looked like he was no longer in pain.

"I want to meet the man in the helicopter," I said. "If he comes to you again, I want you to tell him about me."

"Tell him what?"

"Tell him I bit you. Tell him I want to meet him. Tell him I'll come back to the burned houses next Friday night. And tell him I didn't know that you . . . that you knew him. If he asks you any questions about me, it's okay to answer. All right?"

"Yeah. What's your name?"

Good question. "Don't bother about a name. Describe me to him. I think he'll know. And don't tell anyone else about either of us. Make up lies if you have to."

"Okay."

I started to get up, but he caught my hand. Then he let it go. "That thing you did," he said, touching the spot I'd bitten. "That was really good."

"It will probably make you feel weak and sick for a while," I said. "I'm sorry for that. You'll be all right in a couple of days."

"Worth it," he said.

And I left feeling better, feeling as though he'd forgiven me. Whoever I was before, it seemed I had had strong beliefs about what was right and what wasn't. It wasn't right to bite someone who had already been claimed by another of my kind. Certainly it hadn't been all right to drain Raleigh to the point of sickness when he wasn't truly responsible for shooting me. Why on earth would one of my own people take the chance of being responsible for a pointless shooting, perhaps even a death?

I jogged back toward the ruin. Eight chimneys, much burned rubble, a few standing timbers and remnant walls. That's what was left. Why did it need guarding? The guarding should have come before the fire when it might have done some good.

Finally, I jogged over to the unblocked part of the private road, coming out where Wright and I had parked the night before. I heard him coming—heard him stop down at the gate, then start again. I waited, making sure it was his car and not some stranger's. The moment I recognized the car and caught his scent, I could hardly wait to see him. The instant he stopped the car, I pulled the passenger door open and slid inside.

He was there, smelling worried and nervous. And somehow he didn't see me until I was sitting next to him, closing the door.

He jumped, then grabbed me and yanked me into a huge hug.

I found myself laughing as he examined me, checked my leg, then the rest of me. "I'm fine," I said, and kissed him and felt alarmingly glad to see him. "Let's go home," I said at last. "I want a hot bath, and then I want you."

He held me in his lap, and I was surprised that he had managed to move me there without my realizing it. "Anytime," he said. "Now, if you like."

I kissed his throat. "Not now. Let's go home."

# seven

A week later, we went back to the ruin.

I wanted Wright to park the car beside the gate to the private road. I thought it would be safest for him to stay with the car while I went in alone. But I had told him the little that Raleigh Curtis had told me, and Wright was adamant. He was going with me.

"You don't know what this guy will do," he said. "What if he just grabs you and takes you away with him? Hell, what if he's the one who torched those houses to begin with?"

"He's of my kind," I said. "Even if he doesn't know anything about me, he'll probably know someone who does. Or at least he can tell me about my people. I have to know who I am, Wright, and what I am."

"Then I have to go with you," he said. "And I think I'd better take my nice new rifle along."

I had not made any effort to get Raleigh Curtis's rifle back to him. If he didn't have it, he couldn't shoot some exploring stranger with it. Wright had kept the gun and had gone out and bought bullets for it.

"This guy is a man of your kind," he told me. "An adult male who is probably a lot bigger and stronger than you. I'm telling you, Renee, he might just decide to do what he wants with you no matter what you want."

He was afraid of losing me, afraid this other man would take me from him. He might be right. And he was probably right in thinking that the man would be bigger and stronger than I was.

That last possibility was enough to make me want Wright to stay with me and keep the gun handy. We left his cabin well before sunset because he wanted to get a look at the ruin in something more than starlight. To be sure he would be able to see well, he took along a flashlight zipped in his jacket pocket—the pocket that wasn't full of bullets.

With my jeans, my shirt, and my hooded jacket, I was reasonably well covered up so I didn't mind the daylight. It was a gray day anyway, with rain threatening but not yet falling. That kind of light was much easier on my eyes than direct sunlight.

"He won't be there yet," I told Wright as he drove. "If he's coming, he'll show up after sundown."

"If?" Wright asked.

"Maybe Raleigh didn't see him and couldn't pass along my message. Maybe he's not interested in meeting me. Maybe he had something else to do."

"Maybe you're getting nervous about meeting him," Wright said.

I was, so I didn't answer.

"You should have gotten Raleigh's phone number. Then you could have called and asked him if he'd passed on your message."

"He might not tell me," I said. "I'm not sure I'd trust him to tell me the truth on the phone." I stopped suddenly and turned to face him. "Wright . . . listen, if this guy bites you, you tell him whatever he wants to know. Do that, okay?"

He shook his head. "I don't think I'll be letting him bite me."

"But if he does. If he does."

"Okay." And after a moment, "You don't want me to suffer like Raleigh did, is that it?"

"I don't want you to suffer."

He gave me a strange little smile. "That's good to know."

We went on for a few minutes, then turned down the side road. By the time we reached the gate, we should have been close enough to the ruin for me to get a good scent picture of it, if only the wind had been blowing toward us.

"Wait here," I said when we reached the gate. "I'm going to make sure Raleigh or someone else isn't waiting for us with another gun."

He grabbed me around the waist. "Whoa," he said. "You don't need to be shot again."

I was half out of the car, but I stopped and turned back toward him into his arms. "I'll circle around and get whatever scents there are," I said.

"Stay here. Don't make noise unless you need help." And I slipped away from him.

I ran around the area, stopping now and then, trying to hear, see, and scent everything. As I expected, there was no helicopter yet. Raleigh had not been near the place recently. Someone else had, but I didn't recognize his scent. It was a young man, not of my kind, not carrying a gun. But he wasn't there now. No one was there now.

I went back to the gate where I'd left Wright and managed to surprise him again. He'd gotten out of the car and was leaning against the gate.

"Good God, woman!" he said when I caught his arm. "Make some noise when you walk."

I laughed. "No one's there. This whole night might turn out to be a waste of time, but let's go in anyway."

We got back into the car and drove in. At the ruin, we spent our time looking though the rubble and finding a few unburned or partially burned things: a pen, forks and spoons, a pair of scissors, a small jar of buttons . . . I recognized everything I found until I discovered a small silver-colored thing on the ground near where Wright had piled burned wood to wall me into my shelter. It must have been under the wood that I had pushed aside when I broke out.

"It's a crucifix," Wright told me when I showed it to him. "It must have been worn by one of the people who lived here. Or maybe the arsonist lost it." He gave a humorless smile. "You never know who's liable to turn out to be religious."

"But what is it?" I asked. "What's a crucifix? I kept running across that word when I was reading about vampires, but none of the writers ever explained what it was except to say that it scared off vampires."

He put it back into my hand. "This one's real silver, I think. Does it bother you to hold it?"

"It doesn't. It's a tiny man stuck to a tiny "†"-shaped thing. And there's a loop at the top. I think it used to be attached to something."

"Probably a chain," he said. "Another perfectly good vampire superstition down the drain."

"What?"

"This is a religious symbol, Renee—an important one. It's supposed to hurt vampires because vampires are supposed to be evil. According to every vampire movie I've ever seen, you should not only be afraid of it but it should burn your skin if it touches you."

"It isn't hot."

"I know, I know. Don't worry about it. It's just movie bullshit." He went to look around the chimneys and examine broken, discolored remains of water heaters, sinks, bathtubs, and refrigerators. As I looked around, I realized that some of the houses were missing sinks and tubs, and I wondered. Perhaps people had come here when Raleigh wasn't on guard and taken them away. Or perhaps Raleigh and his relatives had taken them. But why? Who would want such things?

Then Wright found something outside the houses more than half buried in the ground near one of the chimneys: a gleaming gold chain with a little gold bird attached to it—a crested bird with wings spread as though it were flying.

"I'm surprised something like this is still here," he said. "I'll bet plenty of people have been through here, picking up souvenirs." He wiped the thing on his shirt, then let it side like liquid into my hand.

"Pretty," I said, examining it.

"Let me put it on you."

I thought about whether I wanted the property of a person who was probably dead around my neck, but then shrugged, handed it back to him, and let him put it on me. He wanted to. And he seemed to like the effect once it was on.

"Your hair is growing out," he said. "This is just what you need to decorate yourself a little."

My hair was growing out, crinkly and black and about an inch long, and my head was no longer disfigured by broken places. I'd had Wright trim the one patch of hair that hadn't been burned off so that now it was all growing out fairly evenly. I thought I almost looked female again.

"Did you ever think I was a boy?" I asked him. "I mean when you stopped for me on the road that first time?"

"No, I never did," he said. "I should have, I guess. You were almost bald and wearing filthy, ill-fitting clothes that could have been a man's. But when I first saw you in the headlights, I thought, 'What a lovely, elfin little girl. What in hell is she doing out here by herself?'"

"Elfin?"

"Like an elf. According to some stories, an elf is a short, slender, magical being—another mythical creature. Maybe I'll run into one of them on a dark road someday."

I laughed. Then I heard the helicopter. "He's coming," I said. "It's early for him to be awake and out. He must be eager to meet me."

"I don't hear a thing," Wright said, "but I'll take your word for it. Shall I get out of sight?"

"No. You couldn't hide your scent from him. Let's wait over by that largest chimney." It was a big brick chimney that rose from a massive double fireplace. It might shelter us if our visitor decided to try to shoot us.

The copter didn't bother about landing in the meadow this time. I wondered why he had landed there before. Habit? Or was this stranger someone who would have come to visit the eight houses when they were intact and occupied?

The copter, looking like a large, misshapen bug, landed in what Wright said must have once been a big vegetable garden. He had been able to identify several of the scorched, mostly dead plants. The copter crushed a number of the survivors—cabbages and potatoes mostly.

The pilot jumped out, ducked under the rotors, and looked around. Once he spotted us, he came straight toward us. Wright, who had been checking the rifle, now stood straight, watching the stranger intently. I watched him, too. He was a tall, spidery man, empty-handed, and visibly my kind except that he was blond and very pale-skinned—not just light-skinned like Wright, but as white as the pages of Wright's books. Even so, apart from color, if I ever grew tall, I would look much like him—tall and lean, probably not elfin at all.

"Shori?" the man asked. I liked his voice at once, and he smelled . . . safe somehow. I mean his scent made me feel safe, although I couldn't say why. Then I realized that he was looking at me, had spoken to me. And what had he meant by that one word?

I stood away from the chimney.

"How did you survive, Shori? Where have you been?"

He was calling me "Shori." I let out a breath. "You know me, then," I said.

"Of course I do! What's the matter with you?"

I breathed a little more, trying to decide what to say. The truth seemed humiliating, somehow, admitting such a significant weakness to this stranger, telling him that I knew nothing at all about myself. But what else could I do? I said, "I woke up weeks ago in a cave not far from here. I have no memory of anything that happened before then. And . . . I don't know you."

He reached out to me, but I stepped back out of his reach.

"I don't know you," I repeated.

Off to one side, I saw Wright come to attention. He didn't point the rifle at the stranger, he pointed it downward. He held it across his body in both hands, his right forefinger near the trigger, so that aiming it at the man would only be a matter of moving it slightly.

The man dropped his hand to his side. He glanced at Wright, then seemed to dismiss him. "My name is Iosif Petrescu," he said. "I'm your father."

I stood staring at him, feeling nothing for him. I didn't know him. And yet he might be telling the truth. How could I know? Would he lie about such a thing? Why?

"And I'm . . . Shori?"

"The name your human mother gave you is Shori. Your surname is Matthews. Your Ina mothers were distant relatives of mine named Mateescu, but in the 1950s, when there was a great deal of suspicion about foreign-sounding names, they decided to Anglicize the name to Matthews."

"My mothers . . . ?"

He looked around at the rubble. "Listen," he said. "We don't have to talk here in the midst of all this. Come to my home."

"I lived . . . here?"

"You did, yes. You were born here. Doesn't this setting stir any memories?"

"No memories. Only a feeling that I'm somehow connected to this place. I came here when I was able to leave the cave where I woke up, but I didn't know why. It was as though my feet just brought me here."

"Home," he said. "For you, this was home."

I nodded. "But you don't live here?"

He looked surprised. "No. We don't live males and females together as humans do."

I swallowed, then asked the question I had to ask: "What are we?"

"Vampires, of course—not that we call ourselves by that name." He smiled, showing his very human-looking teeth, except for the canines, which looked a little longer and sharper than the other people's, as my own did. If his teeth were like mine, they were all sharper than other people's. They had to be. He said, "We have very little in common with the vampire creatures Bram Stoker described in *Dracula*, but we are long-lived blood drinkers." He looked at Wright. "You knew what she was, didn't you?"

Wright nodded. "I knew she needed blood to live."

Iosif sighed, then spoke wearily as though he were saying something he had to say too many times before. "We live alongside, yet apart from, human beings, except for those humans who become our symbionts. We have much longer lives than humans. Most of us must sleep during the day and, yes, we need blood to live. Human blood is most satisfying to us, and fortunately, we don't have to injure the humans we take it from. But we are born as we are. We can't magically convert humans into our kind. We do keep those who join with us healthier, stronger, and harder to kill than they would be without us. In that way, we lengthen their lives by several decades."

That got Wright's attention. "How long?" he asked.

"How long will you live?"

"Yes."

Iosif took a deep breath, then said, "Barring accident or homicide, chances are you'll live to be between 170 and 200 years old."

"Two hundred . . . I will? Healthy years?"

"Yes. Your immune system will be greatly strengthened by Shori's venom, and it will be less likely to turn on you and give you one of humanity's many autoimmune diseases. And her venom will help keep your heart and circulatory system healthy. Your health is important to her."

"Sounds too good to be true."

"It is mutualistic symbiosis. You know you're joined with her."

Wright nodded. "It scares me a little. I want it to be with her, need to be with her, even though I don't really understand what I'm getting into." After a moment, he asked, "How long do your kind live?"

"Long," Iosif said. "Although we're not immortal anymore than you are. How old do you think your Shori is?"

"I've been calling her Renee," he said. "I'm Wright Hamlin, by the way."

"How old is she?"

"I thought she was maybe ten or eleven when I met her. Later, I knew she had to be older, even though she didn't look it. Maybe eighteen or nineteen?"

Iosif smiled without humor. "That would make things legal at least."

Wright's face went red, and I looked from him to Iosif, not understanding.

"Don't worry, Wright," Iosif said after a moment. "In fact, Shori is a child. She has at least one more important growth stage to go through before she's old enough to bear children. Her child-bearing years will begin when she's about seventy. In all, she should live about five hundred years. Right now, she's fifty-three."

Wright opened his mouth, but didn't say anything. He just stared, first at Iosif, then at me. I knew that Wright was twenty-three, sexually mature, and aware of much that went on in the world. If Iosif was telling the truth, I was almost twice Wright's age, and yet I knew almost nothing. Someone had taken away most of my fifty-three years of life.

"Who did this?" I asked, gesturing at the ruin. "Who set the fire? Did anyone else survive?"

"I wasn't here," Iosif said. "I don't know who did it. And I haven't found . . . any other survivors. I've arranged for the other people who live in this area to keep their eyes open."

That got my attention. "You were careless. Raleigh Curtis wasn't just keeping his eyes open. He was going to shoot Wright. He did shoot me."

"Accident. He didn't know you were one of us. If he'd seen you clearly, he wouldn't have fired."

"Why would he want to shoot Wright?"

"He didn't know Wright was with you."

"Iosif, why shoot anyone over this rubble? Only the people who did this should be punished."

He stared at me. "Someone burned your mothers and your sisters as well as all of the human members of your family to death here. They shot the ones who tried to get out, shot them and threw most of them back into the fire. How you escaped, I have no idea, but we found the others, burned, broken . . . My people and I found them. We were coming for a visit, and we actually arrived before the firemen, which meant we were able to get control of them and see to it that they recalled this place as abandoned. When the fire was out, we cleaned up and covered up because we didn't want the remains examined by the coroner. We searched the area for several nights, hunting for survivors and questioning the local humans, finding out what they knew and seeing to it that they only remembered things that wouldn't expose or damage us. In fact, the neighbors didn't know anything. So we didn't catch the killers. We thought, though, that some of them might come back to enjoy remembering what they'd done. Criminals have done that in the past."

"To enjoy the memory of killing . . . How many people?" I demanded.

"Seventy-eight. Everyone except you."

I wet my lips, looked away from him, remembering the cave. "Maybe only seventy-seven," I said. I wanted badly not to say it, but somehow, not saying it would have made me feel even worse.

Iosif touched me, put his hand on my chin and turned my head so that I faced him. He or someone else had done that before. It felt familiar and steadying. He had straight, collar-length white-blond hair framing his sharp, narrow face and large gray eyes with their huge dark-adapted pupils. He still didn't look familiar. I didn't know him. But his touch no longer alarmed me.

I said, "Someone found me as I was waking up in the cave. I don't know how long I'd been there. Several days, at least. But finally, I was regaining consciousness, and someone found me. I didn't know at the time that it was . . . a person, a man. I didn't know anything except . . . I killed him." I couldn't bring myself to say the rest—that I'd not only killed the man, but eaten him. It shamed me so much that I moved my face away from his fingers, took a step back from him. "I still don't know who he was, but I remember the sounds he made. I heard them clearly, although at the time I didn't even recognize what he said as speech. Later, when I was safe with Wright, I was able to sort through the memories and understand what he said. I think he knew me. I think he'd been looking for me."

"What did he say?" Wright asked. He had moved closer to me.

It was terrible that he was hearing this. I shut my eyes for a moment, then answered his question. "He said, 'Oh my God, it's her. Please let her be alive.'"

There was silence.

Iosif sighed, then nodded. "He wasn't from here, Shori, he was from my community."

I looked at him and saw his sorrow. He knew who the man was, and he mourned him. I shook my head. "I'm sorry."

To my surprise, Wright pulled me against him. I leaned on him gratefully.

"I sent my people out to hunt," Iosif said. "We thought you would have survived, if anyone did. Only one of my men didn't come back from the search. We never found him. Where is your cave?"

I turned to look around, then described as best I could where the cave was. "I can take you there," I said.

Iosif nodded. "If his remains are still there, I'll have them collected and buried."

"I'm sorry," I repeated, my voice not much more than a whisper.

He stared at me, first with anger and grief, then, it seemed, only with sorrow. "You are, aren't you? I'm glad of that. You've forgotten who and what you are, but you still have at least some of the morality you were taught."

After a while, Wright asked, "Why did you think she had a better chance of surviving?"

"Her dark skin," Iosif said. "The sun wouldn't disable her at once. She's a faster runner than most of us, in spite of her small size. And she would have come awake faster when everything started. She's a light sleeper, compared to most of us, and she doesn't absolutely have to sleep during the day."

"She said she thought she was an experiment of some kind," Wright said.

"Yes. Some of us have tried for centuries to find ways to be less vulnerable during the day. Shori is our latest and most successful effort in that direction. She's also, through genetic engineering, part human. We were experimenting with genetic engineering well before humanity learned to do it—before they even learned that it was possible."

"We, who?" I asked.

"Our kind. We are Ina. We are probably responsible for much of the world's vampire mythology, but among ourselves, we are Ina."

The name meant no more to me than his face did. It was so hard to know nothing—absolutely nothing all the time. "I hate this," I said. "You tell me things, and I still don't feel as though I know them. They aren't real to me. What are we? Why are we different from human beings? Are we human beings? Are we just another race?"

"No. We're not another race, we're another species. We can't interbreed with them. We've never been able to do that. Sex, but no children."

"Are we related to them? Where do we come from?"

"I think we must be related to them," he said. "We're too genetically similar to them for any other explanation to be likely. Not all of us believe that, though. We have our own traditions—our own folklore, our own religions. You can read my books if you want to."

I nodded. "I'll read them. I wonder if they'll mean anything to me."

"You've probably suffered a severe head injury," Iosif said. "I've heard of this happening to us before. Our tissue regenerates, even our brain tissue. But memories . . . well, sometimes they return."

"And sometimes they don't."

"Yes."

"I know I had a head wound—more than one. The bones of my skull were broken, but they healed. How can we survive such things?"

He smiled. "There's a recently developed belief among some of our younger people that the Ina landed here from another world thousands of years ago. I think it's nonsense, but who knows. I suppose that idea's no worse than one of our oldest legends. It says we were placed here by a great mother goddess who created us and gave us Earth to live on until we became wise enough to come home to live in paradise with her. Actually, I think we evolved right here on Earth alongside humanity as a cousin species like the chimpanzee. Perhaps we're the more gifted cousin."

I didn't know what to think—or say—about any of that. "All right," I said. "You said the Ina people live in single-sex groups—men with men and women with women."

"Adults do, yes. Young males leave their mothers when they're a little older than you are now. They live the last years of their childhood and all of their adult years with their fathers. I'm the only surviving son of my father's family so my sons have only one father. Our human symbionts may be of either sex, but among us, sons live with brothers and fathers.

Daughters live with their mothers and sisters. In a case like this, though, since you're not fully adult, you would be welcome to join my community for a while—until you get your memories back or relearn the things you need to know and until you come of age."

"I live with Wright."

"Bring him with you, of course, and any others you've come to need. I'll have a house built for you and yours."

I looked at Wright and was not surprised to see that he was shaking his head. "I have a job," he said. "Hell, I have a life. Renee . . . Shori will be all right with me."

Iosif stared at him with an expression I couldn't read. "And you will teach her about her people and their ways?" he said. "You'll teach her her history, and help her into the adulthood she is approaching? You'll help her find mates and negotiate with their family when the time comes?" He stood straight and gazed down at Wright. He wasn't that much taller than Wright, but he gave the impression of looking down from a great height. "Tell me how you will do these things." he said.

Wright glared at him, his expression flickering between anger and uncertainty. Finally, he looked away. After a moment, he shook his head. "Where?" he asked.

"A few miles north of Darrington."

"I'd want to keep my job."

"Of course. Why not?"

"It's a long way. We'd . . . have a house?"

"You'd be guests in my house until your house is finished. We're interested in keeping Shori safe and teaching her what she needs to know to get on with her life. You're already a greater part of her life than you realize."

"I want to be with her."

"I want you with her. But tell me, what's your life been like with her? What do your friends and neighbors think about your relationship with her?"

Wright opened his mouth, then closed it again. He stared an Iosif angrily.

Iosif nodded. "You've been hiding her. Of course you have—lest someone think you were having an improper relationship with a child. Once you're living with us, there will be no need to hide. And to us, there is nothing improper about your relationship."

# eight

That same night, Iosif flew Wright and me up to see the community that was to become our new home. As we arrived, we could see from the air five large, well-lit, two-story houses built along what was probably another private road. There were also two barns, several sheds and garages, animal pens, and fields and gardens, all a few miles north of the lights of a small town—Darrington, I assumed.

Iosif promised to fly Wright and me back to the ruin later that night so that we could pick up Wright's car and go back to his cabin. If things went as Iosif intended, we would move in a week. He gave us each a card that showed his address and phone numbers and that gave directions for driving to his community. He said he would send a truck and two people to help load Wright's things onto it. Anything that didn't fit in our temporary quarters could be stored in one of the barns until our house was ready.

"You live in such out-of-the-way places," Wright complained. "This is even more isolated than the other one. I'm going to have a hell of a commute. I don't know whether it's going to be possible."

Iosif ignored him. When we landed on a large paved area not far from the largest of the houses, he said, "You need to know that it's best to avoid cities. Cities overload our senses—the noise, the smells, the lights . . . They overload us in every possible way. Some of us get used to it, but others just get sick."

"That's a surprise," Wright said. "The movies I've seen and the books I've read say vampires like cities—that their large populations makes it easy for vampires to be anonymous."

Iosif nodded. "Vampires in books and movies usually seem to be trying to kill people or trying to turn them into vampires. Since we don't do either of those things, we don't need cities. Fortunately." Iosif turned and jumped out of his side of the helicopter, while Wright slid out the other side, then reached in and lifted me out. Then Wright quickly caught up with Iosif and stood in his path like a human wall.

"I want to know what's going to happen to me," he said. "I need to know that."

Iosif nodded. "Of course you do." He glanced at me. "How long have you two been together?"

"Eleven days," I said.

"My God," Wright said. "Eleven days? Is that all? I feel as though I've had her with me for so much longer than that."

"And yet you're healthy and strong," Iosif said. "And you obviously to want to keep her with you."

"I do. I'm not entirely sure that it's my idea, but I do. What will I become, though? What have I become? You said she'll . . . find a mate. What happens to me then?"

"You are her first symbiont, the first member of her new family. Her mating can't change that. She'll visit her mates and they'll visit her, but you'll live with her. No one could separate the two of you now without killing you, and no one would try."

"Killing me . . . ? Why would I die? What would I die of?"

"Of the lack of what she provides."

"But what—?"

"Come into the house, Wright. I'll see that you get all the answers you need. You might not like them all, but you have a right to hear them."

We walked from the side to the front of the large house. Iosif's community was clearly nocturnal. The Ina were naturally nocturnal, and their symbionts had apparently adjusted to being awake at night. There were lights on in all the houses, and people—human symbionts and their children, I guessed—moved around, living their lives. A red-haired woman was backing a car out of a garage. She had a small, red-blond baby strapped into a special seat in the back. Two little boys were raking leaves, and pausing now and then to throw them at one another. They were my size, and I wondered how old they were. A little girl was sweeping leaves from a porch with a broom that was almost too big for her to manage. A man was on a ladder, doing something to the rain gutter of one of the houses. Several adults stood talking together in one of the broad yards.

Wright and I followed Iosif into the biggest house and found ourselves in a room that stretched from the front to the back of the house. Wright's whole cabin might have filled a third of it. There were several couches, several chairs large and small, and several little tables scattered around the room.

Iosif said, "We meet here on Sunday evenings or when there's something that needs community-wide discussion."

There was a broad picture window on the backyard side of the great room; it ran across the top half the wall from one end of the room to the other. At one of the end walls, there was a huge fireplace where a log burned with much snapping and sparking. Books filled built-in bookcases on the two remaining walls.

In a corner near the fireplace, two men and a woman—all human— sat at a small table, their heads together, talking quietly. There were steaming cups of coffee on the table. There was no light in the room except the fire. Iosif walked us over to the three people.

"Brook, Yale, Nicholas."

They looked up, saw me, and were on their feet at once, staring. "Shori!" the woman said. She came around her chair and hugged me. She was a stranger as far as I was concerned, and I would have drawn away from any possibility of a hug, but she smelled of Iosif. Something in me seemed to accept her. She smelled of someone I had decided was all right. "My God, girl," she said, "where have you been? Iosif, where did you find her?"

Both men looked at me, then at Wright. One of them smiled. "Welcome," he said to Wright. "Looks like Shori was able to take care of herself."

Iosif put his hand on my shoulder as the woman let me go. "Is any of this familiar to you? Do you know these people, this house?"

I shook my head. "I like the room, but I don't remember it." I looked at the three people. "And I'm sorry, but I don't remember any of you either."

All three of them stared at Iosif.

"She was very badly injured," he said. "Head injuries. As a result, she's lost her memory. And she was alone until she found Wright Hamlin here. I'm hoping her memory will return."

"Don't you have your own medical people?" Wright asked. "People who know how to help your kind?"

"We do," Iosif said. "But for Ina, that tends to mean someone to fix badly broken bones so that they heal straight or binding serious wounds so that they'll heal faster."

"You don't want to see what they mean by 'a serious wound,'" one of the men said. "Intestines spilling out, legs gone, that sort of thing."

"I don't," Wright agreed. "Shori told me she had been badly burned as well as shot. But she healed on her own. Not a scar."

"Except for not knowing herself or her people," Iosif said. "I would call that a large scar. Unfortunately, it's not one we know how to fix."

"Did I have friends here?" I asked. "People who might know me especially well?"

"Your four brothers are here," he said. He looked at the three humans. "Look after Wright for a while," he said. "Answer fully any questions he asks. He's with Shori now. He's her first, but he knows almost nothing." He took my arm and began to lead me away.

"Renee?" Wright said to me, and I stopped. It eased something in me to hear him call me by the name he had given me. "You okay?" he asked.

I nodded. "Yell if you need me. I'll hear."

He nodded. He looked as though my words eased something in him.

I followed Iosif down a long hallway.

"These bedrooms belong to me and my human family," he told me. "They're the three you just met and five others who aren't here right now. They've all been with me for years. Eight is a good number for me, although at other times in my life I've had seven or even ten. I'm wealthy enough to care for all of them if I have to, and they feed me. They're free to hold jobs away from the community, even live elsewhere part time, and sometimes they do. But at least three of them are always here. They work out a schedule among themselves."

We went through a door at the end of the hallway and out onto a broad lawn. I stopped in the middle of the lawn. "Do they mind?" I asked.

"Mind?"

"That you need eight. That none of them can be your only one." I paused. "Because I think Wright is going to mind."

"When he understands that you have to have others?"

"Yes."

"He'll mind. I can see that he's very possessive of you—and very protective." He paused, then said, "Let him mind, Shori. Talk to him. Help him. Reassure him. Stop violence. But let him feel what he feels and settle his feelings his own way."

"All right."

"I suspect this kind of thing needs to be said more to my sons than to you, but you should hear it, at least once: treat your people well, Shori. Let them see that you trust them and let them solve their own problems, make their own decisions. Do that and they will willingly commit their lives to you. Bully them, control them out of fear or malice or just for your own convenience, and after a while, you'll have to spend all your time thinking for them, controlling them, and stifling their resentment. Do you understand?"

"I do, yes. I've made him do things but only to keep him safe—mostly to keep him safe from me—especially when Raleigh Curtis shot me."

He nodded. "That sort of thing is necessary whether they understand or not. How many do you have other than Wright?"

"I've drunk from five others, but Wright doesn't know about any of them." I paused, then looked at him. "I don't know whether they've come to need me. How will I be able to tell about the others? Will you look at them and tell me?"

"It isn't sight," he said, "it's scent. Did you notice Brook's scent?"

"She smelled of you."

"And Wright smells of you—unmistakably. The scent won't wash away or wear away. It's part of them now. That should give you some idea of how we hold them."

"Something, some chemical, in our saliva?"

"Exactly. We addict them to a substance in our saliva—in our venom—that floods our mouths when we feed. I've heard it called a powerful hypnotic drug. It makes them highly suggestible and deeply attached to the source of the substance. They come to need it. Brook and Wright both need it. Brook knows, and by now, Wright probably knows, too."

"And they die if they can't have it?"

"They die if they're taken from us or if we die, but their death is caused by another component of the venom. They die of strokes or heart attacks because we aren't there to take the extra red blood cells that our venom encourages their bodies to make. Their doctors can help them if they understand the problem quickly enough. But their psychological addiction tends to prevent them from going to a doctor. They hunt for their Ina—or any Ina until it's too late."

"Until they die or until they're badly disabled."

"Yes. And even if they find an Ina not their own, they might not survive. They die unless another of us is able to take them over. That doesn't always work. Their bodies detect individual differences in our venom, and those differences make them sick when they have to adapt to a new Ina. They're addicted to their particular Ina and no other. And yet we always try to save their lives if their Ina symbiont has died. When I realized what had happened to your mothers' community, I told my people to look for wounded human symbionts as well as for you. I knew my mates were dead. I . . . found the places where they died, found their scents and small fragments of charred flesh . . ."

I gave him a moment to remember the dead and to deal with his obvious pain. I found that I almost envied his pain. He hurt because he remembered. After a while, I said, "You didn't find anyone?"

"We didn't find anyone alive. Hugh Tang, the man you killed, found you, but we didn't know that."

"All dead," I whispered. "And for me, it's as though they never existed."

"I'm sorry," he said. "I can't even pretend to understand what it's like for you to be missing so much of your memory. I want to help you recover as much of it as possible. That's why we need to get you moved into my house and dealing with people who know you." He hesitated. "To do that, we need to clear away the remnants of the life you've been living with Wright. So think. Which of the humans you've been feeding from has begun to smell as much like you as Wright does?"

I carefully reviewed my last contact with each of the humans who had fed me. "None of them," I said. "But there's one . . . she's older—too old to have children—but I like her. I want her."

He gave me a long sad look. "Your attentions will keep her healthy and help her live longer than she would otherwise, but with such a late start, she won't live much past one hundred, and it's going to be really painful for you when she dies. It's always hard to lose them."

"Can she stay here?"

"Of course. There's a large guest wing on the side of the great room opposite my family rooms. You and yours can live there in comfort and privacy until we get your house built."

"Thank you."

"You'll need more than two humans."

"I don't like the others that I've been using. I needed them, but I don't want to keep them."

He nodded. "It goes that way sometimes. I'll introduce you to others. I know adult children of our symbionts who have been waiting and hoping to join an Ina child. Some of them can't wait to join us; others can't wait to leave us. But before you meet them, you'll have to spend the next week going once more to each of the ones you don't want. You'll have to talk to them, tell them to forget you, and become just a romantic dream to them. Otherwise, chances are they'll look for you. They don't need you, but they'll want you. They might waste their lives looking for you."

"All right."

We began to walk again. He said, "I'm taking you to see your youngest brother, Stefan, because you were close to him. You spent the first twenty-five years of your life with him at your mothers' community. The two of you were always phoning each other after Stefan moved here. While you're with him, though, don't mention Hugh Tang."

"All right."

"Did you kill Hugh because you'd gone mad with hunger? Did you eat him?"

". . . yes."

"I thought so. He was Stefan's symbiont. He had met you several times, and Stefan chose him to be part of the search party because he knew Hugh would recognize you. I'll tell your brother what happened later."

We entered one of the smaller houses through the back door. In the kitchen, we found three women working. One was stirring and seasoning something in a pot on the stove, one was searching through a huge, double-doored refrigerator, and one was mixing things in a large bowl.

"Esther, Celia, Daryl," Iosif said, gesturing toward each of them as he said their names so that I would know who was who. Two of them, Esther and Celia, had skin as dark as mine, and I looked at them with interest. They were the first black people I remembered meeting. And yet the genes for my dark skin had to have come from someone like these women. The women turned to look at us, saw me, and Esther whispered my name.

"Shori! Oh my goodness."

But they were all strangers to me. Iosif told them what had happened to me, while I examined each face. I could see that they knew me, but I didn't know them. I felt tired all of a sudden, hopeless. I followed Iosif into the living room where he introduced me to my youngest brother, Stefan, and to more of his human symbionts—two men and two women. The symbionts left us as soon as they'd greeted me and heard about my memory loss. I did not know them, didn't know the house, didn't know anything.

Then I did know one small thing—something I deduced rather than remembered. I could see that Stefan was darker than Iosif, darker than Wright. He was a light brown to my darker brown, and that meant . . .

"You're an experiment, too," I said to him when we'd talked for a while.

"Of course I am," he said. "I should have been you, so to speak. We have the same black human mother."

I smiled, comforted that I had been right to believe that one of my mothers had been a black human. "Did I know her?"

"You were her favorite. Whenever I did something wrong, she'd shake her head and say I wasn't really what she had in mind anyway." He smiled sadly, remembering. "She said I was too much like Iosif."

"And someone murdered her," I said. "Someone murdered them all."

"Someone did."

"Why? Why would anyone do that?"

He shook his head. "If we knew why, we might already have found out who. I don't understand how this person was able to kill everyone—except you. Our Ina mothers were powerful. They should have been . . . much harder to kill."

"Could it have happened because humans thought we were vampires?" I asked. "I mean, if they thought we were killing people, they might have—"

"No," Stefan and Iosif said together. Then Iosif said, "We live in rural areas. People around us know one another. They know us—or they think they do. No one had died mysteriously in my mates' home territory except my mates themselves and their community."

"I don't mean that we have been killing people," I said. "I mean ... what if someone saw one of us feeding and ... drew the wrong conclusions?"

Iosif and Stefan looked at one another. Finally Iosif said, "I don't believe that could have happened. Your mothers and sisters were even more careful than we are."

"I don't believe humans could have done it," Stefan said.

"I was burned and shot," I said. "Anyone can use fire and guns."

Iosif shook his head. "I questioned several of the people who live near your mothers' community. There was nothing wrong, no trouble, no suspicions, no grudges."

"When I went to the ruin today," I said, "someone had been there. He was human, young, unarmed, and he'd walked all around the ruin. Did you notice?"

"Yes. He prowls. He lives in your general area but down toward the town of Gold Bar. He's sixteen, and I suspect he prowls without his parents' knowledge." He shook his head. "We combed the area very thoroughly. He was one of the people we checked. He didn't know anything. No one knows anything."

I sighed. "They don't and I don't." I looked from one lean, sharp face to the other, realizing that they had drawn away from me a little, and now they looked oddly uncomfortable. They fidgeted and glanced at one another now and then.

I said, "Tell me about my family, my mothers. How many mothers did I have anyway? Were they all sisters except for the human one? How many sisters did I have?"

"Our mothers were three sisters," Stefan said, "and one human woman who donated DNA. Also, there were two eldermothers—our mothers' surviving mothers. The two eldermothers were the ones who made it possible for us—you in particular—to be born with better-than-usual protection from the sun and more daytime alertness."

"They integrated the human DNA with our own somehow?"

"They did, yes. They were both over 350 years old, and biology fascinated them. Once their children were mated, they studied with humans from several universities and with other Ina who were working on the problem. They understood more about the uses of viruses in genetic engineering than anyone I've ever heard of, and they understood it well before humans did. They were fantastic people to work with and talk to." He paused, shaking his head. "I still can't believe that they're dead—that someone would murder them that way."

"Could their work be the reason they were murdered?" I asked. "Did anyone object to it or try to stop it?"

Stefan looked at Iosif and Iosif shook his head. "I don't believe so. Shori, our people have been trying to do this for generations. If you could remember, you'd know what a celebrity you are. People traveled from South America, Europe, Asia, and Africa to see you and to understand what our mothers had done."

"There are Ina in Africa, and they haven't done this?"

"Not yet."

"Was anyone visiting just before the fire?"

"Don't know," Iosif said. "I hadn't spoken to your mothers for a week and a half. When I phoned them in the early morning and told them I wanted to visit the next night, they said they would be expecting me. They said if I came, I had to stay a few days." He smiled, apparently taking pleasure in his memories, then his expression sagged into sadness. "They told me to bring at least five symbionts. I took them at their word. The next night, I gathered five of my people and drove down there. Vasile had wanted to use the helicopter for something so I took one of the bigger cars. When I got there, I found smoke and ashes and death." He paused, staring out into nothing. "Once I'd seen it and understood it, I called home to get Stefan and Radu to come down with some of their symbionts to help clean things up, to hunt for survivors, and to keep our secrets secret."

So that was how Hugh Tang had wound up at the cave looking for me. "What have you learned since then?" I asked.

He turned away from me, paced a few steps away, then the same few back. "Nothing!" The word was a harsh whisper. "Not one goddamned thing."

I sighed. Suddenly, I'd had enough. "I think I need to go home," I said. "Let's go get Wright, and you can take us back to the ruin."

"You are home." He stood in front of me and looked down at me with an expression I couldn't read, except that it wasn't an altogether friendly expression. "You must think of this place as your home."

"I will," I said. "I'll be glad to come back here and learn more about my life, my family. But I'm tired now. I feel . . . I need to go back to things that feel familiar."

"I was hoping to convince you to stay here until tomorrow night," he said.

I shook my head. "Take me back."

"Shori, it would be best for you to stay here. Wright has hidden you successfully for this long, but if anything went wrong, if even one person spotted you with him and decided to make trouble—"

"You promised to give us a week," I said. "That was the first promise you made me."

He stared down at me. I stared back.

After a while, he sighed and turned away. "Child, I've lost everyone but you."

Stefan said, "All of our female family is dead, Shori. You're the last."

I wanted more than ever to go home, to be away from them and alone with Wright. And yet they pulled at me somehow—my father and my brother. They were strangers, but they were my father and my brother. "I'm sorry," I said. "I need to go."

"We Ina are sexually territorial," Iosif said. "And you're a little too old to be sharing territory with the adult males of your family—with any adult Ina male since you're too young to mate. That's what's bothering you."

"You mean I feel uncomfortable with you and Stefan just because you're male?"

"Yes."

"Then how can I live here?"

"Let's go back to Wright. I think you'll feel better when you're with him." He led me away from Stefan toward a side door. I looked back once, but Stefan had already turned away."

"Is he feeling territorial, too?" I asked.

"No. He's willing for you to be here because he fears for you—and for himself. And you're not mature yet, so there's no real danger . . ."

"Danger?"

He led me through the door, and we headed back across the lawn.

"Danger, Iosif?"

"We are not human, child. Male and female Ina adults don't live together. We can't. Mates visit, but that's all."

"What is the danger?"

"As your body changes, and especially as your scent changes, you will be perceived more and more as an available adult female."

"By my brothers?"

He nodded, looking away from me.

"By you?"

Another nod. "We won't hurt you, Shori. Truly, we won't. By the time you come of age, I'll have found mates for you. I was already talking to the Gordon family about you and your sisters ... Now ... now I intend to sell your mothers' land. That money should be enough to give you a start at a different location when you're a little older."

"I don't think I want to live here."

"I know, but it will be all right. It will only be until you look more adult. Your brothers and I have our genetic predispositions—our instincts—but we are also intelligent. We are aware of our urges. We can stand still even when the instinct to move is powerful."

"You said I'm a child."

"You are, now more than ever with your memory loss. You can play sexually with your symbionts, but you're too young to mate. You can't yet conceive a child, and you're not yet as large or as strong as you will be. Your scent right now is interesting, but for us, it's more irritating than enticing."

We went back into his house. "You'll take us back to the ruin tonight," I told him. "You said you would. Were you speaking the truth?"

"I was, but I shouldn't have said it. I'm afraid for you, Shori."

"But you'll do it."

There was a long silence. Finally he agreed. "I will."

We went down the long hallway again and into the great room. There, Wright sat alone in one of the large chairs. The other three humans had left him. I went up to him, wanting to touch him from behind, wanting to lay my hands on his shoulders, but not doing it. I wondered what Iosif's symbionts had said to him, what they had made him feel about being with me. I walked around and stood in front of him, looking down, trying to sense his mood.

He looked up at me, his face telling me only that he was not happy. "What happens now?" he asked.

"We go home," I said.

He looked at Iosif, then back at me. "Yeah? Okay." He got up, then spoke to Iosif. "You're letting her go? I didn't really believe you would do that."

"You thought I was lying to you?" Iosif said.

"I thought your . . . paternal feelings might kick in and make you keep her in spite of your promise."

"She's tough and resilient, but I fear for her. I'm desperate to keep her."

"So . . . ?"

"She wants to go . . . and . . . I understand why. Keep her hidden, Wright. Except for my people and hers, I don't believe anyone knows she's alive. I even got that boy, Raleigh Curtis, to forget about her. Keep her hidden and bring her back to me on Friday."

Wright licked his lips. "I don't understand, but I'll bring her back."

"Even though you don't want to?"

". . . yes."

They looked at each other, each wearing a similar expression of weariness, misery, and resignation.

I took Wright's hand, and the three of us went out to the copter. Wright said nothing more. He let me hold his hand, but he did not hold mine.

# nine

W right and I didn't talk until we reached the car. We had flown all the way back to the ruin in silence, had said good-bye to Iosif and watched him fly away. When we got into the car and began our drive home, Wright finally said, "You have others already, don't you? Other . . . symbionts."

"Not yet," I said. "I've gone to others for nourishment. I can't take all that I need from you every night. But I haven't . . . I mean none of the others . . ."

"None of the others are bound to you yet."

"Yes."

"Why am I?"

"I wanted you." I touched his shoulder, rested my hand on his upper arm. "I think you wanted me, too. From the night you found me, we wanted each other."

He glanced at me. "I don't know. I never really had a chance to fig-ure that out."

"You did. When I was shot, I gave you a chance. It was . . . very hard for me to do that, but I did it. I would have let you go—helped you go."

"And you think I could have just gone away and not come back? I had to leave you lying on the ground bleeding. You insisted on it. How could I not come back to make sure you were all right?"

"You knew I would heal. I told you you weren't bound to me then. I offered you freedom. I told you I wouldn't be able to offer it again."

"I remember," he said. He sounded angry. "But I didn't know then that I was agreeing to be part of a harem. You left that little bit out."

I knew what a harem was. One of the books I'd read had referred to Dracula's three wives as his harem, and I'd looked the word up. "You're not part of a harem," I said. "You and I have a symbiotic relationship, and it's a relationship that I want and need. But didn't you see all those children? I'll have mates someday, and you can have yours. You can have a family if you want one."

He turned to glare at me, and the car swerved, forcing him to pay attention to his driving. "What am I supposed to do? Help produce the next generation of symbionts?"

I kept quiet for a moment, wondering at the rage in his voice. "What would be the point of that?" I asked finally.

"Just as easy to snatch them off the street, eh?"

I sighed and rubbed my forehead. "Iosif said the children of some symbionts stay in the hope of finding an Ina child to bond with. Others choose to make lives for themselves outside."

He made a sound—almost a moan. For a while, he said nothing.

Finally, I asked, "Do you want to leave me?"

"Why bother to ask me that?" he demanded. "I can't leave you. I can't even really want to leave you."

"Then what do you want?"

He sighed and shook his head. "I don't know. I know I wish I had driven past you on the road eleven nights ago and not stopped. And yet, I know that if I could have you all to myself, I'd stop for you again, even knowing what I know about you."

"That would kill you. Quickly."

"I know."

But he didn't care—or he didn't think he would have cared. "What did those three people tell you?" I asked. "What did they say that's made you so angry and so miserable? Was it only that I take blood from several symbionts instead of draining one person until I kill him?"

"That probably would have been enough."

I rested my head against his arm so that I could touch him without looking at him. I needed to touch him. And yet, he had to understand. "I've fed from you and from five other people—three women and two men. I'll keep one of the women if she wants to stay with me. I think she will. The others will forget me or remember me as just a dream."

"Did you sleep with any of them?"

"Did I have sex with them, you mean? No. Except for the one

woman, I fed and came back to you. I stayed longer with her because something in her comforts and pleases me. Her name is Theodora Harden. I don't know why I like her so much, but I do."

"Swing both ways, do you?"

I frowned, startled and confused by the terrible bitterness in his voice. "What?"

"Sex with men and with women?"

"With my symbionts if both they and I want it. For the moment, that's you."

"For the moment."

I reached up to slip my hand under his jacket and shirt to touch the bare flesh of his neck. It was unmarked. I had only nipped him a little for pleasure the night before, then I went to one of the others while he slept. He had healed by morning. Tonight, I had intended to do something that wouldn't heal nearly as fast.

And yet when we reached his cabin, we went in and went to bed without saying or doing anything at all. I didn't bite him because he clearly didn't want me to. I fell asleep fitted against his furry back, taking comfort in his presence even though he was angry and confused. At least he didn't push me away.

Finally, some time later, he shook me awake, shook me hard, saying, "Do it! Do it, damnit! I should get some pleasure out of all this if I don't get anything else."

I put my fingers over his lips gently. When he fell silent, I kissed first his mouth, then his throat. He was so angry—so filled with rage and confusion.

He rolled onto me, pushing my legs apart, pushing them out of his way, then thrust hard into me. I bit him more deeply than I had intended and wrapped my arms and legs around him as I took his blood. He groaned, writhing against me, holding me, thrusting harder until I had taken all I needed of his blood, until he had all he needed of me.

After a long while, he rolled off me, sated for the moment in body if not in mind.

"Did I hurt you?" he asked very softly.

I pulled myself onto his chest and lapped at the ragged edges of the bite. "You didn't hurt me," I said. "Were you trying to hurt me?"

"I think I was," he said.

I went on lapping. There was more bleeding than usual. "Did I hurt you?" I asked.

"No, of course not. What you do ought to hurt, but except for that first instant when you break the skin, it never does." He slipped his arms around me, and it was more the way he usually held me.

"It's good to know we don't hurt each other even when we're upset."

"I don't know how to deal with all this, Renee ... Shori. It's like being told that extraterrestrials have arrived, and I'm sleeping with one of them."

I laughed. "That may be true, except that if we arrived, it must have happened thousands of years ago."

"Do you believe that—that your people come from another planet? I remember your father said something about a theory like that."

"According to Iosif, some younger Ina believe it. Some don't. He doesn't. I don't know what to think about it. If I could get my memory back, then maybe I'd have an opinion that was worth bothering about."

"Do you believe Iosif is your father?"

I nodded against his chest. Then the sweet smell of his blood made me go on licking at the bite.

"Why? If he's a stranger to you, why do you believe him?"

"I don't know. Maybe it's something about his manner, his body language. But more likely it's his scent. I kept hoping to remember something while I was with him, any little thing. But there was nothing. He introduced me to my brother Stefan, and still, there was nothing. But I never doubted that they were who they said they were. And all their human symbionts recognized me."

"Yeah," Wright said.

"You talked to three symbionts. Do you think they were lying?"

"No, I don't think they were lying." He ran his hand over my head and down my back. "They said I was lucky to have you—lucky to be your first. That was when I realized that ... of course you'd have to already have others, even though I didn't know about them. Then the woman, Brook, told me all Ina have several symbionts."

"How much blood do you think you could provide?"

"You ... you taste me just about every day."

"Just a little. I crave you. I do. And I enjoy pleasuring you."

"That's the right attitude," he said. He rolled over, trapping me beneath him and thrust into me again. This time I was the one who could not let out a groan of pleasure. He laughed, delighted.

Later, as we lay together, more satisfied, more at ease, he said, "They'll be coming for us next Friday."

"Yes," I said. "I don't want to go live with them, but I think we have to."

"I was going to say that."

"I need to learn how to set up my own household—how to make it work. When I can do that, when I've learned the things I need to know to do that, we'll go out on our own."

"How big a household?" he asked.

"You, me, five or six others. We don't all have to live in the same house the way my brothers do with their symbionts, but we need to be near one another."

"It'll be rough to live together in your father's house."

"He says he'll sell my mothers' property, and when I'm older, the money will give me a start somewhere else."

"And he'll hook you up with a male Ina, or rather, with a group of Ina brothers. My God, a group of brothers . . ."

I said nothing. My mothers had lived together in the same community, shared a mate, and worked things out somehow. It could be done. It was the Ina way. "That will all happen in the future," I said. "Next week, we'll be in rooms at Iosif's house, you and I and Theodora. She's one of our neighbors, a few doors down. You might know her."

There was a long silence. Finally he asked, "Is she pretty?"

I smiled. "Not pretty. Not young either. But I like her."

"Are you going to tell her to join us . . . or ask her?"

"Ask her. But she'll come."

"Because she's already fallen so far under your influence that she won't be able to help herself?"

"She'll want to come. She doesn't have to, but she'll want to."

He sighed. "I think the scariest thing about all this so far is that all three of those symbionts seem genuinely happy. What do you figure? Old Iosif told them they were living in the best of all possible worlds, and they bought it because as far as they're concerned, he's God?"

"He didn't," I said.

"You asked?"

"He told me that it was wrong, shortsighted, and harmful to symbionts to do such things. I didn't ask. I had already figured that out."

"So you believe that's what he believes?"

"I do, at least on this subject."

"Shit."

I kissed him and turned over and went to sleep.

      ◎     ◎     ◎

During the next week, I visited each of my people, fed from them, and said good-bye. I became a dream to them, as Iosif had suggested, and I left them. Finally, on Thursday, I visited Theodora.

I paid attention to her house and waited until shortly after sunset when she was alone. Then I visited her.

I hadn't seen her for a while, but as I looked at her large, handsome house, it occurred to me that in spite of what I had said to Wright, perhaps I should not ask Theodora to join me until I had a home, something more than rooms in Iosif's house to offer her. The thought surprised me. It occurred to me after I reached her front door and rang the doorbell.

I heard her come to the door. Then there was a long pause while, I suppose, she looked out through the peephole and tried to figure out who I might be. She had never seen me before. I had visited her in darkness three times and had not allowed her to turn on a light. She must have gotten an idea of my general size, but she had never seen my face, my coloring, or the fact that I looked so young.

Finally, she opened the door, looked down at me questioningly, and said, "Hello there."

"Hello," I said, and as she recognized my voice, as her expression began to change to one of shock, I said, "Invite me in."

At once, she stood aside and said, "Come in."

This was a bit of vampire theater. I knew it, and I was fairly sure she knew it, too. She had probably been brushing up on vampires recently. Of course, I didn't need permission to enter her home or anyone else's. I did find it interesting, though, that human beings made up these fantasy safe-guards, little magics, like garlic and crucifixes, that would somehow keep them safe from my kind—or from what they imagined my kind to be.

I walked past her into the house. There was, near the front door, a broad staircase on one side and a living room almost as large as Iosif's on the other. The walls were a very pale green, and the woodwork was white. All the furniture was, somehow, exactly where it should be and exactly what it should be. Iosif's living room was more lived-in, more imperfect, more comfortable to be in. I began to feel even more uneasy about asking Theodora to come with me.

She came up behind me, and when I turned to face her, she stopped, staring at me with a kind of horror.

"Is it my skin color or my apparent age that's upsetting you so?" I asked.

"Why are you here?" she demanded.

"To talk with you," I said. "To have you see me."

"I didn't want to see you!"

I nodded. "It will make a difference," I said, "but not as great a differ-ence as you think." I went to her, took her arm, tried to lead her into the perfect living room.

She pulled back and said, "Not here." She took my hand and led me up the stairs into a room whose walls were covered with books. There was a sofa and two chairs also piled high with books and papers. In the middle of the room was a large, messy desk covered with open books, papers, a computer and monitor, a radio, a telephone, a box of pencils and pens, a stack of notebooks and crossword puzzle magazines, a long decorative wooden box of compact discs, bottles of aspirin, hand lotion, antacid, correction fluid, and who knew what else.

I stared at it and burst out laughing. It was the most disorderly mass of stuff I had run across, and yet it all looked—felt—familiar. Had I once had an equally messy desk? Had one of my mothers or sisters? I would ask Iosif. Anyway, it was the opposite of the living room downstairs, and that was a relief.

Theodora had been clearing books off a chair so that I could sit down. She stopped when I laughed, followed my gaze, and said, "Oh. I forget how awful that must look to strangers. No one ever sees it but me."

I laughed again. "No, this is who you are. This is what I wanted to see." I drew a deep breath, assuring myself that she was still free of me, still unaddicted. She was, and that was a good thing, although it felt like a flaw I should fix at once.

"I write poetry," she said. She almost seemed embarrassed about it. "I've published three books. Poetry doesn't really pay, but I enjoy writing it."

I took some of the books off the sofa and piled them on the chair she had been clearing for me, then took her hand and drew her to the sofa. She sat with me even though she didn't want to—or she didn't want to want to. I felt that she was teaching me about herself every moment. I turned her to face me and just enjoyed looking at her. She had waist-length, dark-brown hair with many strands of gray. Her eyes were the same dark brown as her hair, and the flesh at the corners of them was indented with arrays of fine lines—the only lines on her face. She was a little heavier than was good for her. Plump might have been the best word to describe her. It made her face full and round. She wore no makeup at all— not even lipstick. She had been at home, relaxing without her family around her.

After a moment, I leaned against her, put my head on her shoulder, and she put her arm around me, then took it away, then put it back. She smelled remarkably enticing.

"I don't understand," she said.

"I don't either," I said. "But the things I don't understand are probably not the same ones giving you trouble. How long do we have before your family comes home?"

"They're visiting my son-in-law's family in Portland. They won't be home until tomorrow." The moment she said this, she began to look nervous, as though she was afraid of what I might make of her solitude, her vulnerability.

"Good," I said. "I need to talk to you, tell you my story, hear yours. Then I have something to ask of you."

"Who are you?" she demanded. "What's your name? What . . . What . . . ?"

"What am I?"

". . . yes." She looked away, embarrassed.

I pulled her down to a comfortable level and bit her gently, then hard enough to start blood flowing on its own so that I could be lazy and just take it as it came. After a while, I said, "You told me I was a vampire."

She had not objected to anything I'd done even when I climbed onto her lap, straddled her, and rested against her, lapping occasionally at the blood. She put her arms around me and held me against her as though I might try to escape.

"You are a vampire," she said. "Although according to what I've read, you're supposed to be a tall, handsome, fully grown white man. Just my luck. But you must be a vampire. How could you do this if you weren't? How could I let you do it? How could it feel so good when it should be disgusting and painful? And how could the wound heal so quickly and without scars?"

"You don't believe in vampires."

"I didn't use to. And I never thought they would be so small and . . . like you."

"I've been called an elfin little girl."

"That's exactly right."

"In a way, it is. I'm a child according to the standards of my people, but my people age more slowly than yours, and I have an extra problem. I may be older than you are in years. As far as my memory is concerned, though, I was born just a few weeks ago."

"But how can that—?"

"Shh." I started to get off her lap, and she tried to hold me where I was. "No," I said. "Let me go." She released me, and I sat beside her and leaned against her.

"Three, maybe four weeks ago," I began, "I woke up in a shallow cave a few miles from here. I'm being vague about when and where because I don't know enough to be exact. During my first days in the cave I was blind and in and out of consciousness. I was in a lot of pain, and I had no memory of anything that had happened before the cave."

"Amnesia."

"Yes." I told her the rest of it, told her about killing Hugh Tang, but not about eating him, told her about hunting deer and eating them. I told her about Wright finding me and taking me in, and about finding my father and brothers. I told her the little I knew about the Ina and about what an Ina community was like. I told her I wasn't human, and she believed me. She wasn't even surprised.

"You want me to be part of such a community?" she asked.

"I do, but not yet."

"Not . . . yet?"

"My father is having a house built for me. Come to me when the house is ready. I'll see to it that there's space for your books and other things—a place where you can write your poetry."

"How long?"

"I don't know. No more than a year."

She shook her head. "I don't want to wait that long."

I was surprised. I had been careful to let her make up her own mind, and I had believed she would come with me, but not so quickly. "I have nothing to offer you now," I said. "I'll be living in rooms in my father's house. He says you can come, but when I saw what you have here, I thought you'd want to wait until you could have something similar with me."

"I have no patience," she said. "I want to be with you now."

I liked that more than I could have said, and yet I wondered about it. "Why?" I asked her. I had no idea what she would say.

She blinked at me, looked surprised, hurt. "Why do you want me?"

I thought about that, about how to say it in a way she might understand. "You have a particularly good scent," I said. "I mean, not only do you smell healthy, you smell . . . open, wanting, alone. When I came to you the first time, you were afraid at first, then glad and welcoming, excited, but you didn't smell of other people."

She frowned. "Do you mean that I smelled lonely?"

"I think so, yes, longing, needing . . ."

"I didn't imagine that loneliness had a scent."

"Why do you want me?" I repeated.

She hugged me against her. "I am lonely," she said. "Or I was until you came to me that first time. You've made me feel more than I have since I was a girl. I hoped you would go on wanting me—or at least that's what I hoped when I wasn't worrying that I was losing my mind, imagining things." She hesitated. "You need me," she said. "No one else does, but you do."

"Your family?"

"Not really, no. This is my home, and I'm glad to be able to help my daughter and her husband by having them come live here, but since my husband died, all I've really cared about—all I've been able to care about—is my poetry."

"You would be able to bring only some of your things to my father's house," I said.

"A few boxes of books, some clothing, and I'll be fine."

I looked around the room doubtfully. "Wright and I will be moving tomorrow. I'll need your telephone number so I can reach you. If you don't change your mind, we'll come back for you and your things the Friday after next."

"Promise me."

"I have."

"Will you stay with me tonight?"

"For a while. Have you eaten?"

"Eaten?" She looked at me. "I haven't even thought of eating, although I suppose I'd better. Do you eat regular food at all, ever?"

"No."

"All right. Come keep me company in the kitchen while I microwave something to eat. I don't think I should miss very many meals if I'm going to be with you."

"Exactly right," I said, and enjoyed every moment of the flesh-to-flesh contact when she bent and kissed me.

# *ten*

No one came for us on Friday.

When the night was half gone, Wright tried to phone Iosif—tried each of the numbers he had given us. At first, there was no answer, then there was a computerized voice saying that the number he was calling was out of service. He made several fruitless attempts.

"We need to go there," I said.

He looked at me for a moment, then nodded. "Let's go," he said.

I grabbed a blanket from the bed, thinking that we might have to spend part of the coming day in the car. I didn't want to think about why that might happen, but I wanted to be ready for it. Thoughts of the burned-out ruin that had been my mothers' community jumped into my mind, and I couldn't ignore them.

Wright was not certain how to reach Iosif's community. His maps didn't show the tiny community, of course. Iosif's card contained a sketch of a map that turned out to be hard to follow. We got onto what seemed to be the right side-road, but found no turn off where Wright had expected one. We tried another side road, then another, but still did not find the community.

Finally, I did what I hadn't wanted to do.

"This is no good," I said. "We're in the right general area. Find a place to park, and I'll go out and find the community. I can find it by scent if not by sight."

He didn't want me to go. He wanted to keep driving around or, if necessary, go home and try again during the day.

I shook my head. "Find a safe place and park. I need to go to them and see that they're all right. And if . . . if they're not all right, if this is anything like what happened to my mothers, you can't be there. If my father or my brothers are injured, they'll be dangerous. They might not be able to stop themselves from killing you."

"And eating me," he said. He didn't even make it a question.

I said nothing for a moment, stared at him. Had the human symbionts told him or had he guessed? I hated that he knew but clearly, he did know. "Yes," I admitted finally. "That's probably what would happen. Park and wait for me."

He parked on the highway at a place where the road's shoulder was wide. "This will do as well as anywhere," he said. "If anyone wants to know what I'm up to, I got sleepy and decided to play it safe and catch a nap."

"If you have to move," I said, "wait for me somewhere south of here along the road. I'll find you. If you have to leave the area—"

"I won't leave you!"

"Wright, hear me. Do this. If you're in danger from the police, from an Ina, from anyone at all, leave me, go home. I'll get there when I can. Don't look for me. Go home."

He shook his head, but he would do it. After a moment, he said, "You honestly believe you could find your way to my cabin from here?"

"I could," I said. "If I have to, I will." I took his hand from where it was still resting on the steering wheel. Such a huge hand. I kissed it then turned to go.

"Shori!" he said.

I had opened the door to get out of the car, but his tone stopped me.

"Feed," he said.

He was right. I was probably going to have to cover a few miles and face I-didn't-know-what. Best to be at full strength. I shut the door and kneeled on the seat to reach him. He lifted me over onto his lap, kissed me, and waited.

I bit him deeply and felt him spasm and go hard under me. I hadn't bitten him this way for a week, hadn't taken a full meal from him. I had hoped we would share this night in our new quarters. I liked to take my time when I truly fed from him, tear sounds from him, exhaust him with pleasure, enjoy his body as well as his blood. But not now. I took his blood quickly, rocking against him, then stayed for just a few minutes more, licking the wound to begin its healing, comforting him, comforting myself. Finally I hugged him and got out of the car. "Stay safe," I said.

He nodded. "You too."

I left him and began to run. We were in the right general area but were, I thought, south of our target. Wright had turned off too soon. I ran along the road, alert for cars and for a telltale wisp of scent. I was moving in a generally northerly direction through woods, alongside a river that sometimes veered away from the road and sometimes came close to it. I passed the occasional house, cluster of houses, or farm, but these were strictly human places.

After a while I did catch a scent. I didn't bother about finding the side-road. I followed the scent cross-country through the woods, past a house that had been almost completely hidden by trees. I didn't care about private property or rugged terrain. All I cared about were the scents drifting in the air and what they could tell me. I stopped every now and then to take a few deep breaths, turning into the wind, sorting through the various scents. Running, I might miss something. Standing still, eyes closed, breathing deeply, I could sort through far more scents—plant, animal, human, mineral—than I wanted to bother with.

There was a gradual change. After a while, what I smelled most was smoke—old smoke, days old, and ash clinging to the trees, stirred up by my feet, by the feet of animals, by cars on the narrow little roads I crossed.

Smoke and burned flesh. Human flesh and Ina flesh.

When I found my father's and brothers' homes, they looked much like the ruin of my mothers' community. The buildings had been completely destroyed, burned to rubble, and then trampled by many feet. My father and my brothers had been there, but they were gone now. I could smell death, but I could not see it. I did not know yet who had died and who had survived. Someone had come for my male family, and whoever it was had been as thorough as they had when they came for my mothers and my sisters.

The place that had been Iosif's community was full of strange, bad smells—the scents of people who should not have been there, who had nothing to do with Iosif or his people. Whose scent was I finding? The arsonists? Firemen? The police? Neighbors? All of these, probably.

I stood amid the rubble and looked around, trying to understand. Was Iosif dead? And Stefan? I hadn't even met my other three brothers and their symbionts. All dead? None wounded and surviving in hiding?

Then I remembered that some of Iosif's symbionts worked away from the community, even lived away from it part of the time. Did they know what had happened? If they didn't, they would be coming back here soon. They would come, needing Iosif or one of my brothers. When they found out what had happened, they would have to find another Ina to bond with just to survive. Could I help? Was I too young? I was definitely too ignorant. Surely they would know of other Ina communities. If they had come home and found only rubble, they might already have taken refuge in some other community.

When had the fire happened? Days ago, surely. The place was cold. Even the freshest human smells I found were all at least a day or two old.

Who had done this and why? First my mothers' community, now my father's. Even Iosif had had no idea who attacked my mothers. He had been deeply angry and frustrated at his own ignorance. If he didn't know, how could I find out?

Someone had targeted my family. Someone had succeeded in killing all of my relatives. And if this had to do with the experiments that had given me my useful human characteristics—what else could it be?—then it was likely that I was the main target.

I began to run again, to circle the community, stopping often to sample scents more thoroughly and hunting for fresh scents, any hint that some member of my family might be alive, hiding, healing. I found the narrow private road that led to where the houses had been, and I followed it out to a two-lane public road. There, I closed my eyes and turned toward where Wright was waiting. I could get back to him in half an hour.

But I didn't want to go back to him yet. I wanted to learn all I could, all that my eyes and my nose could tell me.

I went back to the rubble—charred planks, blackened jagged sections of wall, broken glass, standing chimneys, burned and partially burned furniture, appliances, broken ceramic tile in what had been the kitchens and the bathrooms, unrecognizable lumps of blackened plastic, a spot where an Ina had died . . .

I stood still at that place, trying to recognize the scent, realizing that I couldn't because it was the wrong scent, that of a dead male whom I had not met, burned to ash and bone, definitely dead.

I had not known him. He must have been one of my brothers but one I had not met. He had died in one of the three houses I had not entered.

I stared at the spot for a long time and caught myself wondering what the Ina did with their dead. What were their ceremonies? I knew something about human funeral services from my vampire research. I had read through a great deal of material about death, burial, and what could go wrong to cause the dead to become undead. It was all nonsense as far as I was concerned, but it had taught me that proper respect for the dead was important to humans. Was it important to Ina as well?

What had been done with the remains of both my male and my female families? Had the police taken them? Where would they take them? I would have to talk to Wright about that and perhaps to Theodora. She worked at a library. If she didn't know, she would know how to find out.

But if I somehow got the remains, what could I do but bury them or scatter their ashes after, perhaps, a more thorough cremation? I didn't know any Ina rituals, any Ina religion, any living Ina people.

I found another place where someone had died—a symbiont this time, a female. I had not met her. I was grateful for that. After a while, I made myself go to the house that had been my father's. I walked through it slowly, found two spots where symbionts I did not know had died. Then I found two that I did know—the two men I had met in Iosif's huge front room, Nicholas and Yale. I stood for a long time, staring at the spots where the two men had died. I had not known them, but they had been healthy and alive only a week before. They had welcomed me, had been friendly to Wright. It did not seem possible that they were dead now, reduced to two smudges of burned flesh that smelled of Iosif and of their own individual human scents.

Then, in the remains of what must have been a large bedroom, I found a place that smelled so strongly of Iosif that it had to be the spot where he died. Had he tried to get out? He was not near a window or a door. I got the impression that he was lying flat on his back when he died. Had he been shot? I found no bullets, but perhaps the police had taken them away. And if there had ever been a smell of gunpowder, it had been overwhelmed by all the other smells of burning and death. Iosif had certainly burned. A small quantity of his ashes were still here, mixed with the ashes of the house and its contents.

He was definitely dead.

I stood over the spot, eyes closed, hugging myself.

Iosif was dead. I'd hardly begun to know him, and he was dead. I had begun to like him, and he was dead.

I folded to the ground in anguish, knowing that I could do nothing to help him, nothing to change the situation. Nothing at all. My family was destroyed, and I couldn't even grieve for them properly because I remembered so little.

"Shori?"

I jumped up and back several steps. I had been so involved with my thoughts and feelings that I had let someone walk right up to me. I had heard nothing, smelled nothing.

At least I could see that I had startled the person who had surprised me. I had moved fast, and it was dark. She was looking around as though her eyes had not followed my movement, as though she did not know where I had gone. Then she spotted me. By then I understood that she was human and that she didn't see very well in the dark, that she smelled of my father and that I knew who she was.

"Brook," I said.

She looked around at the devastation, then looked at me, tears streaming down her face.

I went to her and hugged her, as she had hugged me when we met. She hugged back, crying even harder.

"Were you here when this happened?" she asked finally.

"No. We were supposed to move in tonight."

"Do you know if . . . ? I mean, did you see Iosif?"

I looked back at the place where Iosif had died, where a very small quantity of his ashes still remained. "He didn't survive," I said.

She stared at me silently, frowning as though I had said words she could not understand. Then she began to make a noise. It began as a moan and went on to become an impossibly long, ragged scream. She fell to the ground, gasping and moaning. "Oh God," she cried. "Oh God, Iosif, Iosif."

Someone else was coming.

Brook had come in a car, I realized. I had been so focused on my own distress that I had missed not only the sound and smell of a person walking up to me, but the noise of a car as well. Now someone else was coming from the car—another human female. This one had a handgun, and she was aiming it at me.

I jumped away from Brook, ran wide around her, leaping through the rubble as fast as I could. I reached the woman with the gun before she could track me and shoot me, and I knocked the gun from her hand before she could fire and grabbed her. I absolutely did not want to spend another day and night recovering from a bullet wound.

This woman was also someone I'd met—Celia, one of Stefan's symbionts. She had been in his kitchen with two other women whose scents I was glad not to have found.

"Celia, it's Shori," I said into her ear as she struggled against me. "Celia!" She lifted me completely off the ground, but she couldn't break my hold on her. "It's Shori," I repeated in her ear. "Stop struggling. I don't want to hurt you."

After a moment, she stopped struggling. "Shori?"

"Yes."

"Did you do this?"

That surprised me into silence. Celia was one of the two black women in the kitchen. She had seemed friendly and interesting. Now there was nothing but grief and anger in her expression.

Brook came up at that moment and said, "Celia, it's Shori. You know she didn't do this."

"I know what she did to Hugh!" Celia said.

I let go of her. Hugh Tang was symbiont with her to Stefan. They were family.

Celia jabbed her fist up, clearly meaning to hit me. I dodged the first jab, then grabbed one fist, then the other. She tried to kick me, so I tripped her and took her to the ground.

She lay stunned for a moment, breathless and gasping since I fell on top of her. She glared up at me. I couldn't think of anything helpful to say so I kept quiet. She and I lay on the ground. After a moment, she looked away from me and her muscles relaxed.

"Let me up," she said.

I didn't move or loosen my hold on her.

"What do you want me to do, say 'please?'"

"I truly don't want to hurt you," I said, "but if you attack me again, I will."
After a moment, she nodded. "Let me go. I won't bother you."

I took her at her word and let her up.

"She says Iosif's dead," Brook said.

Immediately, Celia confronted me. "How do you know he's dead? Were you here when all this happened? Did you see?"

I took both their hands, although Celia tried to snatch hers away, and led them over to the place where Iosif had burned. "He died here," I told them. "I can smell that much. I don't know whether it was only the fire or whether he was shot, too. I couldn't find any bullets. But he died here. A few of his ashes are still here."

I looked at one woman, then the other. Both now had tears streaming down their faces. They believed me. "I don't remember anything about Ina funerals or beliefs about death," I said. "Do either of you know other Ina families—Iosif's mothers perhaps—who would be able to do what should be done?"

"His mothers were killed in Russia during World War II," Brook said. She and Celia looked at one another. "We went to Seattle to shop and visit our relatives. That's why we weren't here. The only Ina phone numbers I know from memory are the numbers of several of the people who lived here and some of your mothers' phone numbers." She looked at Celia.

"I knew some of our community's numbers and Shori's mothers' numbers too," Celia said. "That's all."

It occurred to me then for no reason I could put my finger on that Celia was much younger than Brook—young enough to be Brook's daughter. Brook was only a few years younger than Theodora but except for very small signs, she appeared to be the same age as Celia. That, I realized, was what happened when a human became an Ina symbiont while she was still young. Wright would age slowly the way Brook had.

I pulled my thoughts back to the rubble we stood in. "When did you go into Seattle?" I asked.

Celia answered, "Five nights ago."

"I won't be able to visit my relatives many more times," Brook said. "My sister and my mother are aging a lot faster than I am, and they keep staring at me and asking me what my secret is."

Celia and I both raised an eyebrow and looked at her in the same way. She noticed it, glanced at the spot where Iosif had died, and whispered, "Oh God."

I took a deep breath, glanced at Celia, then left them and walked toward Stefan's house. They followed, saying nothing. Then they stood outside the site of the house while I walked through the rooms, finding five symbionts, including the two I'd met when I met Celia. And I found a misshapen bullet inside a charred plank. I had to break apart what was left of the plank to get at it, but once I had it, I found a faint blood scent. One of the symbionts. The bullet had passed through the man's body and gone into the wood.

Finally, I found the place where Stefan's body had fallen and burned in one of the bedrooms near part of the window frame. Had be been trying to get out or . . . might he have been firing a gun at his attackers? I couldn't be certain, but it seemed likely to me that he died fighting against whoever had done this.

I went back to Celia and shook my head. "I'm sorry. He didn't survive either."

She glared at me as though I'd killed him—a look filled with grief and rage.

"Where," she demanded. "Where did he die?"

"Over here."

They both followed me to the place where Stefan had died curled on his side, limbs drawn tight against his body.

"Here," I said.

Celia looked down, then knelt and put her hands flat in the ashes, taking up some of what remained of Stefan. For a long time, she said nothing. I glanced to the east where the sky was growing a little more light.

After a while, Celia looked up at Brook. "He was shooting back at them," she said. "He could have made himself do it, even if they came during the day. Days were hard on him, but he could wake up enough to shoot back."

Brook nodded. "He could have."

"That's what I thought," I said.

Celia glared at me, then closed her eyes, tears spilling down her face. "You can't tell for sure?"

"No. But I know there was shooting. I found a bullet that smelled of one of the other members of his household. And Stefan's position . . . somehow it seemed that he might have been shooting back. I hope he hit some of them."

"He had guns," Celia said. "Iosif didn't like guns, but Stefan did."

It hadn't helped him survive.

"It's almost dawn," I said. "Will you drive me back to where Wright is waiting? I can direct you."

They looked at each other, then at me.

"Drive me to Wright, then follow us to his cabin," I said. "Although we'll have to find another place soon. The cabin is almost too small for two people."

"Iosif owns—owned—a house outside Arlington," Brook said. "Some of us used it to commute to jobs or to entertain visiting family members. There are three bedrooms, three baths. It's a nice place, and it's ours. We have a right to be there."

I nodded, relieved. "That would be better. Could other symbionts be there already?"

Brook looked at Celia.

"I don't use it," Celia said. "I haven't kept up with the schedule."

"I don't think anyone's there," Brook said. "If there is . . . if some of us are there, Shori, they need you, too."

I nodded. "Take me back to Wright. Then we'll go there."

During the sad, silent trip back to Wright's car, I had time to be afraid. These two women's lives were in my hands, and yet I had no idea how to save them. Of course I would take their blood. I didn't want to, but I would. They smelled like my father and my brother. They smelled almost Ina, and that was enough to make them unappetizing. And yet I would make myself take their blood. Would that be enough? Iosif had told me almost nothing. What else should I do? I could talk to them. What I told them to do, they would try to do, once I'd taken their blood. Would that be enough?

If it wasn't, they were dead.

# *eleven*

To get to the house that my father had bought for his symbionts and my brothers', we followed the highway through dense woods, past the occasional lonely house or farm, past side roads and alongside the river. I asked Wright whether the river had a name.

"That's the north fork of the Stillaguamish," he told me. "Don't ask me what 'Stillaguamish' means because I have no idea. But it's the name of a local Native American tribe."

Eventually we reached more populated areas where houses and farms were more visible, scattered along the highway. There were still many trees, but now there were more smells of people and domestic animals nearby. In particular, there was the scent of horses. I recognized it from the time I'd spent prowling around Wright's neighborhood. Horses made noises and moved around restlessly when I got close enough to them to be noticed. My scent apparently disturbed them. Yet their scent had become one of the many that meant "home" to me.

Wright and I followed the women's car talking quietly. I told him what had happened to my father's community and that Celia and Brook had survived because they were in Seattle.

He shook his head. "I don't know what to make of this," he said. "Your kind have some serious enemies. What we need to do is find some place safe where we can hunker down, pool information, and figure out what to do. There's probably a way to tip the police to these people if we can just figure out who they are."

As he spoke, I realized that I was willing to go further than that. If we found the people who had murdered both my male and my female families, I wanted to kill them, had to kill them. How else could I keep my new family safe?

My new family . . .

"Wright," I said softly and saw him glance at me. "Celia and Brook will be with us now. They have to be."

There was a moment of silence. Then the said, "They're not going to die?"

"Not if I can take them over. I'm going to try."

"You'll feed from them."

"Yes." I hesitated. "And I don't know what's going to happen. I don't remember anything about this. Iosif told me it had to be done when an Ina died and left symbionts, but he didn't tell me much. He couldn't know . . . how soon I would need the information."

"Maybe Brook and Celia know."

I turned away from him, looked out the window. The sun was well up now, and in spite of the threatening rain clouds, it was getting bright enough to bother me. I reached into the backseat, grabbed the blanket I had brought, and wrapped myself in it. Once I'd done that, except for my eyes, I was almost comfortable.

"Look in the glove compartment there," Wright said gesturing. "There should be a pair of sunglasses."

I looked at the glove compartment, decided how it must open, opened it, and found the glasses. They were too big for my face, and I had to keep pushing them up my nose, but they were very dark, and I immediately felt better. "Thank you," I said and touched his face. He needed to shave. I rubbed the brown stubble and found even that good to touch.

He took my hand and kissed it, then said, "Why don't you want to ask Brook and Celia what they know?"

I sighed. Of course he had not forgotten the question. "Embarrassment," I said. "Pride. Imagine a doctor who has to ask her patient how to perform a life-saving operation."

"Not a confidence builder," he said. "I can see that. But if they know anything, you need to find out."

"I do." I drew a deep breath. "Brook is older. Maybe I'll feed from her first and find out what she knows."

"She can't be much older. They look about the same age."

"Do they? Brook is older by about twenty years."

"That much?" He looked skeptical. "How can you tell?"

I thought about it. "Her skin shows it a little. I guess it's as much the way she smells as the way she looks. She smells . . . much more Ina that Celia does. She's been with my father longer than Celia's been with my brother. I think Celia is about your age."

He shook his head. "Brook doesn't have any wrinkles, not even those little lines around the eyes."

"I know."

"No gray either. Is her hair dyed?"

"It isn't, no."

"Jesus, am I still going to look that young in twenty years?"

I smiled. "You should."

He glanced at me and grinned, delighted.

"I think we're here," I said.

The car ahead of us had turned and pulled into the driveway of a long, low ranch house. There were no other houses in sight. We turned down the same driveway, and when Brook stopped, Wright said, "Hang on a moment." He jumped out and went to speak to the two women. I listened curiously. He wanted them to pull into the garage that I could see farther back on the property. It bothered him that this house was connected with Iosif's family. He thought the killers might know about it.

"You heard that didn't you?" he asked me when he came back.

I nodded. "You may be right. I hoped we could settle here for a while, but maybe we shouldn't. Even the police might come here to look for information about Iosif."

He pulled the car into the garage alongside Brook's. The garage had room enough for three cars, but there was no other car in it. "True," he said. "But we won't be able to use my cabin for long either. I already told my aunt and uncle that I was leaving." He hesitated. "Actually, they sort of told me I had to go. They know . . . well they think that I've been sneaking girls in."

I laughed in spite of everything.

"My aunt listened at the door a few nights ago. She told my uncle she heard 'sex noises.' My uncle told me he understands, said he was young once. But he says I've got to go because my aunt doesn't understand."

I shook my head. "You're an adult. What do they expect?"

He pulled me against him for a moment. "Just be glad they haven't seen you."

I was. I got out of the car and stood waiting, wrapped in my blanket, in the shadow of the garage until Brook had opened the back door, then I hurried inside. There was, even from the back, not another house in sight. There were other people around. I could smell them. But they were a comfortable distance away, and the many trees probably helped make their houses less visible.

Inside, the rooms were clean, and there were dishes in the cupboard. There were canned and frozen foods, towels, and clean bedding.

"The rule," Brook said, "is to leave the place clean and well-stocked. People tend to do that. Tended to do that."

"Let's settle somewhere," I said to Celia and Brook. "I need to talk with you both."

Wright had walked down the hallway to look out the side door. Now he was wandering back, looking into each of the bedrooms. He looked up at me when I spoke.

I shrugged. "I changed my mind," I told him.

"About what?" Celia demanded. I looked at her and noticed that she was beginning to sweat. The house was cool. As soon as we got in, Brook had complained that it was cold. She had reset the thermostat from fifty-five to seventy, but the house had not even begun to warm up. Yet Celia was hot. And she was afraid.

I waited until we'd all found chairs in the living room. "About our becoming a family," I said.

Both women looked uncomfortable.

"If you know any other Ina, and you would prefer to go to them, you should do it now, while you can," I said. "If not, if you're going to join with me, then I need your help."

"We're here," Celia said. She wiped her forehead with a hand that trembled a little. "You know we don't know anyone else."

"And you know I have amnesia. I have no memory of seeing or hearing about the handling of symbionts whose Ina has died. Iosif told me a little, but anything either of you know—anything at all—you should tell me, for your own sakes."

Brook nodded. "I wondered what you knew." She took a deep

breath. "It scares me that you're a child, but at least you're female. That might save us."

"Why?" I asked.

She looked surprised. "You don't know that either?" She shook her head and sighed deeply. "Venom from Ina females is more potent than venom from males. That's what Iosif told me. It has something to do with the way prehistoric Ina females used to get and keep mates." She smiled a little. "Now females find mates for their sons, and males for their daughters, and it's all very civilized. But long ago, groups of sisters competed to capture groups of brothers, and the competition was chemical. If a group of sisters had the venom to hold a group of brothers, they were more likely to have several healthy children, and their sons would have a safe haven with their fathers when they came of age. And their daughters were more likely to have even more potent venom."

"The sons would have more potent venom, too," Wright said.

"Yes, but among the Ina, the females competed. It's like the way males have competed among humans. There was a time when a big, strong man might push other men aside and marry a lot of wives, pass on his genes to a lot of children. His size and strength might be passed to his daughters as well as his sons, but his daughters were still likely to be smaller and weaker than his sons.

"Ina children, male and female, wind up with more potent venom, but the female's is still more potent than the male's. In that sense, the Ina are kind of a matriarchy. And a little thing like Shori might be a real power." She took a deep breath and glanced at Celia. "Ina men are sort of like us, like symbionts. They become addicted to the venom of one group of sisters. That's what it means to be mated. Once they're addicted, they aren't fertile with other females, and from time to time, they need their females. Need . . . like I need Iosif."

She knew more about Ina reproduction and Ina history than I did. She should, of course, after so many years with Iosif. But still, hearing it from her made me uncomfortable. I tried to ignore my discomfort. "You were with Iosif a long time," I said.

"Yeah." She blinked and looked off into the distance at nothing. "Twenty-two years," she said. She covered her face with her hands, curled her body away from me on the chair, crying. Like Celia, she was a lot bigger than I was, but for a moment, she seemed to be a small, helpless person in deep distress. Yet I didn't want to touch her. I would have to soon enough.

She said through her tears, "I always *knew* that I would die before him and that was good. I was so willing to accept him when he asked me. God, I loved him. And I thought it meant I would never be alone. My father died when I was eight. I had a brother who drowned when he was seven. And my sister's husband died of cancer when they'd been married for only two years. I thought I had finally found a way to avoid all that pain—a way never to be alone again." She was crying again.

"I'm Iosif's daughter," I said. "I hope that my venom is strong and that you'll come to me. It won't be the same, I know, but you won't be alone. I want you with me."

"Why should you?" Celia demanded. "You don't know us."

"With my amnesia, I don't know anyone," I said. "I'm getting to know Wright. And there's a woman named Theodora. I'm getting to know her. And, Celia, I'm only beginning to know myself."

She looked at me for several seconds, then shuddered and turned away. "I hate this," she said. "Damn, I hate this!"

And this was the way a symbiont behaved when she was missing her Ina. Or at least this was the way Celia behaved—suspicious, short-tempered, afraid. Brook and Celia were both grieving, but Celia must have been longer without Stefan than Brook had been without Iosif.

I got up and went to Celia, trying to ignore the fact that she clearly didn't want me to touch her. She was sensible enough not to protest when I took her hand, drew her to her feet, and led her away into one of the bedrooms.

"I hate this," she said again and turned her face away from me as I encouraged her to lie down on the huge bed. She smelled more of Stefan than she had before, and I truly didn't want to touch her. Where I would have enjoyed tasting Theodora or Wright, I had to force myself to touch Celia.

She turned back to face me and caught my expression. "You don't want to do it," she said. She was crying again, her body stiff with anger.

"Of course I don't," I said, and I slid into bed next to her. "Stefan has posted olfactory keep-out signs all over you. Didn't you ever wonder why Ina can live together without going after one another's symbionts?"

"It happens sometimes."

"But only with new symbionts, right?"

"You have amnesia, and yet you know that?"

"I'm alive, Celia. My senses work. I can't help but know." I unbuttoned her shirt to bare her neck. "What I don't know is how this will be for you. Not good, maybe."

"Scares me," she admitted.

I nodded. "Bear it. Bear it and keep still. Later, when I can, I'll make it up to you."

She nodded. "You remind me of Stefan a little. He told me I reminded him of you."

I bit her. I was more abrupt than I should have been, but her scent was repelling me more and more. I had to do it quickly if I were going to be able to do it at all.

She gave a little scream, then frantically tried to push me away, tried to struggle free, tried to hit me . . . I had to use both my arms and my legs to hold her still, had to wrap myself all around her. If she'd been any bigger, I would have had to knock her unconscious. In fact, that might have been kinder. I kept waiting for her to accept me, the way strangers did when I climbed through their windows and bit them. But she couldn't. And strangely, it never occurred to me to detach for a moment and order her to be still. I would have done that with a stranger, but I never thought to do it with her.

She managed not to scream anymore after that first strangled sound, but she struggled wildly, frantically until I stopped taking her blood. I had only tasted her, taking much less than a full meal. It was as much as I could stand. I hoped it was enough.

I gave her a moment to understand that I had stopped, and when she stopped struggling, I let her go. "Did I hurt you?" I asked.

She was crying silently. She cringed as I leaned over to lick the bite and take the blood that was still coming. She put her hands on my shoulders and pushed but managed not to push hard. I went on licking the bite. She needed that to help with healing.

"I always liked that so much when Stefan did it," she said.

"It should be enjoyable," I said, although I wasn't enjoying myself at all. I was doing what seemed to be my duty. "And it helps your wounds heal quickly and cleanly. It will be enjoyable again someday soon."

She relaxed a little, and I thought I might be reaching her. "Maybe," she said. "Maybe you've got some kind of keep-out sign on you, too—as far as I'm concerned, I mean. I panicked. I couldn't control myself. Your bite didn't hurt, but it was . . . it was horrible." She drew away from me with a shudder.

"But do you feel better?" I asked.

"Better?"

"You've stopped shaking."

"Oh. Yeah. Thanks . . . I guess."

"I don't know exactly how long it will be before we can take pleasure in one another, but I think it's important that you do feel better now. Next time will be easier and more comfortable." Now that I'd bitten her, it would. It seemed best to tell her that.

"Hope so."

I left her alone in the huge bed. She wouldn't have been able to sleep if I'd stayed. I wouldn't have been able to sleep if I'd stayed.

I went to the bathroom, washed, and then just stayed there. I knew I had to go to Brook soon. The longer I waited, the harder it would be. Maybe Brook would have an easier time since she hadn't seemed so needy. Or perhaps it would be worse because she'd been with Iosif for so long. Was twenty-two years a long time when she would live to be maybe two hundred? If only I knew what I was doing.

I sat on the side of the bathtub for a long time, hearing Celia cry until she fell asleep, hearing Wright moving around the kitchen, hearing Brook breathing softly in one of the bedrooms. She was not asleep, but she was not moving around either. She was sitting or lying down—probably waiting for me.

I got up and went to her.

"I thought you could wait," she said when she saw me. "If you wanted to, you could wait until tomorrow. I mean, I'm all right now. I'm not getting the shakes or anything."

I didn't sigh. I didn't say anything. I only went to the bed where she lay atop the bedspread and lay down beside her. Her scent was so much like my father's that if I closed my eyes, it was almost as though I were lying in bed beside Iosif, and even though I had begun to trust Iosif and even to like him, I had not found him appetizing in any way at all.

"We will get through this," I said. "What you feel now will end."

She sighed and closed her eyes. "I hope so," she said. "Do it."

I did it. And when I was finished, I left her crying into a pillow. She was no more able to take comfort from me than Celia had been, and there was no comfort for me in either of them. I went out, hoping to find the comfort I needed with Wright. He was in the living room, eating a ham sandwich and a bag of microwave popcorn and watching a television that I had not noticed before. He aimed the remote and stopped the program as I came in.

"No cable," he said, "but movies and old TV shows galore." He gestured toward the shelves of tapes and DVDs in the cabinet. Then, after a moment, he asked, "How are things?"

I shook my head and went to sit next to him on the arm of his chair. I had worried that he would draw away from me, resent my bringing two strangers into our family, but he reached up, lifted me with a hand under one of my arms, and put me on his lap. I made myself comfortable there, his arms around me. I sighed with contentment.

"Things were horrible," I said. "But they're better now."

That was when I heard the people outside, first two of them, then, as I sat up and away from Wright's chest and the beat of his heart, I heard more. I couldn't tell how many.

Then I smelled the gasoline.

# twelve

I turned to speak very softly into Wright's ear. "The killers are here." I covered his mouth with my hand. "They're here now. They have guns and gasoline. Go wake Brook and Celia— quietly!—and look after them. Keep them safe. Watch the side door. When I clear a way, get them out of here. Don't worry about me. Don't try to help me. Go. Now."

I slid off his lap, avoided his grasping hands, grabbed my blanket and glasses, and ran for the side door. There were men—human males—at the front and back doors, and at least one was heading for the side door at the end of the hall, but no one reached it before I slipped out of it and down the three concrete steps to the ground.

The men were spreading gasoline all around the house, quietly splashing it on the wood siding so that it puddled on the ground. I threw my blanket on the ground alongside an oak tree that was losing its leaves. It was probably overhanging the house too much to survive what was to come. It gave me shade, though, and kept me from burning. I put the glasses on, then turned toward the sounds of a man who was approaching from the front yard, spreading his gasoline as quietly as he could.

He was like the deer I had killed—just prey. He was my first deer that day. Before he realized I was there, I was on his back, one hand over his nose and mouth, my legs around him, riding him, my other arm around his head under his chin. I broke his neck, and an instant later, as he collapsed, I tore out his throat. I wanted no noise from him.

He'd had a gun—a big strange-looking one. I picked it up by the barrel, thrust it into the house through the door I'd come out of. Then I moved the dead man's gasoline can to the oak tree.

Another man was coming around from the backyard, and he was my second deer, as quickly dispatched as the first. It was almost a relief to use my speed and strength without worrying about hurting someone. And it was good to kill these men who had surely taken part in killing my families.

Someone in the house opened the side door a crack, and I beckoned with both hands, calling them out. That same instant, someone threw something through two or three of the windows, smashing them. Someone in the backyard lit the gasoline, and flames roared around the house on every side but the one I had cleared. Through a window, I could see that there was fire inside the house, too.

Wright, Celia, and Brook spilled noisily out of the house, but the roar of the fire probably drowned out the noise they made at least as far as the gunmen were concerned. Wright had the gun I had left for him. I snatched up the second man's gun and thrust it into Celia's hands. Of the two women, I thought she would be more likely to know how to use it. She started to say something, but I put a hand over her mouth.

She nodded and positioned herself so that she and Wright had Brook and I between them. She watched the front while Wright watched the back.

I went to Wright who was edging away from the heat of the fire, but still looking toward the backyard. He glanced back at me.

I touched his mouth briefly with my fingers to keep him silent, then stepped ahead of him, acting on what I had heard and he had not. For the second time that day, I had to evade his hands. One more gunman was coming around the house, around the fire at a run, perhaps to see what had happened to his friends. He was my third deer. Best not to make noise until we had to.

How many gunmen were left? How many had there been? There hadn't been time for me to listen and estimate, but I tried to think back to what I had heard. Then my concentration was shattered by the sudden, deep, quick spitting of Celia's gun. She had shot a man who had come around the house from the front.

The man fell, and even if no one had heard the strange spitting sound of Celia's gun, someone must have seen him go down. The element of surprise was gone.

I snatched the gun of the man I'd just killed, shouted to the others, and all of us sprinted for the shelter of trees. They would give us cover when the other gunmen came to see what the shooting was about.

We all reached the trees in time. I was with Brook behind the oak, which, high above, was already catching fire where it overhung the house. I gave her the gun and she frowned, studying it. Meanwhile, Wright and Celia were already firing. I could see men firing back from both the front and the backyards, but they could not aim very well because they lacked cover where they were. We had trees, but they had only the burning house. If they had tried to reach trees that might have shielded them, Wright or Celia would have gotten a clear shot at them. If we survived, I would get Wright and Celia to teach me to shoot.

Then there was the sound of sirens in the distance. I heard it and froze, wondering how we could avoid being caught either by the gunmen or by the police. Then Brook looked up from her gun, and I realized she was beginning to hear the sirens, too.

And the gunmen heard them. The shooting from the other side dribbled away to silence. Wright and Celia stopped their very careful firing because suddenly they had no targets.

I could hear the remaining gunmen running, their footsteps going away from us, toward the street. I showed myself, walking out away from the tree, providing a target for anyone who had stayed behind.

No one shot me.

I ran to the garage, lifted one of the doors, and glanced toward the side of the house, where I hoped Wright, Celia, and Brook were paying attention.

They were coming, all three of them, at a run.

I opened the other garage door and waited until they were all in the cars. Then I got in and we fled.

We fled slowly. Wright said we shouldn't speed, shouldn't do anything that might make us memorable to anyone who saw us or bring us to the attention of the police. He was leading this time so his judgment kept Brook's speed down. There were no neighbors near enough to see the house or report that we'd left it (and left several corpses) just after the fire began. In fact, the guns had made so little noise that I wondered whether human ears had heard them with the houses so far apart. It was almost certainly the smoke that had caught someone's attention. That meant the emergency call probably went to the fire department. Firemen would arrive, begin to put out the fire, find the bodies, and then call the police. They would also find the gas cans. We had to avoid getting involved in the investigation that would surely follow. I had seen too many police programs on Wright's television to believe there was any story we could tell the police about this that would keep us out of jail.

"Where are we going?" I asked Wright.

"God," he said. "I don't know. Back to the cabin for now, I guess."

"No," I said. "Your relatives are there in the front house. Let's not lead anyone to them."

"Do you think that's likely? Whoever these people are, they don't know anything about me." He shook his head. What he had been through seemed to be too much for him suddenly. "Whoever they are ...Who the hell are they? Why did they try to kill us? I've never shot at anyone before—never even wanted to."

"We're all alive," I said.

He glanced at me. "Yeah."

"We should find a place to stop when we've gotten a few miles farther away. We need to talk with the others, find out if they know of another place where we can stay for a while."

"Any place they know is probably as dangerous as the place we just left."

I sighed and nodded. "We need to be far away from all this," I said. "I can't believe that Brook was with Iosif for twenty-two years, and yet she knows of no relatives but my mothers, no friends or business associates."

"I was wondering about that," he said. "Do you think she's lying?"

I thought about that for a moment, then said, "I don't think so. I just think she knows more than she realizes she knows. Maybe Iosif told her not to remember or not to share what she knows with anyone outside his family. I mean, as things are, I don't know where to begin a search for more of my kind. I don't even know whether I should be looking for them. I don't want to get people killed, but I have to do something. I have to find out who these murderers are and why they want to kill us. And I have to find a way to stop them." I paused, then fidgeted uncomfortably. I already had the beginnings of a burn on my face and arms, and had left my jacket in the house. "Wright, would you be cold if I used your jacket?"

"What?" He glanced at me, then said, "Oh." I helped him struggle out of his jacket, pulling it off of him while he drove. Once I had it, I covered myself with it as though it were the blanket that I had lost, probably leaving it beside the oak tree. The jacket was warm and smelled of Wright and was a very comfortable thing to be wrapped in.

"You and I are conspicuous together," he said. "But you could go into a clothing store with Celia and pass as her daughter. You could get yourself some clothes that fit and another jacket with a hood, maybe a pair of gloves and some sunglasses that fit your face."

"All right. We should get food, too, for the three of you. It should be things you can open and eat right here in the car. I'm not sure when we'll dare to settle somewhere."

"I should be back at work on Monday."

I looked at him, then looked away. "I know. I'm sorry. I don't have any idea when this will be over."

He drove silently for a few minutes. We were, I realized, still headed southwest toward Arlington. Once we arrived in Arlington, he seemed to know his way around. He took us straight to a supermarket where we could buy the food we needed. Once we were parked, we moved over to the larger car to talk with Celia and Brook.

"Don't you need to sleep?" Brook asked me as soon as we got into the backseat. "Doesn't the fact that it's day bother you at all?"

"I'm tired," I admitted. "You're probably all tired."

"But don't you sleep during the day?" Celia asked. It occurred to me that they had been discussing me. Better that than terrifying themselves over the fact that several men had just tried to murder us.

"I prefer to sleep during the day," I said, "but I don't have to. I can sleep whenever I'm tired."

Brook looked at Celia. "That's why we're not dead," she said. "They came during the day, thinking that any Ina in the house would be asleep, completely unconscious."

"Why didn't it help her save her mothers?" Celia asked.

Brook looked at me.

"I don't know," I said. "Have either of you ever heard of a community being destroyed the way my parents' communities were? I mean, has it happened before anywhere else?"

Both women shook their heads. Brook said, "Not that I know of."

"Maybe that's it then." I thought for a moment. "If no one was expecting trouble, probably no one was keeping watch. Why would they? I don't know whether I usually slept during the day. My mothers did, so I probably did, too, just because it was more convenient to be up when they were. I'll bet the symbionts had adapted to a nocturnal way of life just as symbionts had in Iosif's community. But I don't know. That's the trouble; I don't know anything." I looked at Brook. "You must have spent time at my mothers' community. Wasn't everyone nocturnal?"

"Pretty much," she answered. "Your eldermothers had three or four symbionts who did research for them. They were often awake during the day. I guess it didn't help."

I looked at Celia. "Did Stefan always sleep during the day?"

"He said he got stupid if he didn't sleep," she answered. "He got sluggish and clumsy."

"Iosif had to sleep," Brook said. "He would go completely unconscious wherever he happened to be when the sun came up. And once he got to sleep, it was impossible to wake him up until after sundown."

Wright put his arm around me. "You're definitely the new, improved model," he said.

I nodded. "I think maybe someone's decided there shouldn't be a new, improved model."

"We were talking about that," Brook said. "About how maybe this is all because someone doesn't like the experimenting that your family was doing. Or someone envied your family for producing you and Stefan. I don't know."

"How could it be about her?" Wright wanted to know. "Those guys were human, not Ina."

"They may be symbionts," Celia said.

"Or one of them might be a symbiont and the rest hirelings," Brook added.

Wright frowned. "Maybe. But it seems to me they could just as easily be ordinary human beings who imagine they're fighting vampires."

"And who have focused only on my family," I said.

"We don't know that. Hell, we're in the same boat you are, Shori. We don't really know anything."

I nodded and yawned. "We probably know more than we realize. I think we'll be able to come up with at least a few answers after we've gotten some rest."

"Why are we in this parking lot?" Brook asked.

"To get food for you," I said. "After that, we'll find a place to park in the woods. We can get some sleep in the cars. Later, when we're rested, we'll see what we can figure out."

"I thought we would go to your house," Celia said to Wright.

"His relatives' home is too close by," I said. "I don't want them to get hurt or killed because someone's after us—or after me. I don't want that to happen to anyone. So no hotel for now."

The two women exchanged another look, and this time I had no idea what they were thinking.

"Let's go buy what we need," Wright said. "Celia, while Brook and I shop for food, can you be Shori's mother or her big sister? There's a clothing store ..." He opened the glove compartment, found a pencil and a small wire-bound notebook. "Here's the address," he said, writing. "And here's how to get there. I did some work here in Arlington last year. I remember the place. This clothing store is only a few blocks from here, and it's a good place for buying cheap casual clothes. She needs a couple of pairs of jeans, shirts, a good hooded jacket, gloves, and sunglasses that will fit her face. Okay?"

Celia nodded. "No problem if you have money. I spent most of what Stefan gave me in Seattle. He's going to—" She stopped, frowned, and looked away from us across the parking lot. She wiped at her eyes with her fingers but said nothing more.

After a moment, Wright got his wallet out of his pocket and put several twenties into her hand. "I see an ATM over there," he said. "I'll get more—enough for a few days."

"We need gas, too," Brook said. She looked at me, then looked past me. "I have my checkbook and a credit card, but they're both Iosif's accounts. I don't know whether using them will attract the attention of the police—or of our enemies. I have enough money to fill our tank, but if this lasts, if we're on the run for more than a few days, money is likely to become a problem." There was an oddly false note in her voice, as though she were lying somehow. She smelled nervous, and I didn't like the way she looked past me rather than at me. I thought about it, and after a moment, I understood.

"Money will not be a problem," I said, "and you know it."

Brook looked a little embarrassed. After a moment, she nodded. "I wasn't sure you knew . . . what to do," she said.

And Wright said, "What do you expect her to do?"

"Steal," I said. "She expects me to be a very good thief. I will be. People will be happy to give me money once I've bitten them."

He looked at me doubtfully, and I reached up to touch his stubbly chin.

"You should get a razor, too," I said.

"I don't want you getting in trouble for stealing," he said.

"I won't." I shrugged. "I don't want to do it. I don't feel good about doing it, but I'll do what's necessary to sustain us." I glanced at Brook, feeling almost angry with her. "Ask me questions when you want to know things. Tell me whatever you believe I should know. Complain whenever you want to complain. But don't talk to other people when you mean your words for me, and speak the truth."

She shrugged. "All right."

My anger ebbed away. "Let's go buy what we need," I said.

"Hang on a minute," Wright said. He wrote something else in the wire-bound notebook. Then he tore out the page and handed it to Celia. "Those are my sizes. If you can, get me a pair of jeans and a sweatshirt."

She looked at the sizes, smiled, and said, "Okay."

We left them. Celia and I took her car—one of Iosif's cars, she said—and drove to the clothing store. She found it easily, following Wright's directions, and that seemed to surprise her.

"I usually get lost at least once and have to stop and ask somebody for directions," she said. And then, "Listen, you're my sister, okay? I refuse to believe I look old enough to be your mother."

I laughed. "How old are you?"

"Twenty-three. Stefan found me when I was nineteen, right after I'd moved out of my mother's house."

"Twenty-three, same as Wright."

"Yeah. And he's your first. You did very well for yourself. He's a decent-looking big bear of a guy, and he's nice. That jacket of his looks like a way-too-big coat on you."

"When he found me, when he stopped to pick me up, I couldn't believe how good he smelled. My memory was so destroyed that I didn't even know what I wanted from him, but his scent pulled me into the car with him."

Celia laughed, then looked sad and stared at nothing for a moment. "Stefan would say things like that. I've always wondered what it would be like to be one of you, so tuned in to smells and sounds, living so long and being so strong. It doesn't seem fair that you can't convert us like all the stories say."

"That would be very strange," I said. "If a dog bit a man, no one would expect the man to become a dog. He might get an infection and die, but that's the worst."

"You haven't found out about werewolves yet, then."

"I've read about them on Wright's computer. A lot of the people who write about vampires seem to be interested in werewolves, too." I shook my head. "Ina are probably responsible for most vampire legends. I wonder what started the werewolf legends."

"I've thought about that," Celia said. "It was probably rabies. People get bitten, go crazy, froth at the mouth, run around like animals, attacking other people who then come down with the same problems . . . That would probably be enough to make ancient people come up with the idea of werewolves. Shori, what did you get mad at Brook about a few minutes ago?"

I looked at her and, after a moment, decided that she had asked a real question. "She touched my pride, I think. She worries that I can't take care of the three of you. I worry that I won't always know how to take care of you. I hate my ignorance. I need to learn from you since there is no adult Ina to ask."

"Before I saw what you did today, I figured we'd be the ones taking care of you."

"You will. Iosif called it 'mutualistic symbiosis.' I think it's also called just 'mutualism.'"

"Yeah, those were his words for it. Before Stefan brought me to meet him, I'd never even heard those words used that way before. I thought he had made them up until I found them in a science dictionary. So you want us to be straight with you even if you don't always like what we say?"

"Yes."

"Works for me. Let's get you some clothes."

I wound up with two pairs of boy's blue jeans that actually fit, two long-sleeved shirts, one red and one black, a pair of gloves, a jacket with a hood, sunglasses, and some underwear. Then Celia used the last of her own money as well as the last of what Wright had given her to get him a pair of jeans and a hooded sweatshirt. Then we headed back to the supermarket to meet Wright and Brook.

"Brook and I are lucky we left our suitcases in the back of the car," Celia said. "A Laundromat would be a good idea for us, but otherwise, we're okay. Did you hear that saleswoman? She said you were the cutest thing she'd seen all day. She figured you were about ten."

I shook my head. I'd said almost nothing to the woman. I had no idea how to act like a ten-year-old human child. "Does it bother you that I'm so small?"

She grinned. "It did at first. Now I kind of like it. After seeing you in action today, I think you'd be goddamn scary if you were bigger."

"I will grow."

"Yeah, but before you do, I'll have time to get used to you." She paused. "How about you? Are you okay with me?"

"You mean do I want you?"

". . . yeah. You didn't exactly choose us."

"I inherited you, both of you, from my father's family. You're mine."

"You want us?"

I smiled up at her. "Oh, yes."

# thirteen

We turned northeast again and drove until we found a place where we could go off a side road and camp in the woods, far enough away from the road and the highway to be invisible. I took a look around before I went to sleep, made sure there was no one near us, no one watching us.

After I got back, I asked Celia to stay awake and keep one of the guns handy until dark. She was a good shot, she'd had some rest, and she said she wasn't very tired. We had the three guns I had taken from the gunmen and Celia's handgun—a semiautomatic Beretta. She told me the gunmen had used silenced Heckler & Koch submachine guns. She said she'd never seen one before, but she'd read about them.

"The gunmen meant to kill us all, but to do it quietly," she said. "I don't think anyone heard the shooting over the noise of the fire and the distance between houses. We need to avoid these people, at least until we find a few more friends."

I agreed with her. But at that moment, I just wanted to sleep. I went to sleep in the backseat of Wright's car and woke briefly as Wright lifted me out and put me down in Brook's car, where someone had folded the back seats down and spread clothing on them to make them less uncomfortable.

"What are you doing?" I whispered.

He climbed in, lay down beside me, and pulled me against him. "Go back to sleep," he said into my ear. I did. The makeshift bed turned out to be not so uncomfortable after all.

Then Brook lay down on the other side of me, and her scent disturbed me, made me want to get up and go sleep somewhere else. I tried to ignore it. Her scent would change, was already beginning to change. I slept.

Sometime later, after dark, I bit her.

She struggled. I had to hold her to keep her still and silent at first. Then, after a minute, she gave a long sigh and lay as I'd positioned her, accepting me as much as she could. She didn't enjoy herself, but after that first panic, she at least did not seem to be suffering.

I had only tasted her before. Now I took a full meal from her—not an emotionally satisfying meal, but a physically sustaining one. Afterward, I spent time lapping at the wound until she truly relaxed against me. She eased back into sleep and never noticed when I got up, stepped over her, and got out of the car.

I closed the door as quietly as I could and stood beside it. Not being fully satisfied made me restless. I paced away from the car, then back toward it. I found myself wondering whether Brook, Celia, and Theodora would be better able to sustain me when they were as fully mine as Wright was. Would they be enough? I was much smaller than my father who had preferred to have eight symbionts. My demands must be smaller.

Mustn't they?

I shook my head in disgust. My ignorance wasn't just annoying. It was dangerous. How could I take care of my symbionts when I didn't even know how to protect them from me?

I stopped beside the car and looked through its back window at Brook and Wright, now lying next to each other, both still asleep. Both had been touching me. Now that I had moved, they were almost touching one another.

My feelings shifted at once from fear for them to confusion. I wanted to crawl between them again and feel them both lying comfortably, reassuringly against me. They were both mine. And yet there was something deeply right about seeing them together as they were.

Celia came up behind me, looked at me, glanced into the car, then drew me away from it. We went to the other car and sat there. "I long for a shower," I said.

"Me too," Celia said. "You mind if I go to sleep now?"

"Go ahead." She had already climbed into the backseat of Wright's car. She put her handgun on the floor and lay on her back on the seat.

"I think I need to say something you won't like hearing," she said.

"All right."

She closed her eyes for several seconds, then said, "Stefan told me what happened to Hugh Tang. He told me and he told Oriana Bernardi because he knew we both loved Hugh."

Loved? I listened to her with growing confusion. I didn't know what to say so I said nothing.

"The relationship among an Ina and several symbionts is about the closest thing I've seen to a workable group marriage," she said. "With us, sometimes people got jealous and started to pull the family apart, and . . . well . . . Stefan would have to talk to them. He said the first time that happened, he was still living with his mothers and one of them had to tell him what to do, and even then he could hardly do it because he was feeling so confused himself. He didn't say 'jealous.' He said 'confused.'"

I nodded. "Confused."

"I don't really understand that, but then, we are different species."

"How did you wind up with Hugh?"

She smiled. "Hugh had been with Stefan for a few years when Stefan asked me to join him. When I'd been there for a while, Hugh asked for me. Stefan said that was up to me, so Hugh asked me. It scared me because I didn't understand at first how an Ina household works, that everyone went to Stefan, fed him, loved him, but that we could have relationships with one another, too, or with other nearby symbionts. Well, I didn't go to Hugh when he first asked, but after a while, I did. He was a good man."

"I'm sorry," I said. "I wish he hadn't found me when he did."

"I know."

I looked at her lying there, not looking at me. "Thank you for telling me," I said.

She nodded and looked at me finally. "You're welcome. I didn't just say it for your benefit, though. I figure I might want to have a kid someday."

I wanted that—a home in which my symbionts enjoyed being with me and enjoyed one another and raised their children as I raised mine. That felt right, felt good.

I left Celia alone so she could sleep, and I checked the area again to make sure we were still as alone as we seemed to be. Once I was sure of that, I set out at a jog, then a run to find out who our nearest neighbors were. I followed my nose and found a farm where two adults and four children lived, along with horses, chickens, geese, and goats. I found three other houses, widely separated along the side road, but without farm fields around them. I found no real community on the territory I covered.

It seemed we had privacy and a little more time to recover and decide what to do. I could question Celia and, in particular, Brook.

I went back to the cars and used some of the disposable wipes that Wright and Brook had bought to clean up as best I could. Then I put on clean clothes. As I got my jeans on, I heard Brook wake up and slip out of the car behind me. She made slightly different noises breathing and moving around than Wright or Celia did.

"God, it's dark out here," she said. "If I weren't a symbiont, I don't think I could see at all. Aren't you cold?"

I wasn't really, but I pulled on an undershirt, then put my long-sleeved shirt on, buttoned it, and pulled on my new jacket. "I'm all right," I said. "I'm glad you're awake. I need to talk to you."

"Sure."

"Eat first. Do whatever you need to do. This will probably take a while."

"That doesn't sound good."

"I hope it won't be too bad. Your neck okay?"

She pulled her collar aside and showed me the half-healed wound. "It . . . wasn't so bad this time."

"It will get better."

"I know."

She pulled open the white Styrofoam cooler they had bought and filled with ice and food. She took out a plastic packet of four strips of pepper-smoked salmon and a bottle of water. She made a sandwich with the salmon and some bread from one of the grocery bags. When she'd eaten that and drunk the water, she got more water from the chest and dug out a blueberry muffin and two bananas from one of the bags. It didn't seem to bother her that I sat in the car watching her—that I enjoyed watching her.

Finally she took the plastic can of wipes and went away into the trees to make her own effort to clean up. While she did that, Wright awoke and stumbled off in a different direction. A few moments later he came back and got another plastic can of wipes, scrubbed his face and hands, then got into the food.

"You okay?" he asked me.

"I'm fine. I'm going to see what I can learn from Brook. I need some idea where to find adult Ina. Now that I know what my parents' communities faced—humans with gasoline and guns—I think I can ask for help without endangering other Ina or their symbionts."

"You didn't think so yesterday."

"I do now. I still don't want to stay at the cabin near your relatives. Anyone I go to will have to post guards, stop shutting down during the day, be willing to fight and kill, be able to plant false stories in the memories of any witnesses, and be able to deal with the police. Ina families with symbionts can do that if they know they should. They can survive and help remove a threat."

He shook his head. "I just can't figure out why human beings would be killing your kind plus a hell of a lot of their own kind unless it's some kind of misguided vampire hunting."

"It may be," I said. "I don't know. But I'm pretty sure it's something to do with my family's genetic experiments. Will you sit with us and speak up whenever you think of anything useful?"

"Sure. Not that I'm going to know what's useful."

"Unless something she says shakes loose some part of my memory, you'll know as much as I do."

"Scary thought," he said. Then, "Here's Brook."

"I'm cold," she said, rubbing her hands together. "Let's get back into the car." Once we had moved the clothing we'd slept on and put the back seats up, we all climbed in, Brook in front and Wright and I in the back. "Okay," she said, "what do you want to talk about?"

"We need help," I told her. "I need to find adult Ina who will help me get rid of these assassins and then help me learn what I need to know to do right by the family I seem to be building. So I need you to tell me whatever you can about Iosif's Ina friends and relatives."

"I told you, I don't know how to contact any of them. Outside of our community, the only ones I had phone numbers for were your mothers."

"But you would have heard of others," I said. "Whether or not you know how to reach them, you would have heard their names, maybe met them."

She shook her head. "Iosif was unusual because he was so alone. He was too young to take part in the various Ina council meetings, and he had no elderfathers to represent his family. His brothers and his fathers, like his mothers and sisters, are all dead. Most of his relatives used to be scattered around Romania and Russia and Hungary. They died during the twentieth century—most of them during and after World War II when a lot of European Ina were killed. His sisters died with his mothers during the war. The Nazis got them. And his brothers and fathers were killed later by the Communists. They were some kind of nobility—had a lot of land taken from them before the war. Afterward, with all the destruction, I guess there was nothing left to take but their lives. Iosif was barely able to get out. They all should have left well before the war, but they were stubborn. They said no one would drive them from their homes."

"Were all Ina originally based in Romania—Transylvania?"

"No, they've been scattered all over Europe and the Middle East for millennia, or so their records say. They claim to have written records that go back more than ten thousand years. Iosif told me about them. I think he believed what he was saying, but I never quite believed him. Ten thousand years!" She shook her head. "Written history just doesn't go back that far. Anyway, now Ina are scattered all over the world. You just happen to be descended from people who lived in what Iosif used to call 'vampire country.' I think some of your ancestors there were outed and executed as vampires a few centuries ago. Iosif used to joke about it in a bitter way. He said that, physically, he and most Ina fit in badly wherever they go— tall, ultrapale, lean, wiry people. They usually looked like foreigners, and when times got bad, they were treated like foreigners—suspected, disliked, driven out, or killed."

"He told Wright and me that there is an Ina theory that claims the Ina were sent here from another world."

"Yes, that's something young Ina have come up with. They read and go to movies and pick up and adapt whatever's current. For a while, there was an idea that Ina were angels of some kind. And there's the old standby legend of the Ina being sent here by a great mother goddess. You're all supposed to be stuck here until you prove yourselves," she said. "Did Iosif tell you that one?"

"He did," Wright said. "It's a little like Christianity."

"It isn't, really," Brook said. "They're not supposed to go home in some spiritual way after they die. Some future generation of them is supposed to leave this world en masse and go to paradise—or back to the homeworld. It might be mythology or it might be that you and I have finally found—and joined—those extraterrestrial aliens that people keep claiming to spot on lonely back roads."

Wright laughed. Then he stopped laughing and shook his head. "There's another intelligent species here on Earth, and they're vampires. What am I laughing at?"

I took his hand and held it, looking at him. He looked at me, put his head back against the seat, and curled his fingers around my hand.

"Didn't other Ina visit Iosif?" I asked. "Did you ever meet others?"

She nodded. "That was scary sometimes."

"Why?"

"Because not everyone treats symbionts as people. I didn't realize that until I'd been with Iosif for a few years, but it's true. I remember one guest—actually, he came back recently to negotiate with Iosif for an introduction to you and your sisters. You weren't old enough yet, but he hoped to win all three of you for himself and his brothers when you came of age. That was never going to happen because your father was smart enough to see what he was."

"There were three of us?" I said, my mind latching on to this new bit of information about my past, about my family. "I didn't know that. I asked Iosif, but I was asking him so many questions . . . he never got around to answering that one."

"There were three of you. This was not a man Iosif would ever have introduced to you or your sisters. This man liked to . . . amuse himself with other Ina's symbionts. He was very careful and protective of his own, but he liked sending them among us with instructions to start trouble, raise suspicions and jealousies, start fights. He liked to watch arguments and fights. His symbionts were so good, so subtle that we didn't realize what was happening at first. It excited the hell out of him when two of Radu's symbionts almost killed one another. He got something sexual out of watching. The symbionts would have died if they hadn't been symbionts—but then, they never would have been endangered if they hadn't been symbionts."

"Radu," I said, remembering that Iosif had mentioned the name.

"Your brothers were Stefan, Vasile, Mihai, and Radu. It was your father's right to name them, and he named them for the dead—his two brothers and two of his fathers who died in Romania. Your mothers liked plainer, American-sounding names. Your sisters were Barbara and Helen. You were lucky. Your human mother claimed the right to name you." She smiled. "'Shori' is the name of a kind of bird—an East African crested nightingale. It's a nice name."

"Oh," Wright said. We looked at each other, then I reached into my shirt and pulled out the gold chain with the crested bird.

"Was this mine before?" I asked, showing it to her. "Wright found it in the rubble of my mothers' houses."

She turned the car's interior light on and looked at the bird, then looked at me. "Your human mother gave you this. I think she loved you as though she had given birth to you herself. Her name was Jessica Margaret Grant."

Jessica Margaret Grant. I shut my eyes and tried to find something of this woman in my memory—something. But there was nothing. All of my life had been erased, and I could not bring it back. Each time I was confronted with the reality of this, it was like turning to go into what should have been a familiar, welcoming place and finding absolutely nothing, emptiness, space.

After a moment, I said, "I wouldn't want to meet the Ina you described. What about others? Who's visited Iosif or one of my brothers recently?"

Brook frowned. "There was one a few months ago. He and Vasile owned some sort of business together. He was interested in joining with you and your sisters, and Vasile thought it might be a good match. Iosif was willing to be convinced so this man—what was his name? One of the Gordon family . . . Daniel Gordon! He had his brothers come to see us. Their ancestors were English, I think. They immigrated first to Canada, then to the United States. All the symbionts of Iosif's community were told to notice them, notice their behavior, talk to their symbionts, and listen to them. We did, and no one spotted anything bad. They seemed to be good, normal people. Shori, you met them yourself and liked them, even though it was way too soon for you to mate. They had heard about you and they wanted to meet you. Iosif went down, collected you, and brought you to stay with us for a few days."

"All because of my dark skin?" I said.

"That's the most obvious reason. You're not only able to stay completely awake and alert during the day, but you don't burn."

"I burn."

"You didn't yesterday."

"I blistered a little. I tried to keep covered up, and it was cloudy yesterday. Did the brothers like me?"

"Have you healed?" Wright asked, interrupting. "I meant to buy you some sunscreen, but I forgot."

"I healed," I said and wondered what all this talk of my mating was doing to him. I looked at him but couldn't read anything more than mild concern in his expression as he examined my face—probably for burns.

"The Gordon brothers were delighted with you," Brook said. "They wished you were a little older, but they were willing to wait. They planned to go down to meet your sisters and your mothers. I don't know whether or not that had happened, but it would have been necessary. Your mothers would have to meet the whole Gordon family and then give or refuse their consent."

"Where do the Gordons live?" I asked.

She hesitated, frowned. "Somewhere on the coast of northern California."

"You don't know exactly where?"

She shook her head. "Their community has a name—Punta Nublada—but it's not a real town. It's only the four brothers and their three fathers and a couple of elderfathers who were born in the sixteen hundreds. It's amazing to meet people like that."

"You met them?" Wright asked.

"I went with Iosif and one of Shori's mothers and some other symbionts to visit them. I loved the trip, but I didn't know where I was most of the time. I know we flew into San Francisco Airport—at night, of course—and a couple of symbionts from Punta Nublada met us in vans and drove us up. It was more than two hours north of San Francisco Airport and on the coast. That's all I know. They have a lot of land. Inland, away from

their community, they own vineyards. They have a wine-making business, which is kind of funny when you think about it."

Wright laughed. "Yeah. I'll bet they still don't drink it."

"What?" I demanded.

"Old joke from a vampire movie," Wright said. "From the Bela Lugosi
version of *Dracula*. Someone offers the Count a glass, and he says, 'I do
not drink . . . wine.'"

I shrugged. Maybe I'd watch the movie someday and see why that
was funny. "We'll go to Punta Nublada," I said. "You'll find it for us,
Brook."

She looked distressed. "I don't know where it is, I swear."

"Did you sleep while you were being driven?"

"No, but it was dark."

"You can see in this darkness—here, under the trees. Your night vision
is good."

"It is. But most of what I saw was headlights and taillights."

I nodded. "They can be a problem. But I think you saw more than you
realize."

"I didn't," she said. "I really didn't."

"We need help, Brook," I said. "Can you think of anyone else—anyone
other than the Gordons—who might help us?"

She faced me and shook her head. "But these people may not help us,
even if we find them. I don't know whether there was a confirmed
agreement between your family and theirs. And even if there was, they
. . . I'm sorry, Shori. They might not want you without your sisters. It's
hard for only children to find mates. Iosif said it would have been hard
for him, but he was already mated when his brothers were killed. His
mates were just smart enough to get out before he did."

I shrugged. "All right, even if the Gordons don't still want to mate
with me, they should be willing to help find and stop the assassins. That's
what I really need help with, after all. Human gangs wiping out two
whole communities of Ina. Any Ina should be willing to do something
about that—out of self-preservation if nothing else."

"They should."

"Then you find them, and I'll put it to them in just that way. Self-
preservation. Iosif must have seen some good in them." I looked at her,

and she looked away. "I feel as though I know humans better than I know my own kind—not that that's saying much. Am I missing something here? Is there some reason these people might not help us?"

She shook her head. "I think they will help, even if they don't want you as a mate. I'm just scared I won't be able to find them for you."

"Yes you will," I said. "You'll find them. Then once we get some peace, we can begin to assemble a household. The Gordons should be able to give us phone numbers and addresses of other Ina—my mothers' brothers, perhaps. Are they alive?"

"Your mothers' brothers? Yes. I've never met them, but you have." Suddenly she put her hands to her face. She didn't cry, but she looked as though she wanted to. "How can I do this?" she demanded. "You can't depend on me. I don't really know anything."

"You can." I said. "You will. Don't worry about it. Just know that you will."

Wright said, "We can drive down—all the way to San Francisco Airport if we have to. From there, we can turn north again, and maybe Brook can find the way."

"We'll start tonight," I said.

He nodded. "What about Celia? She might know something."

"She needed to sleep. We'll tell her when she wakes up, and I'll find out what she knows."

"We need maps," Wright said. "I don't know the way, except that we'll be going south, probably on I-5. We'll make San Francisco Airport our destination, so when we reach California, we should stick to a coastal route—probably U.S. 101—until we reach the airport or until Brook recognizes something."

"We should go back to your cabin first," I said, "or if you don't want to do that, you can let me out a few blocks from there. I need to talk to Theodora and see whether or not she should come with us."

He nodded. "I need to talk to my uncle anyway, to let him know that I haven't just disappeared on him and that I want my job. I want him to be willing to hire me again when this is over. I want to get some of my stuff, too. Hell, I was all packed to leave anyway."

"Let's go now," I said. "We've got hours of darkness left. By daybreak, we should be well on our way."

# fourteen

Once we got back to Wright's cabin, I went to visit Theodora. I slipped into her bedroom by way of her balcony, woke her, and told her what had happened and what we were going to do. Her scent was still mostly her own so I knew I could leave her, lonely but safe.

"I want to go with you!" she protested.

"I know," I told her. "But it will be better if you wait. I can't protect you now. I don't even have the prospect of a home now, and I have no Ina allies. It was only luck that none of us was hurt or killed at the Arlington house."

"You protected them."

"Luck," I said. "They could so easily have been burned or shot. Wright could have left the television on, and I might not have heard the intruders until it was too late. I want you with me, and you will be. But not yet."

She cried and wanted me to at least stay the rest of the night with her. I bit her a little—only to taste her—then held her and lapped at the wound until she was focused on the pleasure. She was like Wright. She had some hold on me beyond the blood. At last, I knew I had to go so I told her to sleep. She resisted briefly, took something from the very back and bottom of the middle drawer in her night table, and put it in my hand. "You might need this," she whispered. "Take it. I've got more." Then she kissed me and let herself drift off to sleep.

She had put money into my hand, a thick roll of twenty-dollar bills with a rubber band around it. I took it back to Wright's cabin. He was in the main house, talking to his uncle. He and the two women had each had a shower. By the time Wright came back, I was having one, and the women were eating the meal they had prepared. We were all wasting time, and I knew it, but I enjoyed my shower and let them enjoy their microwaved mugs of vegetable soup, slabs of canned ham, and dinner rolls heated in the convection oven—simple, quickly prepared food.

They finished, cleaned up, took out the trash, and made sandwiches of the last of the ham and some cheddar cheese Wright had had in his refrigerator. Meanwhile, I put Wright's two suitcases and the canvas travel bag he had given me for my things into his car. Wright already had a book of maps called *The Thomas Guide: King and Snohomish Counties*—we were in Snohomish—and a map of Pierce County. We would get whatever else we needed as we traveled, although, according to Wright, all we really had to do was get on I-5 and stay on it until we got to California, then switch over to U.S. 101. None of that meant anything to me. I meant to look at the relevant maps in *The Thomas Guide* while we traveled. I needed, for my own comfort, to have some idea of where we were going.

Wright came out ahead of the two women, and I put the money Theodora had given me into his hand. "Take this," I said. "If I get separated from the rest of you, you take care of Brook and Celia. All of you would have to find other Ina as quickly as possible."

His hand closed around the money, then he looked at it in the light from the back door of the cabin. His mouth dropped open. "Where did you get this?"

"From Theodora. She said we might need it, and we might."

He put the money in an inside pocket of his jacket and zipped the pocket. "I'll use it to keep us all as safe as I can," he said. "But don't imagine I would just drive off and leave you, Shori. I wouldn't. I couldn't."

"I hope it won't be necessary. But if it is necessary to keep you safe, to keep Celia and Brook safe, you'll do it. You will do it!"

He drew back from me, angry, wanting to dispute, yet knowing he would obey. "Sometimes I forget that you can do that to me," he said.

"I do it to save your life," I said.

After a while he sighed. "You're a scary little person," he said.

I had no idea what to say to that so I ignored it. "Theodora wanted to come, too," I said. "I couldn't let her, even though I wanted her to. The only person I want more is you. I need you to be safe, and I need you to keep Brook and Celia safe."

He shook his head, then put his arm around my shoulders, his expression going from angry to bemused. "That is the most unromantic declaration of love I've ever heard. Or is that what you're saying? Do you love me, Shori, or do I just taste good?"

"You don't taste good," I said, smiling. "You taste wonderful." I grew more serious. "I would rather be shot again than lose you."

"More and more romantic," he said and shook his head. He bent, lifted me off my feet, and kissed me. I nipped him, tasted him, and heard him draw a quick breath. He held me hard against him, and I closed my eyes for a moment, submerged in the scent, the feel, and taste of him.

Then Brook came out with her own suitcase. She had taken it from the back of her car to get at her toiletries. "We'd better get going," she said, noticing the way Wright and I held each other, then looking away.

We sighed. Wright put me down, and we let each other go.

Celia came out carrying the sandwiches, each bagged with the apples and bananas that Wright had had in the cabin. She handed a bag to Wright and one to Brook, then said, "You guys got everything?"

We nodded, and Wright went to turn off the lights and lock the door.

We drove, Wright with me in one car and Celia with Brook in the other. We drove through what was left of the night and into the day. By daybreak we had reached Salem, Oregon. We were still, according to the maps, hundreds of miles north of San Francisco Airport. We got two motel rooms at a place that did not force us to park our cars where they could be seen from the street—just in case someone was hunting us. We picked up a map of the area, the others ate the food they had brought, and we all went to bed.

I lay awake for a while next to Wright, wondering whether I should even be in bed. Perhaps I should stay awake, keep watch. But I couldn't quite believe that humans would have been able to follow us without my noticing them. And I couldn't believe they would be willing to kill a motel full of humans unrelated to Ina if they did find us. Also, the motel was filled with windows—eyes—and perhaps with curiosity. Our enemies liked concealment and quiet. I could sleep. In fact, this was an excellent place to sleep. I let myself drift off.

Once Wright had slept off some of his weariness, he woke me up and told me to try biting him now and see what happened.

I laughed and bit him. I didn't take much blood because I had taken a full meal from him only two days before. Still, I was eager to see what happened, and he didn't disappoint me.

After a few hours, we got up and got on the road again. We didn't hurry. We stopped for meals, stayed within the speed limit, and, as a result, spent one more night in a motel. This time I was hungry enough to leave the room while Wright was asleep and wait until I spotted a stranger letting himself into his room. I slipped in with him before he realized I was there. I bit him and had a nourishing, but unsatisfying, meal. Afterward, I told him to keep the bite mark hidden until it healed and to remember only that he'd had an odd dream.

Sometime later, after we got underway on our third night, I realized that I should be riding with Brook to do what I could to encourage her memory. I didn't really know whether she would remember more clearly or focus her attention more narrowly if I were there to prod her, but I meant to find out. When we stopped for gas, I switched cars.

"Do you want me to send Celia to keep you company?" I asked Wright. "Or would you rather have some time to yourself?"

He hesitated, then said, "Send her. I'll ask her questions and find out more about this symbiont business."

I looked at him and saw that he wasn't asking me to send Celia to him, he was daring me. And he was smiling a little as he did it.

"Ask," I said. "I'm afraid for you to talk to them and learn what they know—because I know so little. But you should talk to them. We're a family, or the beginnings of one. We'll be together for a very long time."

"It's all right," he said, immediately contrite. "A little solitude might be good for me."

"No," I said. "Talk to her. Get to know her. Ask your questions. It isn't all right, but it will be." I walked away to where Brook was putting gas into her car.

"What?" she asked.

"I'm switching cars," I said. "I want to do what I can to prod your memory."

She sighed. "I'm still afraid I won't remember."

"I'll drive, then," Celia said through her open window. "We're more likely to survive the trip if the driver isn't looking all around trying to remember stuff."

She was right. Brook hadn't been driving when she visited these people before. Best for her not to be driving now. I went back and told
Wright he would be driving alone after all and told him why.

He grinned. "Decided you didn't want me to know everything, then,"
he said.

I grinned back at him. "That must be it."

They went into the store that was attached to the gas station and
bought more maps, food, bottled water, and ice. Then Wright and Celia
consulted over the new maps. Somewhere in Sonoma or Mendocino
County in California we decided to use State Route 1 instead of U.S.
101 as we'd planned because Brook said State Route 1 "felt" like the
right road. This apparently had to be discussed again. Then, finally, we were
on our way. Celia led off.

Brook and I sat in the backseat, and she studied a huge, sheetlike map.
Finally she put the map down and looked at me. "We're close enough,"
she said, "but I don't recognize anything yet."

"Are you still worried about your memory?" I asked.

She nodded. "Of course I am."

"You will remember," I said. "When you see things you've seen before,
you're going to recognize them. You've been to this place before. You've
seen the way, going and coming. Now you'll see the way a third time, and
you'll get us there. Look out the windows. Don't worry about the map."

She took a deep breath and nodded.

And yet we drove all the way to the Golden Gate Bridge before she
began to see things that looked familiar to her. By then we had to cross
the bridge, then find a place to turn back. On our way back, though, she
kept seeing familiar landmarks, businesses, signs.

"I think I paid more attention when we were traveling to Punta
Nublada from the airport," she said. "We were headed north, the way
we are now, and I know this place now. It all seemed so new to me when
I came this way with Iosif. I hadn't been anywhere far from home for a
long time. I was so excited."

Just over two hours later, a newly confident Brook had us turn down
a narrow paved road that took us to a gravel road that led, finally, to
Punta Nublada, a community of eleven large houses with garages and
several other buildings scattered along either side of the road. It was

almost a village. Behind some of the houses, I could see the remains of large gardens, most of them finished for the year, stark and empty. The community was dark and still, as though it were a humans-only place and everyone were asleep. I wondered why. I could smell Ina males nearby.

"Which house belongs to the oldest son, or perhaps we should see one of the elderfathers?" I asked, then had another thought. "Wait, which is the home of Daniel Gordon, the one you said first approached Iosif."

"Daniel?" Brook asked. "He is the oldest son."

"Show me which home is his."

"Third house on the right."

We stopped there. I got out and understood something interesting and frightening at once. There were people—human and Ina—watching us with guns. I smelled the guns, I saw some of the people hiding in the darkness. I smelled them and knew they were all strangers to me, but I sorted through them anyway. The scents of the Ina were very disturbing. These people were nervous. Some of the humans were frightened. At least none of the humans present had been among those who attacked Wright, Celia, Brook, and me. That possibility had not occurred to me until I smelled all the guns.

"Don't get out yet," I said to Celia and Brook. But behind us, Wright had already gotten out and come to stand beside me. It frightened me how vulnerable he was, how vulnerable we all were, but if these people wanted to shoot us, surely they would already have done it.

I took Wright's hand, or rather, I touched one of his huge hands and allowed it to swallow mine, and we walked to the front porch of Daniel Gordon's house.

"This the guy who wants to be your mate?" he asked in a soft voice that I thought he tried hard to keep neutral.

"Things have changed," I said, knowing that he was not my only listener. "I don't know what they want now. But for the sake of the past, I hope they will speak with me and not just point guns at me."

Wright froze, drew me closer to him, and I realized he had known nothing of those who watched us. He saw no one until the tall, male Ina stepped into view on the broad front porch.

"Shori," he said, making a greeting of my name.

Of course, he was a stranger to me. "You're Daniel Gordon?" I asked. He frowned.

"If you and your people are this alert," I said, "you must know what's happened to my family—to my mothers, my sisters, my brothers, and my father. It almost happened to me, too. I had a serious head injury. Because of it, I don't remember you at all. I don't remember any part of my life before getting hurt. So I have to ask: Are you Daniel Gordon?"

After what seemed to be a long while, he answered, "Yes, I'm Daniel."

"Then I need to talk with you about what's happened to my family and, very nearly, to me and my symbionts."

Daniel looked at Wright, at our joined hands, at the two women in the car. Finally, he nodded. "You and your people are welcome here," he said.

There was an almost-silent withdrawal of armed watchers. I saw a few of the humans around Daniel's house and the houses of his nearest neighbors lower their guns and turn away. I turned to the car and beckoned to Brook and Celia.

They came out of the car and up to us, and Daniel looked at them, lifted his head and sampled their scent, then looked at me again. He recognized them. I could see that in his expression—realization and surprise.

"Those two . . ." He frowned. "They aren't yours, Shori."

"They were my father's and my brother Stefan's. They're with me now." I knew they smelled wrong, but if he knew what had happened to my family, he must know why they smelled the way they did—of both the dead and the living.

"We must question them," he said. "We've heard what happened on the radio, read about it in the newspaper, seen it on television. Two of my fathers even went up to look around. And yet even they don't understand any of this. Who did these things?"

"We'll share everything we know," I said, "although that isn't much. We came here because we need help against the assassins."

"Who are they? Do you have any idea?"

"We don't know who they are, but we killed some of them when they attacked us." And I repeated, "We'll tell you all we can."

"How did you survive?"

I sighed. "Call your brothers and your fathers from the shadows, and let's go into your house and talk."

His fathers and brothers had gathered around us in near silence and just far enough away to prevent my symbionts from seeing them. They were listening and sampling our scents and looking us over. I didn't see that it would do them any harm to examine us in comfort and with courtesy.

Perhaps Daniel thought so, too. He turned, opened his door, switched on a light, and stood aside. "Come in, Shori," he said. "Be welcome."

We went up the steps into the house, into a large room of dark wood and deep green wallpaper. A large flat-screen television set covered much of one end wall. Beneath it on shelves was a large collection of tapes and DVDs. At the opposite end of the room was a massive stone fireplace. Along one side wall there were three windows, each as big as the front door, and between them and alongside them, there were tall bookcases filled with books. On the other side wall there were photographs, dozens of them, some in black and white, some in color, most of them of outdoor scenes—woods, rivers, huge trees, rock cliffs, waterfalls. They would have been beautiful if they had not been so crowded together.

There were a great many chairs and little tables around the room. We and the brothers and fathers who came in after us found places to sit. Wright, Celia, Brook, and I sat together on a pair of two-person seats at the fireplace end of the room. The fathers and brothers Gordon sat around us, surrounding us on three sides, crowding us. Our world was suddenly filled with tall, pale, vaguely menacing, spidery men, and I was annoyed with them for being even vaguely menacing and scaring my symbionts. I watched them, wondering why I was not afraid. They seemed to want me to be afraid. They stared at the four of us in silence that was as close to hostile as silence could be. Or maybe they only wanted my symbionts to be afraid.

My symbionts *were* afraid. Even Wright was afraid, although he tried to hide it. He couldn't hide his scent, though. Celia and Brook didn't try to hide their fear at all.

I looked at Daniel who sat nearest to me. "Do you believe that I or my people murdered my families?"

He stared back at me. "We don't know what happened."

"I didn't ask you what you knew. I asked whether you believe that I or my people murdered my families?"

He glanced back at his fathers and brothers. "I don't. I don't even believe you could have."

"Then stop scaring my symbionts. If you have questions, ask them."

"You're a child," one of the older men said. "And the two women with you are not your symbionts."

I looked at him with disgust. He had already heard me answer this. I repeated the answer exactly: "They were my father's and my brother Stefan's. They're with me now."

"You don't have to keep them," he said. "They can have a home here . . . if you took them only out of duty."

"They're with me now," I repeated.

The older man took a deep breath. "All right," he said. "Tell us what you know, Shori." And the pressure on us eased somehow, as it had when the guns were lowered outside. I felt it, even though I hadn't been afraid. I looked at my symbionts and saw that they felt it, too. They were relaxing a little.

I turned back to face the Gordons and sighed. After a moment of gathering my thoughts, I summarized the things that had happened to me. I talked about awakening amnesiac in the cave, about Hugh Tang, finding the ruin, finding Wright, and later finding my father, who told me that the ruin had been the community of my mothers, then losing my father and all of his community except Celia and Brook, going to the Arlington house and almost dying there, discovering that our attackers were all human . . .

One of the Gordons interrupted to ask, "Were you able to question any of them?"

I shook my head. "We killed several of them. The rest escaped. We only just escaped ourselves. The fire had attracted attention, and I didn't want to have to deal with firemen or the police."

"You weren't seen," Daniel said. "Or if you were, it's being kept very secret. There's been nothing in the media about cars escaping the scene, and none of the sources my fathers created have phoned to tell us about anyone escaping. The police seem very frustrated."

"Good," I said. "I mean I didn't know whether or not we were seen. We spent the next night in our cars in the woods. Then, because Brook had been here once, I thought I could get her to bring us back here."

A Gordon who looked about fifty and who was, almost certainly, one of the two oldest people present spoke with quiet courtesy: "May we question your symbionts?" He had a British accent. I had heard BBC reporters on Wright's radio back at the cabin talking the way this man did.

I looked at Celia and Brook, then at Wright. "It's all right," I said. "Tell them whatever they want to know." They looked alert but not afraid or even uncomfortable. I nodded to the older man. "All right," I said. "By the way, what's your name?"

"I'm Preston Gordon," he said. "I'm sorry. We should all introduce ourselves." And they did. Preston and Hayden were the two oldest. They were brothers and looked almost enough alike to be twins, except that Hayden was taller and Preston had a thicker mop of white-blond hair. Their sons were Wells, Manning, Henry, and Edward. And they in turn were the fathers of Daniel, Wayne, Philip, and William. William was, I suspected, only fifteen or twenty years older than I was. Although no one said so, I got the impression that I'd met most of them, perhaps all of them, before. What did it say to them that I couldn't remember any of them now? It embarrassed me, but there was nothing I could do about it.

Preston directed his first question to Brook. "Did you recognize anyone among those your group killed? Had you seen any of them before?"

"No," Brook told him. "I didn't get to see all their faces, but the ones I saw, I had never seen before."

William asked, "How many did you kill, Shori, you personally, I mean."

"Three," I said surprised. "Why?"

"Three men," he said and grinned. "You must be stronger than you look."

I frowned because that was a foolish thing to say. Of course I was stronger than I looked, just as he was stronger than he looked.

Daniel said, "Shori, we didn't know about your mothers. There was apparently no news coverage. Do you know why that was?"

"Iosif and two of my brothers covered it up. He said they did. And even so, there was some local coverage. He convinced local reporters and apparently the police that my mothers' community had been abandoned, that someone burned a cluster of abandoned houses. That's news, but it's not important news. And he saw to it that some of my mothers' neighbors kept an eye on the place. He thought the killers might come back to gloat."

Preston shook his head. "I see. Iosif must have worked very hard to keep things quiet. Brook, did he say anything to you about his effort to cover up and, perhaps, about his effort to investigate?"

"He told me what happened," she said. "He didn't understand how it could have happened, who could have been powerful enough to do it. He said it must have happened during the day—that that was the only way Shori's mothers could have been surprised. And he thought Shori might have survived if anyone did. But . . . I don't believe he thought of it as something that would happen again. I never got the impression that he was worried about it happening to our community."

Celia nodded. "Stefan flew down with him to help with the neighbors. They took Hugh Tang and some other symbionts with them to search for survivors. They really did think it was just a single terrible crime. I mean, you hear about people committing mass murder—shooting up their schools or their workplaces all of a sudden—or you hear about serial murders where someone kills people one by one over a period of months or years, but serial mass murder . . . I don't think I've ever heard of that except in war."

"Iosif didn't know anything," I said. "I talked to him about it. He was frustrated, grieving, angry . . . He hated not knowing at least as much I hate it."

There was a brief silence, then Daniel spoke to Wright. "What about you? You're the outsider brought into all this almost by accident. What are your impressions?"

Wright thought for a moment, frowning a little. Then he said, "Chances are, this is all happening for one of three reasons. It's happening because some human group has spotted your kind and decided you're all dangerous, evil vampires. Or it's happening because some Ina group or Ina individual is jealous of the success Shori's family had with blending human and Ina DNA and having children who can stay awake through the day and not burn so easily in the sun. Or it's happening because Shori is black, and racists—probably Ina racists—don't like the idea that a good part of the answer to your daytime problems is melanin. Those are the most obvious possibilities. I wondered at first whether it could be someone or some family who just hated Shori's family—an old fashioned Hatfields and McCoys family feud—but Iosif and his sons would have known about anyone who hated them that much."

Philip Gordon, younger than Daniel, older than William, said, "You're assuming that if Ina did it, they used humans as their daytime weapons."

"I am assuming that," Wright said.

"We don't do that!" Preston said, his mouth turned down with disgust.

"I'm glad to hear it," Wright told him. "Of course I didn't think that anyone Iosif would introduce to his female family would do that. But there are other Ina. And your species seems to be as much made up of individuals as mine is. Some people are ethical, some aren't."

I watched the Gordons as he spoke. The younger ones listened, indifferent, but the older ones didn't much like what he was saying. It seemed to make them uncomfortable, embarrassed. I wondered why. At least no one tried to shut Wright up. That was important. I wouldn't have wanted to stay in a community that was contemptuous of my symbionts.

I also liked the fact that Wright wasn't afraid to say what he thought.

The Gordons talked among themselves about the possibilities Wright had offered, and they didn't seem to like any of them, but I suspected that their objections came more from wounded pride than from logic. Ina didn't use humans as daytime weapons against other Ina. They hadn't done anything like that for centuries.

And Ina were careful, both Preston and Hayden insisted. No Ina would leave evidence of vampiric behavior for humans to find. And according to Daniel, Ina families all over the world were happy about my family's success with genetic engineering. They hoped to use the same methods to enable their own future generations to function during the day.

And the Ina weren't racists, Wells insisted. Human racism meant nothing to the Ina because human races meant nothing to them. They looked for congenial human symbionts wherever they happened to be, without regard for anything but personal appeal.

And of course, there was no feud. According to Preston, nothing of that kind had happened for more than a thousand years. Nothing of the kind could happen without a great many people knowing about it. Iosif certainly would have known, and he and his mates would have been on guard.

"Speaking of being on guard," I said loudly.

The Gordons stopped and one by one turned to look at me.

"Speaking of being on guard," I repeated, "it's good that you have people guarding this place now, but are you also keeping watch during the day?"

Silence.

"We haven't been," Edward said at last. He was probably the youngest of the fathers. "We'll have to now." He paused. "And, Shori, you'll have to stay with us until this business is over, until we've found these killers and dealt with them."

"Thank you," I said. "I came here hoping for help and refuge. If I stay, I might be most useful as part of your day watch."

That seemed to interest them. "You can stay awake all day, every day and sleep at night?" William asked me.

I nodded. "I can as long as I get enough sleep," I said. "If I'm allowed to sleep most of the night, I should be all right during the day. And . . . it will keep me out of your way."

There was an uncomfortable silence. I had noticed that a couple of the unmated sons were already beginning to fidget as my scent worked on them. And Daniel tended to stare at me in a way that made me want to touch him. I liked his looks as well as his scent. I wondered whether I had liked him before, when my memory was intact.

"I'll need you to tell your day-watch symbionts to listen to me. When the killers attacked the Arlington house, they were fast and coordinated. If I'd been just a little slower or if Wright had been slower to wake up Celia and Brook and get them out, we might have died."

"We'll talk to our symbionts," Preston said. "We'll introduce them to you and tell them to obey you in any action against attackers, but Shori . . ." He stopped talking and just looked at me.

"I'll do all I can to keep them safe," I said.

# fifteen

The Gordons had a guest house at Punta Nublada. It was a comfortable two-story, five-bedroom house, smaller than the sprawling family houses but easily large enough for us and as ready to be lived in as Iosif's guest house had been. It was usually used by visiting Ina and their symbionts or visiting members of the Gordon symbionts' families. Daniel said such people imagined that their relatives lived in a commune that had somehow survived from the 1960s. Then he had to tell me something about the 1960s. I might not have asked, but I found I enjoyed hearing his voice.

My symbionts and I moved our things from the cars into the house and relaxed for the rest of the night. There was canned and frozen food, as there had been in the Arlington house, and Wright, Celia, and Brook put together a meal. A short time later we were all asleep.

Just before dawn, though, I left the bed I was sharing with Wright and went to the room Celia had chosen. I was hungry but didn't want to be in too much of a hurry with her. I slipped into her bed, turned her toward me, and kissed her as she woke. Once the surprise and stiffness had gone out of her, I found the place on her neck where I could feel her pulse most strongly. I licked the dark, salt-and-bitter skin where I would bite her. She didn't struggle. Her body jerked once when I bit her, then it was still. Afterward, she dozed off easily, resting against me while I licked the wound I had made. Like Brook, she still wasn't enjoying herself, but at least she was no longer suffering.

When she was asleep, I got up, showered, dressed, and went outside while it was still comfortably dim. I meant to wander around, take a look at the place. But I found Preston sitting on a seat that swung from chains attached to the ceiling on the front porch of the guest house. He looked up at me, smiled, and said, "I hoped you would get up before I got too drowsy. I'm here to speak with you on behalf of the son of one of my symbionts."

I sat down next to him. "All right," I said.

He smiled. "We love our mates," he said. "Their venom never lets us go. We would be lost if it did. But our symbionts . . . they never truly understand how deeply we treasure them. This boy . . . I still miss his mother."

I waited, very curious. I liked him. That was interesting. I didn't know him, but I liked him. He smelled good somehow, not in the slightest edible, not even sexually interesting, but good, comfortable to be with.

"One of my symbionts had a son," he said. "Then about ten years ago, she was killed in a traffic accident in San Francisco. She had gone there to visit her sister. I might have been able to help, but I wasn't notified until she was dead. Her husband is still alive, still here. He's one of William's symbionts. But in this matter . . . Well, I promised father and son I would speak to you. The son is twenty-two and just out of college. He's heard about you and seen your picture. Last night when you arrived, he saw you for the first time. He says he would like to join with you if you'll have him. He has a degree in business administration, and I think you'll eventually need someone like him to help you manage the business affairs of your families."

I drew a deep breath and smiled sadly. "I don't know about that, but I think I need more symbionts soon. I don't believe three is enough, and I'm worried about hurting the ones I have."

"I wondered whether you were aware of the danger," he said. "You do need more people quickly. In fact, you need three or four more symbionts."

"I left one back in Washington. We have an emotional connection, but that's all so far. I refused to bring her because I didn't know what I would find here, and I didn't know whether I could protect her."

"With our help, you should be able to do that."

"And I have no home," I said. "I'll have to start from nothing. I'll do that, but with my memory gone, I'll need a lot of information from you. I don't really know how to be Ina."

"You do, I believe, even though you don't realize that you do. Your manner is very much that of an intelligent, somewhat arrogant, young Ina female. I think you learned long before you lost your memory that you could have things pretty much your own way." He smiled.

"You see that in my behavior?" I asked surprised.

"Yes, I do. Don't worry about it. A little self-confidence may be just what you need right now."

"I have nothing to be confident about," I said. "I really do need to learn all I can from you and your family."

"Of course you do. Ask us any questions you like. Best to ask only the fathers. You won't torment us quite so much."

I nodded. "I'm sorry about that. I know my scent bothers you."

"Do you remember?"

"No. Iosif told me."

"I see. Will you have my symbiont's son?"

"Of course I will, if it turns out he and I like each other. What's his name?"

"Joel Harrison. I think you'll like him, and as I've said, he's seen you and he wants to be with you. And as a bonus, his father saw you last night, too. They were both on guard. He got a look at you and liked the way you stood up for your symbionts. He said you would take care of Joel."

"As best I can," I said. "But—"

"You're with us now. You aren't alone. And what you said earlier about having nothing . . . that probably isn't true. Your mothers and your father owned large tracts of land, several apartment buildings in Seattle run by a management company, and interests in several businesses. They had substantial incomes. Daniel was involved in some sort of business venture with one of your brothers. He knows something about their affairs, and we can find out more. Eventually, what they owned will be yours."

"Thank you," I said. "I knew they owned the land they lived on, but I didn't have any idea what else there was or how to find out about it." I frowned, remembering something I had read about on Wright's computer. "Would they have left wills?"

He frowned. "Well, yes, but they would never have foreseen being so completely wiped out. We'll find out. Somewhere along the line, there will be a lawyer or two who's been bitten and who, as a result, will be very helpful and very honorable about seeing that your rights are respected."

I nodded and repeated, "Thank you."

He stood up, and it was as though he suddenly unfolded, tall and lean. "You're welcome, Shori. Now, I think I'd better introduce you to Joel so that I can get to bed." He raised his arm and beckoned. A young man emerged from one of the houses across the road. The man was as tall as Wright, but not as heavily muscled. And this man was as dark skinned as I was and had hair like mine. He walked toward me with a little smile on his face. I got the impression he was excited—both happy and very nervous.

I liked the way he looked—strong and wiry and healthy and brown, striding as though there were springs in his legs.

"You will have to talk to your first," Preston said.

I glanced up at him, startled.

"You don't want them fighting or competing with one another in ways that make the rest of you miserable. Each must find a way to accept the other. Each must find a way to accept the other's relationship with you. You must help them do this."

I sighed.

The young man came up to me, towering over me, smiling down.

"Shori Matthews, this is Joel Harrison," Preston said. "I believe the two of you will be very good for one another."

"Thank you," I said to him. And to Joel, "Welcome."

"I've been looking forward to meeting you," Joel said. Slowly, deliberately, he extended his arm, wrist up, clearly not so that we could shake hands.

I laughed, took the hand, kissed his wrist, and said to him, "Later."

"Date," he said. "Is there room for me over here?"

"There's room."

"I'll get my stuff."

I watched him walk away, then said to Preston, "He smells wonderful."

Preston crooked his mouth in something less than a smile. "Yes. He's been told that, I'm afraid. Be good to each other."

He had started to walk away from me when I stopped him. "Preston, do you know whether I had my own family of symbionts before . . . before the fire?"

He looked back. "Of course you did. You can't remember them at all?"

"Not at all."

"Good."

I stared at him.

"Child . . . you have no idea how much it hurts when they die. And you've lost all of yours. All seven. If you remembered them, the pain would be overwhelming . . . unbearable."

"But they were mine, and I don't recall their scents or their tastes or the sounds of their voices or even their names."

"Good," Preston repeated softly. "Let them rest in peace, Shori. Actually, that's all you can do." He walked slowly away to the house Joel had gone into. I watched him go, wondering how many symbionts he had lost over the years, over the centuries.

The sun was rising now and growing bright enough to be uncomfortable even through the low clouds. I went back inside and found Celia frying frozen sausages from the refrigerator.

"How are you?" I asked.

"I'm good," she said. "How about you? You didn't hurt me, but you filled up on me, didn't you?"

"I did." I looked at the sausages. "Do you need more food? You can get things from one of the other houses." That felt right. No one here would wonder why a symbiont needed to eat well.

"Some butter?" she asked. "There are frozen waffles in the refrigerator, and there's syrup in the cupboard—good maple syrup—but no butter."

"Go to the house next door and tell whoever answers that you're with me. If they don't have what you want, they'll tell you who does."

She nodded. "Okay. Don't let my sausages burn." And she ran off to the nearest house, introduced herself, and asked not only for butter, but for fresh fruit and milk as well. I listened while turning her sausages. Wright hadn't managed to teach me to cook, but he had cooked food around me often enough for me to be able to keep pork sausage from burning. The symbiont who answered Celia just said sure, introduced herself as Jill Renner, put the things Celia wanted into a bag, and told her to have a good breakfast. Celia thanked her and brought them back to the guest-house kitchen. Brook came in just then, and she dove right into the bag, took out a banana, and began to peel and eat it.

"A new symbiont will be coming in sometime soon," I told her. "Offer him breakfast, would you?"

"Ooh," Brook said. "*Him?*"

"Damn," Celia said and sighed. "See, now here's where I don't envy you guys. You're going to go upstairs and kick that nice hairy man of yours right in his balls, aren't you? A new man already! Damn."

"Keep the new guy down here until I come back," I said.

I left them and went up to talk to Wright.

Wright had showered and was shaving. There was another sink in the bathroom—one that had a chair in front of it and a large low mirror with lights around it. I sat down in the chair and watched him shave before a similar, higher mirror. He had collected his electric razor from his cabin when we stopped there and was using it now to sweep his whiskers away quickly and easily.

Then he looked at me. "Something wrong?" he asked.

"Not wrong," I said. "But perhaps something that will be hard for you." I frowned. "Hard on you. And I don't want it to be."

"Tell me."

I thought about how to do that and decided that directness was best. "Preston has offered me another symbiont, one whose mother, when she was alive, was one of Preston's symbionts. The new one's name is Joel Harrison."

He turned his shaver off and put it on the sink. "I see. Is Preston the father?"

I stared at him in surprise. "Wright, that's not possible."

"I didn't think it was, but I thought I'd ask, since you didn't mention the father."

"I don't know who Joel's father is, but he's here. He's one of William's symbionts. Joel's mother was killed in a traffic accident ten years ago."

"What does the father think about his son coming to you?"

"He wanted his son to come to me. He asked Preston to introduce us."

"So he's pimping his own son."

I hesitated. "I don't know what that means, but your voice says it's something disgusting. Joel's father hasn't done anything disgusting,

Wright. He and Joel both looked at me and decided I would be good for Joel. He's been away at school. He could have stayed away, could have come back now and then to visit his father. But he chose a life with the Ina, with us. I'm glad of it. I need him."

"For what? You need him for what?"

I looked at him, wanting to touch him, knowing that at that moment he did not want to be touched. "Three of you aren't enough to sustain me for long without harm to you. I'm going to try to have Theodora brought here, too."

He shook his head angrily. "I don't mind the women so much I guess. I kind of like the two downstairs. I was hoping you'd get all women— except me. I think I could deal with that." He turned around, filled with energy and violence, and punched the wall, breaking it, leaving a fist-sized hole. And he had hurt his hand. I could smell the blood. But he did not seem to notice. "Hell," he said, "you don't even know Harrison. Maybe you'll hate him."

I shrugged. "If I don't like him, I'll have to find someone else and soon."

He looked at me sadly. "My little vampire."

"Still," I said.

He stepped over to me, picked me up with a hand under one arm, sat down, and sat me on his lap. I took his injured hand and looked at it, licked away the blood, saw that he hadn't done himself much damage. It would heal overnight like a shallow bite.

"I could get a lot more pissed with you if you were bigger," he said softly.

"I hope not," I said.

He wrapped both arms around me, held me against him. "I don't think I can do this, Shori. I can't share you."

I leaned back against him. "You can," I said softly. "You will. It will be all right. Not now, perhaps, but eventually, it *will* be all right."

"Just like that." The bitterness and sorrow in his voice was terrible.

I turned on his lap, straddled him, and looked up at him.

After a moment, he said, "I want you for myself. It scares me how much I love you, Shori."

I pulled his head down and kissed him, then rested my forehead against his chest, savoring his scent, his wonderful furry body, the beat of his heart. "Preston says our symbionts never know how much we treasure them," I said.

"You treasure me?"

"You know I do."

He held me away from him and looked at me. "You've taken over my life," he said. "And now you want me to share you with another man."

"I do," I said. "Share me. Don't fight with him. Don't hurt the family by fighting with him. Accept him."

He shook his head. "I can't."

"You can," I repeated. "You will. He's part of the family that we must form. He's one of us."

When I left him and went down to the kitchen, I found Joel sitting at the table drinking coffee with Brook and Celia.

"Hey," he said when I came in. He had two large rolling suitcases parked near his chair.

"Hey," I said reflexively. "Come talk to me." I took his hand and led him to the other end of the house to what I had been told was the "family room."

"Don't you mean that *you're* going to talk to *me*?" Joel asked as he sat down in one of the large leather-covered chairs. I sat on the arm of his chair.

"First things first," I said and took the wrist he had offered earlier. He watched me raise it to my mouth and kiss it a second time, and he smiled. I bit him.

He was delicious. I had intended only to taste him and get a little of my venom into him, but he was such a treat that I took a little more that a taste. And I lingered over his wrist longer than was necessary.

Finally, I looked up at him and found him leaning back bonelessly in the chair. "God," he said. "I hit the jackpot."

"How have you managed to stay unattached?" I asked. "Didn't anyone here want you?"

He smiled. "Everyone wanted me. Everyone except Preston and Hayden. They said I was too young to join with them. The others . . . they left me alone when I asked them to, but before that, they were all after me. And I didn't want to join with a man. There's too much sexual feeling involved when you guys feed. I wanted that from a woman. Preston said he would check with nearby female families after I finished college, and he's taken me to see a couple of them, but I wasn't interested. You are the only Ina I've ever been attracted to."

"After seeing me only once?"

"Yeah. I didn't even see you when you were here before . . . before your parents died. I had gone to San Francisco to spend time with some friends from college." He shook his head. "I liked your looks when I saw the pictures the Gordons had of you and your sisters. When I saw you last night, I didn't have a chance."

I didn't know what to make of that. "I'm only beginning to form my family," I said. "You would probably have an easier life with anyone here or any of the female families you've seen. You know my memory only goes back a few weeks."

"I heard."

"And when I leave the Gordons, I'll be alone."

He nodded. "Then let me help you make a new family."

I looked at him and saw that his expression had changed, had become more serious. Good. "I want you to be part of my new family," I said. "More than that, I need you. But you and my first will have to accept each other. You will accept him. There will be peace between you. No fighting. No endangering the rest of us with destructive competitions."

"All right. I doubt that your first and I will ever be anything like friends, but I know how it is. I suppose you told him the same thing."

"Of course." I paused. "He helped me, Joel. When I had no one else, when I had no idea who or what I was, he helped me."

"I wish I had had the chance to do such a thing." He reached up and touched my face. "Like I said, let me help you make a new family."

◎      ◎      ◎

A little later that morning, I put on my hooded jacket, sunglasses, and gloves and walked around to each of the houses of the community. I spotted the guards from outside, then went into the houses to do what I could to help them be less easily spotted. Being easily spotted by the kind of attackers my symbionts and I had faced would mean easily shot.

The Gordon symbionts greeted me by touching me—my shoulders, arms, hands. I found that I was comfortable with that, although I had not expected it. It was as though they had to touch me to believe that I could be Ina and yet be awake.

"You aren't drowsy at all?" a woman named Linda Higuera asked. She was a nervous, muscular brown woman, at least six feet tall and leaning on a rifle. We were on the third floor of William's house, and she was one of his symbionts. From what I had seen, William preferred big, powerful-looking symbionts, male and female. Wise of him.

"I'm not drowsy," I said. "As long as I don't get too much sun, I'm fine."

She shook her head. "I wish William could do that. I would feel safer if he could at least wake up if we need him."

I shrugged. "Your turn to keep him safe."

She thought about that, then nodded. "You're right. Damn. He's so strong, I've just gotten used to depending on him. Guess it ought to work both ways." She stopped and thought for a moment. "Do you have a phone?"

"There are phones in the guest house."

"I mean a cell phone."

"No, I don't." I wasn't entirely sure what a cell phone was.

"You should have one so we can talk to each other if something happens. The house phones are too easy to disable."

That made sense. "Is there one I can borrow?"

She sent me down to wake up a huge man named Martin, a man so brown he was almost black. Martin not only supplied me with a charged cell phone, but saved several numbers on it and made me repeat the names that went with them and whose house each person was in. Then he showed me how to make a call, and I made a practice call to the guard at Daniel's house. Finally, he dug out a charger and showed me how to use that.

"Here's your number," he said, making it flash across the phone's small screen, "just in case you have to give it to somebody."

"Thank you," I said, and he grinned.

"No problem. How's Linda doing up there?"

"Doing well," I said. "Alert and thoughtful."

"And how about my son?" he asked in a different tone. "How's he?"

I looked at him, startled. "You're Joel's father?"

"Yep. Martin Harrison. Joel move into the guest house yet?"

"He has, yes. I like him."

"Good. You're what he wants. If you take care of him, he'll take care of you."

I nodded and left him feeling much better about the safety of the Gordon community. With or without me, these people would not be caught by surprise and murdered, and now I could communicate with them in a quiet, effective way.

I walked around the community once more, stopping now and then to listen to the activity around me. There were symbionts eating meals, making love, discussing children who were away at boarding schools, discussing the vineyards and the winery, pruning nearby trees, washing dishes, ordering audiobooks by phone, typing on computers . . . There were little children playing games and singing songs in a room at Hayden's house. It seemed that here some symbionts still carried on most of their activities during the day while others had switched to a nocturnal schedule to spend more time with their Ina.

As I wandered back toward the guest house, I found myself paying attention to a conversation that Wright and Brook were having there.

"They take over our lives," Brook said. "They don't even think about it, they just do it as though it were their right. And we let them because they give us so much satisfaction and . . . just pure pleasure."

Wright grunted. "We let them because we have no choice. By the time we realize what's happened to us, it's too late."

There was a long pause. "It's not usually that way," Brook said. "Iosif told me what would happen if I accepted him, that I would become addicted and need him. That I would have to obey. That if he died, I might die. Not that I could imagine him dying. That seemed so impossible . . . But he told me all that. Then he asked me to come to him anyway, to accept him and stay with him because I could live for maybe two hundred years and be healthy and look and feel young, and because he wanted me and needed me. I wasn't hooked when he asked. He'd only bitten me a couple of times. I could have walked away—or run like hell. He told me later that he thought I might run. He said people did run sometimes out of superstitious fear or out of the puritanical belief that anything that feels that good must have a huge downside somewhere along the line. Then he had to find them and talk them into believing he was a dream or an ordinary boyfriend."

Wright said, "By the time Shori asked me—or rather, by the time she offered to let me go—I was very thoroughly hooked, psychologically if not physically."

"That was probably because of her memory loss."

Wright made an "mmmm" sound of agreement. "I suppose. She's shown herself to be a weirdly ethical little thing most of the time. It still bothers me, though, and now there's this new guy she told me about . . ."

"Joel," Brook said. "You haven't met him yet?"

"She didn't hang around to introduce us. I met him in the upstairs hall. He had the nerve to ask me which bedrooms were empty. You know she never even told me he was black."

"They're not human, Wright. They don't care about white or black."

"I know. I even know she needs the guy—or at least, she needs a few more people. But I hate the bastard. I'm not going to do anything to him. I'll deal with this somehow, but Jesus God, I hate him!"

"You're jealous."

"Of course I am!"

"You aren't sure you want her, but you don't want anyone else to have her."

"Well, it's not like I can leave. Hell, I can feel the hold she's got on me. I can't even think of leaving her without getting scared."

"Would you change that?" Brook asked. "If you could escape her, would you?"

". . . I don't know."

"I think you do. I've seen you with her."

"I can't imagine being without her, but I'm not sure I would have begun if I'd known what I was getting into." There was a silence, then he asked, "What about you? How do you feel about the way she claimed you?"

"Better," Brook admitted.

"Better?"

"She got us out of the Arlington house alive, and she shouldn't have been able to do that. And she stood her ground last night. The Gordons were pushing her, trying to intimidate her a little just to see what she would do, what she was like. Well, she's strong, and it matters to her how other Ina treat us. We can trust her. Celia said we could, but I wasn't sure."

"You're saying you want to be her symbiont, not some man's? I mean, I thought that after choosing to be with Iosif . . ."

There was another short silence, then Brook said, "I would probably have chosen a man if I'd had a choice initially. But I'm okay with Shori. I can find myself a human man if I need one. I can't believe what she's done for Celia and me. I've seen symbionts who've lost their Ina. An old Ina who was visiting died while he was with us. I saw his symbionts in withdrawal, and I heard them screaming when other Ina tried to save their lives by taking them over. It was bad. Convulsions, pain, helpless fear and revulsion for the Ina who is only trying to help. It went on for days, weeks. It was really horrible. One of the symbionts died. But with Shori . . . she's fed from me twice, and already it doesn't hurt anymore. It's not fun, but it's not bad. I can't wait to know what it will be like when I'm fully her symbiont."

"So . . . they don't all feel the same when they bite?"

"No more than we all look the same. Their venom is different—very individual. I suspect her bite is spectacular. That's why she was able to get you the way she did."

"And she's only a kid," he said.

They said nothing more. I listened for a few moments for more conversation, then for outsiders, intruders. When I knew that the community was safe, for the moment, I thought about what Brook and Wright had said. What they had said, over-all, was that, except for Wright's problem with Joel, they were content with me. It felt remarkably good to know this. I was relieved, even though I had not realized I needed relief. Wright would have to find his own way to accept Joel, and Joel would have to do the same with Wright. There would be a period of unease that I would have to pay attention to, but we would get through it. Other families of Ina and symbionts proved that it could be done.

That day, there were no intruders. The symbionts kept watch, with fresh guards arriving every three hours so that no one got too tired or drowsy. I met a few more of them and liked their variety—a dentist, an oceanographer, a potter, a writer who also worked as a translator (Mandarin Chinese), a plumber, an internist, two nurses, a beautician who was also a barber, and, of course, farmers and winegrowers. And those were just the ones I met. Some no longer did the work they had trained to do except on behalf of the people of Punta Nublada. Some worked in nearby towns or in the Bay Area two or three days out of the week. Some worked in the vineyards and the winery that the Gordons owned. Some, who were self employed, worked in Punta Nublada. Three of the buildings I had mistaken for barns or storage buildings proved to be full of offices, studios, and workshops.

"We fill our time as we please," Jill Renner told me during her watch at Wayne Gordon's house, next to the guest house. "We help support the community whether we have jobs away from it or stay here, whether we bring in money or not." She was the daughter and granddaughter of symbionts and had been much relieved when Wayne Gordon took an interest in her and asked her to accept him. She had a half-healed bite just visible on the side of her neck. I realized that she wanted it to be seen. She was proud of Wayne's obvious attentions to her. Interesting.

That night Wayne and Manning, one of Wayne's fathers, drove to a local airfield where they kept a private plane. Each took two symbionts with him, so I assumed they expected to be gone for two full nights—not that they couldn't graze on strangers if they had to. The Gordons called it grazing. It was what I'd done when I lived with Wright at his cabin, except for Theodora. Ina often found new symbionts when they grazed.

Wayne and Manning came to the guest house before they left to tell me that they were going up to Washington to begin to work out the legal affairs of my male and female families and to look at the ruins of their former communities in the hope that they would see something that we had missed. I had Brook tell them the exact address of Iosif's guest house near Arlington. Let them look at that, too.

"Shall I go?" I asked them. "Won't you need me as daughter and only survivor? Anyway, I think I'd like to collect Theodora."

"We won't need you yet," Wayne said. He was tall even for an Ina, the tallest in his family. He towered over even his tallest symbionts. "We'll have to produce you eventually, but for now, we just want to find out who handled Iosif's and your mothers' legal affairs. Then we'll bite them and see how quickly all this can be sorted out. The land should be yours whether or not you want to live on any of it. If you like, you can sell one parcel and use the money to get a couple of houses started on the other. And your parents owned apartment houses in Seattle and quite a bit more than just the land their communities stood on. We need to learn all we can about their business affairs before you can even begin to decide what to do."

I nodded. "Can you collect Theodora?"

"Give us her address."

I called Wright, described Theodora's location three doors east of his uncle's house, and he told Wayne how to find her.

"Theodora Harden," I said. "I'll phone her and tell her you'll be there . . . when?"

They worked that out. They would pick up Theodora on their way home on the third night.

"Thank you," I said. "Be careful. Someone should always be awake and on guard."

They nodded and went out to their huge, boxy car. Joel told me it was called a Hummer and that it cost more money than some houses.

Then they were gone.

The next day, Punta Nublada was attacked.

# sixteen

The attackers arrived just after ten the next morning. Except for me, all Ina were asleep. I had spent nearly an hour on the phone with Theodora and was thinking about her, wanting her, looking forward to seeing her. Then I heard the cars.

They drove into the community in three large, quiet cars, each almost as big as the Gordons' Hummer, and I heard them before I was able to see them from my perch at one of the dormer windows in the guest-house bedroom that Wright and I shared. I didn't know who the newcomers were. They weren't talking among themselves. They weren't making much noise of any kind, but the moment I heard their approach, I was suspicious. I phoned two other houses and told the symbionts there to alert everyone else.

"Wake everyone," I said. "Wrap your Ina in blankets and be ready to get them out of the house. These people like to set fires. Watch. If they carry large containers, if they try to spread any liquid, shoot them."

I was worried about innocent visitors being killed by frightened symbionts, but I was even more worried about the Gordons and their symbionts being killed in their sleep, perhaps because of me or something to do with my family.

I pulled on my hooded jacket and put on my sunglasses and gloves. The sun was shining outside. There were no clouds. Finally I ran downstairs and found Wright in the kitchen. He hadn't spoken to me at all today because I had spent part of the night with Joel. I grasped his arms. "This may be an attack," I said. "Get Brook, Celia, and Joel. Get guns. Watch! Don't show yourselves and don't fire unless you see gas containers or guns."

I needed to be outside so that I could keep an eye on things and take whatever action was needed. I went out the back door. I had my phone in my pocket—set to vibrate, not ring—but no gun. I would kill quietly if I had to kill.

The cars came down the private road that led to the Gordon houses. They stopped before they reached the first house—the guest house—and men spilled out of the doors. Each carried some burden in his hand, and at once I could smell the gasoline.

I phoned the nearest house—Wayne's house—and said, "Shoot them. Now!"

There was a moment when I thought they would not obey me. Then the shooting started. The symbionts had a wild mixture of rifles, handguns, and shotguns. The sound was a uneven mix of pops, thunderous roars, and intermediate bangs. Somehow, most of the invaders went down in that first barrage. They were used to taking their victims completely by surprise, setting their fires, and shooting the desperate who awoke and tried to run. Now it was the raiders who were running—at least those still able to run.

I heard someone running my way, around the side of the guest house toward the back, away from the road. The runner was human and smelled strongly of gasoline. He was spilling gasoline as he ran. He never saw me.

I let him come around the house to me, let him get completely out of sight of his friends, and then hit him with my whole body. As he went down, I broke his neck. He was too slow to understand fully what was happening. He made no noise beyond the rush of air from his lungs when I hit him.

I left his gun and his gasoline can out of sight behind a garage, then I ran along the backs of the houses, hoping that if anyone saw me, I would be moving too fast for them to aim and shoot. I ran around the community, killing three more men as the symbionts went on shooting and as someone set fire to Henry's house, then to Wayne's.

I saw that Henry was being looked after—three of his symbionts were carrying him from his house thickly wrapped from head to toe in blankets. They took him into William's house. The rest of Henry's symbionts poured out of his house, too, and three of them found hoses and began to fight the fire. The other two guarded them with rifles.

I felt a particular duty toward Wayne's symbionts because he had gone up to Washington to help me. I made sure everyone was out of his house, checked with the symbionts flowing out the doors, and told them to count themselves. All were present and healthy, three of them carrying young children whom they took to William's house. The rest got hoses and shovels and began to fight the fire. They needed no help from me.

I went through the community, looking everywhere. There was no more shooting. All the intruders seemed to be dead or wounded. Then I heard footsteps and caught an unfamiliar scent. I realized there was at least one intruder still alive and trying to get back to one of their cars. I spotted him moving behind the houses. He took off his shirt as he slipped past Preston's house. He wanted to blend in, look, at least from a distance, like one of the male symbionts who had been awakened unexpectedly and were now fighting the fires or tending the wounded, shirtless.

Shirtless or not, this man smelled of gasoline and alienness. He was an outsider. There was nothing of the Gordon community about him.

I ran after him as he sprinted from the back of Preston's house toward one of the buildings that housed offices and studios. This did not take him closer to any of his group's cars. He couldn't have reached them without running across a broad open space. But the building was unlocked, and it would have given him a place to hide and bide his time. It was his bad luck that I had seen him.

I caught up with him, tripped him, and dragged him down just as he reached the building. He fell hard and knocked himself out on the concrete steps in front of the building. I was glad of that. I wanted him unconscious, not dead. I had questions to ask him. I took a full meal from him while he lay there. I didn't need it yet in spite of the running around and fighting I'd done, but I needed him cooperative.

He came to as I finished and tried to buck me off him.

"Be still," I said. "Relax."

He stopped struggling and lay still as I lapped at the bite just enough to stop the bleeding and begin the healing.

"All right," I said. "Let's go see how things stand between your people and mine." I stood up and waited for him to get up. He was a short, stocky, black-haired man, clean shaven but disfigured by the beginnings of a big lump over his left eye and a lower lip rapidly swelling from a blow that had probably loosened some of his teeth.

He stumbled to his feet. "They'll kill me," he said, mumbling a little because of the swelling lip and looking toward the clusters of people putting out the fires, gathering weapons, moving cans of gasoline away from the houses, checking dead or wounded raiders, keeping children away from the bodies.

"Stay close to me and do as I say," I told him. "If you're with me and if you don't hurt anyone, they won't kill you."

"They will!"

"Obey me, and I won't let anyone hurt you."

He looked at me, dazed. After a moment he nodded. "Okay."

"How many of you were there in those three cars?" I asked, glancing back at the cars. None of this group should escape. Not one.

"Eighteen," he said. "Six in each car."

"That many and your gear. You must have really been packed in."

I walked him back toward the houses, made him pick up his shirt and put it on again. Then I spotted Wright. He came toward me, looking past me at the raider.

"Don't worry about him," I said. "Are Celia, Brook, and Joel all right?"

"They're fine."

I nodded, relieved, and told him where to find the men I'd killed and their guns and their gasoline. "Get other symbionts to help you collect them," I said. "There should be a total of eighteen raiders, living and dead, including this one."

"Okay," he said. "Why is this one still alive?"

"I've got questions for him," I said. "Are any of the rest of them alive?"

"Two. They're shot, and they've been kicked around a little. The symbionts were pissed as hell at them."

"Good. Make sure the dead, their cars, and the rest of their possessions are gathered and shut up out of sight in case the noise or the smoke attracts outside attention." The Gordons had no neighbors who could be seen from the houses, but the noise might have reached some not-too-distant farm. And the smoke might be seen, although there was much less of it now. The fires were almost out. Two houses had been damaged, but none of them had been destroyed. That was amazing. "Where are the survivors?" I asked.

He pointed them out in the yard where they had been laid, then he said with concern, "Shori, your face is beginning to blister. You should get inside. If it gets any worse, you might have scars."

I touched his throat just at the spot I had so often bitten. "I won't scar anymore than you do when I bite you. Thank you for worrying about me, though." I left him. My raider followed me as though I were leading him with a rope.

The two surviving raiders were battered and unconscious. They lay on the grass in front of Edward's house. "Don't hurt them any more," I told the symbionts who were guarding them. "When they can talk, your Ina will want to question them. I will, too."

"Our doctor will look at them when she gets around to them," a man named Christian Brownlee said. He stared at my raider, then ignored him. My raider inched closer to me.

"Are all the symbionts alive?" I asked.

He nodded. "Five hurt. They're in Hayden's house."

I knew the Gordons had a doctor and two nurses among the ninety or so adult humans in the community, and I went to Hayden's house, expecting to find her at work there. She was.

The doctor was one of Hayden's symbionts. She was an internist named Carmen Tanaka, and she was assisted not only by the two nurses, a man and a woman, but by three other symbionts. She was busy but not too busy to lecture me.

"You stay out of the sun," she said. "You're blistering."

"I came to see whether I could be of use," I told her. "I don't know whether there is anything I can do to help heal symbionts not my own, but I want to help if I can."

Carmen looked up from the leg wound that she was cleaning. The bullet had apparently gone straight through the man's calf. "If any of them were in danger or likely to be in danger before their Ina awake, I'd ask for your help," she said. "But as things are, you'd just cause them unnecessary pain and create problems between them and their Ina."

I nodded. "Let me know if anything changes," I said. "I'm going to do what I can for the raiders who survived. We're going to want to talk to them later."

"Is this one?" she looked at my companion.

"Yes."

She looked at the bite wound on the man's neck and nodded. "If you bite the others, you'll help them avoid infection and they'll heal faster and be more manageable."

I nodded and went out to tend to the raiders. Once I finished with them, I took my raider back to the guest house, gave him a cold bottle of beer from the stock we'd found in the pantry, and sat down with him at the kitchen table.

"What's your name?" I asked him.

"Victor Colon."

"All right, Victor. Tell me why you attacked this place."

He frowned. "We had to."

"Tell me why you had to."

He frowned, looking confused. It was a kind of confusion that worried me since it seemed to me that it could mean only one thing.

Celia and Brook came into the kitchen, saw us, and stopped.

"Come in," I said. "Did you come to get food?"

"We missed lunch," Brook said. "We probably shouldn't be hungry after all this, but we are."

"It's all right," I said. "Eat something. Fix some for Victor here, too. And sit and talk with us."

They didn't understand, but they obeyed. They cooked hamburger sandwiches for themselves and one for Victor Colon. They had found loaves of multigrain bread, hamburger meat, and bags of French fries in the freezer, and had put the meat and bread in the lower part of the refrigerator to thaw. Now, they fried the meat and the potatoes in cast-iron pans on the stove. There was salt and pepper, mustard and catsup, and a pickle relish in the cupboard but, of course, no fresh vegetables. At some point we were going to have to find a supermarket.

Once they all had food and bottles of beer from the refrigerator, and I had a glass of water, the confused man seemed more at ease. As he ate, he watched Celia and Brook with interest. He was seeing them, I thought, simply as attractive women. He stared at Celia's breasts, at Brook's legs. They knew what he was doing, of course. It seemed to amuse them. After a few glances at me, they relaxed and behaved as though Victor were one of us or, at least, as though he belonged at our table.

Celia asked, "Where do you come from?"

Victor answered easily, "L.A. I still live there."

Brook nodded. "I went down to Los Angeles a few years ago to visit my aunt—my mother's sister. It's too hot there."

"Yeah, it's hot," Victor said. "But I wish I were there now. This thing didn't go down the way it was supposed to."

"If it had, we'd be dead," Celia said. "What the hell did we ever do to you? Why do you want to kill us?" Oddly, at that moment she handed him another bottle of beer. He'd already finished two.

Victor frowned. "We had to," he said. He shook his head, reverting to that blank confusion that so worried me.

"Oh my God," Brook said. She looked at me, and I knew she had seen what I had seen.

Celia said, "What? What?"

"Victor," Brook said, "who told you and your friends to kill us?"

"Nobody," he responded, and he began to get angry. "We're not kids! Nobody tells us what to do." He drank several swallows of his beer.

"You know what you want to do?" Brook said.

"Yeah, I do."

"Do you want to kill us?"

He thought about that for several seconds. "I don't know. No. No, I'm okay here with you pretty ladies."

I decided he was getting too relaxed. "Victor," I began, "do you know me? Who am I?"

He surprised me. "Dirty little nigger bitch," he said reflexively. "Goddamn mongrel cub." Then he gasped and clutched his head between his hands. After a moment, he put his head down on the table and groaned.

It was clear that he was in pain. His face had suddenly gone a deep red.

"Didn't mean to say that," he whispered. "Didn't mean to call you that." He looked at me. "Sorry. Didn't mean it."

"They call me those things, don't they?"

He nodded.

"Because I'm dark-skinned?"

"And human," he said. "Ina mixed with some human or maybe human mixed with a little Ina. That's not supposed to happen. Not ever. Couldn't let you and you . . . your kind . . . your family . . . breed."

So much death just to keep us from breeding. "Do you think I should die, Victor?" I asked.

"I . . . No!"

"Then why try to kill me?"

Confusion crept back into his eyes. "I just want to go home."

"Victor." I waited until he sat up and faced me. "If you leave here, do you think they'll send you after me again?"

"No," he said. He swallowed a little more beer. "I won't do it. I don't want to hurt you."

"Then you'll have to stay here, at least for a while."

"I . . . can I stay here with you?"

"For a while." If I bit him a time or two more and then questioned him, I might get the name of our attackers from him—the name of whoever had bitten him before me, then sent him out to kill. And if I got that name, the Gordons would probably recognize it.

"Okay," he said. He finished his beer. Celia looked at me, but I shook my head. No more beer for now.

"You're tired, Victor," I said. "You should get some sleep."

"I am tired," he said agreeably. "We drove all night. You got a spare bed?"

"I'll show you," I said and took him upstairs to our last empty bedroom. I had intended to give it to Theodora. We would have to get rid of Victor soon. Maybe one of the other houses would have room for him. "You'll sleep until I awaken you," I told him.

"Will you bite me again?" he asked.

"Shall I?" I didn't really want to, but of course I would.

"Yeah."

"All right. When I awaken you, I will."

"Listen," he said when I turned to leave. "I didn't mean to call you . . . what I called you. My sister, she married a Dominican guy. Her kids are darker than you, and they're my blood, too. I would kick the crap out of anyone who called them what I called you."

"You only answered my question," I said. "But I need more answers. I need to know all that you can tell me."

He froze. "Can't," he said. "I can't. My head hurts." He held it between his hands as though to press the pain out of it somehow.

"I know. Don't worry about it right now. Just get some sleep."

He nodded, eyelids drooping, and went off to bed. I felt like going off to bed myself, but I went back down to the kitchen where Celia and Brook were waiting for me. Wright and Joel had joined them. Wright spoke first.

"All eighteen attackers are accounted for," he said. "No one got away."

I nodded. That was one good thing. None of them would be running home to tell the Ina who had sent them that they had failed, although that would no doubt be obvious before long. And what would happen then? I sighed.

Joel seemed to respond to my thought. "So some Ina is sicking these guys on us," he said. "When he sees it didn't work this time, he'll send more."

"It seems that way," I said wearily. I sat down. "I don't know my own people well enough to understand this. I feel comfortable with the Gordons, but I don't really know them. I don't know how many Ina might be offended by the part of me that's human." I wanted to put my head down on the table and close my eyes.

"The Gordons will help you," Joel said. "Preston and Hayden are decent old guys. They can be trusted."

I nodded. "I know." But of course I didn't know. I hoped. "Tonight we'll talk to the prisoners. Maybe we'll all learn something."

"Like which Ina have been trying to kill you," Celia said.

I nodded. "Maybe. I don't know whether we can find that out yet. It may be too soon. But Victor isn't really injured, so we can begin questioning him tonight. The others, though, they might need time to recover, and they might know things that Victor doesn't. Or we might just use them to verify what Victor says."

"You're sure you can make Victor tell you what he knows?" Wright asked.

"I can. So could the Gordons. It will hurt him, though, stress him a lot. It might kill him. I don't believe any of this is his fault, so I don't want to push him that far."

"You remember that," he asked, "that your questioning him could kill him?"

I nodded. "I saw his face when I asked him who I was, and he answered. It hurt him. In that moment, I knew I could kill him with a few words. But he's only a tool—one of eighteen tools used today."

"What makes you so sure he's not a willing tool?" Celia asked.

"His manner," I said. "He's confused, sometimes afraid, but not really angry or hateful." I shrugged. "I could be wrong about him. If I am, we'll find out over the next few days."

"You're sure it's all right to leave him alone upstairs?" Wright said.

"He'll sleep until I wake him," I said. "And when he wakes, I won't be the only one wanting to question him."

# seventeen

I went upstairs feeling tired and a little depressed. I didn't know why I should feel that way. I was close to finding out who was threatening me, and I had taken a full meal from Victor, which should have restored my energy after all my running around in the sun and blistering my face until it hurt. Somehow, it hadn't.

I had taken off my shoes and was lying down on the bed Wright and I usually shared when Brook looked in and said, "Come to my room and lie down with me for a little while."

The moment she suggested it, it was all I wanted to do. I slid from the bed and went down the hall to her room.

I lay down beside her, and she turned me on one side and lay against me so that I could feel her all along my back.

"Better?" she asked against my neck. "Or is this hurting your face?"

I sighed. "Much better." I pulled one of her arms around me. "My face is healing. Why do I feel better?"

"You need to touch your symbionts more," she said. "Temporaries like Victor don't matter in the same way, and Joel isn't yours yet. You need to touch us and know that we're here for you, ready to help you if you need us." She brought her hand up to my hair and stroked gently. "And we need to be touched. It pleases us just as it pleases you. We protect and feed you, and you protect and feed us. That's the way an Ina-and-symbiont household works, or that's the way it *should* work. I think it will work that way with you."

I brought her hand to my mouth and kissed it. "Thank you," I said.

"Sleep a little," she said. "It isn't likely that there will be any more danger today. Take a nap."

I drifted off to sleep in utter contentment.

⊚    ⊙    ⊚

"Shori?"

I awoke sometime after dark and disentangled myself from Brook as gently as I could. I got up, listening. Someone had called my name. Daniel's voice, not speaking loudly, not in the room with me, not even in the house, but clearly speaking my name to me.

I didn't want to wake Brook so I went to the bathroom down the hall. The window there faced the road and the other houses.

"Yes," I said aloud, eyes closed, listening.

"Bring your captive to my house for questioning," he said. "You can act as his protector, as some of us will scare him."

"Other Ina ordered him to kill us," I said. "He's their tool, not a willing volunteer."

Silence. Then, "All right. Bring him anyway. We won't hurt him any more than we have to."

"We'll be over in a few minutes."

I went to Wright's and my bedroom and got my shoes from beneath the bed. Wright was there, snoring softly. I didn't disturb him. I went back to the bathroom, put my shoes on, and washed my face, all the while thinking about how easily Daniel and I had spoken. I had heard him even though he had not left his house, and he had known that I would hear him. I stood for a moment in the bathroom and listened, focusing my listening first on the guest house where Victor and my four symbionts were all asleep, breathing softly, evenly. Then I focused on Preston's house and heard a female symbiont tell a male named Hiram that he should telephone his sister in Pittsburgh because she had phoned him while he was out helping with the wounded. A male was trying to repair something. He was cursing it steadily, making metallic clattering noises, and insisting, apparently to no one at all, "It's not supposed to do that!" And a woman was reading a story about a wild horse to a little girl.

Of course I had been focusing my listening almost since I awoke in the cave, but I had not been around other Ina enough to know how sensitive our hearing could be. It had never occurred to me that someone could awaken me and get my full attention just by calling my name in a normal voice from another house across and down the road. Had I heard because on some level I was listening for my name? No, this couldn't have been the first time people talked about me when I wasn't present or wasn't awake.

But it probably was the first time someone so far away had spoken *to* me as I slept. And perhaps that small thing, the tone of Daniel's voice alone, had been enough to catch my attention.

I went to Victor's room and woke him. Then, because I had promised and because it would help me get information out of him later, I bit him again, tasting him, taking only a little blood. He lay writhing against me, holding me to him, accepting the pleasure I gave him as willingly as I accepted his blood. I found myself wondering whether anyone had ever investigated the workings of Ina salivary glands or tried to synthesize our saliva. It was no wonder that Ina like my father worked so hard to conceal our existence.

When the bite wound had ceased to bleed, we got up, and I took him over to Daniel's house where all of the Gordons, except those who had flown up to Washington, waited.

"What's going to happen to me?" he asked as we went. He seemed frightened but resigned. He had been in Ina hands long enough to know that there was no escape, no way of refusing his fate, whatever it turned out to be.

"I don't know," I said. "You do your best for us, and I'll do my best for you. Relax and answer all questions truthfully."

When we reached Daniel's house, I saw that the Gordons had gathered in the living room. There were no symbionts present. That was interesting. I had not even thought of awakening my symbionts to bring them along. If Victor died tonight, I didn't want them to see it happen. I didn't want to confront them with the reality of what could happen to them if some Ina who hated me got hold of them. But they knew, of course. They were all intelligent people. They even had some idea of what I could do to them if I were to lose my mind and turn against them. But they trusted me, and I wanted—needed—their trust. They didn't have to see the worst.

I sat with Victor. He was alone and afraid, actually shaking. He needed someone to at least seem to be on his side. He was the alien among us, the human being among nonhumans, and he knew it.

"His name is Victor Colon," I told the Gordons when we were settled. "Victor," I said and waited until he looked at me. "Who are they?"

He responded in that quick, automatic way that said he wasn't thinking. He was just responding obediently, answering the question with information he had been given. "They're the Gordon family. Most of it." He looked them over. "Two are missing. We were told there would be ten. Ten Gordons and you." He glanced at me.

I nodded. "Good. Relax now, listen to their questions and answer them all. Tell the truth." I looked at the Gordons. They must know more than I did about questioning humans who had been misused by Ina. I would leave it to them as much as possible.

Preston said, "What else are we, Victor? What else do you know about us?"

"That you're sick. That you're doing medical experiments on people like the Nazis did. That you are prostituting women and kids. I believed it. Now, I don't know if it's true." He was trembling more than ever. He jumped when I put my hand on his arm, then he settled down a little. "They said we all had to work together to stop you."

"How many of you were there?" This was from Hayden, the other elder of the group. They were centuries old, Hayden and Preston, although they looked like tall, lean, middle-aged men in their late forties or early fifties, perhaps. Their symbionts had told me they were the ones who had emigrated here from England, arriving at the colony of Virginia in the late eighteenth century.

"There were twenty-three of us at first," Victor said. "Some got killed. Jesus, first five guys dead and now just about everyone else . . . Today there were eighteen of us.

"Eighteen." Hayden said nodding. "And were they your friends, the other men? Did you know them well?"

"I didn't know them at all until we all got together."

"They were strangers?"

"Yeah."

"But you joined with them to come to kill us?"

Victor shook his head. "They said you were doing all this stuff . . ."

"Where were you?" Preston asked quietly. "Where did you get together?"

"L.A." Victor frowned. "I live in L.A."

"And how were you recruited? How were you made part of the group that was to come for us?"

Victor frowned. He didn't appear to be in pain. It was as though he were trying hard to remember and understand. He said, "It almost feels like I've always been working with them. I mean, I know I wasn't, but it really feels like that, like nothing really matters but the work we did together. I remember I had been watching TV with my brother and two of my cousins. The Lakers were on. Basketball, you know? I needed some cigarettes. I went down to the liquor store to buy some, and this tall, skinny, pale guy pulled me into an alley. He was goddamn strong. I couldn't get away from him. He . . . he bit me." Victor looked down at me. "I thought he was crazy. I fought. I'm strong. But then he told me to stop fighting. And I did." He stopped talking, looked at me, suddenly grabbed me by the shoulders. "What do you people do to us when you bite us? What is it? You're goddamn vampires!"

He shook me. I think he meant to hurt me, but he wasn't really strong enough to do that. I took his hands, first one, then the other, from my arms. I held them between my hands and looked into his frightened eyes.

"Answer us honestly, Victor, and you'll be all right. Relax. You'll be all right."

"I don't want you to bite me again," he said.

I shrugged. "All right."

"No!" he shouted. And then more softly, "No, I'm lying. I do want it again, tomorrow, now, anytime. I need it!" His voice dropped to a whisper. "But I don't want to need it. It's like coke or something."

I suddenly felt like hugging him, comforting him, but I didn't move. "Relax, Victor," I said. "Just relax and answer our questions."

The Gordons watched both of us with obvious interest. Daniel, in particular, never looked away from me. I supposed that I was as much on trial as Victor was but in a different way. What did I remember? How well did I compensate for what I didn't remember?

Did they still want me? I thought Daniel did. His scent pulled at me. His brothers smelled interesting, but his scent was disturbing. Compelling.

I sighed and dragged my attention back to Victor. I looked from Preston to Hayden. The others had left the questioning to them so far.

"Victor," Preston said, "where were you taken after you were bitten for the first time?"

"The guy had a big Toyota Sequoia. He told me to get in and just sit there. I did, and he just drove around. He was spotting other guys and picking them up. I guess I was his first catch of the night. He caught five more guys, then he took us all out to some houses up above Altadena, up in the San Gabriel Mountains, kind of all by themselves on a dead-end road. His family was there. They all looked like him—tall, lean, pale guys. And there were a lot of other just ordinary people."

There was a stir among the Gordons. They didn't say anything, but I could see that they knew something. Most likely, they knew which Ina family lived above Altadena in the San Gabriel Mountains. I had no idea how far away these places might be, but they did.

"Victor," Hayden said, "when did all this happen? When were you taken and bitten for the first time?"

He frowned. "More than a month ago? Yeah, it was that long. Maybe six weeks."

I could see what was coming. I stared at the rug, needing to hear more, needing to hear everything, but not quite wanting to hear it. It was only reasonable that Victor had been one of those used to kill both my families.

"So you've done other jobs, then, haven't you?" Hayden continued.

"Up in Washington State, yeah," Victor agreed. "We did three jobs up there."

"How did you get there?"

"They flew us up in private planes with all our gear. Then we rented cars. Followed the maps we were given."

"So they gave you new identities? Credit cards?"

"Not me. Five of the other guys. And they gave them plenty of cash. They had cell phones, too. They'd call in when we were ready to do a job and tell us to go ahead. Then they'd call in afterward and we'd be told what to do next, which was mostly to get motel rooms and wait for the call to get into position for the next job. The five guys they chose, they were all ex-military. One used to be Special Forces. They told the rest of us what to do."

So by now, with no phone call, their bosses must have realized that something was wrong. I wondered how long it would take these enemy Ina to collect new human tools and send them out to try again.

"You said you did three jobs," Preston said. "Where in Washington did you do those . . . jobs?"

"One a few miles outside a little town called Gold Bar. Another not too far from a town called . . . Darlington? No, Darrington. That's it. And one at a house near the town of Arlington. That's all up in western Washington. Pretty country. Trees, mountains, rivers, waterfalls, little towns. Nothing like L.A."

"You were successful in Washington?"

"Yeah, mostly. We hit the first two, and everything went the way it was supposed to. Something went wrong at the third. People got killed. The cops almost got us."

"Weren't people supposed to get killed?"

"I mean . . . our people got killed. We didn't know what happened at first. Later we heard on the radio that two got shot and three had their throats ripped out. The rest of us never saw what did that—a dog, maybe. A big dog. Anyway, the cops were coming, and we had to run."

I thought about telling him exactly what had killed his friends, then decided not to. None of it was his doing, really. Even so, I didn't want to be sitting next to him any longer. I didn't want to know him or ever see him again. But he was not the one who would pay for what had been done to my families. He was not the one I had to stop if I were going to survive.

I took a deep breath and spoke to Preston. "Do you know who's doing this?"

He looked at Victor. "Who are they, Victor? What's the name of the family who recruited you and sent you to kill us?"

Victor's body jerked as though someone had kicked him. He looked at me desperately, confusion and pain in his eyes.

Hayden picked up the question. "Do you know them, Victor? What is their family name?"

Victor nodded quickly, eager to please. "I know, but I can't say . . . please, I can't."

"Is the name 'Silk'?"

Victor grabbed his head with both hands and screamed—a long, ragged, tearing shriek. Then he passed out.

I didn't to care. It was clear from the Gordons' expressions that they didn't care. But I had bitten him twice. I didn't want him, wouldn't have kept him as my symbiont, but I did care what happened to him. I couldn't ignore him. It seemed that the bites made me feel connected to him and at least a little responsible for him.

I listened to his heartbeat, first racing, then slowing to a strong, regular beat. His breathing stuttered to a regular sleeping rhythm. "What can we do with him?" I asked Preston. "I can talk him into forgetting all this and send him home, but what if the Silk family picks him up again?"

"You feel that you need to help him, in spite of everything?" he asked.

I nodded. "I don't want him. I don't like him. But none of this really has anything to do with him."

He looked around at his brother and his sons. Most of them shrugged.

Daniel said, "I don't think the Silks will bother about him. They won't know he survived. They probably don't even know exactly where he lived before they picked him up. He's just a tool. They might have rewarded him if he survived, but if they think he's dead, that will be the end of it. We need to check what he's said with what the other prisoners say. If their stories agree, they can all go home. You can send them back to their families."

I nodded. "I'll fix Victor. Do you want me to fix the others, too?"

"Once we've questioned them, you might as well. You've already bitten them." He didn't sound entirely happy about this. I wondered why.

"Is there transportation back to L.A. from somewhere around here?" I asked.

"We'll get them back." Daniel looked uncomfortable. "Shori, I think your venom is the reason this man is still alive, the reason he was able to answer as many questions as he did."

This was obvious so I looked at him and waited for him to say something that wasn't obvious.

"I mean, *your* venom. If one of us had bitten him instead of you, I think he'd be dead now."

I nodded, interested. That was something I hadn't known.

"And that means that if the Silks do get him again somehow and question him, he won't survive. There may be female relatives of the Silks—sisters or daughters—with venom that's as strong as yours. They could question him, but chances are, they won't. And he wouldn't survive being questioned by males. Their venom would make it necessary for him to answer but not really possible. The dilemma would kill him. He'd probably die of a stroke or a heart attack as soon as they began."

I looked at Victor and sighed. "Is there anything we can do to keep him safe?"

"No," Preston said. "It really isn't likely that the Silks will pick him up again. He'll probably be all right. But unless one of us wants to adopt him as a symbiont, we can't keep him safe. Daniel only wanted you to know . . . everything." I heard disapproval in his voice, and I didn't understand it. I decided to ignore it, at least for now.

I looked at Daniel and thought he looked a little embarrassed, that he was staring past me rather than at me. "Thank you," I said. "So much of my memory is gone that I'm grateful for any knowledge. I need to know the consequences of what I do."

Daniel got up and left the room.

I looked after him, surprised, then looked at Preston. "When should Victor be ready to go?"

"A couple of nights from now. After we've questioned the others."

"All right," I paused. "Can one of you take him? I don't want him back at the guest house."

Preston glanced at the doorway Daniel had gone through. "Don't worry," he said. "We'll take care of him."

"Thank you," I said with relief. Then I changed the subject and asked a question I had been wanting to ask since I arrived. "Are there . . . do you have Ina books, histories I could read to learn more about our people? I hate my ignorance. As things stand now, I don't even know what questions to ask to begin to understand things."

It was Hayden who answered, smiling. "I'll bring you a few books. I should have thought of it before. Do you read Ina?"

I sighed and shrugged. "I honestly don't know. We'll find out."

# eighteen

To my surprise, I did read and speak Ina.

Hayden brought me three books and sat with me while I read aloud from the first in a language that I could not recall having heard or seen. And yet as soon as I opened the book, the language seemed to click into place with an oddly comfortable shifting of mental gears. I suppose I had spoken English from the time I met Wright because he and everyone else had spoken English to me. If I had heard only Ina since leaving the cave, I might not know yet that I spoke English.

I shook my head and switched back to English. "I wonder what else I'll remember if someone prods me."

"Do you understand what you've read, Shori?" Hayden asked.

I glanced at the symbols—clusters of straight lines of different lengths, inclined in every possible direction, and often crossed at some point by one or more S-shaped lines. They told the Ina creation myth. "Iosif told me a little about this," I said. "It's an Ina myth or legend. The goddess who made us sent us here so that we could grow strong and wise, then prove ourselves by finding our way back home to her."

"Back to paradise or back to another planet," Hayden said. "There was a time when Ina believed that paradise was elsewhere in this world, on some hidden island or lost continent. Now that this world has been so thoroughly explored, believers look outward either to the supernatural or to rather questionable science."

"People truly believe this?" I frowned. "I thought the story was like one of the Greek or Norse myths." I had run across these in Wright's books.

"There was a time when those were believed, too. A great many of us still believe in the old stories, interpreted one way or another. What you're holding could be called the first volume of our bible. Your parents believed the stories were metaphors and mythologized history. We do, too. None of us are much interested in things mystical. I don't believe you were either before, but now I suppose you'll have to read the books, talk to believers as well as nonbelievers, and make up your mind all over again."

"How old is this book?" I asked.

"We believe that its oldest chapters were originally written on clay tablets about ten thousand years ago. Before that, they had been part of our oral tradition. How long before that had they been told among us? I don't know. No one knows."

"So old? Are there human things ten thousand years old?"

"Writings, you mean? No. There were wandering family bands, villages of human farmers, and there were nomadic human herders. They left behind remnants of their lives—stone tools, carved stone figurines, pottery, woven matting, stone and wood dwellings, some carving on bone and stone, painting on cave or cliff walls, that sort of thing."

I nodded, interested. "What signs did we leave?"

"We had already joined with humans ten thousand years ago, taking their blood and safeguarding the ones who accepted us from most physical harm. I suspect that by then we had already been around for a very long time. Whenever we evolved or arrived, it was much longer ago than ten thousand years. Ten thousand years ago, we were already thinly spread among human tribes and family bands. Even then, that was the most comfortable way for us to live.

"Our earliest writings say that we joined humans around the rivers that would eventually be called Tigris and Euphrates and that we had scattered north and west into what's now Russia, Ukraine, Romania, Hungary, and those regions. Some of us wandered as nomads with our human families. Some blended into stationary farming communities. Either way, we were not then as we are now. We were weak and sick. I don't know why. The stories say we displeased the goddess and were suffering her punishment. The group that believes in an outer-space origin says that our bodies needed time to adjust to living on Earth.

"For a while, it seemed that we might not survive. I think that's when some of us began to find a new use for the writing we had developed for secret directional signs, territorial declarations, warnings of danger, and mating needs. I think some of us were writing to leave behind some sign that we had lived, because it seemed we would all die. We weren't reproducing well. Our children, when they were conceived, often did not survive their births. Those who did survive were not strong. Few mated families managed to have more that one or two children of their own. Everyone took in orphans and tried to weave new families from remnants of the old. We suffered long periods of an Ina-specific epidemic illness that made it difficult or impossible for our bodies to use the blood or meat that we consumed, so that we ate well and yet starved. We believe now that the disease was spread among us by Ina nomads and by families traveling to be near mates.

"Our bodies were no better at dealing with this illness than our human contemporaries were at dealing with their illnesses. But while our attentions helped them deal with their infections, defects, and injuries, they could not help us deal with ours. We died in greater numbers than we could afford. It got harder and harder for us to find mates. Then, gradually, we began to heal. Perhaps we had simply undergone a kind of microbial winnowing. The illness killed most of us. Those left were resistant to it, as were their children.

"Even when we were fit, though, we had to be careful. Nonsymbiont humans might attack us and murder us to steal our possessions or because we were careless and lived too long in one place without seeming to age." He shrugged. "Some humans wanted to know how we could live so long. What secret magic did we possess to avoid growing old? What could be done to us to force us to share our magic with them?

"Suspicions about us grew out of control now and then down through the ages, and we had to run or fight, or we were tortured and murdered as demons or as possessors of valuable secrets. Sometimes they hacked at us until they thought we were dead, then buried us. When we healed, we came out of our graves confused, mad with hunger . . . perhaps simply mad. Well, that's how in some cultures we became the 'walking dead' or the 'undead.' That's why they learned to burn or behead us."

"What about the wooden stake through the heart?" I asked.

"That might work or it might not. There's nothing magical about wood. If the stake leaves enough of the heart intact, we heal. One of my fathers was buried with a stake in his heart. He lived and . . . killed six or seven people when he came out of his grave. As a result, my families had to leave Romania and change their names. That's how my brothers and I happened to grow up in England."

He sighed. "Even in the most savage of times, when there were Ina family feuds that were like small wars, it almost never happened that we wiped out whole families. What is happening now, what happened to your families, Shori, is rare and terrible."

"And by coming here, I've brought it to your family," I said. "I'm sorry for that. I just . . . didn't know what to do or where else to go. And I was afraid for my symbionts."

Hayden nodded, watching me. "I don't believe my sons' sons would have wanted you to go to anyone else, although you're already making Daniel's life uncomfortable."

I wasn't surprised, but I didn't know what to say.

He smiled. "You didn't know, did you?"

"I thought I might be. I'm sorry."

"You needn't be. It's normal. Daniel apologizes for his behavior. He knows you're much too young to make the kind of commitment he's thinking of. And your efforts and warnings have kept us safe so far. No one is seriously hurt. What we do next, though . . . well . . ." He sighed. "I suppose we will do what we must. These murders must be stopped."

He wouldn't talk about what he and his family meant to do next. He only told me to keep the books as long as I needed them and to come to him when I wanted more or if I wanted to talk about what I'd read.

When he was gone, instead of reading more, I went up to where Wright lay sleeping. I undressed and climbed into bed beside him. He awoke enough to curl his body around mine.

"You okay?" he asked, his chin against the top of my head.

"Better," I said. "Better now."

"Do they know who killed your family or, rather, who's idea it was?"

"They know one family name, and where they live. The two injured captives can't be questioned yet."

"Is Victor alive, Shori?"

"He is." I swallowed. "Even though he remembers helping to murder both of my families. He even remembers attacking the house at Arlington where you and I and Celia and Brook could have died."

"But it wasn't his idea."

"It wasn't. So far, the Silk family seems to be guilty of all three attacks."

"Silk," he said. "Interesting name. I wonder if you knew them before."

"I don't think so. None of the Gordons mentioned any connection between them and me, and I think at least one of them would have."

"What will be done to them?"

"I don't know. Hayden wouldn't tell me. But I don't think anything will be done until the other two prisoners are questioned."

"You bit them."

"I did. It will help them heal quickly."

He moved me so that we lay eye-to-eye and took my face between his hands. "It will help you question them."

"Of course it will."

"What will happen to them after that, to Victor and the other two captives?"

"When we've finished questioning them, I'll help them forget us because I'm the one who bit them. Then they'll be sent back to their families." I rubbed his shoulders. "They're not anyone's symbionts, Wright. They're only someone's tools. People who never wanted them, never cared about them, kidnapped them and used them to kill my families."

He nodded. "I understand that, but . . . they did what they did."

"The Silks are responsible, not Victor and the others."

He nodded again. "Okay."

He didn't sound happy. "What?" I asked.

"I don't know exactly. I guess I'm just learning more about what I've stumbled into and become part of."

I was silent for several seconds, then asked, "Shall I let you alone tonight? I can go sleep with one of the others."

"Not with Victor?"

I drew back, staring at him.

"Where is he?" he asked.

"At Daniel's house. Daniel had room for him, and Theodora will be here soon. And . . . I didn't want him here."

After a while, he nodded.

"Shall I go?"

"Of course not." He pulled me against him. He caressed my face, my throat. Then, as he kissed me, he slipped his free hand between my thighs. "Are you hungry?" he asked.

I shook my head against him. "No, but I want to be close to you anyway."

"Do you? Good. If you taste me, I want you to do it from my thigh."

I laughed, surprised. "I've heard of doing it that way, although I don't know whether I ever have. You've been talking to someone!"

"What if I have?"

I found myself grinning at him. A instant later, I threw the blankets off him and dove for his thigh. He had nothing on, and I had him by the right thigh before he realized I had moved. Then I looked up at him. He looked startled, almost afraid. Then he seemed to catch my mood. He laughed—a deep, good, sweet sound. By touch and scent I found the large, tempting artery. I bit him, took his blood, and rode his leg as he convulsed and shouted.

❂    ❂    ❂

The next night, the Gordons and I questioned the other two prisoners. Hayden and Preston questioned them while I prodded and reassured them. I had bitten each of them twice. They trusted me, needed to please me.

They, too, told us about what sounded like members of the Silk family abducting them at night. One had been in downtown Los Angeles, looking for one of his girls—one of the prostitutes who worked for him. He was angry with her. He didn't think she was working hard enough, and he meant to teach her a lesson. Hayden had to explain this to me, and at last I found out what a pimp was. The explanation made me wonder what other unsavory things I didn't remember about human habits.

The other captive had been on his way to the Huntington Memorial Hospital in Pasadena to pick up his mother who was a nurse there and whose shift was ending. Her car had stopped running the day before, and he had promised to meet her and give her a lift home.

One prisoner was a pimp. The other was a college student keeping a promise to his mother. Both had been collected by members of the Silk family and sent north to kill my family and me. Neither had any information beyond what Victor had already told us.

When both captives were unconscious, much stressed by being made to talk about things that they had been ordered not to talk about, the Gordons and I looked at one another. Again, except for the captives, the company was all Ina.

"What can we do?" I took a deep breath and looked at the younger Gordon males—men who might someday be the fathers of my children. "These people have killed my family. Now they've come after you. They'll probably come after you again."

"I believe they will unless we stop them," Hayden said.

Daniel nodded once. "So we stop them."

"Oh my," Preston said, his head down, one hand rubbing his forehead.

"What else can we do?" Hayden demanded.

"I know." Preston glanced at him sadly. "I'm not disagreeing. I'm just thinking about what it will mean, now and in the long run."

Hayden made a growling sound low in his throat. "They should have thought about what it would mean."

Wells, one of Daniel's fathers, said, "I've been thinking about it since yesterday. We need to start by talking to the Fotopoulos and Braithwaite families, and perhaps the Svoboda and the Dahlman families as well. The Dahlmans are related to the Silks through Milo, aren't they? All these people are related in one way or another to the Silks and to Shori."

And I thought, *I still have relatives*. I didn't know them, didn't know whether they knew me. But they were alive. What would that mean?

"Don't phone the Dahlmans yet," Preston said. "Make them your eighth or ninth call. Try the Leontyevs and the Akhmatovas, and perhaps the Marcu and Nagy families."

"You believe we'll have time to bring together a Council of Judgment before they try again to kill us?" Daniel demanded.

Hayden and Preston looked at one another—the two elderfathers of the Gordons. Apparently they would decide.

"As soon as we get agreement from seven of the thirteen families, I'll call the Silks," Preston said. "I know Milo Silk, or I thought I did. How he and his sons have gotten involved in all this, I can't imagine. Anyway, once they've been notified that we're calling a Council of Judgment, that we have the first seven families, they won't instigate another attack. They won't dare."

"Why not?" I asked.

Everyone looked at me as though I'd said something very stupid.

I stared back at them. "My memory goes back a few weeks and no further," I said. "I ask because I don't know, and I don't want to make assumptions about anything this important." And because I was annoyed. I let my tone of voice say, *You should all realize this. I've explained it before.*

Hayden said, "If they attack us after we've called for a Council, the judgment will automatically go against them. Our legal system is ancient and very strong. That part of it in particular is absolute. It's kept feuds from getting out of control for centuries."

"And what does that mean?" I asked. "What would happen to them if they attacked you again?"

"The adults would be killed, and their children dispersed among us to become members of other families." He stared down at me. "We would bring the adults to you. You are the person most wronged in all this and the only surviving daughter. I think you could manage it."

"Manage . . . I would be their executioner?"

"You would be, yes. You would bite them and speak to them, command them to take their lives. I suspect that you would grant them a gentler death than they deserve."

For a moment, I was shocked speechless. Of course I knew I could kill humans directly by destroying their bodies or indirectly by biting them and then telling them to do things that were harmful to them, but kill Ina just by biting them and ordering them to die?

"I was almost tempted not to tell you," Hayden said. "Your youth and your amnesia make you both very attractive and very frightening."

"I can really do that? Bite another Ina and just . . . tell him to kill himself?"

They all looked at one another. Preston said, "Hayden, damnit—"

Hayden held up both hands, palms outward. "She needs to know. We've had a chance to see what sort of person she is. And let's face it, it's too dangerous for her not to know. If not for the crime that took her memory, she would know." He looked at me. "When you're physically mature, you'll take blood from your mates, and they'll take blood from you. That's the way you'll bond. The only other reason for you to take blood from an Ina male would be to kill him."

I thought about that for several seconds, then asked an uncomfortable, but necessary, question: "It wouldn't work on an Ina female?"

"It might. Your handling of the human captives says you're strong. But if you go against another Ina female, you might die. Even if you manage to kill her, you might die, too."

I thought about this. It dovetailed with what Brook had told me. "Do you know," I said, "I have no memory of ever having seen or spoken to an Ina female. I've only seen my father, one of my brothers, and you. I try to picture a female, and I can't."

"They learn early to be careful of what they say," Hayden told me. "It's one of their first and most important lessons. I believe that's a lesson you've remembered in spite of your amnesia."

I nodded. "I was always careful with my symbionts, even before I understood fully why I should be. But now . . . I might have to kill the Silks?"

"Probably not," Hayden said. "That kind of thing hasn't happened in living memory. The Silks will respect the call for a Council of Judgment."

"I hope so," I said. "What can I do now to help?" They were beginning to get up. Some of them took phones from their pockets. Daniel went to the kitchen and brought back a cordless phone for Hayden.

"Nothing yet," Hayden told me. "You'll have to speak at the Council."

"All right. But shouldn't we keep the three captives? Shouldn't they speak, too?"

He shook his head. "Who would believe them? By now you could have taken them over completely and taught them to say—and to believe—anything at all."

"All right. But why should the Council believe me—or you for that matter?"

He smiled. "I don't think they would believe me. I'm 372 years old. I think they might feel that someone my age might be able to lie to them successfully. You're a child. They'll assume that they'll be able to read your body language well enough to know whether or not you're lying."

"Will they be your age?"

"Some will be older."

I sighed. "They're probably right then. It doesn't matter. I haven't felt inclined to tell lies. So far, my problem is ignorance, not dishonesty."

# nineteen

There was a great deal of telephoning, conference calling, faxing, and e-mailing.

First, what Hayden called "the rule of seven" had to be satisfied. Seven families with whom both the Silks and I share a common ancestor within seven generations of the oldest living Silk or Matthews had to agree to send representatives to Punta Nublada for a Council of Judgment that would judge the accusations that I and the Gordon family were making against the Silk family. Once that was done, Preston phoned the Silk family. First Russell Silk, one of the elderfathers, denied all responsibility for wiping out my families, denied any knowledge of it. Then Milo Silk, the oldest living family member, came on and he denied everything, too. They had both heard of a mass murder in Washington State but had not realized that it involved two Ina communities. They were very sorry for me, of course, but none of it had anything to do with them.

Preston put the call on speaker phone and let all of us hear it.

"Nevertheless," he told Milo Silk, "we've heard evidence that your family is responsible, and we've called for a Council of Judgment. We've met the rule of seven."

"This is madness," Milo argued. "We didn't do it, Preston. I swear to you. Look, we don't care for the genetic engineering experiments that the Matthews and Petrescu families have been carrying out, and we've made no secret of it, but—"

"Milo," Preston said, "this is the required notification. The first seven families are Braithwaite, Fotopoulos, Akhmatova, Leontyev, Rappaport, Nagy, and Svoboda. We will also be asking the Dahlmans, the Silvesters, the Vines, the Westfalls, the Nicolaus, and the Kalands. Do you object to any of these?"

"I object to all of them," Milo said angrily. "This is insanity!"

"The rule of seven has been met," Preston repeated.

After a moment of absolute silence, Russell's voice replaced Milo's. "I object to the Vines," he said. "They are not friends of the Silk family, even though they are related to us. During the ninth century, their family fought ours in a long feud."

Preston stared at the floor, thinking. "Will you accept the Marcus?"

There was another silence, longer this time. Then finally, "Yes. We accept the Marcus. We also object to the Silvesters. Three of my sons had a financial dispute with two of them five years ago. It was not settled amicably."

Preston looked at Hayden. Hayden asked, "Will you accept the Wymans?"

"No!" a third voice said. "Not that pack of wolves. Do you realize—" Then the voice was cut off, and there was a long silence. Finally Milo came on again.

"We will not accept the Wymans," he said. And after a pause, he said, "Individual animus." He had a deep, quiet voice that somehow made everything he said sound important.

"The Andreis?" Preston asked, looking at his own family as though he were asking them. His family offered no objection.

There was a silent pause from the Silks. Finally, Milo said, "Fine."

"Are you content with the list now?" Preston asked.

More silence.

"The Kalands," Russell said. "We would prefer the Morarius."

Preston stretched out a long forefinger and pressed the button on the phone marked "hold." "Objections to the Morarius?" he said.

The Gordons looked at one another.

"I don't like them," Daniel said. They're proud people with not that much to be proud of. But I don't suppose that's reason enough to object to them."

The others shrugged.

Preston touched the hold button again and said, "We accept the Morariu family, Milo. Ten nights from tonight, we will all meet here at Punta Nublada for a Council of Judgment. You should begin to prepare for your family's journey. And maybe you should talk to your sons, especially the younger ones. You may not know everything." He switched the phone off.

⊙      ⊙      ⊙

Just before dawn, Manning and Wayne drove in with their symbionts and Theodora.

She got out of the Hummer and looked around at the houses. All of them were still lit from within in the early-morning darkness. There were people moving around both inside and out, and although she could not know it, there were people watching. I had been asleep, but I awoke at the sound of the car coming in. I looked out, saw her climb out of the car and look. Quickly, I put on jeans, pulled a T-shirt over my head, and ran out shoeless to meet her. She didn't see me until I reached her and took her hand.

She jumped, turned, saw me, and to my surprise, grabbed me, lifted me off the ground, and hugged me hard against her.

I found myself laughing with joy and hugging her back. When my feet were on the ground again, I took her into the guest house. "Have you eaten?" I asked. "Brook and Celia went shopping yesterday so we have plenty of food." Joel had taken them to a distant mall where they could get groceries, some more clothes, and whatever else they might need. Wright and I had each provided them with a list so we were all taken care of for a while.

"I had a late dinner," Theodora said. "The other people, the symbionts—is that what they're called?"

"It is, yes. It's what you'll be called, too, if you stay with me."

She gave me a shy smile and looked downward. "They said I should have a hearty meal before I reached you."

I laughed again, hungry for her, suddenly eager. "Come on upstairs. How are you? Is everything all right with your family?"

She got ahead of me and stopped me, hands on my shoulders. "I'm going to have to phone my daughter in a few hours. She's worried about me. She tried to stop me from leaving. Sometime soon, she's going to want to visit."

"Phone her whenever you like," I said. "I have to tell you more of what's going on here so you'll understand why she won't be able to visit you for a while. But you can go see her."

"Sounds like bad news."

"Difficult, I think, but not bad. This is a time to be careful. We've found out who has been attacking us, and we're going to have something called a Council of Judgment to deal with them."

She looked at me as though she were trying to read my expression. "Is there danger right now?"

In the early-morning darkness with all the Gordon men awake and alert? With the Council of Judgment already being organized? "No, not now."

"Good," she said. "Then tell me about it in the morning."

I smiled. "It is morning. But you're right. First things first."

I took her to the spare room. I had changed the bedding myself and made certain that the room was clean and ready for her. "I know I promised you more than this," I said as she looked around. "I will keep my promise. It's just going to take longer than I thought."

"I want to be with you," she said. "It's all I've wanted since you first came to me. I don't truly understand my feelings for you, but they're stronger than anything I've ever felt, stronger than anything I ever expected to feel. We'll find a way."

I shut the door, went to her, and began to undo her blouse. "We will," I said.

⊙     ⊙     ⊙

The next night I met with Wayne and Manning to find out what I could about my families' land and business affairs.

"Your mothers and father understood how to live by human rules," Manning said. "Their affairs are very much in order. You will have to work through the lawyers, but everything your families owned will be yours, and there's cash enough for you to be able to pay your taxes without selling anything you don't want to sell."

"I don't know what I want to do, really," I said. "I mean, I don't know anything." I looked at Manning—one of the fathers of Daniel, Wayne, William and Philip. He was a quiet, kindly man, and there was something about his expression that looked uncomfortably close to pity.

"Tell me about the lawyers," I said quickly. "Are there one or two who would make good symbionts?"

Manning shrugged. "I'm not sure what a good symbiont might be for you. Your Theodora is too old, but she loves you absolutely. She's exactly the kind of person I would expect to be able to resist one of us—older, educated, well-off—but she couldn't wait to get to you."

"She was lonely," I said. "Tell me about the lawyers."

"One of the ones I bit might be good for you," Wayne said.

I liked Wayne's long, quiet face. He was the only one of the four sons who towered over me even when he was sitting down. "Tell me about that one," I said.

He nodded. "She's thirty-five. She has a good reputation among the others at her firm. She's a good attorney even though she hates her work. She feels that she made a mistake going to law school, but now, she doesn't know what else she might do. She's an orphan with a brother who died six years ago. She's divorced and has no children."

"You investigated her. You planned to suggest that I go after her."

"Yes. You'll need a lawyer. She'll help you, she'll teach you, she'll be your connection to the rest of the legal world, and once you have her—if you're as right for each other as I think—she'll be completely loyal to you." He took a folded paper from his pants pocket and handed it to me. "Her name, home address, and work address."

"Thank you," I said and put the paper in my own pocket. "I don't think I'll be able to go see her until after the Council of Judgment."

"I think that would be best," Manning said. "The lawyers Wayne and I bit will look after your interests until then. But you should find her as soon as the Council ends. You need more than five symbionts."

◎     ◎     ◎

I continued to keep watch every day. I didn't believe there would be another attack, but why take chances?

I saw the bodies of the attackers buried with a great deal of a powder called quicklime in a long, deep trench dug by a small tractor around one of the gardens well away from the houses. I saw the attackers' cars driven away by gloved symbionts, followed by a Punta Nublada car. And, of course, only the Punta Nublada car returned.

I saw the three living attackers taken away to San Francisco where they would be three ordinary men catching three different Greyhound buses back to southern California where they lived. They wouldn't attract attention. No one would be likely to remember them. The Gordons had supplied them with money, and I had supplied them with the outline of a memory of going north to do some work driving trucks, hauling cargo up and down the coast. They could each fill in the details according to their own past work experience. As it happened, they had all driven trucks of one kind or another professionally, so they would be able, as Hayden put it, to confabulate to their hearts' content. But they would not remember one another, Punta Nublada, my families' communities, or the house near Arlington. I told them to forget those things completely and to remember only the truck-driving job. It was unnerving to see that I could do such a thing, but clearly, I could. I did. I even helped the pimp decide that he was sick of abusing women for a living. His cousin had a landscaping company. He would work for his cousin for a while or for someone else and then go back to school. He was only twenty-one. I made him tell me what he believed he should and could do. Then I told him to go do it.

Meanwhile, the Gordons and their symbionts worked hard to prepare for the fact that they were soon going to have a great deal of company. The Silk family—all their Ina and most of their symbionts—would be coming. Two representatives from each of thirteen other families would be coming, each bringing three or four symbionts. A Council of Judgment traditionally lasted three days.

Most of the Gordon symbionts were excited and looking forward to meeting friends and relatives they hadn't seen for months or even years. Would Judith Cho sym Ion Andrei be there? Or Loren Hanson sym Elizabeth Akhmatova? Did anyone know? What about Carl Schwarcz sym Peter Marcu? No one bothered asking me since it was clear that I knew nothing, but they chattered among themselves around me, happily ignoring me except to say that it was a shame I wouldn't get to enjoy any of the parties.

Only a few of them were apprehensive. To most, the Council of Judgment was an Ina thing that had little to do with them. Their Ina had disputes to settle. The symbionts planned to have parties. I enjoyed watching and listening to them. It was comforting somehow.

Several went out to buy the huge amounts of food and other supplies that would be needed to keep well over a hundred extra symbionts comfortable. Others prepared the guest quarters in each of the houses and transformed offices, studios, storage space, and even space in the two barns into places fit for human and Ina habitation. Every house had guest quarters—three or four bedrooms and a couple of bathrooms. These would be enough for a couple of traveling Ina and a few symbionts. And then there was the guest house itself, intended especially for human guests. My symbionts and I had arrived at a time when the Gordons' symbionts had no guests visiting, so we had had the whole guest house to ourselves. Now we would have to share the kitchen and the dining room and give up the downstairs bathroom, as well as the living room and family room.

The Council meetings would be held in one of the metal storage buildings. Martin Harrison, Joel's father and William's symbiont, the man who had given me a cell phone and taught me to use it, now seemed to be in charge of preparations for the visitors. Once I understood that, I found him and asked if I could follow him around for a while to see what he did and to ask him questions.

"I really want you to tell me if I'm in the way or if I'm being too irritating, because I can't always tell," I said, and he laughed. It was a loud, deep, joyful-sounding laugh that was a pleasure to hear even though I knew he was laughing at me.

"All right, Shori, I'll do that," he said. "I was a high-school history teacher when Hayden found me. It will be good to have a student again."

"Hayden found you? Not William?"

"Hayden found me *for* William." He shook his head. "William hadn't yet come of age, and Hayden thought the boy could stand to learn more of human history. Hayden thought I'd make a good bodyguard, too, since William goes completely unconscious during the day. He said I smelled right, for godsake. I understand that now, but I didn't then. I wanted to believe he was crazy, but he'd bitten me by then, and I couldn't just ignore what he told me."

"Did you mind that you would be symbiont to another man?" I asked, remembering the question that Wright had asked Brook.

He gave me an odd look. "You don't care what you pry into, do you?"

I didn't answer—since I didn't know what to say.

"There are plenty of women here," he said. "I married one of them shortly after I decided to stay." He lifted an eyebrow. "How's your new symbiont—the one who came in last night?"

"Theodora?" I smiled, seeing the connection. "She says she doesn't understand her feelings for me but that they are important to her."

"I'll bet. I saw you two. You were all over each other. That's the way it goes. It doesn't seem to matter to most humans what our lives were before we meet you. You bite us, and that's all it takes. I didn't understand at all. Hayden ambushed me as I got home from work one day. He bit me, and after that I never really had a chance. I didn't have any idea what I was getting into."

"Are you ever sorry you got into it?"

He gave me another strange look, this broad, tall black man. Joel had his coloring but would never have his size. Martin just stood, looking down at me as though trying to decide something. After a while, he said, "The Gordons are decent people. Hayden brought me here, showed me around, introduced me to William, who was tall and spindly but looked almost as young as you do now. Hayden let me know what was going to happen if I stayed. He let me know while I could still leave, and I did leave. They didn't stop me. William asked me to stay, but that made me run faster. The whole thing was too weird for me. Worse, I thought it sounded more like slavery than symbiosis. It scared the hell out of me. I stayed away for about ten months. I'd only been bitten three times in all, so I wasn't physically addicted. No pain, no sickness. But psychologically . . . Well, I couldn't forget it. I wanted it like crazy. Hell, I thought I was crazy. All of a sudden, I lived in a world where vampires were real. I couldn't tell anyone about them. Hayden had seen to that. But I knew they were real. And I wanted to be with them. After a while, I quit my job, packed my things, put what I could in my car, gave the rest away, and drove here. God, it was a relief." He stopped and smiled down at me. "Your first doesn't want any other life, girl, no more than Joel does. The only difference is Joel knows it. Wright is still finding out."

"You've talked to him?"

"Yeah. He'll be all right. How's he getting along with Joel?"

"When he can, he pretends Joel isn't there. When he can't do that, he's civil."

"It's rough on him. Rough on both of them, really. Ease their way as best you can. This Council of Judgment should help a little—distraction, excitement, new people, plenty to do."

"It scares me a little."

"The Council? Sensory overload for you and the other Ina. That's why Councils are only three days long."

"No, I mean . . . having Wright and Joel as well as Brook, Celia, and Theodora. It scares me. I need them. I care about them more than I thought I could care about anyone. But having them scares me."

"Good," he said. "It ought to. Pay attention. Help them when they need help." He paused. "Only when they need help."

I nodded. "I will." I looked into his broad dark face, uncertainly. "Do you want your son to be with me?"

"It's what he wants."

"Is it all right with you?"

"If you treat him right." He looked past me at nothing for several seconds. "I wanted him to live in the human world for a few years, get more education than we could give him here. He did that. But to tell the truth, I wanted him to stay out there, make a life for himself, forget about vampires. Then he comes back, and all he wants to do is find himself a nice vampire girl." He smiled, and it wasn't an altogether happy smile. "I think he'll want to do more once he's been with you for a while. He'll want to write or teach or something. Too much energy in that boy for him be to just some kind of house-husband."

"Theodora wants more, too. Once this Council of Judgment is finished, I'll have to decide what to do, how best to build a home for us all. When that's done, my symbionts will be able to do what they want to do."

"Good girl." He took a deep breath and started toward the nearest building of offices and studios. "Now let's go figure out how many people can be jammed into these studios. Thank God the weather hasn't gotten cold yet."

# twenty

The night before the Council was to begin, members of the Leontyev family arrived. I didn't know them, of course, and until they arrived and Martin mentioned it, no one had bothered to tell me that Leontyev was the name of my mothers' male family—the family of their fathers, elderfathers, brothers, and brothers' sons.

The Leontyevs and their symbionts arrived in two cars—a pair of Jeep Cherokees—while I was coming back from showing the very cool and distant Zoë and Helena Fotopoulos and their symbionts to their rooms in one of the office complexes. Martin had given me a list of who was coming and where they were to sleep. He said, "If you want to learn, you might as well help. This will give you a chance to meet people." He was, I had noticed, good at putting people to work.

The Leontyevs were older males, Konstantin and Vladimir, each with three symbionts. Martin intended them to stay with Henry Gordon. I came to get them, introduced myself, and realized from their expressions that something was wrong.

"I've had a serious head injury," I told them. "As a result of it, I have amnesia. If I knew you before, I'm sorry. I don't remember you now."

"You don't remember . . . anything?" the one Martin had pointed out to me as Konstantin asked.

"Not people or events. I remember language. I recognize many objects. Sometimes I recall disconnected bits about myself or about the Ina in general. But I've lost my past, my memory of my families, symbionts, friends . . . The people of my families who are dead are so completely gone from me that I can't truly miss them or mourn them because, for me, it's as though they never existed."

Konstantin gazed down at me with almost too much sympathy. A human who looked that way would surely cry. After a moment, he said, "Shori, we're your mothers' fathers. You've known us all of your life."

I looked at them, took in their tall leanness, trying to find in them something I recognized. They looked more like relatives of Hayden and Preston Gordon—just two more pale blond men who appeared to be in their mid-to-late forties but who were actually closer to their mid–four hundreds.

And suddenly, I found myself wondering what that meant. What had their lives been like so long ago? What had the world been like? I should ask Martin who had once been a history teacher.

The faces and the ages of these two elderfathers—my elderfathers, my mothers' fathers—triggered no memories. They were strangers.

"I'm sorry," I told them. "I'll have to get to know you all over again. And you'll have to get to know me. I can't even pretend to be the person I was before the injury."

"I'm grateful the Gordons were able to take you in and care for you," the one called Vladimir said. "How did they find you?"

I stared at him, surprised, suddenly angry. "I found them. I've survived three attacks, and twice helped fight the attackers off. I helped to question the surviving attackers who came here a few days ago. Only my memory of my life before I was hurt is impaired."

They looked at each other, then at me. "My apologies," Vladimir said. He lifted his head a little and smiled down his long nose at me. He managed to look more amused than condescending. "Whether you remember or not, you still have my Shori's temper."

I took them to the rooms that Henry Gordon had set aside for them in his house. Before I left, I showed them Martin's list and asked one more question. "Are any of these people close female relatives of mine?"

They looked at the list, then looked at one another, each of them frowning. In that moment, they looked almost identical. Then Vladimir said, "I believe your closest surviving female blood relatives are too young to be involved it this. They're children or young women busy with children. For instance, your brothers were mated and had two girls and a boy, all of whom are still very young children. Your mothers' brothers have adult female children, but those children are too young for Council duty."

"Wouldn't they be around my age or older? Some of them must be adults."

"Yes. They're mated so the youngest of them is years older than you. But, unless they're directly involved, people aren't usually called to Councils of Judgment unless their children are adult and mated."

That explained why everyone I'd seen so far seemed to be around the ages of Hayden and Preston.

"All right," I said. "I've been told that all Council members are related to me in one way or another. Who among the women members are my closest relatives? And did any of them know me before?" I asked.

Again the two paused to think. At last, Konstantin said, "The Braithwaites. The Braithwaite eldermothers are Joan, Irene, Amy, and Margaret. Two of them will be coming. They're the daughters of your second elderfathers."

I frowned trying to understand that.

"They are the daughters of your father's father's father," Vladimir clarified. "They know you, knew you before. You can talk to them. But, Shori, you can talk to us, too. We are your family. We've come here to see that your interests are protected and that the people responsible for what happened to you and to so many of our relatives pay for what they've done."

I remembered hearing from Hayden that Joan and Margaret Braithwaite would be coming. In fact, they were arriving tonight. "Thank you," I said. "I . . . I just need to see and talk to an Ina female. I have no memory of ever doing that before today. I've met several males since my injury, but until I met Zoë and Helena Fotopoulos this morning, no females. It's very strange to be an Ina female and yet have no clear idea of what Ina females are like."

Konstantin smiled. "Talk to the Braithwaites then. Elizabeth I was on the throne of England when Joan and Irene were born, so I'm not sure you'll learn much from them about being a young Ina woman now. But all four sisters have met you, Shori, and I think they like you. Go ahead and talk with them when they come."

I kept watch for the Braithwaite women, pestering Martin to look whenever female Ina drove in. The Braithwaites arrived just after midnight. Before I could ask Martin about them, Daniel came out to welcome them. I heard him call them by name. I watched as he stood talking with them.

Joan and Margaret Braithwaite were a head shorter than Daniel, but still taller than Celia or Brook. They were very straight, very pale women in white shirts and long black skirts. Their hair was twisted and pinned up neatly on their heads. One was brown-haired—the first brown-haired Ina I'd seen—and one was blond. Their chests, beneath their clean, handsome, long-sleeved shirts, were as flat as mine. I suspected that that meant I would not be growing the breasts Wright liked on women. Yet as ignorant as I was, even I wouldn't have mistaken these two for men. There was something undeniably feminine and interestingly seductive about them, even to me. Was it their scents? Did my scent make me seem interesting to other people?

I realized that I wanted Joan and Margaret to think well of me, to like me. That was important somehow. Their scent was definitely influencing me. Was it something they were doing deliberately, I wondered. Could they control it? Could I? I would ask them if I could manage to be alone with one of them.

"Shori?" the brown-haired one said to me as I stood off to one side, almost hiding in the shadows, watching them. Daniel had called the blond woman Joan, so this one must be Margaret.

I was immediately ashamed of myself for hiding and staring. "I'm sorry," I said, stepping forward. "I have no memory of seeing Ina females before today. I've been waiting for you because I was told you are my closest female relatives on the Council."

Daniel looked at me with that strange, strained look of his that ranged between hostility and hunger. I had come to see that look more and more as my stay with the Gordons lengthened. I had seen it on Daniel, William, Philip, and Wayne. Without saying a word, Daniel turned and walked away. I was fairly sure his longing made him seem even more ill-mannered than my ignorance made me. We would have to talk, Daniel and I. If my presence was disturbing him so much, we should at least take a few moments to speak privately together, to get to know each other a little.

"That was interesting," Joan Braithwaite said. She looked at Daniel's retreating back.

"When this is over, I'm hoping I can leave here for a while and stop irritating Daniel and his brothers," I said.

Margaret said, as though we'd known one another for a long time, "Will you mate with them?"

"I think so. I was afraid at first that they might not want me, now that I have to get to know everything all over again . . . and now that I'm alone."

"You truly don't remember anything about your mothers, your sisters?" Margaret asked. "You don't remember any other women?"

"I don't remember anyone," I said. "As I said, I haven't seen an Ina woman since my injury until today. I've only seen males."

The two Braithwaite sisters looked at one another. After a moment, Margaret said, "Take us to our quarters, then I'll talk with you."

I hesitated, remembering the list. "Your quarters are in the offices. This way." I took them and their six symbionts, each carrying a suitcase or a garment bag or both to the offices and the studio that were to be their living quarters. The symbionts were four men and two women. All four of the men were large and strong looking. They must have smelled very interesting before the Braithwaites claimed them. Two of the men were brown with very straight, very black hair. They were enough alike to be brothers. The other two were pale, muscular men. One of the women—the smallest of them—was startlingly beautiful. She was smaller than Celia, my smallest symbiont, and I'm not sure I would have chosen her as a symbiont out of fear that I would take too much blood from her. The other woman was tall and strong looking and deeply interested in one of the brown men.

"Those two got married last week," Margaret told me when we had left the symbionts in their rooms and Joan in hers. I was alone with Margaret in the office she had chosen as her bedroom. Her arrangement seemed to be to have a room of her own and have her symbionts come to her when she needed them. "Eden, the young woman, is mine and Arun is Joan's," she said. I realized she had noticed me noticing the affectionate pair.

"Do they mind sharing each other with you and Joan?" I asked. "I mean, are they still content to be symbionts?"

"Oh yes." She smiled. "Symbionts usually choose to mate with one another because, as symbionts, they share a life that other humans not only couldn't understand or accept, but . . . well, think about it, Shori. Symbionts age much more slowly than other humans, depending on how young they are when then accept us. How could they have a long-term relationship with someone who ages according to the human norm? People have tried it, but it doesn't work."

I nodded. "I have no coherent idea of what does work. I'm still finding out how Ina families live. I know I should leave here as soon as I can, but then what? I can provide for myself and my symbionts, but I don't know how to be part of the web of Ina society that obviously exists. How can I offer my symbionts the contacts they'll need with other symbionts?" I sighed. "I've forgotten almost everything I spent fifty-three years learning."

"But you're still a child," Margaret Braithwaite said. "You could be adopted into one of your secondary families. Once this business with the Silks is attended to, you'll be welcome in a number of communities."

"If I did that, what would happen to my connection with the Gordons?"

She thought about that, then shook her head. "If you're adopted into another community, you mate where they mate unless you could convince them to accept the Gordons. And you'd have to find a community with unmated daughters so that you can join them before the group of you mated. First adoption, then mating."

"My family was negotiating with the Gordon sons to mate with my sisters and me, and the Gordons have helped me, taken risks for me."

"You want to mate with them, then? It isn't just that at the moment, they're all you've got?"

"I think I do. I like them. But it's true that right now, I don't know any other eligible mates."

"Then you'll have to do what your father did. He lost his family in the European wars. Your mothers lost a few people, too. You had five eldermothers. Three were killed. At that point, your mothers left eastern Europe. Did you know that you were the only one of your sisters to be born here in the United States?"

"I didn't know. The others were born in Romania?"

"Two in Romania and one in England. I met your mothers in England. They had young children, and two of them were pregnant when they reached England. They made themselves over, became English women, and begged your fathers to join them. But your fathers had once owned a great estate in Romania until it was taken from them after

World War I and broken up and sold to small farmers. Your fathers' family had lived there for at least two thousand years under several different names, and they truly didn't want to leave. My own family lived there long enough for my mothers to mate with the fathers of your elderfathers. Eventually, though, we went to Greece, then to Italy, then to England. We were always willing to move to avoid trouble or to take advantage of opportunity. From England, we moved to the United States just after World War I. My mothers said there would be another war soon, and they wanted to avoid it as much as possible. No place on Earth was safe, of course, and we lost people, but we were never winnowed down to one person as your father's family was. He had absolutely no primary relatives left who were of his age or older."

"He said my mothers were his distant relatives," I said.

"You remember him?" Margaret asked.

"I met him after my injury." I told her about finding my father, my brothers, then almost at once losing them again.

When I'd finished, she shook her head. "You'll tell of that several more times during the nights of the Council." She drew a deep breath. "Your father fled Romania just before the Communists took over. Most Ina had already left or died. I don't believe any stayed after the war, and I don't think any family has gone back.

"Anyway, your father went to your mothers. He and his four remaining symbionts had little more than their clothing and a few pieces of jewelry that had belonged to his mothers, who were dead. He and your mothers and their symbionts left England for the United States shortly after he joined them. When your mothers settled in the state of Washington, they invited him to live with them for a while, until his oldest son came of age, but your father chose to follow our ways and live apart from his mates. Until his sons grew up, he was alone with his symbionts, acquiring property and money, building his first houses, and acquiring a few more symbionts—people who could help him establish a community and help prepare his sons for adult life."

"So that when his sons were men and went to him, he was able to help them begin their adult lives," I said.

"Yes. He must have been very lonely, but he was a proud man. He did what he believed he should do."

I watched her as she spoke. "It's not the same for me," I said at last. "When my father's kinsmen were killed, he was an adult, already mated, and most of his children already born. I'll be alone with my symbionts, growing up, then bearing and raising my children. I'll have no one to help me, no one to teach them how to be an adult Ina."

She nodded. "That will happen if you permit it. It would be wiser, though, to make friends with several communities of your female secondary families and work for them. Learn from them. I've been told that you can stay awake during the day and go out in the sun like humans. Is this true?"

"I can stay awake," I said, "but when I go outside, I need to cover as much skin as possible and wear dark glasses. Otherwise, I burn, and I can't see very well except with very dark glasses. The sun hurts my eyes."

"But you've walked in it?"

"I have. I think it makes me hungrier to walk it in, though. I burn a little—my face mostly—then I have to heal. My first wants me to wear sunblock, and one of the Gordon symbionts told me I should get something called a ski mask to cover my face. With that and with dark glasses and gloves, I would be completely covered, but I think I would look very strange."

"That's . . . Child, do you understand your uniqueness, your great value?"

"The Silks don't see me as valuable."

She closed her eyes and shook her head. "Stupid, stupid people," she whispered almost to herself. Then to me, "Are you sleepy during the day? Is it hard to stay awake? Hard to think?"

"No, I'm alert," I said. "I tire faster during the day than I do at night, but it isn't important. I mean, it doesn't stop me from doing anything. And I can sleep as comfortably at night as during the day."

"You are a treasure. You would be an asset to any community since most of humanity works during the day. Most human troublemakers cause trouble during the day. We've evolved methods for dealing with this, but there isn't a community that wouldn't be happy to have an Ina guardian who could be awake and alert during the day. I know of several cases where it would have saved lives."

"It didn't save my families," I said. "It did save the Gordons, although

I'm pretty sure that it was my being here that put them in danger to begin with."

"Only because some of us are fools." She looked at me for several seconds, then said, "When this business is over, spend a year or two with each of your secondary families if they'll permit it. They can teach you and you can guard them. Later, when you come of age, you might even adopt a sister from among their more adventurous young daughters before you mate. Find a young girl who feels lost among too many sisters and eager to go out on her own." She paused. "Do you remember how to read?"

"I read English and Ina," I said. "Those are the only two languages I've seen in written form since my injury."

"You read Ina? Excellent! I hope you'll teach your children that skill. Some of our people don't bother to teach their children to read Ina any longer. Some day our native language will be forgotten."

I frowned. "Why should it be forgotten? It's part of our history."

"Shori," she said sadly, wearily, "what do you know of our history?"

"Almost nothing," I said, echoing her tone. "I've been reading it, though. Hayden loaned me some of his books. That's how we found out that I could read Ina."

"I see," she said, and she seemed happier. "What are you reading?"

"*The Book of the Goddess*," I said. "I don't know yet how much of it is truly history. It seems to be some combination of religion, metaphor, and history."

"Perhaps. But that's a very long conversation in itself. Someday, when you've had time to relearn more of what you've lost, I would love to discuss it with you."

She gave me a card that contained her name and address, her phone number, her fax number, and her e-mail address. She laughed as I looked it over. "We used to be so isolated from one another," she said. "We sent messages by travelers or hired humans to carry messages or packages. We rarely traveled because it was so uncomfortable and so dangerous. Not only were there highwaymen, but local authorities who had to be bribed, and there was always, always the sun. Now travel and communication are so easy. If you need to talk, call me."

I thanked her and turned to go but then stopped at the door for a last question. "I wanted to ask you something that is probably very personal, but I think I need to know."

She nodded, waiting.

"Your scent . . . do you deliberately use it to influence people? I mean, can you control the way it effects people or who it affects?"

She laughed aloud, laughed for several seconds, stopped, then laughed again. Finally, she said, "Shori, child, I'm an old woman! My scent is barely interesting compared to yours. I don't want to imagine what you'll be like by the time you come of age."

## twenty-one

I ran into Daniel on my way out of the building where the Braithwaites were staying. I got the impression he was waiting for me. "Leave the greeting of guests for a little while," he said. "You and I should talk."

I agreed with him, so I followed him back to his house, enjoying the dark, smoky scent of him. It contrasted oddly with his pale, almost translucent skin and his white-blond hair. There were more people than ever milling around the grounds. Peter and Thomas Marcu and their several symbionts were hauling suitcases into Daniel's guest quarters. Daniel led me past them back toward his own rooms. He kept almost taking my hand. He would reach a little, then catch himself, and drop his hand to his side.

His quarters were two large wood-paneled rooms, a room-sized closet, and a big bathroom. He sat down in a tall chair and said nothing while I explored. In the bathroom was a huge tub—large enough for two, perhaps three people. There was also a huge walk-in shower with a built-in seat and two shower heads. One shower head was fixed to the tile-covered wall, and the other could be held like a hair dryer and directed anywhere. I had no memory of ever having seen such an opulent bathroom, but there was nothing in it that confused me.

The bedroom contained a huge bed in the middle of the floor surrounded by bookcases, a stereo system, and a large television.

I went back to the first room where Daniel waited, looking impatient but not complaining. There was a desk there, a computer, more bookcases, a telephone, file cabinets—like Theodora's office but much tidier. There were other tall chairs. I pulled one of them close to him, placing it in front of him, and I sat down.

"Is there any way for me to be here without tormenting you?" I asked.

"No," he said. "But it doesn't matter. I want you here. I've wanted you here since I first saw you before you lost your memory. You will mate with us."

"I will if you and your brothers still want me."

He seemed to relax a little, to let his body sag in the chair. "Of course we do."

"Hayden says I'm too young to make such a commitment," I said.

He shook his head. "Hayden says a great many things. He says you're too great a risk because you're all alone. He says we should look around, find a family with several unmated females. He says you might leave us with only one son or none. He says he would welcome you in a moment if you had even one sister, but you alone . . . He says it's too dangerous for our family."

I drew a deep breath, and I think I sagged a little, too. "I thought he liked me, that he wanted me as your mate."

"Did he say he did?"

"He didn't. But he seemed . . . I don't know."

"Preston wants you. He thinks you're worth the risk. He says your mothers made genetic alterations directly to the germ line, so that you'll be able to pass on your strengths to your children. At least some of them will be able to be awake and alert during the day, able to walk in sunlight. Preston says you have the scent of a female who will have no trouble producing children. His sense of smell is legendary among Ina. I believe him." He paused, leaned forward, took my hands. "My brothers and I will mate with you."

I smiled and answered, "I will mate with you and your brothers." It felt like the thing I should say. It felt formal and right.

Daniel closed his eyes and took a deep breath. Then he opened them and without warning came to his feet, pulling me up with him, lifting me off the floor to wrap me in a rough, hard embrace. Nothing more. It didn't frighten me, didn't even startle me. On some level, I had expected it. I accepted it. I touched my closed lips to his face, his throat, but not his mouth. I gave him small, chaste kisses. I didn't bite him. I was surprised that I wanted to. He was Ina, not human, not a potential symbiont, not a temporary food source. And yet, I wanted very much to bite into the tender flesh of his throat, to taste him, to let the sweet, smoky scent of him become a flavor as well.

I rubbed my face against him, caught up in his scent and my unexpected longing. Then I drew back. He didn't put me down, but held me comfortably against him. "Why do I want to bite you?" I asked.

He grinned. "Do you? Good. I thought you might actually do it."

"Shall I?"

"No, little mate, not yet. Not for a few more years. I admit, though, that I half-hoped you would, that maybe with your memory gone, you would simply give in to my scent, my nearness. If you had, well . . . If you had, no one could prevent our union. No one would even try."

"You would be tied to me, wouldn't you? You would be infertile with other Ina."

"I'm already tied to you."

"You're not. I haven't tied you to me. I won't until I'm fully adult. I'll come to you then, if you and your brothers are still unmated and if you still want me. If I live to become adult, then I'll tie you to me."

"Of course you'll live!"

I kissed his neck again. This time I licked his throat. He shuddered and let me slide down his body to the floor. "I'll live if this Council of Judgment is able to stop the attempts on my life," I said. "Can we just sit and talk about the Council for a few minutes, or would it be easier on you if I went to Preston?"

"Stay here," he said. "I'd rather have you with me for a little longer. Here, I can touch you without people thinking that I'm a selfish monster who doesn't care about his family."

I smiled, thinking about the feel of his hands. "You can touch me. You can trust me." He smelled even more enticing than Joel, but I would not taste him.

He sat down, reached out with his long wiry arms, caught me around the waist, and lifted me onto his lap. Wright did the same thing whenever he could, and Joel had begun to do it. I decided I liked it and wondered whether I would someday grow too big for them to be able to do it. I hoped not. I leaned against him, content, listening to the deep, steady beat of his heart. "What will happen?" I asked. "Tell me about the Council."

"I've witnessed seven Councils of Judgment," he said. "Hayden and Preston take me or one of my brothers along whenever they're invited to one. They want us to experience them. We won't be called to serve until we're around their age, but at least we can begin to understand how things work. We can see that our Councils aren't games like the trials humans have. The work of a Council of Judgment is to learn the truth and then decide what to do about it within our law. It isn't about following laws so strictly that the guilty go unpunished or the innocent are made to suffer. It isn't about protecting everyone's rights. It's about finding the truth, period, and then deciding what to do about it." He hesitated. "Have you seen or read about the trials that go on in this country?"

I thought for a moment, hoping some memory would come to the surface, but none did. "I don't remember any," I said. "Except on a fictional show I saw on Wright's TV."

"Good and bad," he said. "Human trials are often games to see which lawyer is best able to use the law, the jury's beliefs and prejudices, and his own theatrical ability to win. There's talk about justice, of course, but if a murderer has a good lawyer, he might go unpunished even though his guilt is obvious. If an innocent person has a bad lawyer, he might lose and pay with his life or his freedom even though people can see that he's innocent. Our judges are our elders, people who have lived three, four, five centuries. They sense truth more effectively than people my age, although I can sense it, too."

He settled me more comfortably against him. At least I was more comfortable.

"The problems arise when friendship or family connections get in the way of honest judgment. That can happen to humans and to us. That's why there are so many on a Council. And that's why everyone on the Council is related to both sides."

"Is a Council ever wrong?" I asked.

"It's happened." He drew a deep breath. "And when it happens, everyone knows it. It's usually a result of friendship or loyalty causing dishonesty. Or the problem might be fear and intimidation. That kind of injustice hasn't happened for over a thousand years, but I've read about it. It dishonors everyone involved, and everyone remembers. Members of the families that profit from it have difficulty getting mates for their young. Sometimes they don't survive as families."

"They are punished?" I asked.

"They are ostracized," he said. "They might survive, but only if they move to some distant part of the world and manage to find mates. Today, with communication so improved, even moving might not work.

"But you need to know procedure and propriety for this trial. Will you remember what I say? Do you have any trouble remembering new things?"

"None at all," I said.

He looked at me for a moment, then nodded. "You will speak after everyone is welcomed and the proceedings are blessed. Preston will welcome them as host and moderator. Then the oldest person present will offer blessing. Then you'll speak. You're making the accusations, so you'll need to tell your story. You must be tired of doing that, but you'll do it one more time, very thoroughly and accurately. No one will interrupt you, and most will remember exactly what you say. The Council will listen. Some of them will just want to learn enough to make a decision based on the truth or falsity of what you say. Others will want to find reason to doubt you so that they can better attack you and defend the Silks. And then there are those who will want to defend you against attack."

"Why should I need to be defended? The Silks need to be defended."

"They will be. And their advocate will probably—"

"Wait a moment. Their advocate? Who's that?"

"You and the Silks will both be asked to choose an advocate from among the Council members. You should think about who you'll want. I suggest you consider Joan Braithwaite, Elizabeth Akhmatova, or either of the Leontyev brothers. We won't know for sure which member of each family will be on the Council until the first session."

"I haven't met Elizabeth Akhmatova at all."

"She's smart, and she was a good friend of your eldermothers'. She or one of the others will help you if anyone on the Silks' side tries to show that because of your memory loss, you may be lying or confused or perhaps not even sane."

I frowned, feeling pulled toward several questions. "Even if I were all those things, it would not make the Silks less responsible."

"But it could, Shori. It could mean that you might not know the difference between lies and truth. You might be delusional, for instance, and able to tell lies that you actually believe. If you're delusional, if you could be shown to be delusional, then anything you say becomes suspect. Anything you've sensed or done may not be as it seems. Tell the complete truth, and remember what you've said."

"Of course. I would have done that anyway. But what about the Silks' lies? If they say they didn't do it, even though they did, how could my being delusional matter?"

"It might not. But you're one small person, one child, and the Silks are a large and respected family. There may be people on the Council who are sorry that your two families are dead and who see the guilt of the Silks, but who don't want to see a third Ina family destroyed. You can count on us—my whole family—to back you up on what almost happened here at Punta Nublada and on what we learned from the prisoners, but you must represent your mothers and your father. You must bring them into the room with you and stand them beside you whenever you can. Do you understand?"

I frowned. "I think so. I wonder, though, if the Ina way is so much better than the one the you say the humans have."

"It's our way," he said. "It's the system you must work within if you're to be safe, if you're to keep your symbionts safe, and if, someday, you're to keep our children safe."

I took one of his long hands and held it in my lap. "All right," I said.

"And don't lose your temper. There will be a lot of questions. Tomorrow, after you've told your story, you'll be questioned by whomever the Silks choose as their family representative, you'll be questioned by the advocate of the Silks, and you'll be questioned by any other member of the Council who chooses to question you. It won't be easy. You shouldn't make it easy on them either. You get to ask questions, too. And you can—should, in fact—call on us to support your memory of what happened here. On the first night, you and the Silk representative will be the ones asking and answering questions. On the second, both of you can call others to support what you've said, and they will be questioned. On the third, the Council will ask any final questions it has, and a decision will be made. This can be flexible. If you or the Silks need to ask more questions on the third day, you can. But that's the way it will go in general." He hesitated, thinking. "It will probably provoke the hell out of you. The Council members can question you or the Silks' representative or anyone either of you call for questioning. So if you get asked the same question ten times or twenty or fifty, give the same answer, briefly and accurately, and don't let it bother you."

"I won't."

"And never answer an accusation that hasn't been made. Even if you believe someone is hinting that you're delusional or otherwise mentally damaged, don't deny what they say unless they make the accusation outright."

"All right."

"Someone might offer you pity and sympathy for your disability. Make them state the disability. Make them say what they mean. Make them support it with evidence. If they say that you're delusional or mentally deficient or too grief stricken to know what you're saying—which, I believe, you definitely would be if your memory were intact—make them explain how they've come to that conclusion. Then, by your questions and your behavior, prove them wrong. If, on the other hand, they can't say what it is they're pitying you for, they must be the ones who are confused. You see?"

"I see."

"Someone might pretend to misunderstand you, might misstate what you've said, then ask you to agree with them. Don't let them get away with it. Pay attention."

"I will."

"Everything will be recorded. Every Ina family gets to see and hear Council proceedings these days. It didn't used to be that way, of course, but now that we can keep an accurate audio-visual record, we do. That means you can ask for a replay if anyone tries to insist on a misstatement of anything you've said."

"How likely is that?"

"I don't know. Most of us have excellent memories. That's why your amnesia will cause some Council members to distrust you at first. Just be yourself. They'll know your intellect is all right as soon as they've heard your story. Anyway, it's dangerous for anyone to lie about someone else's questions or answers. I've seen it happen, though. People feel that things are going against them. They're afraid. We have no prisons, after all."

I thought about that and found that I knew what prisons were. Humans often locked up their lawbreakers in cages—prisons. "No Ina prisons? Why?"

"None of us are willing to spend our lives in prison with the lawbreakers. Maintaining a prison isn't quite as unpleasant as being a prisoner in one, but it's bad enough. And levying fines would be meaningless. It's too easy for us to get money from the human population. For lesser crimes, most likely we amputate something. An arm, a leg, both arms, both legs . . . If the sentence is death, we decapitate the lawbreakers and burn their bodies."

"Decapitate?" I stared up at him. "Amputate . . . ? Cut off people's heads, arms, or legs?"

"That's right. Amputations and executions are also recorded. Amputations are punishments of pain, humiliation, and inconvenience. Limbs grow back completely in a few months, maybe a year or two for legs taken off at the hip. Of course, when it's done, people are given nothing for the pain, and the pain is terrible. It hurts for a long time, although once people are returned to their families, the families can help them with the pain. They're permitted to, not required to."

"You're sure that arms and legs cut off . . . grow back?"

He held his left hand in front of me. "I was in a traffic accident ten years ago. I lost three fingers and part of my hand. In about a month and a half, I had a whole hand again."

"That long?" I hesitated, then asked, "Did you eat raw meat?"

"At first. I don't digest it well, though. If I had been able to eat more of it, I probably would have healed faster."

"You probably would have," I said. And I wondered if he would heal more quickly once he was mated with me. I thought I would like to give him that.

He continued: "The Silks won't be having anything amputated, though. What they've done is too serious for that. If the Council condemns them, they'll either be killed—the adults will be killed, I mean—or they will be broken up as a family. Their youngest members will be scattered to any families that will have them, and the older ones will be left to wither alone. They might try anything they can think of to avoid those possibilities."

"They . . . they would lose their children?"

"Yes. They would not be seen as fit to raise them."

"That seems cruel to the children. And . . . what if they have more children?"

"It might happen. Or their mates might shun them, blame them for the loss of young sons who have been separated and sent to live thousands of miles apart, probably on different continents. Adoption is not cruel, by the way. There are blood exchanges to ease it and seal it. People miss one another, of course, but by letter, phone, and computer, they can keep contact. I hear they tend not to, but they can. Adoptees are truly accepted and accepting once they're in their new circumstances. But for the adults, it's the end. What adult wouldn't fear such a thing and do almost anything to avoid it?"

"If they had let my families alone, they wouldn't be facing it."

"They must have felt very strongly compelled to do what they did. And . . . Shori, if you had been anyone else, they would have succeeded. You not only survived twice, but you came to us with what you knew, and you led the fight to destroy most of the assassins and to question the survivors. They thought mixing human genes with ours would weaken us. You proved them very wrong."

We sat together for a while longer in warm, easy silence. I felt that I had known him much longer than the few days that I'd been living at Punta Nublada.

I turned toward him and opened his shirt.

"What are you doing?" He was shocked, but he did nothing to stop me.

"Looking at you. I wanted to see whether you had hair on your chest." He didn't.

"We tend not to have much body hair."

He had very smooth skin. I kissed it and ran my hands over it, loving the feel of him. Then I stopped and slipped down off his lap because I wanted so badly to taste him, drink him, to lie beneath that tall, lean body and feel him inside me.

He watched me, left the decision to me. If I tried to bite him, even now, he would let me do it. And then what? If I died, he, at least, might age and die childless. His brothers might mate elsewhere, but he could not. "How can you risk yourself this way?" I whispered.

"I know what I want," he said.

I decided that I had better protect him from his wants. He wouldn't send me away, and he should have. I took his hands, his broad hands with long, long fingers that were almost unlined, that were like, but unlike, the hands of my symbionts, larger versions of my own. I took his hands and I kissed them. Then I left him.

◎        ◎        ◎

On the first night of the Council of Judgment, proceedings were to begin at nine.

They would be held in a large storage building a few dozen yards beyond the last house—Henry's—along the private road. The building had been emptied, and the equipment usually stored in it was sitting outside in the cold, rainy weather—two pickup trucks, two small tractors, a small crane that I'd heard called a cherry picker. Lesser tools had been stored in other buildings. Stacks of metal folding chairs and tables had been rented and trucked in. All this had been done quickly and efficiently by the Gordons and their symbionts with my symbionts and me helping where we could.

Attending were all thirteen of the Silks, all ten of the Gordons, of course, and two representatives each from the thirteen other families, all strangers to me, or near strangers like the Leontyevs and the Braithwaites. They would judge the Silks ... and me and perhaps make it possible for me to get to know myself again and get on with my life without having to be on guard every day against another attack.

Could a Council of Judgment really do that? What if it couldn't?

The thirteen families were Fotopoulos, Marcu, Morariu, Dahlman, Rappaport, Westfall, Nicolau, Andrei, Svoboda, Akhmatova, Nagy, and of course, Leontyev and Braithwaite. One representative would act as a Council member and the other as a substitute. There were six male families and seven female. I asked Preston whether the balance of sexes meant anything.

"Nothing at all," he told me. I was working with my symbionts to set up rows of metal chairs, and he was doing something to one of the video cameras that would be recording the Council sessions. "You heard how the decisions were made. The Silks traded names with us until we had a group that both would accept. We have acted as your representative in this because you no longer know these people."

"Did I know them all before?" I asked.

"You knew them. Some you knew well. Others you knew only by family and reputation."

"If you tell me about them now, I'll remember what you say."

"I don't doubt it. But for now, you shouldn't know them. They must see that you don't know them, see how much has been taken from you. Just be yourself. They should see that you have been seriously wounded, but that it hasn't destroyed you."

"It has destroyed who I was."

"Not as thoroughly as you think, child." He gave me a long, quiet look. "Did you taste Daniel's blood?"

The question surprised me. "I will taste it," I said. "I will when I've survived all this," I said. "When I believe I can join with someone and not have it be a death sentence for either of us. And when I've grown a little more."

"He said he offered himself to you."

"And I promised that I would mate with him and his brothers. But not now."

He smiled. "Good. Even alone, you're the best mate my sons' sons could hope for. They all want you."

"Daniel said that Hayden—"

"Don't worry about Hayden. He likes you, Shori. He's just afraid for the family, afraid for so much to depend on one tiny female. Once we get through this Council, I'll convince him."

I believed him.

He left us—Wright, Joel, Theodora, Celia, Brook, and me—to finish making neat rows of a hundred and fifty chairs. There was room for more, and there were more chairs if it turned out that more symbionts wanted to observe, but most of them had intended to be outside roasting meat over contained fires—barbeque pits—and eating and drinking too much. With the rain, many were partying inside the houses. There was even a small party for the children of the Gordon symbionts.

Wright had decided to stay with me through the proceedings, although I had told him he could go enjoy himself if he wanted to. After the chairs and the folding tables had been set up as Preston had instructed, I told Celia, Brook, Joel, and Theodora that they could go or stay as they chose. Joel stayed, probably because he knew Wright was staying. Brook and Celia went off to renew old friendships, and Theodora went with them. Theodora seemed cheerful and excited.

"I've moved to Mars," she told me. "Now I've got to go learn how to be a good Martian. Who better to teach me than the other immigrants?"

It surprised me that I understood what she meant. And it pleased me that she was so happy. There was no feeling of stress or falseness about her; she was truly happy.

"She's exactly where she wants to be," Wright said when she was gone. "She's with you, and you're going to keep her with you. As far as she's concerned, she's died and gone to heaven. People keep falling in love with you, Shori—men, women, old, young—it doesn't seem to matter."

I looked up at him, surprised that I understood him, too. "Why don't you want to learn from the other immigrants?" I asked.

"Oh, I do," he said and grinned at me. "Of course I do. But right now, I want to learn from the Martians themselves."

"You want to see how the Council works."

"Exactly."

"So do I, although I wish I were doing it as just an interested spectator." We finished our part of the preparation—bringing trays with covered pitchers of water and plastic cups to the storage building. We distributed them among the front tables for the Council members and put some on the tables next to the wall in the back for everyone else. Then we chose seats in the first row. I thought I should be in the front so that I could stand and speak when necessary, and I wanted Joel and Wright beside me since they'd chosen to stay.

"Have you ever been to one of these Council meetings?" Wright asked Joel, surprising me. With me encouraging them, giving them small commands, they had recently begun to speak to one another beyond what was absolutely necessary.

"I never have," Joel said. "There's never been one here during my life-time, not while I was at home, anyway."

There was something comforting about having them on either side of me. They eased the stress I had been feeling without their doing any-thing at all.

Ina and some symbionts had begun to come in and choose seats. This first night of the Council was to begin at nine and run until five the next morning.

There was no special clothing worn by members of the Council or by audience members except for the many jackets and coats. The build-ing was unheated, and the symbionts seemed to need extra clothing over their jeans and sweatshirts, their casual dresses, or their party clothing. Several symbionts came in from their parties, apparently deciding that they preferred to watch the proceedings of the Council to eating, drinking, and dancing. Earlier that evening, just after it was fully dark, Joel and I had wandered into the noisiest party—the one at William's house—for a few moments to see, as Joel said, what was going on. It was the first time I could remember seeing people dance to music that was being played on a stereo.

"It looks like fun," I said.

Joel smiled. "It is fun. Want to learn?"

"I do," I said. "But not now. Not tonight." And we had gone back to help with the preparations. I looked back, though, liking the joy and the sweat and the easy sexiness of it all, wishing I could have stayed and let him teach me.

# twenty-two

Ironically, the oldest person present was Milo Silk. He was 541 years old—ancient even for an Ina. According to the world history I had been reading, when he was born, there were no Europeans in the Americas or Australia. Ferdinand and Isabella, who would someday send Christopher Columbus out exploring, were not yet even married. All Ina were in Europe and the Middle East, traveling with Gypsies, blending as best they could into more stationary populations or even finding their ways into this or that aristocracy or royal court. That world was Mars to me, and if Milo Silk were anyone else, I would have wanted very much to spend time with him and hear any stories he would tell about the worlds of his childhood and youth.

As things were, though, I had avoided him and his family until now. And yet, he was asked to bless the opening of Council proceedings. I thought they should have changed the custom and invited an elder who was less involved in causing suffering and death to speak what Preston had told me should be words of unity and peace. But everyone seemed to expect Milo to do it. After all, he hadn't been judged guilty of anything—yet.

Milo Silk stood up in his place directly across from where I had eventually been told to sit. He and I were at opposite ends of a broad arc of cloth-draped, metal-framed tables. Twelve members of the Council sat two to a table. The odd Council member, Peter Marcu, had a table to himself, as did Milo Silk and I and Preston Gordon, who sat at the center of the arc and who was moderating and representing the host family.

The Gordon symbionts had set up a sound system. They'd scattered speakers along the length of the big room and put on each of the tables a slender, flexible microphone for each person. There was also a stand-alone microphone centered between the two prongs of the arc of tables.

Martin Harrison had shown me how to use my microphone—how to turn it on or off, how to take it from its stand and hold it if I wanted to, how close to it I should be when I spoke into it. Wright and Joel had watched all this, looking around as the other Council members and Milo were seated. Then Wright kissed me on the forehead and said, confusingly, "Break a leg." Then he'd gone back to his seat in the front row where he had left his jacket holding his chair and sat there alone.

Joel had stayed with me a little longer, holding my hands between his. "Are you afraid?" he asked.

I shook my head. "Nervous, but not afraid. I wish it were over."

He grinned. "You'll impress the hell out of them." He kissed the palms of my hands—each of them—then went back to sit one seat from Wright, my former seat empty between them.

No one had told them they couldn't sit at the table with me, and I would have been happy to have them there. Even before I sat down at the table, it had looked like a lonely place. But both men had seen, as I had, that there were only Ina at the tables, and they had drawn their own conclusions. They were probably right. Moments later, Brook came in and sat down between them.

Then Preston stood up, introduced himself, welcomed everyone, and asked Milo to bless the meeting.

Milo stood up and, microphone in hand, began to speak.

"May we remember always that we are Ina," he said in his deep, quiet voice. "We are an ancient and honorable people with more than ten thousand years of recorded history. We are a proud and powerful people, well aware of our duty to our families, to our kind, and to the truths that make us who we are. May we look after our human symbionts with kindness and firmness. May we care for them and keep them from harm. May we be loving, loyal, and generous to our mates. May the proceedings of this Council of Judgment be carried on with honor, justice, and truth. May we remember and honor the Goddess as we strive to do and to be all that she expects of us. May we put aside those things that do not honor her. May we put them aside and take care never again to be touched by them, never seduced by them, never soiled by them. May we remember always that our strength flows from our uniqueness and our unity. We are Ina! That is what this Council must protect. Now, then! Let us begin." He closed his straight line of a mouth and sat down.

Milo had looked directly at me as he spoke his last few sentences. He was straight bodied and white haired, six and a half feet tall, and even leaner than most Ina. He was sharp featured and fierce looking somehow. If he were human, I wouldn't have been surprised to hear that he was sixty, perhaps sixty-five years old. He had, I thought, spoken condescendingly of human symbionts and contemptuously of me, and yet in his deep voice, his words had had a majestic sound to them.

Preston Gordon straightened in his seat at the center of the arc. I got the impression Preston was actually enjoying his position. He repeated his welcome to the members of the Council, their deputies, and their symbionts. He assured them that if they needed or wanted anything at all, they had only to speak to a member of the Gordon family. Then he introduced each Council member, although probably everyone knew them except me, some of the newer symbionts, and, ironically, some of the younger Silks. I listened carefully and remembered. Preston had already told me a little about each of the visiting families. Now I was getting a chance to put faces to the names.

There was Zoë Fotopoulos, whose family had once lived in Greece, but who, for a century now, lived on a cattle ranch in Montana.

There was Joan Braithwaite, whom I was glad to see again and whose family lived in western Oregon where they raised, among other things, Christmas trees.

There was Alexander Svoboda, whose family had come from what was, at the time, Czechoslovakia a few years before World War II to establish a community in the northern Sierra Nevada Mountains where they now owned a vacation resort.

Peter Marcu had come down from British Columbia where his family owned several tourist-oriented businesses, including one that helicoptered tourists to isolated areas and guided them on memorable mountain hikes.

Vladimir Leontyev and his family had lived in Alaska since Alaska was still Russian territory. They owned a fleet of fishing boats and interests in a cannery and a plant that processed frozen food.

Ana Morariu's family were neighbors of the Gordons, living only about two hundred miles away in Humboldt County where several of her people were teachers, writers, and artists and owned two hotels that served people visiting the national and state parks.

Katharine Dahlman's family ran a ranch that was a tourist resort in Arizona, but they were planning to move to Canada, away from the sun and toward the longer nights of northern winters. Katharine and her sister Sophia were noticeably short for Ina women. In fact, that was the first thing I noticed about them. Other Ina females who had come to the Council were at least six feet tall. But the Dahlmans were only Celia's height, and Celia had told me she was five feet seven inches tall. She'd said she liked being around me since other Ina females made her feel short. She had measured me gleefully and discovered I was an inch under five feet tall. But I still had some growing to do. I wondered how Katharine and Sophia Dahlman felt about their height.

Alice Rappaport's family had a ranch in Texas where she was, for legal reasons, actually married to her first. He had taken her name legally and was enjoying himself, doing what he had always wanted to do: run a ranch and run it profitably. Alice, her sister, and the six symbionts they had brought with them were using the living, dining, and family rooms of the guest house as their quarters so I'd had a chance to talk to them. According to Alice, female Ina families had passed for human for thousands of years by marrying male symbionts and organizing their communities to look like human villages.

Harold Westfall was also married to his first for legal as well as social reasons. He lived in South Carolina and felt that anything he could do to seem normal and unworthy of notice was a good thing. He and his family had been in South Carolina for 160 years, and yet I got the impression that he still was not comfortable there. I wondered why he stayed.

Kira Nicolau and her family had left Romania for Russia, then left Russia just before the Communist Revolution in 1917, and had eventually settled in Idaho in a valley so isolated that they felt they had no reason to put on a show of human normality. They'd dug wells, cut their own logs, built their own cabins. They used the wind and sun to make their electricity, planted their crops and kept enough chickens, hogs, goats, and milk cows to supply their symbionts with food and make a small profit. They shopped maybe twice a year to buy the things they either couldn't make or didn't want to bother making. If they hadn't had to visit their mates and attend the occasional Council of Judgment, they might have vanished completely from the awareness of other Ina.

Ion Andrei, on the other hand, lived in a suburb of Chicago. His family, too, were planning to move to Canada. They owned interests in several Chicago businesses. They had been in the Chicago area for over a century, but now they were beginning to feel swallowed by the growing population.

During the northern hemisphere's winter, Walter Nagy and his family lived on a farm on Washington's Olympic Peninsula. During the southern hemisphere's winter, the whole family moved to a ranch in Argentina. In fact, they had just gotten back from Argentina. "We could get even more hours of darkness if we moved farther north and farther south," he had told me when I met him. "But we like comfort, too. We don't mind a little cold weather, but do mind snow and ice." His family also owned income property in New York City and in Palo Alto and San Francisco. The few among them who bothered to work were artists, writers, and musicians.

Finally, there was Elizabeth Akhmatova, whose family lived in Colorado in a Rocky Mountain community. They had gradually developed the land surrounding their community, building houses, stores, shops, and a nearby resort area until a fair-sized town had grown around them. They had held on to the property until it became popular and highly valued, and now, they were gradually selling it off at very high prices. She and her family had come to North America in 1875, and they were about to make their third major move, this time to Canada. They liked to find areas with potential, acquire vast stretches of land, and develop it.

Preston introduced them all, then introduced me and welcomed me. Finally, he asked me to stand and tell my story.

I stood, holding my microphone the way Milo had. I began my story with my first memory of awakening in the cave, confused, in pain, without my memory, and racked with intense hunger. I told them about Hugh Tang—all of it—about the ruin that I had not recognized as my home, about Wright and my father and the destruction of my father's community—the whole story up to and including the raid on the

Gordons and the capturing and questioning of Victor and his two friends. The telling took more than an hour.

At last, I finished and sat down. There were several seconds of absolute silence. Then Milo Silk stood up. "Does this child have an advocate?" he demanded. He spoke the word "child" as though he wanted to say a much nastier word but restrained himself.

Before I could say that I didn't yet have an advocate, Vladimir Leontyev spoke up.

"I am one of the fathers of Shori Matthews's mothers," he said. "I believe I'm her nearest living relative on the Council. My brothers and I may be her nearest living relatives period. If Shori wishes it, I will be her advocate."

I leaned forward so that I could see him and said, "I must ask questions because of my memory loss. I mean no offense, Vladimir, but if you become my advocate, will it be a problem that you and I don't really know each other anymore?"

"It won't be a problem," he said. "Family is what matters here. You are of great importance to me because you are one of my descendants."

"Will you speak for me or will you help me understand rules and customs so that I can speak for myself?"

"Both, probably," he said, "but I would prefer the latter."

I nodded. "So would I. I understand that the Silks will also have to have an advocate."

Vladimir gave me a small smile, then looked at Milo Silk. "Who on the Council will be your family's advocate, Milo?"

"I speak for my family," he said.

Preston Gordon said, "Milo, in our negotiations with your family, one of your sons mentioned that a member of the Dahlman family might be persuaded to be your advocate."

"When have you known me to need someone to speak for me?" he demanded.

Preston looked at him, looked down at his own spidery hands resting on the table, then faced Milo again. "Let me advise you, just this once. Your family needs more protection than you can give it. Don't let your pride destroy your family."

Milo looked away from him, kept quiet for several seconds. After a while, he said, "Katharine Dahlman is the oldest daughter of my sisters," Milo said. "I ask that she be my advocate."

Katharine Dahlman managed, by sitting very straight, to look not only important, but a little taller. She lowered her head in a slow nod. "Of course," she said in a deep, quiet contralto—a female version of Milo's voice. It was the voice of a larger woman, somehow. "Will you question the child, Milo, or shall I?"

Milo looked down at the table, and I remembered that he had been writing while I spoke. Perhaps he had not trusted the two video cameras that were being used to record the session. Perhaps he had made notes of the questions he wanted to ask me. Or perhaps he had his own memory problems. I faced him across the arc, ready to be questioned, but he turned his body and tried to face Preston.

"I have my doubts, Preston, whether this child should even be here," he said. "She has suffered terrible losses, and she admits that she hasn't recovered from her injuries."

I resisted an impulse to say that I had recovered, or had recovered as much as I was likely to. Instead, I waited to see what Preston would say. He looked at me, then at Vladimir.

Vladimir said, "Shori, have you recovered from your injuries?"

"I am recovered," I said. "My memory may or may not return. I'm beginning to relearn what I've lost, and I remember clearly all that has happened to me since I awoke in the cave." I looked across at Milo and decided that he would speak directly to me in a minute or two. He didn't want to, but he would.

"Has the child been examined by a physician?" Milo asked. "I understand there is a human physician among the symbionts here. If not, one of my family's symbionts is a physician."

That was too much. I had been at Punta Nublada long enough to recognize that Milo was being openly insulting. He was saying that my body was not Ina enough to heal itself, that the human part of me had somehow crippled me.

"Milo!" I said, not loudly, but sharply. He looked at me before he could stop himself and then looked away smoothly, as though he had only glanced at me by accident. I leaned forward, facing him across the arc. "I am Ina, Milo."

He stared at me, then turned again to Preston. "For the child's own sake, I request that she be examined by a physician."

I said, "What are those notes you're making there, Milo? No one else is taking notes. Are you having difficulties with your memory, too?"

He glared at me. Katharine Dahlman glared at me.

"I am Ina, Milo, and if the doctor must examine me, then for your own sake, I request that she also examine you."

"You're not Ina!" he shouted. He slammed his palm down on the table, making a sound like a gunshot. "You're not! And you have no more business at this Council than would a clever dog!"

People jumped. Katharine Dahlman said, "Preston, could we break for a few minutes?" She didn't wait but stood up and went around to Milo who had risen to his feet and was leaning forward, fists on the table, glaring at me.

"Fifteen minutes," Preston said and glanced at his watch.

People poured themselves glasses of water, got up to stretch their legs, or turned to talk to one another. At first no one on the Council spoke to me. Most didn't even look at me.

Some went to speak to audience members, and Wright, Joel, and Brook took this to mean that they could come talk to me. They reached me at the same moment as Vladimir Leontyev and Joan Braithwaite.

The two Ina and the three humans stared at one another for a moment, then Joan leaned on the table, clicked off my microphone, and said, "Shori, there are people in this room who have loved that old man for centuries."

I focused on her and bit back all the things I could have said. She knew them as well as I did. That old man either ordered my families killed or sat by and watched while his sons did it. That old man had just told me I was no better than a dog because I had human as well as Ina genes. That old man is not sane. All true, all obvious.

"What should I have done?" I asked her.

She looked surprised. "Nothing," she said. "Nothing at all."

"You should have let me do it," Vladimir said. "I'm only about ninety years younger than he is. A rebuke from me would have been more easily accepted."

"Would you have done it?" Wright asked him.

Vladimir took a deep breath. "Eventually."

"It's done," I said. "What happens now?"

"You didn't think of that question before you humiliated him?" Joan asked. "You didn't wonder what would happen afterward?"

"I didn't humiliate him," I said, finally stating the obvious. "I would not have humiliated him. I just stood back and let him humiliate himself."

"Others won't see it that way."

"Are we rid of him?" I asked. "Will he step aside and let one of his sons represent the family?"

She looked at me as though she didn't particularly like me. "He might," she said. "What good do you imagine that will do you?"

"Perhaps the new representative will at least dislike me as one-individual-to-another, and not as man-to-animal."

"And no doubt that will make you feel better," she said. "But it won't help you. You've shown your teeth, Shori. They're sharp and set in strong female jaws. You are now less the victim and more the potentially dangerous opponent. You begin to overshadow your dead."

I thought about that, although I didn't want to think about it. I wanted to go on feeling angry and justified. But finally I sighed. "You're right. What shall I do?"

She nodded. Apparently I had asked the right question. "Remember your dead," she said. "Keep them around you. And remember what you want. What do you want?"

"To punish them for what they've done," I said. "To stop them from hunting me. To stop them from killing anyone else."

She nodded once, then turned and walked across the arc toward where people were very gently arguing with Milo.

"She's right," Wright said to me, "but she's cold."

"She's just female," Joel said.

"And oldest sister," Brook added. "I'll bet the younger one, Margaret, is gentler."

"She is," I said.

"Nevertheless, Joan's advice is good," Vladimir told me.

"I know," I said.

"The truth is your best weapon," he said. "Put aside that temper of yours. Use the truth intelligently." He turned and went back to his place in the arc.

Brook watched him go. Then she stepped behind me and put her hands on my shoulders. She massaged my neck and shoulders so that I began to relax before I realized I needed to. I looked up at her.

"Good?" she asked.

"Good," I said.

Joel laughed. "Ina need to be touched, especially young Ina. I don't think you always realize how much you need it, Shori."

"We'll have to see that she gets what she needs," Wright said, looking at me. The look made me smile and shake my head.

"You should all go back to your seats," I said. "They're about to start the Council again."

They went back to their seats, and on the other side of the arc, another of the Silks—Russell, I had heard him called—sat down in Milo's place.

# twenty-three

$R$ussell Silk had no story to tell. He denied all involvement in the death of my families and in the attacks on the Arlington house and on the Gordons. He denied that his family was involved in any of it. He suggested that I was confused or mistaken or that the humans who had been used as weapons had been given false information intended to incriminate the Silk family—which happened to be the only male Ina family in Los Angeles County. Who would create such a fiction? He did not know. He and his family were victims . . . just as I was.

That was a sickening enough lie to make me wonder if I would have been able to keep my temper had I not lost my memory. If I could remember my mothers, my sisters, and my symbionts, if I could recall my father and my brothers as anything more than kindly strangers, I might not have been able to bear it. I thought Russell might have said it hoping to make me angry, hoping to pay me back for what I said to Milo.

Vladimir Leontyev spoke up. "Russell, are you saying that you know as a matter of fact that neither your father, your brothers, your sons, or their sons were involved in collecting a group of human males, making them your tools, and then sending them to kill the Petrescu, Matthews, and Gordon families?"

Russell looked offended. "I don't believe any member of my family would do such a thing," he said.

Vladimir shook his head. "That isn't what I asked. Do you know for a fact that no member of your family did this?"

"I haven't investigated my family," he said. "I'm not a human police detective."

"So you don't know for certain whether or not members of your family did this?"

"I don't believe they did!" He paused and looked away from Vladimir. "But I don't know with absolute certainty."

I didn't believe him. I don't think I would have believed him even if I hadn't helped to question Victor and his friends. Russell knew what his relatives had been up to, and now he was lying about it. By his silence or by his active participation, he had helped to murder my families.

"I have a question for Shori," Katharine Dahlman said.

I looked at her with interest. I hadn't made up my mind about her yet. How close was she to the Silks and what they had done?

"I'm sorry to ask you about things that may be painful to you," she said, "but what do you remember about your mothers and your sisters?"

"Nothing," I said. "Nothing at all."

"Their names?"

"I've been told that my sisters were named Barbara and Helen."

"And your mothers? Your eldermothers?"

"I don't know."

"Your symbionts . . . how many symbionts did you have?"

"I'm told I had seven. I don't remember any of them."

"You recall no names? Nothing?"

"Nothing."

"So you feel nothing for these people who were once closer to you than any others?"

I looked downward. "It's as though they're strangers. It's terrible to me that I can't recall them even enough to mourn them. I hate that they are dead—my families—but for me, it's as though they never lived."

"Thank you for your honesty," she said. I still didn't know what to think of her. She didn't like me, but she was polite. Did she dislike me because what I said endangered the Silks? Or did she dislike me because I was part human?

"Do you know how old you are, Shori?" Russell asked.

"My father told me I am fifty-three."

"And . . . do you know how tall you are, how much you weigh?"

"I'm 4 feet 11 inches tall. I don't know what I weigh."

"Do you know what the average height is for an Ina female your age?"

"I have no idea."

"The average is 5 feet 6 inches. What does that say to you?"

I stared at him, then gave the 5 foot 7 inch Katharine Dahlman a long look. Finally, I faced him again. At least I wasn't the only person who asked questions without fully considering the effects of the answers. "I'm not sure what you want me to say," I told him.

He glared at me for a moment, then said, "Apart from what you say the three captive human captives told you, do you have any evidence at all that the Silk family has done anything to harm your families?"

"Three humans questioned separately and all telling the same story? Yes, that's all I have, Russell."

We questioned each other repeatedly, Russell Silk and I and our advocates. Factual questions only. Were you told . . . ? Did you see . . . ? Did you hear . . . ? Did you scent . . . ? Did you taste . . . ?

No speeches were permitted, no arguments except through questions, no interrupting each other. Preston Gordon could and did cut us off, though, whenever he heard us stray from these guidelines. He did this with a fairness that infuriated both Russell and me, and he paid no attention when we glared at him.

The Council members could ask us questions and question our answers. The purpose of accused and accuser questioning one another was to give the Council the opportunity to make use of their formidable senses. They watched, listened, and breathed the air as we spoke. Together, they had thousands of years of experience reading body language.

When our questions to one another waned, we began the second night's work early. By mutual agreement, we began to question others, first Russell, then me. Any of the Silks or the Gordons could be asked to speak. If asked, they could not refuse. I intended to work my way through the two youngest of the four generations of Silks—four fathers and five unmated young sons—and have them come to the free-standing microphone one by one to answer my questions and any that Russell or the Council members might want to put to them. The unmated young ones were of the greatest interest to me. They were the ones I most wanted to be heard and seen by the Council. I thought my own scent would reach them and trouble them, and perhaps they would have a harder time keeping their minds on any lies they meant to tell. But now it was Russell Silk's turn. The first person he called was Daniel Gordon.

"Did you actually see the attack on your community that the child Shori Matthews says she defeated?" Russell demanded.

"She did not say she defeated it," Daniel answered. "She and several Gordon symbionts worked together to defeat it."

"Did you see this!"

"It happened during the day," Daniel said. "No Ina other than Shori could have seen it. Over half of our symbionts saw it, though. They not only helped fight off the attack, but captured two of the attackers alive so that they could be questioned. Shori captured the third. She prepared the captives for interrogation but did not touch any of our symbionts."

Russell stared at him, frowned as though he did not believe him, and changed the subject. "Have you ever known Shori to seem confused or uncertain of her surroundings, her intentions, her perceptions?" he asked.

Daniel shook his head. "Never."

"Have you ever heard Shori show disregard for the welfare of other Ina?"

"No, never."

Russell shook his head, as though in disgust. "And yet, isn't it true, Daniel, that Shori Matthews has bound you to her as her mate?"

"She has not," Daniel said.

Russell looked at the Council members. "I believe this to be untrue," he said. "He was seen taking the child into his quarters."

There was a moment of silence. Council members looked carefully at Daniel, breathing deeply to examine his scent. Finally two of them spoke.

"He is not bound," Alexander Svoboda said.

Elizabeth Akhmatova echoed, "He is not bound."

They were, according to what I'd heard, the oldest male and female Council members. One by one, the other members of the Council nodded, either accepting their elders' perceptions and judgment or coming to the same conclusion by way of their own senses. Alice Rappaport took several deep breaths, making a show of taking in Daniel's scent and judging it. She was the last to nod.

I wondered who had seen Daniel and me together, come to their own conclusions about what we were up to, and then run to tell the Silks all about it. Had it been the Marcu family who was staying in Daniel's house? Or perhaps it had been someone outside who saw him approach me and take me into his house. Or was it a Silk symbiont? If symbionts could be used as weapons, they could also be used as spies.

Russell looked surprised by the Council's conclusion. "You have no connection with Shori then?" he asked Daniel.

"We are promised to one another," Daniel said. "When this is over, when she's older and physically mature, my brothers and I will mate with her." He looked at me and smiled. I couldn't help smiling back at him.

Council member Ana Morariu said, "Do you believe the things Shori has told us tonight?"

"I do," Daniel said. "I've seen some of it for myself. I was present when the captives were questioned. Shori and my fathers and elderfathers questioned them. I saw, I heard, I breathed their scent. Because of that, I believe her."

"Are you sure that's why you believe her?" Russell demanded. "Would you believe her if Shori were already mated with other people or if you were?"

He repeated, "I was present when the captives were questioned. I know what I saw and heard."

They didn't make him say it a third time. I think they saw that they could not move him, and their senses told them that he believed that he was speaking the truth. Martin Harrison, of all people, had explained this to me days before. "Of course, the Ina can't sense absolute truth," he'd said. "At best, they can be fairly certain when someone fully believes what he's saying. They sense stress, changing degrees of stress. You do that yourself, don't you? You smell sweat, adrenaline, you see any hint of trembling, hear any difference in the voice or breathing or even the heartbeat."

"I do," I said. "I notice those things and others that I don't always have names for, but I don't always know how to interpret what I sense."

"Experience will take care of that," he said. "That's why the older Ina are so good at spotting truth and untangling lies. They use their senses, their intelligence, and their long experience."

"How can you know all that?" I asked him.

"It's what we all do, Ina and human," he said. "The Ina are just a lot better at it. They do it consciously and with more acute senses. They usually have better memories, and they can pile up more years of practice than humans can. We humans do a little of it and give it names like 'intuition' or 'instinct' or even 'ESP.' In fact, it's just good old conscious and unconscious use of your senses, your experience, and your intelligence."

I asked Preston about it later, and he grinned. "Been talking to Martin?"

"I have," I said. "Is he right?"

"Oh, yes. The man loves to teach. You're a blessing to him."

"How can he know what very old Ina are doing? Did you tell him?"

"No, he just keeps his eyes and ears open. His nose is no better than most other humans', but his intelligence is first-rate. His son is a lot like him."

That left me thinking again of Joel and wondering how like his father he would turn out to be.

The first day of the Council of Judgment ended with an effort on the part of the Silks to make me look irresponsible (at best) and make Daniel and, by extension, the Gordons look as though they were lying. They failed in both efforts. They would have one more day to try to undermine us. On the third day, judgment would be argued, truth acknowledged, and the Council would say, according to Ina law, what must be done.

That was all. It seemed almost . . . easy. Would the Silks simply give themselves up to be killed or allow their unmated young sons to be sent away to other communities? Could anyone do that?

As the Council ended its session just a hour before dawn, I felt the need to talk to someone. Then Brook, Wright, and Joel came to collect me, and I realized I was almost weak with hunger. Joel and Brook both recognized the signs, though I don't think Wright did yet.

"Let's go home," Brook said.

I nodded. I wanted to go find Martin Harrison and ask him questions, but I thought that might be better done during the day when other Ina could not listen.

I let my symbionts walk me home, then kissed each of them, and went to find Celia. I had not touched her for four nights. Tonight she would be expecting me. She was not entirely mine yet, not bound to me, as Daniel would say. Not quite. Tonight would be her turning point. Her scent told me she was almost there. Tonight, she would be mine.

She was asleep, warm and smelling of the soap she had used when she bathed earlier that night. In spite of her bath, she also smelled of the man she had had sex with before washing. I took in the scent and, after a moment, was able to picture the man—a symbiont of Peter Marcu's. He was a short, muscular man with very smooth skin—skin so dark it looked truly black. Someone had said he was from Ghana and that his name was Kwasi Tuntum. He had tired her out, made her sleepy. Eventually I would wake her up. I didn't think she would mind.

But when I slipped into bed beside her, she opened her eyes. I didn't think she could see me, but she said, "Hey, Shori, I thought you forgot about me."

"You didn't think that," I said. "You were enjoying yourself too much with Kwasi to worry about me forgetting you."

She froze next to me. I could feel her body go rigid.

I kissed her face, then her mouth. "Do you really care that I know?" I asked. "I can't help knowing."

"You . . . don't mind?"

"Should I mind?"

She shrugged against me. "Stefan didn't mind. He said I had the right to have human partners and have kids if I wanted them. After all, he couldn't give me kids." She frowned.

I said, "Why did it bother you that he didn't mind?"

She was silent for a long time. I used the time to explore what Kwasi had done with her. He had kissed her mouth and her neck and her breasts. He had kissed her between her breasts and taken her nipples into his mouth . . . I tried that, and she giggled. I'd never heard her giggle before. Then her scent changed, and she made a different sort of noise in her throat.

"What are you doing?" she asked.

"Learning," I said after a moment. "Why did it bother you that Stefan didn't mind your having sex with other people?"

"I think I wanted him to love me more—love me so much that he couldn't not care that I went with another guy."

"He cared. I'm female and I care. But if you're mine, I can accept the rest. And you do have the right to have your own human mate, your own children, or just have pleasure with a man when that's what you want." I lay on my back and moved her so that her body rested against mine. "I know how to take my pleasure with you," I said. "Will you teach me to pleasure you?"

"You will pleasure me this time, I think. I want you to feed. I love the feel of you against me. I almost feel the way I did when I knew Stefan wanted me, when I wanted him."

I smiled, hungry for her, starved for her, but taking my time enjoying the anticipation as much as I would soon enjoy feeding.

She looked up at me, perhaps able to see me a little now. "I'll teach you more when this Council thing is over. And you can teach me what else I can do to make you feel good. But for now, you're hungry. You have that scary, gaunt look." She rubbed the back of my neck. "You'd think I'd be afraid of you when you look like that, wouldn't you? Come here to me." She rolled us over onto our sides, facing one another, holding me against her, so welcoming that I couldn't wait any longer. I bit her deeply, hurt her a little, but also pleased her. She held me as though she thought I might leave her too soon. She held me as though laying claim to me.

◎     ◎     ◎

That afternoon, right after Celia and I got up, Martin Harrison came to see me. I had intended to find him eventually. I was surprised that with all the work he had to do satisfying the Gordons' guests, he had time to come looking for me. And I was surprised at the way he looked—tired, angry, sad, but struggling to keep his expression under control.

"You and I have gotten to know each other a little," he said. "I've come to you now because I believe it's better for you to hear what you have to hear from someone who isn't a stranger."

I stared back at him suddenly afraid, although I didn't know what I was afraid of. His expression made me not want to know.

"Hear what?" Celia asked. She spoke to Martin, but she was looking at me. She got up and came over to stand beside me. I had been keeping her company while she cooked and ate a huge meal and took vitamins and an iron supplement that she'd had in her luggage. She said Stefan had always made her take vitamins and an iron supplement because she had been his smallest symbiont, and he worried about her health. She had stopped taking them when he died. Now she had dug them out of her suitcase and begun using them again.

She was wearing a pullover sweater that fully displayed her half-healed bite. As it happened, Martin also had a half-healed bite on his neck. It showed just above the collar of his shirt. "What do you want her to hear?" Celia asked again. Wright, Joel, and Brook came in just then, flanked by two Gordon symbionts. I realized suddenly that the Gordon symbionts had gone out and found my symbionts and brought them to me, and I could see by their faces that they didn't know why any more than I did.

Martin glanced at them, then looked at Celia—a kind look. A frighteningly kind look. "Stay close to her today and tonight," he said to Celia. "All of you, stay close. She'll need you."

"What do you mean?" Celia demanded.

Suddenly, it occurred to me that someone was missing. "Theodora!" I said. "What's happened to Theodora?"

Martin sighed and turned to face me. "Carmen was going into San Francisco today," he said. "She needed some medical supplies, and she wanted to see her youngest sister who's just had twins. Carmen found Theodora lying on the ground between Hayden's house and his garage. Theodora's dead, Shori."

# twenty-four

**S**everal Gordon symbionts had gathered around Theodora's body, but they had not touched it. Only Carmen had done that, checking to see whether Theodora was alive, whether she could be helped . . .

Martin told me that when Carmen told him Theodora was dead, he asked her to stay with the body and keep everyone else away while he went to find me and send others to find the rest of my symbionts.

I was not fully in control of myself as I approached Theodora. I had demanded that Martin take me to her, but I was not truly seeing or understanding what was happening around me. I could not believe my Theodora was dead. It made no sense that she would be dead. None. Then I touched her cold flesh.

"She's been dead since early this morning," Carmen said behind me.

My own eyes and nose had already told me that much. Hours dead. Dead well before sunrise. Dead while Russell Silk and I tore at one another. Dead while I lay making Celia my own. Dead.

I found myself on my knees beside Theodora making sounds I could not recall ever having made before. She had come to me because she trusted me, loved me. She had been so happy when I asked her to join me here at Punta Nublada where she should have been safe. I had promised her a good life, had had every intention of keeping my promise. I would have kept her with me for the rest of her life. How could she be dead?

I wanted the people around me gone. I wanted to be let alone to examine Theodora, to understand her death. I must have made some gesture because the watching symbionts all took a few steps back. I knelt on the ground alongside Theodora, selecting out scents that were not her own, separating them into odors and groups of odors that I recognized. Theodora had gone to at least one of the parties, and that made for a confusion of scents—sweat, blood, aftershave, cologne, food and drink of several kinds, sexual arousal, many personal scents. There were fourteen distinct, personal human scents.

The odor that screamed loudest at me was the strong blood-scent in Theodora's hair—her blood. I looked and found the wound there. Her hair was stiff and matted with dried blood. Dead blood. I touched her head, ran my fingers over it, and found the place where there was a softness, an indentation. Someone had hit her so hard that they broke her skull.

Someone had murdered her.

Who had done it? Why? No one knew her here. No one had reason to harm her. No one would have harmed her . . . except, perhaps, to harm me. Would someone do that? Murder one person in the hope of causing pain to another? Why not? Someone—the Silks, surely—had murdered nearly two hundred people, human and Ina, in the hope of killing me, killing all that my eldermothers had created.

I closed my eyes, tried to quiet my thoughts and focus on Theodora. After a moment, I breathed deeply again and continued sorting through the scents. She had been in contact with fourteen different humans— Gordon symbionts and visitors. I didn't recognize all of them, but six I could picture. These were people I had met or had had pointed out to me. The others . . . the other scents I would remember. When I found the people they belonged to, I would know them. Any of them could have killed her, or perhaps they had only brushed against her at one of the parties. Perhaps they had danced with her or touched her in some other casual way. She had not had sex with anyone recently.

There seemed no way to tell which of the fourteen might have hit her, but . . . Had her blood splashed on the killer? Had the killer kept the weapon used to kill her? Had the killer touched her at all beyond battering her to death, perhaps to examine her to be certain she was dead?

I put my face down closer to her broken, bloody head. But then the scent of dead blood, of Theodora's beloved body, ten or more hours dead, became all that I could smell, and I had to turn away from it after a moment. I stood up and stepped a short distance away, gasping, sick, desperate for clean air.

Someone spoke to me, came near, and I shouted, "Let me alone! Get away from me!" A moment later, I realized that I had shouted at Wright, my first. I had told him to go away. Stupid of me. Stupid!

I looked up at him, saw that he was already backing away, not wanting to go but going.

"I'm sorry," I said. "Stay here, Wright. Stay near me while I finish this."

I breathed deeply for a moment, then turned back to Theodora and tried again. I rolled her from her back onto her side so that I could see and smell whatever had been trapped under her. The significant odors were more blood, of course, and the scents of five more people. Again, I recognized some of them—three of the five. Through the night, then, nineteen people had had enough contact with Theodora to leave their scents on her—nineteen people, any one of whom might be her murderer. I would have to find each of them and speak to them or to their Ina.

I stood up, finally, and went on looking at my dead Theodora. I would have to go to her daughter and son-in-law and tell them that she was dead. They couldn't know everything, but they had a right to know that. After I found her killer, I would go to her family.

I looked around for Martin. He was still there. The onlookers had gone away, but Martin and my four symbionts still waited.

"Has anyone left the community today?" I asked.

He shook his head. "Not that I know of."

"Could someone have left without your knowing?"

"Of course. I have to sleep, too, girl."

And William Gordon had bitten him early this morning. I looked back at Theodora. "I don't know what should be done with the dead, Martin."

"She should be cleaned up, given a funeral, and . . . well, buried. We have our own cemetery here."

I still didn't know what to do. Theodora should be prepared for burial. A memorial service of some kind should be arranged. Her killer should be caught, should be killed. And yet in a few hours the Council of Judgment would begin its second night, and I would have to be there.

"Shori, girl," Martin said. He spoke with such gentleness that I wanted to run away from him. I could not dissolve emotionally and lose myself in grief. I did not dare. There was no time.

"Shori, we'll take care of her body. We'll prepare her for burial. We can have services for her after the Council is over. You go find out who did this. That's what you want to do, isn't it?"

I looked at him, and all I could do was nod.

"Leave her to us." He almost turned away, then stopped and drew a deep breath. "Two things, Shori. They're important."

"All right," I said.

He looked down and met my gaze with a different expression— harder, unhappy, but determined.

"Tell me, Martin," I said. "You've been a friend. Go ahead and say whatever it is that you don't want to say."

He nodded. "Don't kill anyone. No matter how certain you are that you've found the right person, don't kill. Not yet. Chances are, the murderer is one of the visitors—one of the Gordon family's guests. You are more than a guest. You'll be mated to the sons of the family in a few years. But still . . . Tell Preston or Hayden what's happened before you take a life."

I stared at him, unable to answer at first. Until that moment, if I had learned that Martin himself had killed Theodora, I'm not sure I could have stopped myself from killing him. And yet, I understood on some murky emotional level and from slivers of recovered memory that it would be a serious offense against the Gordons to kill one of their guests. I couldn't remember anyone ever doing such a thing, but I felt enough horror and disgust at the thought of doing it to know that I must not.

"I won't kill anyone," I said finally.

Another nod.

"And don't bite anyone."

That one was even harder. But I could see the reason for it. If I found the killer, he or she would be the symbiont of someone here. Again, I knew—again without understanding fully how I knew—that it would be wrong to interfere with someone else's symbiont.

"The Ina might be the guilty one," I said. "Probably would be."

"All the more reason not to abuse the symbiont."

"I won't bite unless someone attacks me," I said. "I would rather bite than break bones or tear flesh." And I walked away from him. My symbionts followed me.

When we were alone, Wright pulled me to him and hugged me and held me for a while. I felt as though I wanted to stay that way, safe with him, breathing his good, familiar scent. It mattered more than I would have thought possible that he was alive, that he loved me and wanted somehow to comfort me. I knew that if I let him, he would take me home and put me to bed and stay with me until I fell asleep. I knew he would do that because I had come to know him that well. I longed to let him do that.

But there was no time. If possible, by the time tonight's Council session began, I wanted to know who had killed Theodora. I wanted to prevent the murderer from leaving or killing anyone else, and I wanted to put this new crime before the Council to see whether they would deal with it. If they didn't, I would.

I pushed back from Wright and realized that he had lifted me off the ground and was holding me so that I could look at him almost at eye level. I kissed the side of his mouth, then kissed his mouth and said, "Put me down."

He set me on my feet. "What do you want us to do?" he asked.

And I almost disintegrated again. He understood. Of course he did. "I need you to stay together," I said. "Protect one another." I looked at each of them, missing immediately the face that was not there. "I don't know whether Theodora's murder has anything to do with the other attempts on us or with Council of Judgment, but it seems likely." I paused. It hurt to say her name. I took a breath and went on. "Go talk to Jill Renner sym Wayne. She spent some time with Theodora last night and left her scent for me to find. She wouldn't have hurt Theodora, but she might have seen her having trouble with someone or leaving a party with someone. Was there a party at Wayne's house last night?"

"Sym Wayne?" Wright said, frowning. "Is that how you say it, then, when someone is a symbiont? That's what happens to our names? We're sym Shori?"

"You are," I said.

"Something you remembered?"

"No. Something I learned from hearing people talk. What about Wayne's house? Was there a party?"

"Not at Wayne's," Celia said. "But there was a party at Edward's and a big party at Philip's. Jill, Theodora, and I were at both of them. Theodora was a little shy at first, and she kind of hung out with me at Edward's. We ate there and talked with a lot of people. But at Philip's she met a couple of guys. They got her dancing, and the three of them just sort of stayed together, dancing and flirting and enjoying themselves."

Wright frowned at Celia as though she had said something wrong, but Celia ignored him.

"Who were the two men?" I asked.

"A couple of older guys. I don't know their names or who their Ina is. They were both graying, maybe five-ten, well built. They could have been brothers. They looked a lot alike."

"Did you touch them?" I asked. "Shake hands or squeeze past them?" She shook her head.

"Tell me what you can about them. See them in your memory, and tell me what you see." We were walking toward Wayne's house where Jill Renner was probably still asleep.

Celia frowned and looked desperate for a moment, as though she were grasping for something that she couldn't quite reach but had to reach. She glanced at me, then closed her eyes, focusing, remembering. Finally she said, "They both had the same salt-and-pepper hair—black with a lot of white. One of them had a mustache. It was salt-and-pepper, too. They aren't with the Gordons. I'm sure of that. Westfall! I think they're the two male Westfall symbionts. The rest of the Westfall syms are women. These guys talk like they've been here for a long time, but every now and then you could hear a little English accent . . ." She let her voice trail away. Then she said, "The one with the mustache, he has a scar on his forehead, or maybe it's a birthmark. I'm not sure which. I don't know how big it is. It starts just below the hairline and goes back into the hair. It's a red oval, or I think it would have been oval if I could have seen all of it."

"All right," I said. "Relax. I know who you mean. I've never spoken to them, but I saw them and got their scent when the Westfalls arrived. Their scents were on Theodora. You're right. They probably are brothers. I'll find them. The rest of you go talk to Jill Renner."

"Let me stay with you," Joel said. "I know a lot of the visitors, and they know me. I might be able to help."

I glanced up at him and nodded. "You three, watch out for one another."

Brook, Celia, and Wright went off to knock on Wayne's door, and Joel and I went down the road to Wells Gordon's house where the Westfalls—Harold and John—were staying with their eight symbionts, including the two who may have been among the last people to see Theodora alive.

I didn't suspect them of killing Theodora. The Westfalls, from what Preston had told me, were not closely related to me or to the Silks, but they were very interested in the success my eldermothers had had mixing human and Ina DNA and giving me the day. They were not offended by it as the Silks were.

I thought about Milo, about his contempt for me and his less lethal, but no less real, contempt for symbionts—probably for all humans. Ina could not survive without humans, and yet Milo seemed to consider them little more than useful domestic animals. What must life be like for his symbionts?

And how did families who thought like the Silks get along with other Ina? Joan Braithwaite had said that there were many who loved Milo. They must have loved him in spite of his arrogance. Or perhaps they loved him for what he had been when he was younger. He was far from lovable now.

I had read in one of the books I'd borrowed from Hayden about the periods of feuding between Ina families during which Ina fought mainly by doing what the Silks had done to my families—using humans as weapons—using them to kill members of one another's families. Hayden said that hadn't happened anywhere in the world for centuries. It was considered as barabaric among Ina as boiling people in oil was among humans.

And yet, somehow it had come back into fashion.

"I need to see the two male Westfall symbionts," I told Dulce Ramos, the Wells Gordon's symbiont who happened to be awake.

She nodded and said, "Okay." Then, "Hey, Joel," and took Joel and me upstairs and into to the house's guest quarters. "Those two are brothers—twins, I think—Gerald and Eric Cooper. Eric's the one with the mustache." She paused. "I heard what happened. I'm sorry."

I nodded. "Thank you."

"Do you think the Westfall syms did it?"

"No. But they might have seen something."

The Westfall symbionts were asleep, keeping the same hours as their Ina. Awakened, the Cooper brothers came out together, short salt-and-pepper hair standing up in spikes all over their heads. They wore handsome robes made of very smooth, deep red material. They were just as Celia had described them, now sleepy but interested.

"I had heard you could stay awake during the day," Eric said. "But I didn't believe it until now."

I shrugged. "I can," I said, "but while I was asleep this morning someone killed one of my symbionts."

Both men went very still. "Theodora?" Gerald asked.

"Theodora," I said.

"Oh my God, I'm so sorry. Killed? Someone killed her? My God."

"Early this morning. She's been dead now for about ten hours."

He nodded. "And you're talking to us because we spent some time talking to her last night."

"I'm talking to you because both your scents are on her," I said.

"We both danced with her," Eric said. "She was so happy, having such a good time. She was a delight."

"She talked mainly about you," Gerald said. "She made us remember what it was like to be in a brand-new symbiosis. She was very much in love with you, said she thought her life was pretty much over until you broke into her house one night, swept her off her feet, and confused the hell out of her."

I wanted to laugh about that. Then I wanted to run away from these strangers, find a dark corner, and huddle there rocking my body back and forth, moaning and mourning. They were speaking honestly about Theodora as far as I could sense, and yet I hated them. They had been with her talking to her, listening to her, touching her during her last hours. They were strangers, and they had been there with her. I had not.

Beside me, Joel took my hand and held it. That helped a little, steadied me a little.

I struggled to keep my voice and my expression neutral because frightening these men would not get me the information I wanted. And

I couldn't just stir their memories by telling them to remember. They weren't mine. The best I could do would be to ask their Ina to nudge their memories when he awoke. For now, I could only try to persuade them. "Do you remember what time it was when you left her?" I asked.

"She left us," Gerald said. "She said she was tired and wanted to go to bed. Said she wasn't used to having a social life again. I think it was around two this morning." He looked at his brother. "Two?"

"Closer to three," Eric said. "We offered to walk her home, but she just smiled and kissed us both and went on her way. I saw her go out the front door. That's the last time I saw her."

"Did you see anyone paying attention to her?" I asked.

Both men frowned, then Eric shook his head. "I was looking at her. I might have missed what someone else was doing." He glanced at me. "No offense, but I would have taken her to bed if I could have."

I nodded. I had understood that. "I don't think she was ready for that yet."

"She wasn't." He paused. "As soon as she was gone, though, two men left. I don't know them or which families they're with. Hell, I don't even know if they were together. They did leave at the same time, though."

"Tell me what you remember about them," I said. "Did you see their faces?"

"Only for a moment," Eric said. "Young-looking men. Brown hair. Medium brown. Both of them."

"Another pair of brothers?" I asked.

They looked at one another, then back at me. "No, I don't believe so," Gerald said. "They were a Mutt-and-Jeff pair."

I frowned.

"A tall fellow and a short one," Gerald explained. "And they didn't look alike at all except for the hair. Just two guys."

"How short was the short guy?" Joel asked.

Gerald frowned. "Too short to be a symbiont, really. I think most Ina would worry about taking on a such a small man."

Mentally, I went through the list of people who had left their scents on Theodora's body. Of the ones I could identify, three of them were brown-haired men. Only one might be called short by everyone except me. Gerald was right. The man I was thinking of was slender and short, actually too small to be a symbiont. Most Ina worried about hurting smaller humans. In great need, even I might take more blood than a small human could survive losing. "Estimate the height of the shorter man," I said, just to be sure.

"He was maybe five-three or four," Eric said.

Joel whistled. "That might mean his Ina was female," he said.

"Jack Roan," I said. "His scent was on Theodora. Jack Roan sym Katharine Dahlman. And Katharine Dahlman and her sister are the shortest adult Ina I've ever seen. Did Jack dance with Theodora at all?"

"If he did, it was before we arrived," Eric said. "We were at another party at Manning's house. She would have had plenty of time to dance with other people before we arrived."

But she probably hadn't. Theodora had not left Celia until Eric and Gerald took an interest. I needed to talk with Jack Roan as soon as possible.

But Jack Roan had gone—had left Punta Nublada. I went to the office complex where the Dahlmans were staying and he wasn't there.

The complex was also where the Braithwaites were staying, and one of Margaret Braithwaite's symbionts, a man named Zane Carter, told me he had seen Roan go—had seen him take one of the Dahlman cars and leave that morning. Carter assumed Roan had been sent out on some errand for Katherine or her sister Sophia.

Also, the other brown-haired man from the party turned up—the one who had left the party at the same time as Roan. He turned out to be someone that I knew or, at least, that I was aware of. He was Hiram Majors sym Preston, and his scent had not been on Theodora. I was relieved to know that once I knew he was with the Gordons. He came to me on his own when he heard that I was looking for Roan . . . and heard why I was looking for him.

"I was talking to Jack last night," he told me when he caught up with me as Joel and I were leaving the office complex. "Turns out he and my sister both went to Carnegie Mellon in Pittsburgh at the same time. He knew her. Saw her in some play—she was a drama major—and then ran into her the next day and invited her to have coffee with him." Hiram shrugged. "I'm cut off from my family out here. It was good to talk to someone from home."

"Did he leave abruptly last night?" I asked.

"Yes," Hiram admitted. "I think he had been watching your . . . Theodora?"

"That was her name."

"I hadn't really noticed her until she walked past us and out the door, and Jack looked at her and said he had to go do something for Katharine. Said he'd forgotten until that minute." Hiram shook his head. "That's why I remember him so clearly."

"God," Joel said. "What a stupid thing for one symbiont to say to another."

"Why?" I asked, not thinking.

They both stared at me. Joel answered, "You don't forget something your Ina tells you to do. You can't. That's one of the first things you learn as a symbiont. Jack Roan was—I guess—so eager to go after Theodora that he told a really stupid lie."

# twenty-five

I asked Layla Cory, Preston's first, to let me know when he was awake.

Then I went back to the guest house to talk with Wright, Brook, and Celia.

"Jill Renner saw Jack talking to Theodora," Brook said when I told them about Jack Roan.

"She recognized him because he's so short," Wright said. "She'd noticed him before."

"Where were they talking?" I asked.

"Outside," he said. "Near Hayden's house. It was around two thirty or three this morning. She was on her way home."

"Jill said she couldn't hear what they were saying," Celia said. "But it didn't look like anything bad was happening. I mean, Jill said he wasn't touching her or anything."

As soon as Layla Cory phoned me, I left my symbionts at the guest house, went to Preston, and told him what had happened and what I had learned. We talked in his den, next to his bedroom. The den was a windowless, wood-paneled room with leather-covered chairs, oriental rugs on the floor, and many shelves of old, leather-covered books. It felt, somehow, like a cave—the cave Preston was born from each day.

"Katharine Dahlman," he said, and he shook his head. "I've known Katharine for three centuries. Her family and mine . . . well, I can't say we've been friends, but we've usually gotten along. Are you sure?" We sat facing one another in the vast leather chairs. I had slipped off my shoes and curled up in the chair because it was easier than sitting with my legs sticking straight out or sitting forward on the edge with my feet dangling well above the floor. It was a comfortable chair to curl up in.

Under different circumstances, I would have been completely content there.

"I'm sure my Theodora is dead," I said, "murdered by being hit so hard that part of her skull was broken. I'm sure Jack Roan sym Katharine Dahlman followed her from the party at Philip's house after lying about why he was leaving the party. Jill Renner went to the same parties as Theodora, and she said early this morning she saw Roan talking to Theodora near Hayden's house. Sometime after that, Zane Carter saw Roan leaving Punta Nublada. I can't claim to know more than that, but that should be enough."

Preston looked at me for a moment, then shook his head.

"I loved Theodora, and she was mine," I said. "She came to me willingly, eagerly. And now, because she loved me, she's dead."

"You don't know that," he said.

"I can't prove it," I said. "But I know it. So do you." I took a deep breath. "I promised Martin Harrison I wouldn't kill anyone before I talked to you or Hayden. And because the Council goes on tonight, I can't try to track Roan." I took another breath. "Preston, what can I do? She trusted herself to me. I want a life for her life. I will have a life for her life."

Preston turned his face away. "Roan's life?"

"Katharine's life!"

"No."

I said nothing more. I would have Katharine Dahlman's life. We would not play the game of killing off one another's symbionts as though they weren't even people, as though they were nothing.

I jumped down from the chair, grabbed my shoes, and started to walk away from him.

"Who will protect the rest of your symbionts if you kill Katharine?" Preston demanded. "Her family will come after you. You'll have stepped outside the law, and they will be free to protect themselves. They'll kill you, and they'll kill your symbionts, too, if they try to help you. And of course they will try. Do you want the rest of your people dead?"

"The Dahlmans are the ones who stepped outside the law!"

"I agree with you; they almost certainly have. But that isn't yet proved."

"My family is gone!" I said, turning to face him again. "My memory of them is gone. I can't even mourn them properly because for me, they never really lived. Now I have begun to relearn who I am, to rebuild my life, and my enemies are still killing my people. Where is there safety for my symbionts or for me?"

"Go on with the Council of Judgment."

If he had been anyone other than Preston, I would have walked away without bothering to comment. But Preston had become important to me. It wasn't only that I liked him. He was Daniel's elderfather. And he favored a mating between his sons and me. "Why?" I demanded. "Why should I wait?"

"Think about why this was done, Shori. Think. You were very much in control of yourself last night. If your memory were intact, you wouldn't have been, you couldn't have been so calm as you sat in the same room with the people who probably had your families killed. I don't think you were expected to be calm. I think the Silks and perhaps the Dahlmans expected you not only to look unusual with your dark skin, but to be out of your mind with pain, grief, and anger, to be a pitiable, dangerous, crazed thing. We Ina don't handle loss as well as most humans do. It's a much rarer thing with us, and when it happens, the grief is . . . almost unbearable."

I looked away from him. "I know what the grief is like!"

"Of course you do. You stand there hugging yourself as though you were trying to hold yourself together. They did this to you, Shori. They want you this way!"

I found myself leaning against the wall, wanting to slide down it, wanting to dissolve to the floor. "What can I do?" I said. "How can Katharine be punished when the Silks are the only ones everyone is paying attention to?"

"The facts are what the Council is supposed to pay attention to."

"But Katharine Dahlman is a member of the Council."

"Challenge her tonight. Tell the Council what has happened just as you told me. Facts only. Let them draw their own conclusions. Let them question you. Then ask that Katharine be removed from the Council."

"And they'll do it? All I have to do is ask, and they'll do it?"

"Yes. They'll question her. Then they'll do it because they'll know you're telling the truth, and they'll decide her guilt or innocence as well as her punishment—if there is to be punishment—tomorrow night, when they decide what to do about the Silks. But once she leaves the Council, someone else will have to go, too. Chances are it will be Vlad."

If there was to be punishment? If? If they didn't punish her, I would. I would kill her. I would find a way to do it, a way that would not leave my symbionts unprotected. Perhaps I could find a human criminal—a murderer—and have him kill her and then die himself before he could be made to say who had sent him. Katharine's people would know as I knew, but if she could get away with it, so could I. I had to do something. What I wanted to do was tear her apart with my teeth and hands. Maybe it would come to that.

Then my mind registered the other thing that Preston had said. Vladimir Leontyev, my advocate, one of my mothers' fathers, off the Council. "Why?" I demanded.

"Numerical balance. All Councils of Judgment must have an odd number of members. If Katharine were to leave the Council because of an injury or an emergency at home, her sister Sophia would take her place. Under the circumstances, I don't think you or your advocate would find Sophia any more acceptable than Katharine."

"I agree," I said. Who knew whether this was something both sisters had agreed to do or something Katharine had thought of on her own.

"Also," Preston said, "it will strike people as reasonable that both you and the Silks lose your advocates."

"It's as though they're playing a game. After all, I'm not trying to get at her because she's the Silks' advocate."

"It's not a game, Shori. The Council will know why Katharine must go. But it will be best for you if you do this according to custom." He frowned, looked at me, then looked away. "You, more than anyone, must show that you can follow our ways. You must not give the people who have decided to be your enemies any advantage. You must seem more Ina that they."

"I don't know how to do that."

"You know enough. When you don't know, ask."

"Who shall I ask? Who will be my advocate now?"

He thought for a moment. "Joan Braithwaite?"

I had to think about that, too. "If Margaret were the Council member, I'd say yes, but Joan ... Just how friendly is she with the Silks?"

"Because of the way she spoke to you last night?"

"That and ... when she finished with me, she went over to talk with the Silks."

"You should have listened to what she said to them, to Milo in particular."

I waited.

"She told him to give his place to one of his sons or she would, before the Council, question his mental stability."

"As he questioned mine."

"Yes. Stupid of him. But as I've told you, you were not what the Silks expected you to be. You should have been, by all reckoning, only a husk of a person, mad with grief and rage or simply mad." He paused. "I wonder if that's part of why your memory is gone, not just because you suffered blows to the head, but because of the emotional blow of the death of all your symbionts, your sisters, and your mothers—everyone. You must have seen it happen. Maybe that's what destroyed the person you were."

I thought about that. I tried to let his words touch off some feeling, some grief or pain, some memory. But those people were strangers. Right now, there was only Theodora and the pain of just thinking her name. "I don't know," I said. "Maybe I'll never know."

"Go talk to Joan, Shori. See her before tonight's session begins."

I looked into his kindly face, and it scared me how much I liked him and depended on him, even though I didn't really know him very well. But then, I didn't know anyone very well. "What would Joan have done differently if she had been my advocate from the beginning?" I asked.

He gave me a faint, unhappy smile. "From what I know of her, I think she would have spoken to you just as harshly as she did speak, perhaps even more so. But she wouldn't have spoken to the Silks at all, and perhaps Milo would have gone on representing his family and eventually offending almost everyone. Go talk to her, Shori. Do it now."

I went, stopping at the guest house to check on Wright, Joel, Brook, and Celia. I needed to see them to be certain they were all right, I needed to touch each of them. They were sharing a meal of roast beef, a mixture of brown-and-wild rice, gravy, and green beans with the six Rappaport symbionts.

"I need all of you to come to the Council tonight," I said. I didn't think I could stand it if they stayed away, if I couldn't see them and know that they were all right for so many hours.

"We figured," Celia said.

"Don't worry," Wright said. "We were going to go to the Council hall as soon as we finished dinner." The storage building had become "the Council hall" overnight.

"Stay together," I said. "Take care of one another."

They nodded, and I left them. I went to the offices that the Braithwaites were using as living space. I would have given a lot just to sit with my symbionts, watch them eat, hear their voices, walk them over to the Council hall where I would make sure they got seats in the front so that I could always see them. Instead, I went to find Joan Braithwaite.

I tripped and almost fell on the steps that lead up into the offices. I hurt my foot enough to stand still for a moment and wait for it to stop throbbing. It occurred to me as I stood there that I could not recall stumbling like that since the day I left the cave and had healed enough to hunt. This was what Preston had meant. Theodora had been murdered so that I would begin to stumble in all sorts of ways.

I stood still for a minute more, breathing, regaining my balance as best I could. Then I went in and found Joan.

She was in the office that was her bedroom, sitting at the desk, writing in a wire-bound notebook. She closed the notebook as I came in. The folding bed that had been moved in for her was heaped with blankets that she had thrown aside. Her clothing, books, and other things were scattered around the room. She kept a messy room the way Theodora had. Somehow, that made me like her a little.

"I suppose you've come to ask me to be your advocate," she said in her quick, no-nonsense way.

"I have," I said, relieved that she already knew. Zane Carter, who had told me about seeing Jack Roan drive away, had probably told both Joan and Margaret everything.

"You haven't hurt anyone?" Joan demanded.

I shook my head. "I promised Martin Harrison that I wouldn't. I said

I'd wait until I talked with Preston or Hayden. When I talked with Preston, he sent me to you."

She turned her chair so that she faced me, hands resting on the arms of the chair. "So you're pretty much in control of yourself, then? You're over the shock?"

I just stared at her.

After a while, she nodded. "When your rage is choking you, it is best to say nothing. How are your remaining symbionts?"

"Fine." Yes. Fine. Putting up with me and my need to hover over them.

"There are people on the Council who are going to ask you much more painful questions than I have so far, Shori. Someone will surely ask you whether you killed your Theodora yourself."

My mouth fell open. "What? I . . . what?"

"And someone will want to know whether she had accepted you fully, whether she was bound to you."

I couldn't say anything for several seconds. On some level, I understood what Joan was doing. I didn't love her for it, but I understood. Still, it took me a while to be able to respond coherently.

"She had accepted me," I said at last. I cleared my throat. "Theodora loved me. I bound her to me here at Punta Nublada. She was mine when she died. Before she arrived several days ago, we hadn't been together often enough to be fully bound, but she wanted to be. She wanted to be with me, and I wanted her. I loved her."

"Do you understand why I ask that?"

"I don't."

She looked downward, licked her lips. "Symbionts—fully bound symbionts—give up a great deal of freedom to be with us. Sometimes, after a while, they resent us even though they don't truly want to leave, even though they love us. As a result, they behave badly. I don't blame them, but—"

"She didn't resent me. She didn't really know what she was giving up yet. And . . . she trusted me."

"Let me finish. Our senses are so much more acute than theirs, we're so much faster and stronger than they are that it's a good thing they have some protection against us. In fact, it's extremely difficult for us kill or injure our bound symbionts. It's hard, very hard, even to want to do such a thing.

"Even Milo hasn't been able to do it. He resents his need of them, sees it as a weakness, and yet he loves them. He would stand between his symbionts and any danger. He might shout at them, but even then, he would be careful. He would not order them to harm themselves or one another. And he would never harm one of them. I think it's an instinct for self-preservation on our part. We need our symbionts more than most of them know. We need not only their blood, but physical contact with them and emotional reassurance from them. Companionship. I've never known even one of us to survive without symbionts. We should be able to do it—survive through casual hunting. But the truth is that that only works for short periods. Then we sicken. We either weave ourselves a family of symbionts, or we die. Our bodies need theirs. But human beings who are not bound to us, who are bound to other Ina, or not bound at all . . . they have no protection against us except whatever decency, whatever morality we choose to live up to. You see?"

I did. And she had just told me more about the basics of being Ina than anyone else ever had. I wondered what other necessary things I didn't know. I took a deep breath. "I see," I said. "Theodora was bound to me. And I never hurt her. I never would have hurt her."

She watched me as I spoke, no doubt judging me, deciding whether I was telling the truth, whether I was worth her time. "All right," she said. "All right, I'll be your advocate when the time comes." She glanced at her watch. "Let's go to the hall."

## twenty-six

When Katharine Dahlman heard what I had to say, she denied everything. Neither she nor her symbiont Jack Roan had anything at all to do with the death of "the person Shori Matthews is attempting to claim as her symbiont."

"They had chosen one another," Vladimir Leontyev said. "We all saw that they had."

"Where is Jack Roan?" Joan Braithwaite asked.

"I don't know," Katharine said. "My other symbionts have told me he had to go—some family emergency. He has family in Los Angeles, in Phoenix, Arizona, and in Austin, Texas." She said all this with an odd, sly, smiling expression that I had not seen before. And, of course, she was lying. Everything she'd said was a lie. I got the impression she didn't care that we knew.

Vladimir looked disgusted. "You're telling us Roan is yours, but you have no idea which of those three large cities in three different states he's gone to visit?"

Katharine gave a small shrug. "It was an emergency," she said. "He couldn't wait until I awoke. I trust my people."

"You should," I said. "Your people are clearly very competent, especially when it comes to murdering an unsuspecting symbiont who's never done them any harm." I looked along the arc at the other Council members. "I request that she be removed from this Council."

"You request!" Katharine seemed to choke on the words. "I request that you be removed from this room! You're a child, clearly too young to know how to behave. And I challenge your right to represent the interests of families who are unfortunately dead. You are their descendent, but because of their error, because of their great error, you are not Ina!

No one can be certain of the truth of anything you say because you are neither Ina nor human. Your scent, your reactions, your facial expressions, your body language—none of it is right. You say your symbiont has just died. If that were so, you would be prostrate. You would not be able to sit here telling lies and arguing. True Ina know the pain of losing a symbiont. We are Ina. You are nothing!"

There was a swell of voices from the audience—much denial, but some agreement. All the visiting and local Ina were present in the audience or on the Council. The rest of the seats were filled by symbionts who also had opinions about me. Not surprisingly, the symbionts who spoke were on my side. It was the Ina who were divided.

Preston stood up. "Listen to me!" he roared in a voice Milo Silk would have been proud of, and the room went utterly silent. After a few seconds, he repeated more quietly, "Listen to me. Shori Matthews is as Ina as the rest of us. In addition, she carries the potentially life-saving human DNA that has darkened her skin and given her something we've sought for generations: the ability to walk in sunlight, to stay awake and alert during the day." He paused, then raised his voice again. "Her mothers, her sisters, her father, and her brothers were Ina, and they have been murdered along with all but two of their symbionts. All of Shori's own first symbionts have been murdered. This Council has met to determine who's responsible for those murders, and now it must also consider the murder of Theodora Harden, one of Shori's new symbionts. We are here to discover the guilt or innocence of those accused of these murders and, if they are found guilty, to decide what is to be done with the murderers. Based on what we've heard so far, I don't believe Katharine Dahlman should be a member of this Council."

Katharine Dahlman sat very straight and stared angrily at Preston. "You want your sons to mate with this person. You want them to get black, human children from her. Here in the United States, even most humans will look down on them. When I came to this country, such people were kept as property, as slaves. You are biased in Shori's favor and not a voting member of this Council. I won't give up my place because you say so."

Preston stared at her, expressionless, still. "Council members, count yourselves for or against Katharine remaining one of you." He paused until all of them had turned to look at him. "Zoë Fotopoulos?" he said, turning to look at Zoë. She sat farthest from me, next to Russell Silk's table.

Zoë looked from Katharine to Preston, then shook her head. "Katharine should go," she said. "And we need to consider what to do about her directing her symbiont to kill Shori's symbiont. Like the Silks, she must be judged."

"She must be judged," Preston echoed. "Joan Braithwaite?"

"Katharine should go," Joan said stiffly. "Her fears have made her stupid. We cannot afford to have stupid Council members. The decisions we make here are important. They should be made with a clear head." She did not look at Katharine as she spoke, but Katharine stared at her with obvious hatred.

"Alexander Svoboda?" Preston continued.

"Katharine should go," he said, "but we'd better decide now who will go with her to keep our numbers right."

"Peter Marcu?"

"She should go," he said. "But she's the Silk advocate. Maybe Vlad should be the other member to go."

"Vladimir Leontyev?"

My elderfather looked angrier than the rest of them. It had taken me a moment and a look from him to realize that he was angry on my behalf. Something more had been done to me, and he was furious about it. "Katharine must go!" he said. "If that means I go, too, then so be it. How could she have imagined that this would be overlooked? Our symbionts are not tools to be used to kill other people's symbionts. Those days are long past and nothing should be permitted to revive them."

"Ana Morariu?"

Ana hesitated and stared down at the table. "Katharine should stay," she said. "Let's take care of one question at a time. After all, Katharine may be telling the truth about her symbiont. We shouldn't judge her so quickly." Several people frowned at her or looked away. Others nodded. Vladimir was right. Katharine had made little effort to make her lies believable—as though she expected at least some of the people present to go along with her because using her symbiont to murder the symbiont of someone as insignificant as I was such a small thing. It was a little sin that could be overlooked among friends. Friends like Ana Morariu.

"Alice Rappaport?"

"She should go." Alice looked at Katharine, then looked away and shook her head. "Over the centuries, I've seen too much racial prejudice among humans. It isn't a weed we need growing among us."

"Harold Westfall?"

"She should go. I, too, have seen more than enough racism."

"Kira Nicolau?"

"Katharine should go. She may be right in what she says about Shori, but she did send her symbiont to kill a human whom Shori called her symbiont. No member of a Council of Judgment should have done such a thing, and no Council of Judgment should tolerate such a thing."

"Ion Andrei?"

"I believe Katharine should stay. If she's made a mistake—*if* she's made a mistake—well, we can look into it another time."

"Walter Nagy?"

"She should go. None of us want to go back to the days of feuds carried on by murdering one another's symbionts."

"Elizabeth Akhmatova?"

"She should go. How can she murder another Ina's symbiont and not think anything of it? What sort of person could do such a thing?"

That was a very good question.

Katharine seemed surprised that the vote went against her. She had truly expected to benefit from what she had done. She had gotten her symbiont out of my reach so that I couldn't track him and kill him before she awoke. In fact, I wouldn't have killed him. His life did not interest me. Hers did. But she didn't know me, and she wasn't willing to take chances with Jack Roan's precious skin. She had imagined that her fellow Council members—all Ina, all around her age—would accept what she had done, even if they didn't like it. She believed I would either lose control and disgrace myself before the Council—possibly by attacking her—or if I didn't, she could use my apparent lack of feeling to point out how un-Ina I was. She won either way. What did the life of my Theodora matter?

Katharine left the table, glaring at me as though I had somehow done her an injury. I hadn't. But I would. I surely would.

After a little more discussion, Vladimir left, too. I was sorry to see him go. Wright called him my granddad. Ina, for some reason, didn't use the words humans used to described kinship—"grandfather," "aunt," "cousin"—but I liked the idea of Vladimir and Konstantin as my elder-fathers. It comforted me that I still had elderfathers, that I was a younger-daughter to someone.

Both Vladimir and Katharine went to sit in the audience. Wayne and Philip Gordon brought them chairs. Once that was done, the Council could return to the question of whether the Silks had killed my families.

The Silks first questioned several of the Gordons, including Preston, who stood up like the others at the free-standing microphone and quietly answered the same offensive questions. He answered them without protest.

No, he was not concerned about allowing his sons to mate with someone who was, among other things, a genetic experiment.

"I've had a chance to get to know her," he said. "She's an intelligent, healthy, likable young female. When she's older, she'll bear strong children, and some of them will walk in sunlight."

Then Russell called Hayden and asked the same question of him.

"I am concerned because she is alone," Hayden said. "I hope that she will adopt a sister before she mates with my youngersons. My brother is right about Shori. She is bright, healthy, and likable. When her sisters were alive, I saw a mating between them and my youngersons as a perfect match—or as near perfect as any joining can be."

I felt better about Hayden after that. He seemed to be telling the truth. I hoped he was. He was old enough to slip a lie past me and perhaps past everyone else in the room. But why should he?

The Silks had brought along a doctor who was one of their symbionts, poor man. Russell asked the Council to allow the doctor to question me about my injuries. It was intended to be offensive, another effort, like Milo's, to treat me as human rather than Ina and, of course, to humiliate me.

"He may be able to give us some insight into Shori's amnesia," Russell said innocently. "Humans are more familiar with memory problems."

Ion Andrei, Russell's new advocate said, "Russell has the right to stand aside and let someone with specialized knowledge speak for him."

Joan Braithwaite sighed. "We could waste a lot of time arguing whether or not to permit the doctor's questions. Let's not do that. Shori, are you willing to be questioned by this man?"

"I'm not," I said.

She nodded, looked at me for a moment. "The implications of the request are offensive," she said. "They're intended to be. Nevertheless, I advise you to let the doctor question you. He means no harm. He's only one more symbiont being used to cause you pain. Ironic and nasty, isn't it? No matter. I advise you to bear the pain so that anyone on the Council who has doubts about you can see a little more of who and what you are."

I did not like Joan Braithwaite. But I thought I might eventually love her. She was one of the few fairly close relatives I had left. "All right," I said. "I'll answer the doctor's questions."

The doctor was called to the free-standing microphone. He was a tall red-haired man with freckles, the first redhead I could recall seeing. "Do you have any pain, Shori?" he asked. "Have any of the injuries you suffered caused you any difficulties?"

"I have no pain now," I said. "I did before my injuries healed, of course, but they've healed completely except for my memory."

"Do you remember your injuries? Can you describe them?"

I thought back unhappily. "I was burned over most of my body, my face, my head. My head was not only burned, but . . . the bones of my skull were broken so that in two places my head felt . . . felt almost soft when I touched it. I was blind. It hurt to breathe. Well, it hurt to do anything at all. I could move, but my coordination was bad at first. That's all."

The doctor stared at me, and his expression went from disbelieving to a look that I could only describe as hungry. Odd to see a human being look that way. Just for an instant, he looked the way Ina do when we're very, very hungry. He got himself under control after a moment and managed to look only mildly interested. "How long did it take these injuries to heal?" he asked.

"I'm not sure," I said. "I slept a lot at first, when the pain let me sleep. I was mostly aware of the pain. I remember all that happened once I was able to leave the cave, but I'm not sure about some of what went on before that."

"But you remember killing and eating Hugh Tang?"

I drew back and stared at the man, wondering how much of what he asked was what he had been told to ask. Were Joan and I wrong? Was the doctor having fun? "I've said that I remember killing and eating Hugh Tang," I said.

He looked uncomfortable. "Could you tell us," he said, "about anything at all that you've been able to remember of your life before you were injured."

"I recall nothing of my past before the cave," I said, as though I hadn't said it a dozen times the night before.

"Does this trouble you?" he asked.

"Of course it does."

"What is your answer to it, then? Do you simply accept your memory loss?"

"I have no choice. I am relearning the things that I should know about myself and my people."

"Do you feel yourself to be a different person because of your loss?"

I had an almost overwhelming impulse to scream at him. Instead, I kept silent until I could manage my voice. Then I spoke carefully into the microphone. "My childhood is gone. My families are gone. My first symbionts are gone. Most of my education is gone. The first fifty-three years of my life are gone. Is that what you mean by 'a different person'?"

He hesitated.

Russell Silk said, "It isn't yet your time to question. Answer the symbiont's question."

I ignored him and spoke to the doctor. "Have I answered your question?"

He did not move, but now he looked very uncomfortable. He did not meet my gaze. "Yes," he said. "Yes, you have."

The doctor went on to ask several more questions that I had already answered in one way or another. By the time he ran out of questions, I thought he looked more than a little ashamed of himself. His manner seemed mildly apologetic, and I was feeling sorry for him again. How had he happened to wind up in one of the Silk households?

"Is the doctor boring you, Shori?" Russell asked, surprising me. He didn't like addressing me directly. It was a family trait.

I said, "I'm sure he's doing exactly what you've instructed him to do."

"I have no more questions," the doctor said. He was a neurologist, Carmen told me later, a doctor who specializes in diseases and disorders of the central nervous system. No wonder he had been so interested in my injuries. I wondered whether he hated the Silks.

Finally, it was my turn to ask questions. I used my turn to call Russell's sons and their unmated young-adult sons to the microphone for questioning. I asked each of them whether they had known that anyone in their family was arranging to kill the Petrescu and Matthews families.

Alan Silk, one of the younger sons of Russell and his brothers, was my best subject—a good-looking, 180-year-old male who hadn't learned much so far about lying successfully but who insisted on lying.

"I know nothing about the killing of those families," he said in response to my question. "My family had nothing to do with any of that. We would never take part in such things."

I ignored this. "Did you help other members of your family collect humans in Los Angeles or in Pasadena, humans who were later used to kill the Matthews and the Petrescus?"

"I did not! None of us did. In fact, I wouldn't be surprised to learn that your male and female families destroyed each other."

Russell winced, but Alan didn't see it because he was glaring at me.

"Is that what you believe?" I asked. "Do you believe that my mothers and sisters and my father and brothers killed one another?"

He began to look uncomfortable. "Maybe," he muttered. "I don't know."

"You don't know what you believe?"

He glared at me. "I believe my family had nothing to do with what happened, that's what I believe. My family is honorable and it's Ina!"

"Do you believe that my families killed each other?"

He looked around angrily, glancing at his new advocate, Ion Andrei, who had apparently decided not to get into this particular foolish argument. "I don't know what they did," he muttered angrily. He held his hands in front of him, one clutching the other.

I sighed. "All right," I said. "Let's see what you believe about something else. Several humans were used to kill my families. How do you feel about that? Are humans just tools for us to use whenever we find a use for them?"

"No!" he said. "Of course not." He looked at me with contempt. "No true Ina could even ask such a question." He suddenly swung his arms at his sides, then held them in front of him again, as though he didn't know what to do with them.

"What are human, then. What are they to you?"

He stopped glaring at me and looked uncertainly at Russell.

Russell said, "What do his opinions of humans have to do with the deaths of your families?"

"Humans were used as the killer's surrogates," I said. "What do you think of using them that way?"

"Me?" Russell asked.

"You," I said.

"Have you finished questioning Alan, then?"

"I haven't. But you did jump in and it's my time to ask questions. You've had yours. If you would like, though, I will question you as soon as I finish with Alan."

He looked both confused and annoyed. Since he didn't seem to know what to say, I returned my attention to Alan.

"Are humans tools, then? Should we be free to use them according to our needs?"

"Of course not!"

"Is it wrong to send humans out to kill Ina and their symbionts?"

"Of course it's wrong!"

"Do you know anyone who has ever done that?"

"No!" He almost shouted the word. The sound of his own voice magnified by the microphone seemed to startle him, and he was silent for a moment. Then he repeated, "No. Of course not. No."

Every one of his responses to my questions about humans were lies. I suspected that his brothers lied when I questioned them. I wanted to believe they were lying. But my senses told me that Alan, with his little twitches and his false outrage . . . Alan was definitely lying.

If I could see it, anyone on the Council could see it.

## twenty-seven

When the second night of the Council ended, I was exhausted and yet restless. I wasn't hungry, and I couldn't have slept. I needed to run. I thought if I circled the community, running as fast as I could, I might burn off some of my tension.

I got up from my table and joined my symbionts. I walked outside with them, and we headed back toward the guest house.

"What's to stop Katharine Dahlman from escaping?" Wright asked. "She could decide to join her symbiont in Texas or wherever he is."

"She won't run," Joel said. "She's got too much pride. She won't shame herself or her family by running. Besides . . ." He paused. I glanced back at him. "Besides," he said to me, "she might believe that she has a better chance of surviving if she stays here and takes her punishment."

I said nothing. I only looked at him.

He shrugged.

At the guest house, the four of them went straight to the kitchen. While they were preparing themselves a meal, I went out to run. I didn't begin to feel right until I'd had done not one, but three laps around the community. I was the only one running. Everyone else, Ina and human, had trudged back to their meals and their beds.

When I came in, I avoided the kitchen and dining room where I could hear all four of my symbionts and the six Rappaport symbionts moving around, talking, eating. I went upstairs and took a shower. I was planning to spend the night with Joel. My custom was that I could taste anyone anytime—a small delight for me and for my symbionts, a pleasure greater than a kiss, but not as intense as feeding or making love. I made sure, though, that I took a complete meal from each of them only every fifth night.

Now it would have to be every fourth. I would soon have to get more symbionts, but how could I think about doing that now?

Dry and dressed in one of Wright's T-shirts, I somehow wound up in Theodora's room. I wasn't thinking. Her scent drew me. I sat down on her bed, then stretched out on it, surrounded by her scent. I closed my eyes, and it was as though she would come through the door any minute and see me there and look at me in her sidelong way and come onto the bed with me, laughing.

A couple of nights after she arrived, she had found me reading one of Hayden's books written in Ina, and I'd read parts of it to her, first in Ina, then in English. She had been fascinated and wanted me to teach her to read and speak Ina. She said that if she was going to have a longer life span than she had expected, she might as well do something with it. I liked the idea of teaching her because it would force me to go back to the basics of the language, and I hoped that might help me remember a little about the person I had been when I learned it.

I lay there and got lost in Theodora's scent and in grief.

I must have stayed lost for some time, lying on the bed, twisted in the bedding.

Then Joel was there with me, taking the bedding from around me, raising me to my feet, taking me to his room. I looked around the room, then at Joel. He put me on the bed, then got in beside me.

After a while, it occurred to me to say, "Thank you."

"Sleep," he said. "Or feed now if you like."

"Later."

"I'll be here."

I turned and leaned up on my elbow to looked down at his face.

"What?" he asked.

I shook my head. "Why did you want me?" I asked.

"What?"

"You know what I am, what I can do. Why didn't you escape us when you could have? You could have stayed in school or gotten a job. The Gordons would have let you go."

He slipped his arms around me and pulled me down against him. "I like who you are," he said. "And I can deal with what you can do." He hesitated. "Or are you thinking about Theodora? Are you feeling responsible for what happened to her? Do you believe that she was killed because she was with you, and so why the hell would I want to be with you?"

I nodded. "She *was* killed because she was with me. She trusted me. Her death is not my doing directly, but I should have left her in Washington, where she was safe, until all this was over. I knew that. I missed her so much, though, and I had to have more symbionts here with me."

"If she hadn't been here, one of the rest of us would have died," he said. "Theodora was probably the weakest of us, the easiest to kill, but I'll bet if she hadn't been here, Katharine would have sent her man after Brook or Celia."

I nodded. "I know."

"Katharine's guilty. Not you."

I nodded against his shoulder and repeated, "I know." After a while, I said, "You knew much more than most would-be symbionts. You really should have stayed away, made a life for yourself in the human world."

"I might have gone away if you hadn't turned up. You're not only a lovely little thing, but you're willing to ask me questions."

Instead of just ordering him around, yes. That would be important to a symbiont, to anyone. "I won't always ask," I admitted.

"I know," he said. He kissed me. "I want this life, Shori. I've never wanted any other. I want to live to be two hundred years old, and I want all the pleasure I know you can give me. I want to live disease free and strong, and never get feeble or senile. And I want you. You know I want you."

In fact, he wanted me right then. At once. His hunger ignited mine, and in spite of everything, I did still need to feed. I wanted him.

I lost myself in his wonderful scent. Blindly, I found his neck and bit him deeply before I fully realized what I was doing. I hadn't been so confused and disoriented since I awoke in the cave. I needed more blood than I usually did. He held me even though I took no care with him. Afterward, when I was fully aware, I was both ashamed and concerned.

I raised myself above him and looked down at him. He gave me a sideways smile—a real smile, not just patient suffering. But still . . . I put my face down against his chest. "I'm sorry," I said.

He laughed. "You know you don't have anything to apologize for." He pulled the blanket up around us, rolled us over, and slipped into me.

I kissed his throat and licked his neck where it was still bleeding.

Sometime later, as we lay together, sated, but still taking pleasure in the feel of skin against skin, I said, "You're mine. Did you know that? You're scent is so enticing, and I've nibbled on you so often. You're mine."

He laughed softly—a contented, gentle sound. "I thought I might be," he said.

◉        ◉        ◉

That afternoon, we were all awake and restless, so Celia suggested we get away from Punta Nublada for a while and take a drive, have a pic-nic—a meal to be eaten outside and away from so many strangers. I liked the idea. It was a chance for us to get to know one another a little bet-ter and a chance to think beyond the last Council night.

While I added my hooded jacket, gloves, and sunglasses to my usual jeans and T-shirt, the four of them prepared a meal from the refrigera-tor. Celia told me I looked as though I were about to go out into the dead of winter.

"Aren't you hot?" she asked.

"I'm not," I said. "The weather is cool. I'll be fine." They felt changes in the weather more than I did.

They took me at my word and packed their food and some cold soda and beer in the Styrofoam cooler that we had bought for our night in the woods in Washington. They had made sandwiches from leftover turkey, roast beef, and cheddar cheese, and took along a few bananas, some red seedless grapes, and the remains of a German chocolate cake. We all fit comfortably in Celia and Brook's car, and Brook drove us out to the highway and then northward toward a place Joel knew about.

We chose a space on the bluffs overlooking the ocean where there was a flat patch of grass and bare rock to sit on and from where we could watch the waves pounding the beach and the rocks below. Brook had thought ahead enough to bring along a blanket and a pair of large towels from the guest house linen closet. Now she spread them on the ground for us, sat down on one of the towels, and began eating a thick turkey-and-cheddar sandwich. The others took food from the cooler and sat around eating and drinking and speculating about whether the Silk symbionts hated their Ina.

"I think they do," Celia said. "They must. I would if I had to put up with those people."

"They don't," Brook said. "I met one of them when they first arrived. She's a historian. She writes books—novels under one name and popular history under another. She says she couldn't have found a better place to wind up. She says Russell's generation and even Milo help her get the little details right, especially in the fiction. She says she likes working with them. Maybe she's unusual, but I didn't get the feeling that she resented them."

Joel said, "I think that doctor who questioned Shori yesterday joined them so he could learn more about what they are and what makes them tick. I wonder what questions he would have asked if he'd had a choice."

"He's definitely hungry to know more," I said. "He wants to understand how we survive terrible injuries, how we heal."

Joel nodded and took a second roast-beef sandwich. "I wonder what he'd do if he discovered something, some combination of genes, say, that produced substances that caused rapid healing. Who would he tell?"

"No one," I said. "The Silks would never let him tell anyone."

"Maybe he just wants it for himself," Wright said. "Maybe he just wants to be able to heal the way Shori did."

I shook my head. "I don't believe anyone would want to go through a healing like that. I can't begin tell you what the pain was like."

They all looked at me, and I realized that the doctor wasn't the only one who wanted to heal the way I did.

I spread my hands. "I'm sharing the ability with you in the only way I can," I said. "You're already better at healing than you were."

They nodded and opened more food, soda, and tall brown bottles of beer.

After a while I said, "I have to ask you something, and I need you to think about the question and be honest." I paused and looked at each of them. "Have any of you had a problem with either of the Braithwaites or their symbionts?" I asked.

There was silence. Brook had lain down on her back on her towel and closed her eyes, but she was not dozing. Celia was sitting next to Joel, glancing at him now and then. Her scent let me know that she was very much attracted to him. He, on the other hand, was glancing at Wright who had sat down next to me, taken my gloved hand, kissed it, bit it a little as he looked at me, then held it between his own hands. He was showing off. And for the moment, I was letting him get away with it.

"The Braithwaites," Celia said. "Joan could cut glass with that tongue of hers, but I think she's really okay. She just says what she means."

"Are you thinking about moving in with the Braithwaites?" Joel asked.

"I am, yes, for a while . . . if they'll have me. That's why I'm asking all of you whether you've seen anything or know anything against them. If you have reason to want to avoid them, tell me now."

"I like them," Joel said. "They're strong, decent people, not bigots like the Silks and the Dahlmans and a couple of the other Council members."

"I barely know the Braithwaites," Brook said. "I danced with one of their symbionts at a party." She smiled. "He was okay, and I got the impression he was happy, that he liked being their symbiont. That's usually a good sign."

I got the impression she thought the Braithwaite symbiont was more than just "okay." Brook might wind up enjoying our stay with the Braithwaites more than the rest of us—if the Braithwaites agreed to let me visit them for a while.

"So you're not thinking of trying to get them to adopt you?" Joel asked.

"I don't believe I want to be adopted," I said. "I can't remember my female family at all, but I'm part of them. I can learn about them and see that their memory is continued by continuing their family. If I'm adopted, my female family vanishes into history just like my male family did. And I've promised to mate with the Gordons." I thought of Daniel and almost smiled. "I don't know whether that will happen, but I hope it will, and I'm not going to do anything to prevent it."

"So you'll wind up having six or eight children all by yourself," Wright said. "Is that the way it will be?"

"Eventually," I said. "But I'm thinking about doing what Hayden said last night—adopting a relative, a young girl from a family with too many girls. That way there will be two of us. Preston says I can't do that until I'm an adult myself, although I can look around. I hope to be able to live with several different families and learn what they can teach me. I'll read their books, listen to their elders."

"You're trying to get yourself an education," Joel said.

I nodded. "I have to re-educate myself. Right now, you probably know more about Ina history and about being Ina than I do. I have to learn. Problem is, I don't know what my re-education will cost."

He smiled. "Better ask," he said. "Although, actually, I think Joan will tell you whether you ask or not. Learning is good, though. My father made sure I picked up as much education as I could even before I went off to college. From what Hayden has told me, I'm one of maybe a few hundred humans in the world who can speak and read Ina."

And Theodora would have been another, I thought.

"It will be a while before we have a home," I said. "But as my families' affairs are sorted out, and we begin to have more money, you'll be able to have the things you want and do what you want to do. Maybe one of you wants to write books or learn another language or learn woodworking or real estate." I smiled. "Whatever you like. And there will be more of you. At least three more, eventually."

"Seven people," Wright said. "I understand the need, but I don't like it."

"I like the idea of moving around for a while," Brook said. "When I was with Iosif, we didn't travel much at all. Except for elders going to Councils of one kind or another, most adult Ina do very little traveling, probably because traveling is such a production, with so many people needing to travel together. I'm definitely ready to do some traveling."

"Once you've traveled for a while, you'll probably be ready to settle down again pretty fast," Celia said. "My father was in the army while I was growing up. We moved all the time. As soon as I made friends or began to like a school, we were gone again. This sounds as though it will be like that. Meet a friend, spot a nice guy, start a project, then you're on your way somewhere else."

"We'll be staying mostly with female families, won't we?" Wright asked.

"We will," I said. "If it doesn't cause trouble, we'll pay short visits to the Gordons and the Leontyevs, but as I understand it, my pheromones are going to give males more and more trouble as I approach adulthood."

"Bound to be true," Wright growled into my ear. The growl made my whole body tingle.

"Stop that," I said, laughing, and he laughed, too.

"So all we have to do," Celia said, "is get through tonight. Then we can get on with our lives."

⊙    ⊙    ⊙

I talked with Margaret Braithwaite that evening. I went to her office-bedroom before the third night of the Council could begin.

"Shori, you shouldn't ask me about this now," she said. "You should have waited until judgment was passed and the Council had concluded its business."

I had found her looking through a book she'd borrowed from Hayden. I hadn't seen her borrow it, but the book smelled deeply of him and only a little of her. One of his older Ina histories.

"Why should I have waited?" I asked. "Have I broken some rule?"

"Oh, no. No rule. It's just that . . . It's just that you might not want to come to us once you hear the judgment."

I thought about that. It seemed impossible that anyone had failed to hear the lies that the Silks and Katharine Dahlman had told. The elders were much more experienced than I was in reading the signs.

"Is it possible that the Council members will fail to see what the Silks have done?" I asked.

"It is not possible," she said. "The problem isn't their guilt and Katharine's. The problem is what to do about it. What punishment to impose?"

"They killed twelve Ina—all of my male and female families—and nearly a hundred symbionts. From what I've heard, none of the people they killed had ever harmed them. How can they be allowed to get away with what they've done?"

"You want them to die."

"I want them to die."

"Would you help kill them?"

I stared back at her. "I would."

She sighed. "They'll die, Shori, but not in the quick satisfying way you probably hope for. That won't happen—except, perhaps, in Katharine's case. She and her family haven't been good about maintaining friendships and alliances. Very stupid of them. But the Silk family will not be killed today."

"Why?"

"Because as terrible as their crimes are, I don't believe the Council vote will be unanimous. Understand, I'm telling you what I believe, not what I know. I might be wrong, although I doubt it. The Council won't want to wipe out an ancient and once-respected family. They'll want to give them a chance to survive."

I didn't say anything for a while. I hated Katharine Dahlman. I would see her dead sooner or later, no matter what anyone said. I hated the Silks, too, but it was a different, less immediate hate. They had killed people I no longer knew, and they had killed without knowing me. I wanted to see the Silks dead, but I didn't *need* to see them dead in the way that I needed to see Katharine dead. That wasn't the way I should have felt, but it was the way I did feel.

I said, "Daniel told me that the Silks' unmated sons might be taken from them and adopted by other families."

Joan nodded. "I think that will happen. If it does, the word will be spread tonight by mail, by phone, and by e-mail to all the world's Ina communities. I'm glad Daniel let you know what could happen."

"What if the Silks decide to come after me again? I was their main target all along because I was the one in whom the human genetic mix worked best. They killed so many just to get to me."

"They have the possibility of rebuilding their family if Russell's sons' generation can convince their mates to try to have more children. They will lose that opportunity if they make another attempt on your life or on the lives of your people—even if they fail. If they try again, they will be killed."

I looked at her for several seconds. "You truly believe this will stop them from secretly trying kill me or perhaps trying to kill my children in the future?"

"Ina are linked worldwide, Shori. If the Silks give their word—and they must give it if they are to leave here alive—and then break it, they will all be killed and any new sons adopted away. Their family will vanish. They know this."

"Then . . . will you permit me to come to you with my symbionts, learn from you for a while, work for you to pay our way?"

She sighed. "For how long?"

I hesitated. "One year. Perhaps two."

"Come back to me when the Council has finished with its business. I believe that we will welcome you, but I can't answer until I've spoken with my sister."

There was a formal feel to all this—as though we had spoken ritual words. Had we? I would find out eventually.

"What about Katharine?" I asked.

She shook her head. "I don't know."

"I don't believe I could let her go."

"Wait and see."

"Theodora wasn't even a person to Katharine. She was just something Katharine could snatch away from me to make me weaker."

"I know. Don't give her what she wants. Wait, Shori. Wait and see."

# twenty-eight

There were no parties on the night of the third Council session. The hall was so full that there was not enough seating for everyone. People stood or brought chairs from the houses. No one seemed to want to sit on the concrete floor. Seats had been roped off for my symbionts in front, as had seats on the opposite side of the hall for the Silks and their symbionts.

The members of the Council seated themselves as usual, in the same order, and when they were all settled, Preston stood up. This was everyone's signal to be quiet and pay attention. Preston waited until silence had worked its way from the front to the back of the room. Then he said, "Russell Silk, do you have anything further to say or any more questions to ask of Shori Matthews or of anyone that you or she has asked to speak to this Council?"

This was Russell's last chance to speak, to defend his family, and to make me look bad. Of course, anyone he called, I could question, too.

Russell stood up. "I have no one else to call," he said, holding his microphone, looking out toward the audience. Then he turned and faced the Council. "I suppose in a sense, I call on all of you to remember that my family has maintained good and honorable friendships with many of you. Remember that the Silk family helped some of you immigrate to this country in times of war or political chaos in your former homes. Remember that in all the time you've known us, we have not lied to you or cheated you.

"What matters most to us, to every member of the Silk family, is the welfare of the Ina people. We Ina are vastly outnumbered by the human beings of this world. And how many of us have been butchered in their wars? They destroy one another by the millions, and it makes no difference to their numbers. They breed and breed and breed, while we live long and breed slowly. Their lives are brief and, without us, riddled with disease and violence. And yet, we need them. We take them into our families, and with our help, they are able to live longer, stay free of disease, and get along with one another. We could not live without them.

"But we are not them!

"We are not them!

"Children of the great Goddess, we are not them!"

He shook with the intensity of his feeling. He had to take several breaths before he could continue. "We are not them," he whispered. "Nor should we try to be them. Ever. Not for any reason. Not even to gain the day; the cost is too great."

He stood for a second longer in silence, then sat down and put his microphone back on its stand. The room had gone completely silent.

Once he sat down, Preston broke the silence. "Shori, is there anyone you would like to question or anything you would like to say?"

"I have questions," I said, standing up with my microphone. I had thought of something as Russell spoke—something prompted by what he had said and by my having seen Joan Braithwaite reading a history book just a short while ago. It seemed to me that Russell had just admitted that his family had killed my families. He wanted us to believe that he had done it for a good reason. I said to Preston, "I want to ask you a few questions, if that's all right."

Preston looked surprised. "All right. Russell questioned me so I do qualify as someone you can question now."

I nodded. "I ask this because of my limited knowledge of Ina law. Preston, is there a legal, nonlethal way of questioning someone's behavior? I mean, if I believed that you were doing something that could be harmful to other Ina, would I be able to bring it to the attention of a council of some kind or some other group?"

Preston did not smile, did not change expression at all, but I got the impression he was pleased with me. "There is," he said. "If you believed I were doing something to the detriment of the Ina, something that was not exactly against law, but that you seriously believed was harmful, you could ask for a Council of the Goddess."

Russell snatched up his microphone and protested. "Council of the . . . That hasn't been done for at least twenty-five hundred years."

"You are aware of it, then?" I asked him.

"It wouldn't have been taken seriously. No one's done it for two thousand—"

"Did you try?"

"Your families made no secret of the fact that they didn't even believe in the Goddess!"

From the hypothetical to the real. Careless of him. "Would that have mattered?" I asked. "Could my family have ignored a call to take part in a Council of the Goddess?"

Russell said nothing. Perhaps he had remembered where he was and exactly what was being argued.

"Preston, would it have mattered?"

"The rule of seven would apply," Preston answered. "If the rule of seven is satisfied and the accused family refuses to attend, the Council would be carried on regardless of its absence. The family would be bound by any vote of the Council, as though it had been present. If the family were ordered to stop whatever they were doing, and they refused to stop, they would be punished."

I stared across at Russell. "Preston, has the Silk family ever tried to assemble a Council of the Goddess to discuss or warn against the genetic work of my eldermothers?"

"Not to my knowledge," Preston said. "Russell?"

Again, Russell said nothing. It didn't matter. Surely he had already said enough. I sat down and put my microphone back in its place.

"Does any Council member have questions?" Preston asked.

No one spoke.

"All right," he said. "Council members, I ask you now to count yourselves. Is the Silk family guilty of having made human beings their tools and sent those human tools to kill the Petrescu and the Matthews families? Are the Silks also guilty of sending their tools to burn the Petrescu guest house where Shori Matthews and her symbionts were staying? Are the Silks guilty of sending their tools to attack the Gordon family here at Punta Nublada? And also, was Katharine Dahlman, the Silks' first advocate, guilty of sending one of her symbionts, Jack Roan, to kill one of Shori

Matthews's symbionts, Theodora Harden?" He paused, then said, "Zoë Fotopoulos?"

I had decided that Zoë was the most beautiful Ina I had ever seen. Her age—over three hundred—didn't seem to matter. She was tall, lean, and blond like most Ina but was a striking, memorable woman. When she arrived, I had asked Wright what he thought of her. He said, "Sculpted. Perfect, like one of those Greek statues. If she had boobs, I'd say she was the best-looking woman I've ever seen."

Poor Wright. Maybe one of the Braithwaite symbionts would have large breasts.

"Shori Matthews has told us the truth," Zoë said. "I have not once caught her in a lie. Either she has been very careful or she is exactly what she seems to be. My impression is that she is exactly what she appears to be—a child, deeply wronged by both the Silk family and Katharine Dahlman. Members of the Silk family, on the other hand, have lied again and again. And Katharine Dahlman has lied. It seems that all this killing was done because Shori's families were experimenting with ways of using human DNA to enable us to walk in daylight. And it seems that no legal methods of questioning or stopping the experiments were even attempted." She took a deep breath. "I stand with Shori against both the Silks and Katharine Dahlman."

"Joan Braithwaite?" Preston said.

"Shori told the truth, and Katharine and the Silks lied," Joan said. "That's all that matters. I must stand with Shori against both."

"Alexander Svoboda?"

"I stand with Shori against Katharine Dahlman," he said. "But I must stand with the Silks against Shori. Shori has told the truth, as far as she knows, as far as she is able to understand with her damaged memory, but I can't condemn the Silks as a family because of what one child, one seriously impaired child, believes."

And yet, every Silk who had spoken to the Council had lied about what he had done, about what he knew, or both. How could Katharine Dahlman be punished for killing one symbiont and the Silks let off for killing twelve Ina and nearly a hundred symbionts? But that was Alexander's less than courageous decision.

"Peter Marcu?" Preston said.

"I stand with Shori," Peter Marcu said. "I don't want to. My family has been friends with the Silks for four generations. There was even a time when we got along well with the Dahlmans. But Shori has been telling the truth all along, and the others have been lying. Whatever their reasons are for what they've done, they did do it, and for the sake of the rest of our people and all our symbionts, we cannot allow this to go unpunished."

"Ana Morariu?"

"I stand with the Silks and with Katharine Dahlman," Ana said. "Shori Matthews is much too impaired to be permitted to speak against other Ina. How can we destroy people's lives, even kill them on the word of a child whose mind has been all but destroyed and who, even if she were healthy, is barely Ina at all? It is a tragedy that the Petrescu and Matthews families are dead. We shouldn't deepen the tragedy by killing or disrupting other families."

She was the one who had said Katharine Dahlman might be telling the truth. Now she seemed to be saying that my families had simply been unlucky and had, for some unknown reason, died, and that it would be wrong to punish anyone for that. Nothing wrong, she seemed to think, with letting your friends get away with mass murder.

"Alice Rappaport?"

"I stand with Shori," Alice said. "Katharine and the Silks are liars, people who use murder but never think to use the law. They know better than anyone here that we can't let them go unpunished. And what about the rest of you? Do you want to return to a world of lawless family feuds and mass killing?"

"Harold Westfall?"

"I stand with Shori," Harold said. "To let this go would be to endanger us all in the long run. Both the Silks and Katharine must be punished for what we all know they've done."

He glanced at me unhappily. I got the impression he didn't want to be here. He didn't want to stand with me. I suspected he didn't even like me much. But he was doing his duty and trying to do it as honestly as he could. I respected that and was grateful for it.

"Kira Nicolau."

"I stand with Shori as far as Katharine is concerned," Kira said. "What Katharine did was completely wrong, and I have no doubt that she did it. I don't believe she even meant to convince us otherwise; it just didn't seem very important to her. But as to the other problem, I must stand with the Silks. I don't believe Shori's memories and accusations should be trusted. I'm not convinced that Shori understands the situation as well as she believes she does. She believes what she says, that's clear. In that sense, she is telling the truth. But like Alexander, I'm not willing to disrupt or destroy the Silk family on the word of someone as disabled as Shori Matthews clearly is."

Nothing about the lies the Silks had told. Nothing about my dead families. And yet, Kira herself was telling the truth as far as I could see. She really seemed to believe that I was so impaired that I didn't know what I was talking about. She had somehow convinced herself of that.

"Ion Andrei?"

There was a moment of silence. Finally Ion said, "I stand with the Silks and with Katharine. I don't want to. I believe the Silks may have murdered Shori's families. It's certainly possible. And Katharine may have sent her symbiont after Shori's symbiont. But, like Kira, I cannot in good conscience base such a judgment on the words of someone as disabled as Shori is."

It was painful to listen to them. I wanted to scream at them. How could they blind all their senses so selectively? And how could they see me as so impaired? Maybe they needed to see me that way. Maybe it helped them deal with their conscience.

"Walter Nagy?"

"I stand with Shori," Walter said. "And I would stand with her even if she were out of her mind because it is so painfully obvious that the Silks and Katharine Dahlman were lying almost every time they answered a question. They have committed murder and, in the case of the Silks, mass murder. If we excuse that in those we like, we open a door that we tried to lock tight centuries ago. Make no mistake. If we ignore these murders, we invite people to settle disputes themselves, and we risk exposure in the human world. We are, every one of us, vulnerable to the fires that consumed Shori's families."

There was a moment of silence. Finally, Preston said, "Elizabeth Akhmatova?"

"I stand with Shori," Elizabeth said. "For all the reasons Walter's just given, I stand with her. And I stand with her because I've watched her. She *is* impaired. I can't imagine what it would be like to lose the memory of nearly all of the years of one's life. Her memory was stolen from her. But her ability to reason wasn't stolen. The questions she's asked—questions that were answered again and again with lies and misdirection—were good, sensible questions. The questions she answered, she answered honestly. The murderers who killed her families and her symbiont, the thieves who stole her past from her—should these people be rewarded because they did such a savagely thorough job? No, of course not. Shori, on the other hand, should be rewarded for using her intellect to protect herself and to find the murderers."

# twenty-nine

And that was that.

There was a moment of silence, then Preston stood up. "The decision is made," he said.

"A majority of seven members of this eleven-member Council of Judgment have stood with Shori Matthews and against both Katharine Dahlman and the Silk family. Therefore, Katharine Dahlman and the Silk family must be punished for the wrongs they have done. But because the decision was not unanimous, their punishment must be other than death.

"For the wrongs the Silk family has done—for their complete destruction of the Petrescu family, for their nearly complete destruction of the Matthews family, and for their attempted destruction of the Gordon family—the penalty, by written law, is the dissolution of the Silk family. The five unmated Silk sons must be adopted by five families in five countries other than the United States of America. Each will mate as the males of his new family mate. They will be Silk no longer."

The room was utterly silent. Even the Silks made no sound. I wondered how they could keep silent. Was it pride? Was it pain? Were they refusing to believe the sentence or only refusing to let others see their pain? I looked across the room at Russell Silk.

He stared back at me with utter hatred. If he could have killed me, I think he would have done it with pleasure. I realized coldly that I felt the same toward him. If he came after me and I could kill him, I would—joyfully.

Preston said, "Russell, you've heard your family's sentence."

Russell managed to turn away from me and direct his hateful stare at Preston.

"Stand," Preston ordered.

Russell made no move to rise. He turned to look at me again. He looked as though he wanted to kill me so badly that it was hurting him.

"Russell Silk," Preston said in that big, deep, clear voice of his. "Stand," he said, "Stand and speak for yourself and your family."

Russell Silk rose slowly, and I watched him. He was at the very edge of his control. If he lost control, he would certainly come for me. He was half again my height and easily twice my weight—an adult Ina male. Not a deer. But he was old. Perhaps not as fast as a deer. Watching him, I decided I could ride him. I could be on him before he could stop me. I could tear out his throat. It wouldn't kill him, although my venom might tame him for me, make him obey. If it didn't, it would surely slow him down, give me a chance to twist his head right off. No one could recover from that. I could do that. I could.

"You must accept the sentence," Preston said. "Then each member of your family must stand and accept it. By your acceptance, you give your word, each of you, that there will be peace between the Silks and the Matthews, peace between the Silks and the Gordons, peace for a period of at least three hundred years from today."

Preston paused, his eyes on Russell as intently as mine were. "The penalty for refusing to accept your sentence or for breaking your word once you've given it is immediate death—death for you, Russell, and for each mated member of your family." He paused and looked at the Silk family waiting in the audience. "Do you accept your sentence?" he demanded.

Russell launched himself toward me.

I stood up and away from the table, ready for him, eager for him. It was like being eager for sex or for feeding.

But before he could reach me, before I could taste his blood, two of his sons and one of his brothers leaped up from the front row, grabbed him, and dragged him down. They held him while he struggled beneath them, screaming. At first, it seemed that he wasn't making words. He was only looking at me and screaming. Then I began to recognize words: "Murdering black mongrel bitch . . ." and "What will she give us all? Fur? Tails?"

He didn't shed tears. I wondered suddenly whether we could cry the way humans did. Russell just lay curled on his side, moaning and choking.

I watched the whole group of Silks, clustered in the first few rows on Russell's side of the room. Milo glared at me, but the others were focused on Russell, who seemed to be slowly regaining his sanity.

Wright and Joel got up and came toward me, but I waved them back to their seats. They couldn't regrow lost parts. Better for them to stay clear.

Milo looked from me to them—a long, slow look. Then he looked at me again. It was an obvious threat.

Daniel Gordon, his fathers, and his brothers came up to stand behind me. In silence, they looked back at Milo.

The pile of Silks on the floor untangled itself, and all four of them stood up. After a moment, Russell went back to his table and stood by it. The rest of his family watched him, as the three who had restrained him went back to their seats.

At the same time, the Gordons behind me melted away and went back to their seats as silently as they had come. I sat down at my table.

Preston repeated in an oddly gentle voice, "Russell Silk, do you accept your sentence?"

It was as though there had been no interruption. Russell looked down at his table, then stared at me. "What is to be done with the Matthews child?" he demanded.

"Nothing at all," Preston said.

"She should be adopted. She's a child. She's ill. She should be looked after, brought into a family that can teach her how to at least pretend to be Ina."

"You created Shori's problems," Preston said. "But solving them is not your concern. Your only concern now is whether you accept your sentence or reject it. Now, for the last time, do you accept your sentence?"

Russell looked at his family—his father, his brothers, his sons, and his five youngersons who would soon be leaving the Silk family to be adopted by others. Adoption was apparently so permanent a thing that there was no possibility of their sneaking back home or uniting as Silks in another country or another part of the United States. For one thing, they would eventually be mated to different families of females. And their sons would never be Silks.

It took Russell almost a full minute to make himself say the words: "I . . . accept . . . the sentence."

"Milo Silk?" Preston said.

Milo stood up. In an ancient, paper-dry voice that I had not heard from him before, he said, "I accept the sentence." Then he sat down again and sagged forward in his chair, staring at the floor, elbows resting on his knees.

Once he had said it, each of the rest of his sons could say it. Then their sons could say it. Finally the youngest, unmated sons—those who were giving their word that they accepted absolute, permanent banishment— could say it. It still seemed wrong to me that they should be the ones to bear the worst of the punishment. Each might never see his fathers or his brothers again, and three of them were children. They were the only ones truly not responsible for what their elders had done to my families.

It occurred to me suddenly that Russell had asked about my being adopted because if I, like his sons, became a member of a different family, he might not be legally forbidden from attacking me. If I were not Shori Matthews, but Shori Braithwaite, for instance, I might be fair game. The Braithwaites might be fair game. I had no intention of being adopted, but I did intend to ask Preston if my suspicions were true.

The Gordons quietly separated the Silks from their unmated sons. The sons' symbionts joined them quickly, and that was a good thing. It would ease their pain to have these loved and needed people with them, people they had probably known most their lives. The sons would be taken from their fathers but not from the humans who were closest to them. In fact, someone would have to collect the rest of their symbionts back at the Silk community and reunite them with their Ina. I was glad to see that one of the son's symbionts was the doctor who had questioned me. It was good that he could be away from the ugly contempt of the adults. The Silk son to whom he was bound was taller than I was, but he looked no older.

The youngest Silks and their symbionts were herded out of the room by several adult Ina—the siblings of those who had served on the Council of Judgment. Perhaps these were the people who would have had to carry out the death sentence if there had been one. Was that the arrangement? One brother or sister passed judgment and the other helped to carry out the sentence?

The adult Silks watched, distraught. Their obvious pain was so much at odds with their utter stillness that it was hard to look at them. They stared at their children, their family's future, walking away, and in that vast room, no one spoke a word.

Then the youngest Silks were gone, and we all sat looking at one another.

Preston coughed—an odd sound from him since he did it to get our attention rather than to clear his throat. "We must also attend to the matter of Katharine Dahlman," he said. He looked at her where she sat near the Silks. "Stand, please, Katharine, and come forward."

Very slowly, she stood up and came to the microphone that stood alone in the arc.

Preston, also standing, faced her. "For the wrong that you've done, Katharine Dahlman—for using your own symbiont, Jack Roan, as a murderous tool, for having him kill Theodora Harden, the symbiont of Shori Matthews—you must, according to written law, have both your legs severed at mid-thigh." He took a breath. "Katharine, do you accept your sentence?"

She leaned forward to speak into the microphone, then had to lower it to her height. "I do not," she said when she had finished. "The punishment is too extreme. It does not fit the minor crime that I committed."

"Minor crime!" I said loudly. "How can murdering a woman who never harmed you, who never even threatened you be a minor crime?"

She didn't even glance at me. "I ask that the members of the Council consider my punishment and count themselves for or against it."

I looked at Preston. I found it intolerable that Katharine would be permitted to live. Now she was whining about having to suffer at all. If she accepted her punishment, in a year or two, she would have legs again and be fine, but Theodora would still be dead. Minor crime?

"I will give up my left hand to pay for my . . . crime," Katharine said. "That's more than justice."

"Or perhaps only a finger!" I said. "Maybe a fingernail would do. But if the penalty is so small, then I should be able to do to you what you did to me. Which of your symbionts shall I take?"

She looked at me with more hatred and contempt than I would have thought she could manage, then she turned away and spoke to Preston. "I demand a count of the Council. I have a right to that."

"There has been a count as to your guilt. Once that vote went against you, your guilt and punishment were decided. You have no right to negotiate, and you know it. You knew the law long before you decided to break it."

She looked away from him, stared past him, and said nothing for several seconds. Finally, she shook her head. "I can't accept it. It's unjust. That human was not a symbiont because Shori is not Ina! And . . . and at my age, the punishment would probably kill me."

What did that mean? Was she saying she thought it was all right to kill innocent human beings who were not symbionts?

Preston hesitated, then spoke gently. "Katharine, this isn't a death sentence. It will be bad. It's supposed to be bad. Consider what you did to earn it. But your family will look after you, and in a year or two, you'll have healed. But refusing the sentence, Katharine . . . that would be death."

She shook her head. "Then kill me! Go ahead. Kill me! I cannot accept the punishment you've ordered."

The two of them, not far apart in age, stared at one another. "We'll take a short break," he said. "Katharine, go talk with your sister and your symbionts. Think about what you're doing." He stepped away from his place at the table and glanced at his silent audience. "We'll resume in one hour."

❂    ❂    ❂

My symbionts hesitated, then came up to me. I didn't know why they hesitated until they stayed back and let Wright be the first to touch me. He took my hand, and when I took his huge hand between both of mine, the others came up to me.

I realized that they were afraid of me. What had I said or done? How had I looked or acted to make these people whom I loved and needed most afraid of me? I stood and hugged each of them, holding Brook for a little longer than the others because she was trembling so.

"The tension in this place is like a bad smell," I said. "Let's go back to the house for a little while."

We left the hall and headed toward the guest house. We weren't talking. I think we all wanted what I had said—a little time away from the anger and hatred and pain in the hall. Joel had put his arm around me and was, I think, deliberately distracting me with his scent. I needed to be distracted. Both he and Brook knew enough about the Ina to do something like that.

I sat with them in the kitchen while they had coffee and cinnamon-apple muffins. Wright was talking about building our first house himself, and the others didn't believe he could do it. I did. I kind of liked the idea.

They dared me to taste the coffee, and I tasted it. It was less appealing than plain water, but not disgusting. I wondered what other human food or drink I could tolerate. When I had more time, I might find out.

We talked for a while longer, then got up and headed back. Suddenly there was confusion and shouting. Not too far ahead of us, people came spilling out of Henry's house. Before I could understand what was going on, Katharine Dahlman was there in front of us. She had run from Henry's house, run faster than a human could, but not that fast for an Ina. She was holding something in front of her, clutched in both hands.

It took a moment for me to understand that she was holding a rifle. She ran ahead of the crowd, then stopped suddenly and leveled the gun at my symbionts and me.

I charged her. I was terrified that she would kill another of my symbionts before I could stop her.

Again, I had not kept them safe.

She fired.

And I felt as though I'd been punched hard, hammered in the stomach by something impossibly strong.

It was as though I hung in midair for an instant, not going forward, not dropping. It didn't happen that way, of course, but I felt as though it did. In fact, my momentum carried me into her. I hit her with my feet, and she started to fall. I hit the rifle with my hand, shoved it upward, and made her next shot go wild. Her weapon was an old bolt-action rifle, perhaps one of those kept handy while the Gordons were worried about being attacked. If it had been automatic like the ones our attackers had used against us, or if Katharine had been quick with it, she might have shot me again before I reached her. She might have battered me down with bullets, then while I was helpless, she could have finished killing me.

Instead, I reached her. As we struggled on the ground I tore the gun from her hands and threw it away. I was surprised that I could. She was an adult and larger than I was, even though she was small for an Ina. I could feel her in my hands as she twisted and tried to push me away, tried to tear herself free of me, tried to bite me.

My own strength was bleeding away. She was winning, holding on to me, pulling me close so that she could bite and tear. With the last of my strength, I rammed my hand upward, hit her hard under the chin, pulled myself up, and bit down hard into the flesh of her throat.

She screamed. Either she was terrified of my getting control of her or her pain overwhelmed her. I had not bitten her for nourishment or out of affection. I meant to destroy her throat, tear it to pieces. She let go of my shoulders to grab my head and push my face away, and in the instant of opportunity that gave me, I went for a better grip on her with my teeth. I bit through her larynx. She would do no more screaming for a while. And I broke her neck—or tried to. I wasn't sure whether I managed it or not because I lost consciousness before the worst of my own pain could catch up with me.

And then it was over.

# epilogue

**I** regained consciousness slowly. It was like struggling up through mud.

I was naked except for one of Wright's big T-shirts. Someone had undressed me and put me to bed. The room was very dark, and I lay alone in bed. I couldn't see well at first. I wasn't in pain from my wound, but I felt weak—weak on a whole different scale from anything I'd felt since the cave. In fact, this felt like awakening in the cave. This time, though, I thought I'd only lost a night or two.

Then I smelled meat somewhere just beyond to bed. I turned toward it, literally starving. My body had used up its resources healing itself and had reached the point of beginning to consume its own muscle tissue as fuel.

I scuttled toward the meat, desperate for it.

Someone said, "Stop, Shori!"

And I stopped. It was Wright. My first.

I pulled back, seeing him now, tall, broad, and shadowy, sitting in a chair next to the bed. I hadn't touched him, wouldn't touch him. I pulled back, away from him, clutching the mattress, whimpering. The hunger was a massive twisting hurt inside me, but I would not touch him. I heard him moving around, then I caught a different scent. Beef. Food.

"Here," he said. "Take it. Eat." He gave me a big dish filled with lean pieces of raw meat. It wasn't as freshly killed as I would have preferred, but it was good enough. I gulped the meat, bit the pieces into smaller chunks, and swallowed them barely chewed, then gulped more. I finished the platter and grabbed the new one that Wright offered me, gulping much of it, then, with growing contentment, finishing the rest more slowly, actually chewing before I swallowed, feeling almost content, finally content.

I put the platter down, leaned back against the headboard, and sighed. "Thank you," I said. "But next time—if this ever happens again—don't stay with me. Just leave the meat."

"I don't see where you put it all," he said. "You're so small. If you were human, I'd expect you to be sick after eating like that."

"I was sick—from the need to eat."

"I know but ... oh, it doesn't matter. I'm just grateful you're all right."

"You shouldn't have been here," I told him again. I shook my head, tried to shake off the memory of Hugh Tang. "How could the Gordons let you stay here with me?"

"They didn't," he said. "They said we should put the meat in a cooler and leave it in here with you. They said none of us should go in, that we should wait until you came out."

"You should have."

He put something in my hands. It turned out to be several disposable wipes. I used them to clean my hands and face. Then he poured water from a pitcher into a glass and handed me the glass. I had seen neither the pitcher nor the glass until he picked them up from the night table. I was focused on him—his scent, the sound of his heartbeat, his breathing, his voice. It was so good to have him nearby even though he shouldn't have been.

I took the glass and drank. "Thank you," I said. "Why did you disobey the Gordons? You know what I could have done."

"I'm not Hugh Tang," he said. "And you didn't have a head wound this time. I knew you wouldn't hurt me."

I stared at him, amazed and angry. "You don't understand. The hunger is so terrible ... Even without a head wound, I might have killed you."

"You stopped the instant I spoke. I don't believe you would have touched me. In fact, without the head injury, I don't think you would have touched anyone else who had the presence of mind to speak to you. I was pretty sure I was safe here."

"You don't know what it's like to be so ... so hungry."

He put his hand on my arm. "I don't. And I wish you hadn't had to go through it. I know you were afraid Katharine was going to shoot one of us." Very slowly, he gathered me to him. I let him because it felt so good, so completely comfortable to rest against him.

"Are the others all right?" I asked, knowing they were. His manner would have been very different if someone had been badly injured. Or killed.

He smiled. "They're fine. They're worried about you. They've been sitting with you when I had to take breaks. It's been three nights. Preston told us it would be at least three nights. Hayden said it would more likely be five or six nights, but Joel said that for Ina medical problems, you can just about always trust Preston."

I shook my head, amazed, thinking about what could have happened. What if I had awakened and scared Celia or Brook or attacked them because they tried to run away? "I'm glad I woke when you were here."

"Me too."

"And . . . what about Katharine?"

"Dead. Wells and Manning took care of it since executions are the business of the host family. They can do it themselves or bring in other families to help. But this time they didn't need help. They beheaded her, then burned both the head and the body. She might have healed from what you did to her. Her throat was already beginning to. But she refused to accept the judgment against her. She preferred death. She said she was just sorry she couldn't take you with her. Her sister Sophia accepted the judgment on behalf of the Dahlman family. Preston says that means we won't have to worry about them coming after us."

"Good. I hope that promise is as good as the Gordons think it is."

"I asked Hayden about that. He's kind of the Gordons' historian. He said we shouldn't worry, that not many people want to risk sacrificing the lives of their whole adult family to violate a judgment. It's supposed to be a matter of honor, anyway. He said the Dahlmans aren't a likable family, but it seems that they are, by their own standards, an honorable one. Sophia Dahlman is the oldest of them now, and she's given her word. They'll keep it."

I sighed. "I wonder how you can be honorable and still kill the innocent?"

"Don't know," he said. "They're your people."

I looked up at him. "We'll have to learn about them together."

"Well," he said, "Katharine was the guilty one, and now she's dead."

He was right. That's what mattered Theodora was avenged and the rest of my symbionts were safe. What about my mothers and sisters, my father and brothers? What about my memory?

They were all gone. The person I had been was gone. I couldn't bring anyone back, not even myself. I could only learn what I could about the Ina, about my families. I would restore what could be restored. The Matthews family could begin again. The Petrescu family could not.

"All the Council members have gone home," Wright said. "Joan and Margaret Braithwaite left you a letter and their addresses and phone numbers. They're okay with us spending a year or two with them after you've straightened out your parents' affairs and talked to Theodora's family. Joan says if you're going to survive on your own, you'll need good teachers, and she's willing to be one of them. She also said she thought you'd make a damn good ally someday."

I thought about that and nodded. "She's right. I will."

# About the Author

OCTAVIA E. BUTLER (1947–2006) was the first black woman to come to international prominence as a science fiction writer. Incorporating powerful, spare language, and rich, well-developed characters, her work tackled race, gender, religion, poverty, power, politics, and science in a way that touched readers of all backgrounds. Butler was a towering figure in life and in her art and the world noticed. A critical force, she received numerous awards, including a MacAuthur "genius grant," both the Hugo and Nebula awards, the Langston Hughes Medal, and a PEN Lifetime Achievement award.

About herself, Octavia E. Butler once wrote: "I am a fifty-three-year-old writer who can remember being a ten-year-old writer and who expects someday to be an eighty-year-old writer. I'm also comfortably asocial—a hermit in the middle of Seattle—a pessimist if I'm not careful, a feminist, a black, a former Baptist, an oil-and-water combination of ambition, laziness, insecurity, certainty, and drive."